Caroline Harvey is the pseudonym of Joanna Trollope, the highly acclaimed author of best-selling contemporary novels. *The Choir, A Village Affair, A Passionate Man, The Rector's Wife, The Men and the Girls, A Spanish Lover, The Best of Friends, Next of Kin* and *Other People's Children* are published under the Black Swan imprint. As Caroline Harvey she has written several historical novels including *Legacy of Love, A Second Legacy, Parson Harding's Daughter, The Steps of the Sun, Leaves from the Valley, The Brass Dolphin* and *City of Gems*, which are all published by Corgi Books.

Joanna Trollope lives in Gloucestershire. She was appointed OBE in the 1996 Queen's Birthday Honours List for services to literature.

CITY OF GEMS

Caroline Harvey

CORGI BOOKS

For David

Mandalay, November 1979

Acknowledgements

I should like to thank Peter Pointon most warmly both for the truly encouraging interest he has shown in this project and for all his invaluable guidelines for my research. I have benefited enormously from his expertise on Burma and also from material most kindly lent to me by David Brown. I am also very grateful to my father whose painstaking research for me has been used to the full in this book.

Glossary

Kalā   foreigner
Thakin   sir, equivalent of 'sahib' in India
Thakin-ma   memsahib
Salun-daw   low backless couch
Kinwoon Mingyi   Prime Minister
Ashin-nammadaw-paya   formal title of the Queen
Poon-dawgi-paya   formal title of the King
Hlutdaw   parliament

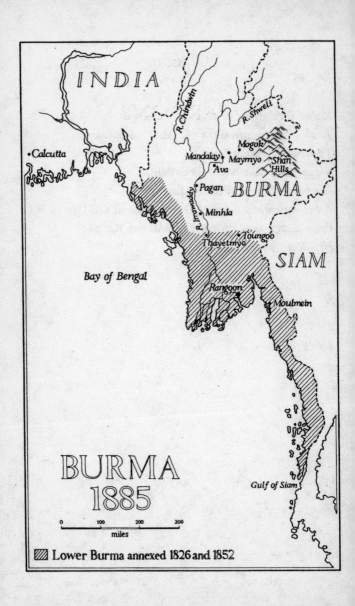

INDIA

• Calcutta

R. Chindwin

R. Shweli

Mogok •

Mandalay • Maymyo

• Ava Shan Hills

Pagan

BURMA

• Minhla

R. Irrawaddy

•• Toungoo

Thayetmyo

SIAM

Bay of Bengal

Rangoon

• Moulmein

BURMA
1885

Gulf of Siam

0   100   200   300
miles

▨ Lower Burma annexed 1826 and 1852

PART ONE

PART ONE

1

On 15 February 1879, the day on which Queen
Supayalat, wife of King Thibaw of the Kingdom
of Ava in Upper Burma, ordered eighty mem-
bers of the royal family to be clubbed to death,
Maria Beresford celebrated her twenty-first birthday in Bombay.

In the furious February sunshine grim pro-
cessions left the rose-brick walls of the royal Gem
City in Mandalay by the ill-omened western gate
and made for the great yellow breadth of the
Irrawaddy, bearing with them red velvet sacks
which were hurled into the slow-moving waters
of the river. In sunshine almost as fierce, tables
had been spread in the shade of trees in the
garden of Hubert Beresford's bungalow in
Bombay, for Maria had been seized by the whim
of a picnic for her birthday and in this, as in
almost everything, her father delighted to indulge
her.

The near-naked men carrying the red velvet
sacks – red velvet because the luckless contents
were of royal blood and also because that same
blood would be less visible on its plushy surface –
were criminals let out of gaol for their grisly duty,

13

armed with sandalwood clubs and primed with a raw local spirit. The people on Hubert Beresford's lawn, retired – or failed – tea-planters like himself, soldiers, civil servants, their wives and daughters, despite the heat, dressed in tight-bodiced gowns of enormous complication, the skirts either elaborately swathed or sporting ruffled trains, ate salmon mayonnaise and cold curried chicken and told each other exhaustedly what a novel idea an al fresco party in a temperature around the hundreds was.

Within six months, Maria Beresford, who had never given Burma a moment's thought in her secluded life, would be congratulating herself on being one of the few European women welcomed at the court in Mandalay.

But this, on the day of Maria's party, was yet to come. Burma had as much significance for Maria that day as Iceland might have done, or the remote islands of the Pacific. She had evolved her plan for a picnic with great care, determined her birthday should be memorable, unlike any-one else's, widely talked of. When she suggested it to her father, she had used her little-girl voice, implying that she needed to be indulged, that he was the protective all-provider who could make her happy.

'Such a little thing, dearest Papa, but such a big thing in terms of its effect! Only think. A mere luncheon party so not a quarter as dread-fully expensive as an evening party might be – and your Maria knows full well how careful we must be and how no-one must know about our carefulness. It is our secret, isn't it Papa? – and outside under the trees so that everyone may walk about and not be stuck with anyone tiresome. And then we shall set up the butts and the croquet and we shall have an archery competition and I shall present the prizes, shan't I, Papa, because it is my day.'

Her day it was, whatever the inconvenience and discomfort for anyone else. She was woken with her customary breakfast tray upon which her father had laid a bunch of flat white Indian roses. She dressed then, in a morning gown of relative simplicity in order to be unimpeded as she swept about the house and garden being commanding to the servants. They had only to put a table down to be told to move it. Tablecloths were declared to be creased, even when freshly ironed, flower arrangements went in and out of the house endlessly as Maria first wished to see their effect in certain places and then insisted that their transient freshness would be gone if they were not kept cool and dark.

Flies descended in thick clusters on servants and furniture. Fruit was ordered out, shrouded first in white muslin, then in flies, and ordered back again. She called for the ice boxes, saw their contents running into the red earth, and commanded them taken away. Glasses were finger-marked, silver improperly arranged, the boys set to fan the whole proceeding with palm leaves were idle and inefficient.

At noon, Maria abandoned the chaos she had created and went in to dress. Hubert, ponderous with significance, waylaid her in the hall.

'One moment only, my dearest.'

His study was dim and hot, the punkah only succeeding in moving clouds of dust about.

She sat down, prettily expectant.

'And did my dearest think I should forget her on such a day?'

She played up to him, eyes wide. 'Oh no, Papa! I know you did not! Those lovely roses on my breakfast tray!'

He said with smiling dismissiveness, 'Oh, roses!' and then he took a red morocco case from his desk and put it in her hands.

She looked up into his face for some moments rather than at the case and then he said, 'Open it! Open it!' delighted at the sweetness of her response, and watched her as she lifted the lid and revealed two pearl earrings, large lustrous teardrops, each swinging from a fleur de lys of diamonds.

She said, 'Oh Papa!' and remained gazing downwards.

'You like them, my own one?'

'More – more than anything I ever saw. But you should not spoil your Maria so, I know you should not. What with my party—'

'Hush,' Hubert said. He lifted an earring from its nest of velvet and deftly screwed it to Maria's ear. She turned her face.

'Now the other one, Papa!'

He surveyed her with pleasure.

'I – don't know how to thank you.'

She rose and put her arms about his neck, so that their handsome profiles were nose to aquiline nose.

'You are the dearest, best Papa in all the world.'

'And you are the dearest and best of daughters.'

Automatically their eyes slid sideways to a dim portrait on the wall, a painting of a sad, faded woman with large pale eyes full of bewildered injury.

'Poor Mamma,' Maria said and sighed.

They smiled at each other.

'Poor Mamma,' Hubert said.

Poor Mamma was scarcely even a memory. She had died when Maria was eleven, protesting faintly as she had done for the previous four years, that Maria should go home, home to England. She had protested, in the same exhausted manner, all her married life, about India, the servants, Hubert's neglect of her and indulgence of Maria, about her health, her loneliness, her boredom. She saw herself as a victim, and it suited her husband and daughter very well to agree with her that she was, indeed, one of nature's victims about whom nothing could be done and of whom little notice need be taken.

She had been very pretty when Hubert married her and had brought with her, apart from her looks and malleable character, twenty thousand pounds. Hubert might have wished that the money had not been made among the potteries of Staffordshire, especially as the pottery concerned made the coarser articles of domestic use, but he needed the money quite enough to blink easily at its origins. He himself brought to the marriage, as he told his admiring bride, such intangible and invaluable qualities as his name, his education, his culture and a family who had lived in the same house in Shropshire for five generations. That his own generation was hopelessly improvident and therefore impoverished he did not choose to tell her, nor that he was, as the third son, destitute and badly in debt. He put the situation to her quite another way.

'And now we shall realize my lifelong dream, together! I have always, all my life, been stirred by tales of India. Indian stories were the chief passion of my boyhood. And what have we to keep us here?'

Fanny Beresford wished to point out that an old mother in Burslem very much wished to keep her there, but did not like to say so.

'Nothing, you see! Nothing at all! We are as free as birds. We shall go to India, we shall buy ourselves a part of India, we shall have our children there. Fanny, it will be our kingdom.'

The Anaimalai Hills had certainly looked like paradise, a fair setting for Hubert's kingdom. The brilliant green slopes around Tirimbatore in southern India had rich, bright earth and rioted with flowers and birds. Hubert bought eight hundred acres and, leaving Fanny miserable as the guest of a formidable colonel's wife at Pondicherry, chose the highest point of his estate where he proceeded to supervise, for almost a year, the building of a magnificent bungalow, luxurious and splendid enough for a viceroy. When the first tea bushes were planted on the surrounding hills and the last rug laid and picture hung, Hubert came to Pondicherry and carried Fanny off to his kingdom. He deposited her in the gleaming bungalow on the hilltop in which absolutely nothing, not even her boudoir, had been of her own choosing, and demanded that she be as elated as he was. She drooped. Alone all day but for the servants, three days' journey from the next Englishman, she began her steady, faint complaining. Hubert, beyond allowing her three months in Madras for Maria's birth, took no notice. He was lord of his domain, always well, vibrant with energy.

Maria was like him. By the time she was four, the missy-baba in her vast sunbonnet was as familiar a figure on the plantation as her father. Her amah came to Hubert for orders; he chose her dresses, taught her French and mathematics, drawing and music, and insisted, after her seventh birthday, that she should sit up to dinner.

When Fanny had said she should go home, she had clung to her father and shrieked.

'Would you break my heart?' Hubert cried.

19

'And hers? Would you tear away our chief of pleasures?'

Fanny had sulked. 'No-one else does. No other children stay. They are all gone by Maria's age. It will look so odd. You have lived up here too long, you have forgotten what people do.'

'Bah!' Hubert cried. 'Convention!'

Maria had stayed, the blue gaze she turned upon her mother ever more scornful and triumphant. She was given duties in the house, instructed in the affairs of the plantation, given a small fiddle as well as her piano and a showy little mare to complement her considerable skill on horseback. Fanny requested a governess and was ignored; suggestions of boarding school, of a companion even, went quite unheard.

'I am Papa's only companion,' Maria informed her mother. 'We do not need anyone else.'

What else was there for Fanny to do but die? She took some mild infection, gave way to it greedily and was buried in Tirimbatore in a ceremony whose elegance owed much to Hubert's reading of elegiac verses. Her going left no mark, indeed it lent an exuberance to meals that her husband and daughter had not felt before; there was an air of holiday about. At eleven, Maria had her own boudoir – it had been her mother's but Hubert let her now have it, redecorated, for herself. He was like a bridegroom. The house must be quite made over. All the old furniture went, all the rugs, all the curtains, most of the pictures, and beautiful things came from Europe to replace them, things that scarcely anyone but Hubert or Maria saw.

Three and four years later, the crops failed. A blight struck the tea bushes withering their brilliant little leaves into rusty uselessness. Hubert had never been a good manager, never prudent with money. For three years more they struggled gallantly on, selling acres to neighbouring plantations, praising each other for small economies. When Maria was eighteen the end came. If they were to have anything to live upon, they must retrench at once. Tirimbatore was sold to a hefty young Scot whose small appraising eyes roused Maria to furious indignation and they took themselves and their possessions to Bombay.

'I shall find employment,' Hubert said. 'I have connections in Bombay.'

If he had, they appeared fairly tenuous. They bought a bungalow on the northern slopes of the city – 'Where else, for my dearest one!' – despite the fact that prices there were the highest, and settled back confidently for offers to pour in for Hubert. None came.

'I don't believe anyone knows you have come,' Maria declared.

She began to call on people; they were asked out to dine. Maria, out of her father's earshot, pleaded prettily with directors of the small trading companies with which Bombay abounded. At last a position was found, much too humble of course, nothing more really than

21

chief clerk in a tea-exporting house, but the money would pay for everyday life and appearances might be kept up.

'You see, my dove, what connections will do for a man.'

Maria said, 'And daughters' silently to herself and put her arms about his neck.

She saw him off to Parsee Bazaar Street every morning and welcomed him home to luncheon. She spoke of his work in the light in which he saw it, not as it actually was, and when an Indian director of the company, one stout and strutting Pranjeevan Jeena, came to complain of the shortness of Hubert's office hours, he found himself confronted by such a terrifying example of English superiority in Miss Beresford that he went away again, mission unaccomplished and his tail between his legs.

'It is of the utmost importance, my darling,' Hubert would say, 'that one puts the highest value upon oneself. The rest of the world, after all, only takes one at one's own valuation.'

With that principle in mind, Maria's birthday guests might have been forgiven for thinking they had really been asked to a viceregal durbar. Maria, always handsome, always much admired by the gentlemen and reluctantly by the ladies, who found her proud and egotistical, was dressed to kill. A new dress had been made for her of blue silk precisely the colour of her fine eyes, its skirt swathed in front, caught up at the sides in

wreaths of white gauze roses and flowing gracefully behind into a train edged with lavish
pleating. The bodice was also edged with gauze
roses, the elbows ornamented with them, and
around her long neck of which she was so proud
was a blue velvet ribbon on which was threaded
the lovely old cameo her father had given her at
Christmas. Her new pearls swung in her ears, her
dark blonde hair curled becomingly on her forehead and then was swept up into curves around a
hat made of yet more gauze roses and blue
ribbons. The ladies of the party, dressed merely
for luncheon and conscious of the damp armpits
and sweat-beaded brows that were inevitably part
of life in India, felt themselves deliberately out-
stripped.

Grace Prior, shyly clinging to her father's arm,
was particularly conscious of the discrepancy between her own appearance and Maria's. If their
circumstances had not been so similar – single
daughters of widowed fathers bravely making
do on insufficient money – she would not have
felt so keenly the endless unhappy comparisons
which blighted her every meeting with Maria. She
looked down at her own dress, a shapeless green
thing she had sewed herself, inspired by the
paintings of Sir Edward Burne-Jones, and felt she
might as well have come dressed in bedclothes
for all it did for her figure. Maria swept up to
them, cool and immaculate, received her father's
hearty congratulations smilingly, glanced briefly
and killingly at Grace's clothes, and swept on,

indicating the laden tables with a graceful gesture of her fan.

'Will you do battle with the flies for a little pilau, my dear?'

Grace smiled lovingly at her father. His great brown beard almost hid his clerical bands, flowing down to meet the waistcoat he was sure to bespatter with food.

'It – it's very grand, Papa. I – I am not at all properly dressed. I had not imagined it would be like this at all. I wonder why we were asked?'

'*De rigueur*, my dear. I am the regulation holy man. Over there is the regulation doctor, and beyond him is, I think, Colonel Browne, who must count as the regulation senior officer, as well as the prize guest. We balance the thing.'

A plate of rice and chicken, liberally sprinkled with flies, was pushed into Grace's hands, speedily followed by a napkin, a fork, a glass of warm champagne. Colonel Browne, coming up to the tables for his own luncheon and seeing her difficulties and her father's equal preoccupation with a similar burden, relieved her of all but her glass and found her a seat in the shade.

'Miss Prior, isn't it? Thought so. Horace Browne at your service, ma'am. We met before you know, at the mission house. I brought along some of my more troublesome boys. Rum do, this, eh?'

'I shan't miss this sort of thing,' Grace said with vehemence.

'Miss it? Miss it? Why, where are you off to? I

thought you were pretty much a fixture here, Prior, Anglican mission humming along nicely and all that. Excellent congregations you get here, I'm told.'

Tom Prior smiled again in the depths of his beard. 'Ah, Colonel, and that's the trouble. Much too excellent. I've no challenge left at all. It might suit a parish priest but not a missionary. It was another matter when we came, you know, my wife and I – we had to leave Grace in England, you know, she only joined me two years ago – empty church, total indifference, nothing doing at all, wonderful, simply wonderful.' He paused, and gazed away, his fork in mid-air, his eyes clouded with memories. He recollected himself with a jerk and dropped a forkful of curry onto his trousers. 'It's too easy now, Colonel. A curate could do it. It's time for me to be off, me and my helpmeet here.'

Grace leaned over and dabbed at her father with a napkin.

'Where are you going?'

Tom Prior's mouth was full but Grace, still scrubbing vigorously, said, 'Mandalay.'

'Good God,' Colonel Browne said, and then added, 'I do beg your pardon, Miss Prior. We soldiers, you know. Mandalay!'

'We have a great man there,' Tom Prior said earnestly, brandishing his fork, 'a true soldier of Christ. Doctor Marks. He has had the most immense influence with the kings, the late king especially. He was permitted to instruct some of the princes even. But he is not so young, he needs another pair of arms, a comrade in God.'

'Buddhists,' Colonel Browne said musingly.

'Yes,' Grace said, giving up the unequal struggle with the flies, and putting her plate down. 'At least they will make a change from Hindus.'

Colonel Browne said, 'Of course, I know Mandalay. First went there in fifty-nine, you know, on one of Phayre's missions, and then led the survey expeditions in sixty-seven. Fascinating business. Took them up into the mountains north-east of Mandalay. First European up there, complete terra incognita. The whole thing would have been a great success except for poor Margary being murdered. He was consul in Shanghai and had come to meet me but insisted on going ahead of the armed escort back to China. Fatal mistake. I've been in and out of Burma for the last twenty years. Extraordinary place. In my view we should annex the whole country, not just content ourselves with Lower Burma. All very useful, of course, a port like Rangoon on the way to Singapore, but I doubt we'll ever really use it. What we need to keep an eye on is the teak. There's going to be trouble over the teak. The French want it. You mark my words, we shall have trouble with Upper Burma before a few years are out. But will the government here or in London listen? Not a bit of it. All eyes on South Africa and Afghanistan. The Resident up in Mandalay is an excellent chap, former tea-planter like Beresford here. He shares my views, says you can't get the government to budge on anything to do with Burma unless it's a question of British dignity, like all that shoe nonsense.'

Grace, who had been suppressing small yawns, she hoped invisibly, into her champagne, looked up. 'Shoes?'

'Yes, my dear, shoes. The court in Mandalay insists all visitors remove their shoes in the presence of the king. Of course that is out of the question for an Englishman.'

'Difficult to,' Tom Prior said, 'to remove, I mean. Eastern sandals are much easier.'

'Just what the Resident said to the Burmese. Do we ask you to take your hats off to us, he said, just because it is a gesture of politeness among us and our hats come off easily? Of course he won. He and the Italian consul were the only foreigners allowed to wear shoes at the late king's funeral. You'll have to watch out for that sort of thing.'

Tom Prior smiled. 'I'm after their souls, not their shoes.'

A cool breath seemed to refresh the air around them. Maria had come over and was standing smiling down on them, particularly at Colonel Browne.

The men got to their feet.

'Are you enjoying my picnic, Colonel?'

'I'm enjoying the company, my dear, but I can't say I'm managing my fodder very well. I'm better off with a table indoors, truth to tell.'

Maria laughed with great good nature and turned to Grace. 'Miss Prior. Do you have everything you want? I am so glad you could come, especially when you are leaving so soon. It is so stupid of me, but I quite forget where you are going.'

'Burma,' Grace said.

'Oh,' Maria said faintly, 'Burma. But I have come to take you away, Miss Prior. I have a lonely young subaltern who needs diverting.'

Captain Murray Shaw of the Queen's Own Bengal Infantry saw Maria coming across the lawn to him with a leap of pleasure. He had three weeks' leave in Bombay, had met Maria at a dinner party on the third night and here he was, two days later, at her birthday party. She was the best-looking girl in Bombay, he thought, perhaps the best-looking in India, but then, he had been stationed in such out-of-the-way spots recently that he fancied he might have found a Hottentot desirable.

Behind Miss Beresford, half hidden by her parasol, trailed a slender discouraged-looking girl in green. Her stalk-like neck seemed to be wilting in the heat as if her small head and fine silky-brown hair were too much of a burden for it to bear. Her dress had no shape to it, nor did her depressed-looking hat from which a tired feather hung. With a sudden sinking sensation, Captain Shaw deduced from Miss Beresford's purposeful walk and bright smile that she was not bringing him the charm of her own company, but rather the doubtful society of the gloomy girl in green.

Maria introduced them with animation. Murray Shaw gave her a glance of deepest reproach, was rewarded by a conspiratorial smile and turned to do his duty by Grace. She was much alarmed by his impeccable appearance in uniform.

'Why do you go to Burma, Miss Prior?'

'I shall accompany my father. He is to run the Anglican mission in Mandalay.'

'Are you not afraid to go? I believe there are very few European women in Burma. Shall you not be lonely?'

'I am used to it,' Grace said, simply. 'We are not going for society you see. We can do our work better if there are difficulties, we can be better Christians.'

Captain Shaw looked at once respectful and mildly embarrassed. A change of subject was imperative.

'Have you known Miss Beresford long?'

Grace followed his longing gaze across the sun-soaked lawn to the tall blue figure deep in conversation with Colonel Browne.

'About two years, I think, but – but we do not see much of each other. She – she is very accomplished.'

'By jove she is,' he said fervently. 'I admire her awfully. I suppose all the fellows do.'

'There are not so many young ones here,' Grace said to encourage him. 'Most are away with their regiments.'

He smiled down at her gratefully and thought that if she had been taller and fairer and better built, she really would not have been a bad-looking girl at all.

Across the lawn, Maria had pinned Colonel Browne between the knotted trunk of a peepul tree and her own slender form. She had presumed upon the slight acquaintance between the colonel and her father, founded in the Malabar Club, to issue an invitation, and had been immensely grateful when it had been accepted. Colonel Browne was highly regarded in both military and civilian circles, with a sound reputation as an explorer and administrator. He was a bigger fish than Maria had hoped to catch for her party and, having caught him, she now wished to make full use of her success.

'Can't think why your father retired,' Colonel Browne said. 'Always imagined those planters led wonderful lives, splendid country, your own man entirely.'

Maria said in a low voice, her eyelids downcast, 'It was circumstances, Colonel, not choice. Leaf blight—'

It was perfectly possible to say leaf blight, but it would have been out of the question, even had she admitted such weaknesses as existing, to add extravagance, careless investment, general improvidence.

'My dear. Forgive me.'

She put her hand on his arm and smiled directly into his eyes. 'There is nothing to forgive.

We are hardly destitute but we must be a little careful. It is not that I mind at all, money means nothing to me, but – but—'

Colonel Browne patted the white glove that rested on his sleeve. 'Can I help you, my dear? Are you in difficulties? You ladies—'

'Oh no!' she said and shook her head. 'It is not that at all. It is not money, Colonel, it – it is more self-esteem. It is for Papa that I care so much, not for myself at all.'

'Suppose you tell me right out, my dear, suppose you tell me just what it is that troubles you.'

She hesitated for a moment and gave her parasol a twirl or two as if she needed to gather courage. 'It – it is his dignity, you see, Colonel. He was, as you say so rightly, his own master. He ruled our little world down there oh so well, Colonel. You cannot imagine how much they all loved him. And then – my mother died and then came the blight and he was forced to sell before the estate was worth nothing at all because we had to keep selling land, you know, to manage. And he came up here – for me really, because I had known no society and nothing, I think – though he is too good to speak of it to me – has quite gone as he had hoped. He was educated at Harrow, Colonel, and then at Cambridge and his family is very old and has produced many distinguished men and here he is, Colonel, scratching away in an office all day like – like any *Indian*. He is so good, he never complains, but he must feel the indignity of it. I know I do. And I wondered, Colonel, since you are a man of such influence, if you would at least remember him when administrative posts need filling. I don't ask for favours outright, I just beg you to keep him in mind.'

Colonel Browne considered her for a moment, shrewdly aware that if she had adopted an artificial pose to plead her father's cause, her desire to help him was genuine enough.

He said, 'As he, your father, my dear, knows nothing of the Civil Service here, I couldn't ever suggest him for anything considerable. I hope I don't offend you.'

She smiled. 'Not in the least. I am perfectly realistic, Colonel. I just don't want to see him perched on a stool with a quill and a ledger for the rest of his working life.'

Hubert's elegant figure was clearly visible to both of them now, stooping to hear something Grace Prior was saying and plainly alarming her by his handsome condescension.

'I understand you, my dear. I do indeed. And if there's a man who might help you I have to say, without undue modesty, that man is myself. Very wise of you to speak to me. And I shan't forget. Never do. Don't expect miracles, Miss Beresford, but I will see what I can do.'

She put out a hand and said, 'Thank you,' in a firm and decided tone, and he thought how splendid it was to meet a young woman who didn't gush. Having made polite speeches about her party, he said, 'Trust me, Miss Beresford,' and pressed her hand and she watched him stride across the lawn with the greatest satisfaction.

Captain Shaw, desperate not to have to leave without the smallest conversation with Maria, found that he had abandoned Grace despite the precepts of his upbringing, and had almost run across the garden to waylay his hostess without having been aware of doing any more than harbouring the desire to be beside her. She shook her fan at him.

'Oh, Captain Shaw, I am going to be very severe with you. How could you leave poor Miss Prior standing all alone like that? I have a good mind to send you straight back again.'

'Then I should disobey,' he said daringly.

She laughed. 'Insubordination in my own garden? That will never do. Tell me what brought you racing over in such a headlong manner.'

He coloured and said something indistinctly, cleared his throat and stammered out a wish to see her, if she would permit it, during the two weeks that remained to him in Bombay.

She raised her eyebrows. 'Permit it? Of course I do. Unless you know some secret reason why I should not? I hope you will dine here on Tuesday. My father will be so much pleased if you would.'

She nodded and smiled again and moved gracefully away, leaving him gazing after her, at once rapturous at the thought of dining with her and cast down that she had only declared how pleased her father would be to see him.

Hubert met his daughter before she descended upon the next group of guests.

'A delightful young man, my dear.'

'Oh, Papa? Is he? What makes him so delightful?'

Hubert leaned a little closer. 'Eldest son of Sir Murray Shaw, baronet, of Battrick, Northumberland, and a present income of three thousand a year which rises considerably on his twenty-fifth birthday, which, I am reliably informed, falls this autumn.'

'Oh Papa, you have been busy!'

'And you, my dearest one? Have you been busy and happy?'

Maria, her mind upon Colonel Browne, glanced over her shoulder to reassure herself that Captain Shaw's admiring gaze followed her still. He did not appear to have moved a muscle since she left him.

'Oh yes, Papa. Very busy – and very happy.'

2

15 February 1879, in the City of London was one of those days that make an Englishman feel that the winter will never end. A raw yellow fog had settled thickly in the courts and passages, blotting out the sky entirely and giving an eerie sensation, on account of the gloom, of its being no particular time of day at all. It was bitterly cold and a thin layer of evil, half-frozen mud made the cobbles alarmingly slippery.

Archie Tennant, the collar of his greatcoat turned up around his ears and his hat jammed down as far as it would go to meet it, had walked from Liverpool Street Station to Austin Friars in order to get his circulation going. The train had been miserably cold and he had had to get up at intervals, all the way from Ipswich, and stamp about and beat his chest until a dyspeptic-looking man in the innermost seat said he thought Archie's fidgets were worse than the cold. Archie, at nineteen easily disconcerted and by nature eager to please, sat down at once and felt the last traces of warmth ebbing for ever from his large and loosely jointed frame.

His mother had said he must go to London.

She had seemed rather tearful at breakfast and refused to tell him why he had been summoned from Oxford in the middle of term. He was used to her being tearful and had always supposed resignedly that widows, without exception, were. So he had eaten his way through an immense breakfast and she had sat behind the coffee pots and sniffed, only remarking now and then that he must not miss the train and cause inconvenience to poor darling Frederick on such a day as this.

'As what?' Archie said through his smoked haddock.

His mother merely sniffed again and said, 'Your brother is so dreadfully busy. I really do not know anyone who works harder and it will be wicked of you, deliberately wicked, to be late and cause him inconvenience.'

Archie did not reply. Nineteen years of being the unsatisfactory son had taught him how useless it was to contradict his mother and nineteen years of close proximity to his elder brother Frederick had taught him equally clearly that he could not bring himself to agree with her about him. He put a good deal of marmalade on a muffin.

'Why does Frederick want to see me at the office?'

His mother looked at him quellingly from behind her battery of silver. 'Where else should he wish to see you? Where else does he ever spend his time, poor hardworking darling?'

The theatre, Archie thought of saying, Epsom,

Newmarket, actresses' bedrooms. Aloud he said, 'I hope he isn't going to go on at me about joining the firm. I have no inclination at all to have anything to do with Far Eastern trade. I want to be a lawyer.'

Mrs Tennant's eyes filled with tears. 'It is as well, Archie, that your beloved father cannot hear you talk with such disgraceful ingratitude, such wicked lack of duty.'

'He was a lawyer,' Archie pointed out reasonably, picking up a second muffin and realizing sadly that even his capacity had its limits. He replaced it reluctantly on its silver dish.

'Only so that he might serve the company better.'

Archie shrugged and stood up. 'I shall go straight back to Oxford tonight, Mother. Straight from London. The drag hounds meet tomorrow.'

'Pleasure!' his mother cried resentfully. 'Pleasure! It's all you ever think of. Not a day passes but I thank God on my knees that He has given me one son at least who is a support to his poor mother, who showers on her the love that your beloved father's passing took from me so cruelly.'

Archie said, his voice a little hardened, 'Hunting is the only pleasure, as you call it, that I do indulge in. I don't gamble, I don't drink much, I only eat because I am always so hungry. I say, Mother, could you lend me twenty pounds?'

'You must ask Frederick. He deals with all the money matters. What I should do without him, I cannot imagine—'

'If I must ask Frederick, I shall have to do without my twenty pounds.'

'Then you must do without,' Mrs Tennant said, and when Archie had left the room in silence, reflected that he had never kissed her goodbye and that Frederick would hardly ever leave the room for a five-minute absence without an affectionate farewell.

Now, on the steps of number 4 Austin Friars, the offices of Tennant Phillipson, Far Eastern traders, Archie remembered he had not said goodbye, and was instantly contrite. He resolved to write a note to his mother and post it at Paddington before catching the train to Oxford. The double doors ahead of him swung open and old Tremlett, who remembered his grandfather, the company's co-founder, said, 'Bad day, Mr Archie,' and held out a trembling hand for Archie's hat.

The reception hall at Tennant Phillipson was panelled in wine-red mahogany, floored in black and white marble and decorated with nothing except two sombre portraits of the founders. There was no fire in the fireplace and Archie didn't wonder that old Tremlett, in his glazed dog kennel by the door, should shake so much.

'How are you, Tremlett? Pretty fit?'

'Not so much as I was, sir. *Anno domini*, sir. Seem to feel the cold so.'

'You should retire, Tremlett, and dig that garden of yours. I'll never forget the raspberries you brought up for me last summer. They deserved an award.'

Tremlett beamed upon him.

'You shall have more this summer, Mr Archie. Mrs Tremlett will be honoured. I'll retire, sir, when I've seen you settled into the company, sir, but not before. I gave my word to your father. And I don't want to lose touch, sir, you see, seeing as how I am a shareholder, sir.'

Archie's father had hit upon the enlightened notion of paying his clerks as little as he could get away with and encouraging them to put their small savings into shares in the company. 'In that way, Tremlett,' he had said thirty years before, 'Tennant Phillipson will pay for your working life and your retirement as well.' It had become a company obligation.

'Is my brother expecting me?'

'Yes, Mr Archie. Mr Frederick said to me this morning, "Now, Tremlett, that young scamp of a brother of mine will be in this morning. Be sure you leave him to cool his heels a while." But I wouldn't do that, sir. I'll get Norris to take you up, sir.'

Archie protested that he could find his way up quite well alone, but Tremlett considered this idea quite unsuitable and so Archie found himself escorted by a spindly boy of fourteen or so whom the company employed as a messenger. When he was announced, Archie heard his brother say, 'Tell him to wait a moment,' and was strongly tempted to cuff the weedy Norris aside and

march in to Frederick's office. He calmed himself
however, and picked up the bound volume of
the company report that lay on the table in the
anteroom outside his brother's office. Such
extraordinary things Tennant Phillipson dealt
in, indigo, fish oil and yak hair, salt and ngape
– what on earth was ngape? Ngape – dried
fish, explained a helpful footnote. The door
opened.

'Come in,' Frederick said abruptly.

Archie followed him into the large square office
furnished with his grandfather's monumental
desk and chair.

'What on earth do you deal in yak hair for?'

'Fly whisks,' Frederick said briefly.

He looked tired and older than his twenty-
eight years. His suit was as beautifully cut as
ever, his linen as immaculate, his meticulously
trimmed whiskers still gave off a faint odour
of bay rum, but his face had an exhausted,
dishevelled look. Archie, whose entire appearance was dishevelled more often than not, cast
himself into a great wing chair opposite his
brother's desk.

'Well, what's up? I'm in the middle of a
particularly thorny patch of Roman law, you
know, and it really wasn't easy to get away.
Mother was crying at breakfast.'

Frederick made a small sound of irritation. 'I
hope she did more than that.'

'Not beyond saying I mustn't be late.'

Frederick said with sudden vehemence, 'Confound it! I expressly asked for you to go home first so that she could – could prepare the way a little. Before you came here.'

Archie was grinning. 'You are the man of the house, you know. All burdens are for you to bear—'

'Take that stupid grin off. What I have to tell you, thanks to Mother, will wipe it off soon enough anyhow. We are washed up, Archie, absolutely done for. The firm is finished.'

Archie, lounging in his chair, froze rigid. 'What do you mean?'

'You wouldn't understand,' Frederick said impatiently. 'You'll simply have to take my word for it. There's not a penny left, all gone. In fact, we are unpleasantly in debt—'

Archie stood up. 'But why?'

Frederick waved his hand. 'Oh, some pretty wild speculation on someone's part. Could happen to anyone. A lot of forward buying of some rather expensive rice and now a bumper harvest in south-east Asia and a bit of a dabble in rhinoceros horn which the Chinese swear by as an – an—'

'Aphrodisiac. I know that perfectly well. But *whose* speculation? *Whose* dabbling? Yours?'

Frederick shrugged. 'Never made a mistake before.'

'Not such a big one, anyhow,' Archie said.

Frederick shouted, 'Don't you preach to me! You're only a boy. You know nothing about trading!'

'No,' Archie said, 'I don't.' He walked to the window and stood looking down at the fog-filled zigzag of Austin Friars, his broad shoulders blocking almost all the light that struggled into the room.

'What happens now?' he said.

'We fold it all up. End of Tennant Phillipson. I've tried to get someone to buy us, but there are no takers. We're too specialized, we don't deal in the big commodities like timber or rubber, nor in the really expert, difficult things like precious stones. The offices will be closed by the end of the month, and I shall sell the building—'

Archie spun round. 'You can't! Have you told the staff? You can't just fold everything up and throw them out on their ears in a fortnight!'

'I'm not asking for your advice, Archie. I'm telling you what is going to happen. No, they don't know. I shall tell them in good time. I'll probably put the proceeds from the building into setting myself up in something in Ipswich. It'll be precious little but it's all I'll have.'

Archie loomed over his brother. 'But your creditors! And the shareholders! What happens to them?'

'Luck of the draw,' Frederick said.

Archie's fist came crashing down on the desk. 'You can't behave like that! You will have to put any monies you receive for the building towards paying debts and shareholders. The law will make you!'

'I'll fight,' Frederick said, 'Why should I be left with nothing? The building is mine in any case, not the company's. I bought it from them some time ago. It's mine to sell. I've sat in this dismal place for nine years now and I'm not going away empty-handed.'

Archie said, 'You are not only unprincipled, but extremely stupid.'

Frederick yawned and looked at his nails. 'I should go if I were you, Archie. There was no reason I had to tell you any of this except that, as you were coming into the company, I thought you should know.'

Archie said furiously, 'I can't wait to be back in Oxford,' and then he realized with a leap of dismay that his Oxford life would presumably crumble with the company.

'Damned annoying,' Frederick said, 'the whole business. I should think number eight out there are laughing themselves sick.'

'Number eight?'

'Wallace Brothers. Number eight Austin Friars. Six of them, four with beards, and trading out of Bombay like nobody's business. Teak, mostly. They are a bunch of canny Scots and they have been waiting to see me fall.'

'What about old Phillipson?' Archie said suddenly.

'I haven't told him yet. He comes up once a year for the board meeting this month, and I can't say I look forward to seeing him.'

Archie remembered an old man in a summerhouse wrapped in a plaid shawl. He had given him a ginger biscuit and told him horrendous stories of the Indian Mutiny.

'Will he have lost a lot?'

Frederick shrugged again. 'Not much. We never saw eye to eye. He managed to palm a lot of his shares off on me seven or eight years ago and then he made a fuss when I bought the building. Rumour has it that he reinvested in Wallace Brothers. He's kept some money with us, "for my father's sake" he always said, the old hypocrite.' He paused and added with bitterness, 'He'll be all right.'

'You must go out to Henley and tell him. You can't just wait for him to struggle up here, believing everything is all right. It would be intolerably cruel.'

Frederick stood up and glared at his brother. 'The whole thing is intolerably cruel! I have to give up the house in Wilton Crescent, my horses, probably my tailor, my wine merchant, everything. I think that's pretty cruel. I don't have, quite frankly, much pity left for a crafty old bachelor with enough money to do just what he wants! If you mind so much, Archie, you can damn well go and see him yourself!'

Two minutes later Tremlett reverently and shakingly assisted Archie into his coat.

'When shall we see you here on a daily basis, sir? When your university time is done, sir?'

Archie took his hat and gazed earnestly into its depths since he could not bear to look at Tremlett's face. 'I don't know about that, Tremlett. I really haven't made up my mind. But I'll be back to see you all very soon, I promise that.'

At Didcot Junction, Archie left the train and ordered a cab to take him to Henley. The fog had trickled up the Thames from London, but hung white and limp here in the river valley having lost the yellow filth of the city. It was even colder however, and the cab was draughty, icy blasts whipping up the fragments of straw that littered the floor and making Archie's boots feel as insubstantial as if they were constructed of paper. He slumped in a corner, plunged in his collars, and continued to fume.

He had been boiling with anger all the way from Austin Friars. At Paddington he remembered his intention to write to his mother, recalled the next moment the knowledge she had withheld from him at breakfast, and her hopelessly partisan feelings for that scoundrel, Frederick, and decided she deserved no letter. He hoped, glaring out of the train window as the red and blue tenements of outer London slid by, that she had spent all day in tears. He could not, even inspired by his fury, think of a fate worthy of Frederick's monstrous incompetence and dishonour. A woman climbed into his compartment at Reading and motioned the child with her to take the seat next to Archie, but the boy, with one alarmed glance at Archie's knotted brows, prudently decided that to disobey his mother was the lesser of two evils, and chose the farthest seat he could.

Even on such a day, Riverdene was a pleasant house. Old Phillipson had built it for himself in the early twenties, intending it to house the ineffably sensible girl with a comfortable fortune whom he had selected as his bride. The sensible girl had spoiled these level-headed plans by running off with an attractive and unprincipled army officer, later to be cashiered, and George Phillipson, adjusting himself to the situation with very little trouble, had shut the house up for thirty years and gone to have a look at business prospects in south-east Asia. He was drawn, like so many young men at that time, to Singapore, established by Sir Stamford Raffles as a free port, free that is of the royal monopolies that so dogged trade with such places as Siam or Cochin China. In Singapore, on the steps of the Malay Institute, George Phillipson met a large, ill-coordinated young man called Frederick Tennant, six months out from England and in search of something more to occupy himself with than a squire's life in Suffolk.

They were chalk and cheese, the two young men, yet wonderfully compatible. George Phillipson, with his unimaginative careful ways, was much attracted to Frederick's inventive brain and impulsive flashes of brilliance. Frederick in his turn found himself steadied and calmed. For three years they travelled together, the large untidy young man with his mass of baggage and boxes full of 'collections' and the tidy and well-organized one, accompanied by the minimum of luggage and the maximum of order.

Nine months of those three years were spent in Hong Kong and nine in Singapore and the experience of both taught Tennant and Phillipson that most of the trading companies mushrooming in the new free economic climate would deal in the most obvious commodities, tea and timber, silk, rubber and rice. It seemed to them that a good many more specialized goods might find an equally hungry market in the West and that in addition, many of these commodities could be traded around the Far East itself, satisfying such curious oriental tastes as dried fish.

They considered setting up an office in Bombay; Riverdene had waited now beside the Thames for five years and could wait longer, and Hasham Hall, Frederick supposed, was quite as competently run by his mother as he could ever manage himself. No, George Phillipson said, there was no point in them both being away from England, no point in their both being in India. He should take a small office in Nesbit Road, Bombay, and Frederick should return home and find somewhere suitable in London. In 1830, Tennant Phillipson was born, operating from number 4 Austin Friars, London, and number 4 Nesbit Road, Bombay, a coincidence which both partners felt to be a good omen.

It was not only a good omen but a good partnership. There were times when Frederick wanted to move faster, take larger risks, buy land, and wrote thunderous letters to Nesbit Road. George moved ahead with sure steadiness, ignoring explosions from London, profiting always from the flashes of imagination that interspersed the expletives in Frederick's letters. The American Civil War eventually proved the great turning point for Tennant Phillipson. The cotton mills of Lancashire, cut off from the supplies in the Southern States of America, turned to Bombay instead, and this time George listened to the urgent recommendations that poured from Austin Friars to buy land for development. He listened and acted and by 1860 the nominal capital of the company had risen to twenty lakhs of rupees, divided into a thousand shares at two thousand rupees each.

By 1860 also, Frederick Tennant had married and was father to one son and seven daughters. George Phillipson possessed a godson of almost thirty he had never met and, motivated by that and a desire to see Riverdene once more before he was too malarial to enjoy it, he sailed for England. The Bombay office was left in the capable hands of its major shareholder besides the two partners, a Parsee merchant who had been responsible for excellent advice to George Phillipson during the cotton boom.

George had come home and stayed at home. Riverdene, with its pleasant rosy bricks and long windows, its lawns and trees and access to excellent fishing, proved the love affair he had been thwarted of thirty years before. His godson had entered the firm eight years previously after reading law at Oxford and had shown himself a worthy successor to the founders. George travelled to London for the three middle days of each working week, slept the nights at his club, and travelled back to Riverdene thankfully on Thursday evenings. Frederick, racked now with gout, had much the same routine, varied only by staying with his son and daughter-in-law in St John's Wood for the nights he had to be in London. Young Frederick worked six days a week, frequently seven, travelled eight times to Bombay in fifteen years, hardly saw the two sons born to him at an interval of nine years and in 1870 followed his gout-ridden father to the grave, felled by a massive heart attack.

Old Phillipson continued to come to the city for a year or so, 'to see the grandson settled' as he put it to himself. The third Frederick resembled his father and grandfather in nothing but name and, within two years, old Phillipson had not only withdrawn the major portion of his money but also himself to Henley, except for an annual excursion to Austin Friars. Riverdene became his life. He kept an indoor staff of ten and an outdoor staff of six. Archie, climbing out of the cab, stiff with cold, thought that despite the gloom cast by the fog, he had never seen a house so utterly, unmistakably cherished, the white window frames gleaming, the creepers up the walls thick and immaculately trimmed, the lawns green and smooth and empty, even in February, of so much as a single dead leaf.

He stamped numbly on the gravel for a while, blowing on his fingers and looking admiringly about him, and then the glossy white front door opened above him and he was asked his business.

'To see Mr Phillipson,' he said.

The old butler, who had looked after Riverdene for the thirty years of his master's absence, inclined his head and looked sceptical. Archie hunted about in his pockets, failed to find a card and was reduced to saying, in more supplicating a tone than he intended, 'I – I'm Archie Tennant. Would you tell Mr Phillipson that I should like to see him?'

At the name of Tennant, the butler's brow darkened. He held the door barely wide enough for Archie to squeeze his bulk into the hall and left him waiting, without taking his hat and coat, to contemplate a handsome pair of elephant tusks that embraced the chimneypiece. There was a fire burning beneath the chimneypiece and a thick Turkey rug on the polished floor, and the panelled walls were painted white and hung with sporting prints of the last century. The air was warm and welcoming and above the scent of firewood and wax polish Archie caught a faint but heady drift of hot buttered toast.

The butler came back and handed Archie a note on a silver tray.

'Which Tennant? What do you want?' old Phillipson had written.

Archie attempted to write a reply but was too much impeded by his greatcoat. Not daring to ask for help, he struggled out of it alone, dropped it clumsily onto a nearby chair, watched implacably by the butler, and with fingers stiffened with cold wrote awkwardly in reply. 'Archie, sir. The company. I am very worried and angry.'

He then thought family loyalty should have precluded the last remark but he could hardly cross it out. He dropped the pen on the tray and remained standing while the butler vanished again. The fire was beginning to thaw him slightly and with returning warmth came courage and a determination not to touch his hat and coat again for himself.

The second note took longer to come but was, for various reasons, much more welcome. 'Come in. Hope you like muffins.'

Old Phillipson, in a velvet dressing-gown, his thin silver hair brushed smooth as metal and his knees covered in a fur rug like a brown bear, was sitting in a room lined entirely with books and looking down to the river. There were several large tables bearing portfolios of prints, a globe, a telescope, objects in ivory and jade, and in the window embrasure a grand piano, open, with music on the rack. Everything, the books, the furniture, the white-painted shelves, gleamed with care.

'You are as large as your grandfather,' old Phillipson said.

'Yes, sir,' Archie said. 'I feel every inch of it. I expect he managed it much better than I do.'

Old Phillipson motioned Archie to a chair. 'No, he didn't. Always knocking things over, chairs, tables, coolies, everything. I'm as old as the century and in all that time I've never met a clumsier man. Tea for Mr Tennant, Ford. You mustn't mind Ford. He thinks all Tennants are like your brother. I expect you had to take off your own coat, eh? He did that to Frederick. Upset him so much he wouldn't even drink his tea. Are you too upset to drink your tea?'

Archie gazed worshipfully at the muffin dish, the fat-bellied tea pot, the rich dark fruit cake. 'I could eat a horse, sir.'

'Then eat one. Talk afterwards. I never did have much appetite, less after India. Your grandfather always ate as if each meal was his last. Remember him?'

Butter running down his chin, Archie nodded vigorously. 'He was pretty lame, sir. But I was ten when he died so I remember him quite well.'

'Worst funeral of my life, that,' old Phillipson said, 'and your father six months later. Terrible year. Fill Mr Tennant's cup, Ford, and then leave us. I'm sure my guest will have the strength then to cut his own cake. Like my house?'

'Enormously, sir,' Archie said with enthusiasm.

'Perfection, ain't it,' old Phillipson said with contentment, 'Perfection. Worth waiting for. Ever been East?'

'No, sir. I'm at Oxford, sir.'

Old Phillipson regarded him with his bright birdlike glance. 'I remember. I gave you ginger-nuts when you were only a little chap. In the summerhouse here. Oriel, isn't it? Undistin-guished college but I suppose that can't be helped. Never seemed to do your father any harm, or your grandfather either for that matter. Another muffin?'

Archie shook his head. Old Phillipson nodded at him. 'Mustn't let your appetite run away with you. All very well when you're young but you don't want a load of extra flesh to haul about when you get older. Your grandfather got heavy, far too heavy, but then, he was too gouty to move about much. You've got his frame. Now then, what are you here for?'

Archie went scarlet. 'I – I thought I ought to come, sir. I went – I went to Austin Friars this morning sir, and – and – I saw Frederick and, well, the fact of the matter is, sir, that something awful has happened and – and I thought – I thought one of us should tell you, sir, and Frederick is so awfully tied up, you see, sir, so I thought that on my way back to Oxford, sir, I would come and, well, and tell you, sir—'

Old Phillipson leaned forward, his pale, well-manicured little paws resting calmly in the brown fur of his rug. 'You may stop now. Have some cake. No? Oh, I should you know, because I am going to tell you my side of the story and you would be much better with something to occupy yourself with.'

Archie gazed at him, the cake knife suspended in his hand. 'Then – then you know, sir?'

'Of course I know. I have my contacts, I haven't lost my touch. Your brother Frederick has got, in common parlance, his comeuppance. That's the fact of it. Always saw Tennant Phillipson as another Jardines, always wanted to be in the first eleven. That was one of the things we fell out about. One of many, mind you. I suppose our worst battle was when he wanted to buy the building in Austin Friars. I should have stopped him, I should have held out, but I'm not as young as I was and he would have his way without my consent. He persuaded all the shareholders. Bombay did their best to keep him in line. Mr Jivanji's a shrewd customer, but what can you do from India, and your brother would never leave London. Miss all his dancing girls? That would never do. So speculate he must and he's been riding for a fall these last five years. Hunt, do you? Good, good. Best thing in the world for the liver. I tell you, young man, the amount your brother knows about rice you could write on a sixpence. He had no business to go experimenting with a commodity where the sums involved are huge and the field is full of experts. It was lunacy. And, of course, he had classic beginner's luck a year ago so he doubled his stake. Bought twice as much at almost twice the price and, as any halfwit in the East could have told him, if he'd only listened, they were heading for the best harvest in years. To cap it all, he'd neglected all the things we'd made our name in, Burmese earth oil, musk, salt, things like that, so of course the producers turned to other traders and there are no markets for him to go back to. What was Frederick's version of all this?'

'He wouldn't explain, sir. Quite rightly, I suppose, since I don't know the first thing about it.'

'Don't defend him to *me*,' old Phillipson said with the first flash of anger he had shown. 'To the world if you must, but not to me. He's an incompetent blackguard, your brother. My money might be safe, young man, but my pride isn't.'

Archie, scarlet again, nodded vigorously in sympathy.

'Nearly half a century,' old Phillipson went on more calmly, 'founded 1830, died 1879. My life work I might say, if I were an emotional man like your grandfather. You're like him. I might also say it if I didn't have this house to console me, if I didn't have something to put my heart into. In fact, young man, I've said it for the last two months to myself but I've scolded myself for doing it. So Frederick refused to be a gentleman and tell me face to face? And you, because you are your grandfather's grandson, felt you should do it? And being an impetuous, headstrong fellow like your grandfather you came straight here from number four without even letting your temper cool?'

Archie hesitated a moment, playing with the cake knife. 'Yes, sir.'

'Thought as much. How d'you like Oxford?'

'Enormously, sir. Law has its dusty side, but everything else is splendid, sir.'

'And who's going to pay for it now?'

'I – I expect it will come to an end.'

'And you will be sorry?'

'Yes, sir.'

'How long have you to go?'

'The rest of this term and four more.'

'And have you been a credit to your brains?'

Archie looked up, caught his host's humorous eye and smiled in relief. 'Two shots at moderations, sir, which wasn't very popular. But I've worked harder since then.'

'And played too? What do you amuse yourself with besides hunting? Share your brother's taste for actresses too, no doubt.'

Archie shifted a little. He had become quite used to paying for the satisfying of his more urgent physical needs, although he came away after every visit to the Jericho slums of Oxford considerably disquieted in mind however much his body had been appeased. He had observed too, without liking to draw conclusions from the fact, that his visits to Jericho were more frequent than a year ago and that he looked forward to each one more eagerly.

'Your grandfather married before he was thirty,' old Phillipson said comfortably. 'I meant to but she wouldn't have me. You Tennants can't do without a woman. Not keeping one, eh?'

Archie shook his head vehemently. 'No, sir. Just – well, you know, sir. There's something else that's worrying me awfully, something apart from your not being told properly about the company. And that's the small shareholders. I don't know much about business, Frederick's quite right, but I do know that most of the clerks in the office have at least part of a share, it was father's policy. Old Tremlett, sir. I mean, what happens to them when the company's bankrupted?'

Old Phillipson looked levelly at Archie. 'When everything has been sold up in Bombay and London, all the buildings, whatever is left in our godowns, the creditors and the shareholders are the first to be paid. But the creditors are in the first place many, owing to your brother's way of doing business, and in the second place, the company debts exceed at this moment its nominal capital. So I shouldn't imagine there will be a brass farthing left.'

'But old Tremlett!'

Old Phillipson shrugged. 'A sad story, young man.'

Archie got up and began to walk about the room rapidly and clumsily, catching his coat tails on piles of books as he strode past.

'Sit down,' old Phillipson said.

'It enrages me,' Archie said from across the room, taking no notice. 'I can't bear to think that that old man who has given so many years' service to the company, who is only waiting for

me to join – although I've told him I never shall –
because he promised Father, I can't bear to think
– it's intolerable—'

'What shall you do?' old Phillipson said com-
posedly.

Archie strode back to the fire. 'How much does
he have in the company, sir? What is he expecting
to see?'

'Five hundred pounds, perhaps. Not more.'

Archie's face broke into a delighted smile.

'Capital, sir! It's just what I have. I was trying
not to touch it because I knew I should need
something to tide me over until I am called to the
Bar. Father left it for me until I am twenty-one,
then I think I shall have – I mean I should have
had – some more. But Tremlett shall have it.'

'And the others?' old Phillipson said. 'Philpotts
has been at number four just as long, Rigby and
Newton forty years to my certain knowledge.'

Archie slumped into his chair in despair. 'I
don't know, sir.'

'I'll strike a bargain with you. You rescue
Tremlett. I will rescue the others.'

Archie leaped to his feet with a shout.

'Sit down!' old Phillipson said commandingly.
'You are quite as noisy as your grandfather. So
that's settled.'

'I think you are – are *splendid*, sir!'

Old Phillipson sighed. 'No,' he said, 'I can
afford it. I took all my money bar a few thousands out of the company. I just left enough to
give myself a seat on the board still. It was a

sentimental thing to do but I could afford it. I can afford to recompense those poor old pen-pushers too. *You* can't though. That five hundred is all you have.'

'I'll manage, sir.'

'Oh yes,' old Phillipson said. 'You will.'

Archie stood up for the third time. 'I must go, sir. You've been awfully good to give me so much time and to have been so generous. Perhaps you would let me call again sometime.'

'I'm not letting you go now, young man. There's one of my own ducks for dinner and it's an abominable night. Comfortable room you'll have here.'

Archie said, stammering, 'But – but I've – I mean, you can't want me, a Tennant—'

'I do. And I want my pound of flesh.'

'I don't understand you, sir.'

'I don't expect you to. I haven't explained myself yet. I'll tell you now and then you can go and fiddle about on my billiard table and think about it. It's a splendid table. I brought the mahogany home from the East with me and I went to Wales myself to choose the slate. Now listen to me, young man, and don't say a word. We'll discuss it at dinner. Don't fuss you've no evening clothes, I didn't ask you to stay for your clothes. I've struck one bargain with you. I'll strike another. I'll keep you at Oxford until you are finished and I'll be liberal with you. A couple of hunters, good rooms, a good cellar. And you in return will do what a son, if I'd had one, would

have pleased me by doing. You'll go to Wallace
Brothers at number eight Austin Friars and offer
yourself as a recruit. They are just about to take
young men on to work up country in Burma
and Borneo for their sister firm in Bombay, the
Bombay-Burmah Trading Corporation, and they
are a first-rate company. They've looked after my
money in a way I couldn't have bettered myself.
Your brother knows that's where I put my
money; it's another reason for his hating me so.
So that's the long and the short of it, Archie. I'll
see you handsomely through the next eighteen
months and you'll give up the law, just as your
father did, and be one of the first young Englishmen Wallace Brothers ever sends to the East.
Now off you go. Don't touch the cue with the
ebony handle. It's mine and it doesn't play the
same if anyone else uses it. I dine at seven.'

3

Four months later, in the decrepit and squalid British Residency in Mandalay, Queen Victoria's official representative in Upper Burma died of rheumatic fever. He was mourned by the Burmese people as a true friend, although his relations with the new young king, Thibaw, had never been as cordial as with Thibaw's father, Mindoon. He had been a diplomatic and scholarly man, had put up patiently with the tyrannical inconsistency of palace dealings, with alternating insult and warm patronage, with knowing how much the Upper Burmese wished to remain on good terms with the British occupiers of Lower Burma and with seeing the Residency of those same British crumble, through lack of funds or interest, into a collection of decaying wooden huts in a compound walled in matting.

His immediate replacement as British Resident in Mandalay was Colonel Horace Browne, fluent Burmese speaker and experienced explorer in up-country Burma. Colonel Browne was in Rangoon when the news of his appointment came, and before setting off up the Irrawaddy in one of the steamers of the Irrawaddy Flotilla Company – a journey of some eight or nine days – he remembered a conversation he had had the previous February with Miss Maria Beresford at her peculiarly uncomfortable birthday party in Bombay.

A telegraph was sent at once to Bombay, followed by a more explanatory letter. Although the appointment of his staff in Mandalay was not altogether a matter for his personal choice, he wrote to Hubert Beresford, it was of course within his power to make warm recommendations. His own appointment was only temporary but he supposed it would occupy a year at the least and as all the assistants at the Residency in Mandalay were young men, he himself would feel the benefit of an older aide. The salary would not be great – rather under a half of his own annual four thousand, though he did not specify this – but the opportunity might in some way compensate for the lack of ample payment. Colonel Browne, having inquired meticulously about Hubert Beresford, had no intention of allowing him much responsibility, but was aware that, first, his slightly rash promise to Maria must be honoured and, secondly, Upper Burma was precisely the place where a man of Hubert's good but idle wits might best profit himself. Colonel Browne intended to introduce him into Burma, and then, tactfully, to withdraw the support of the government of India and leave him to his own devices.

Thus it was on a stifling hot July morning,
a morning drenched with the steam heat of
the monsoons, that Maria looked out from the
steamer as it drifted, hooting, in towards
the riverbank at Mandalay and saw with irritation
Grace Prior, in a hideous cape of green rubber,
waving to her from the top of the bund. In
addition to the cape, Grace wore a monstrous
matching hat-cover of her own devising which
did away with the encumbrance of an umbrella,
and she was attended by a crowd of chattering
Burmese with whom she seemed much at ease,
and this, as well as her clothes, made Maria stare
disagreeably back at her.

Maria's temper had been sorely tried of late, in
any case. She had felt triumph and a thrill of
secret power when Colonel Browne's letter had
arrived in Bombay, and had derived enormous
pleasure from the ostentatious packing up of the
bungalow on account, as she put it to anyone
foolish enough to ask, of her father's 'diplomatic
appointment'. The few good possessions that
remained to them from palatial days in Tirimbatore would accompany them to Mandalay where
Maria envisaged them standing about graciously
on the gleaming floors of the British Residency.
Colonel Browne was a bachelor; he would, without the smallest doubt, be thankful for her talents
as hostess. She saw herself at the head of a
long table glittering with silver and glass, having
managed the servants with serene confidence and

receiving, as awed and grateful guests climbed reluctantly into their carriages after magnificent parties, the warmest tributes of gratitude from the Colonel, a gratitude not untinged with respect . . .

Buoyed up by these visions of their new life together and the public role she would play in it, Maria invested in as many new clothes as she dared, and sailed for Rangoon with Hubert in the best of spirits. Not only had there been a flattering number of farewell parties at which she found herself the undisputed centre of attention, but the day they departed she had received from Bengal a letter from Captain Murray Shaw, now back with his regiment. He heard of her going, he wrote, with the deepest regret, and was consoled only by the rumour that her father's appointment was likely to be temporary. Maria felt quite sure that if Murray Shaw's twenty-fifth birthday had already come, bringing with it his accession to a comfortable income, the letter would have been an open offer of marriage. As it was, it would do very well for the present, and she put it among her numerous personal possessions to be carried onto the ship. Once on board she found herself the only lady. Her new muslins were delightful for the bright breezy days on deck and the captain came as near to flirting with her as he dared. She stepped down onto Burmese soil with every expectation of finding red carpets and a brass band.

There was nothing. Rangoon was pleasant

enough in an unutterably provincial way and would presumably, in view of the amount of European Gothic building going on, be a place of some presence in ten years or so. But now it was a low-built, unfashionable town, boilingly, steamingly hot, the river fringed with godowns, the streets pitted with holes. There was nowhere like Marine Drive in Bombay, to show oneself off, nowhere to see or be seen. The only object that could possibly arouse interest was the Shway Dagon pagoda and that, with its smooth, soaring pinnacle of brilliant gold tinkling and winking with bells, Maria considered hopelessly vulgar. She was taken to visit it by no less a person than the Chief Commissioner of Lower Burma and when she discovered that to step onto the pagoda platform she must remove her shoes, she turned to her guide with a laugh that was not entirely without irritation.

'Mr Aitchison! You cannot suppose I should really take off my shoes! Look at the pavement. It is indescribably filthy and in any case the Burmese walk all over it – in bare feet!'

The Chief Commissioner shrugged and said that in that case he had brought her on a long climb to no purpose. They descended the steps from the platform to his carriage in silence and Maria was left with the feeling that if a mistake had been made that afternoon, it most certainly was not hers. When she drove past the Shway Dagon three days later to board the steamer for Mandalay, she gave it a quelling and reproving glance and resolved to put all memories of Rangoon behind her.

There was precious little to remember in any case, no garden parties, no receptions, no dinners, not even anyone to tea. She had been subjected to an awful performance – again by Mr Aitchison who, for all people said he was a sahib, had clearly lived too long among native peoples – called a *pwe*, where girls with barbarously painted faces and hideous tawdry costumes stiffened into ludicrous points on shoulders and hips, danced in a fashion that was scarcely even decent and sang screechingly to the accompaniment of tuneless gongs. Maria had had an agonizing headache throughout and there had been no European woman in the audience who came even halfway to being a lady. In fact there were very few women at all beyond a garrulous contingent of American female missionaries whose sartorial neglect affronted Maria quite as much as the winged costumes of the dancers.

It will all be all right she promised herself, when I am on the steamer. That is when it will become our new life, that is when everything will be elegant and suitable and deferential. The steamer, one belonging to the Irrawaddy Flotilla Company, was a huge three-decked affair, the top deck screened with awnings as much against the thick black smoke from the funnel as against the furious rains or the blazing sun. Behind the steamer were towed two vast flats piled with dried fish with a smell so violent that

Maria declared at first that she could not stand it.

'Make them take them off,' she cried to her father, angry-eyed across a scented handkerchief. 'Explain who you are! Insist they are removed!'

The flats and their stinking fish remained. Maria, exhausted by the disappointment of Rangoon and the heat and the wet, retired to her tiny none-too-clean cabin and burst into tears. She refused to come out to look at the little villages they stopped at, refused to admire the charming children playing in the river shallows or the pretty little Burmese women in their bright cottons who brought fruit on board in baskets whenever they moored, refused, in fact, to do anything but sit in her cabin and complain. She complained at the mould growing daily on her shoes, at the coarse food provided on board, at the jovial, beery manners of the captain, at the ceaseless melancholy chant of the leadsmen up in the bows, testing the depths of the river with long poles as they steamed onwards.

Hubert made promises about Mandalay.

'You will see, my dearest, you will see. A place of wonderful primitive beauty, the kind of beauty you knew in your childhood! The presence of royalty always gives a place an air. What could you expect of Rangoon? It's a place for petty provincial administrators, the dullest sort of civil servant. But Mandalay will be another world!'

And here now was that other world. All she could see from the taffrail was the huge, ugly, ochre breadth of the Irrawaddy dimpled with rain and stretching away to her left to some undistinguished dun-coloured hills. To her right was the high river bund, crowned with dripping trees, its steep flanks crowded with brown Burmese, some of whom were washing clothes in water the colour and substance of liquid mud. She could see no roof, no tower, no pinnacle. Certainly no palace.

She turned to exclaim her disappointment to her father and caught for a fleeting moment on Hubert's face a look of intense apprehension directed at her and that look, so vulnerable, so beseeching, so quickly gone, transformed her dismay at once to resolve.

'So, Papa! Here we are! And there is Grace Prior looking exactly like a toad in that dreadful arrangement of green rubber and, if I am not mistaken, there is Colonel Browne to welcome us. Just as I thought he would. Well, Papa, is this not exciting? A royal city!'

Hubert straightened his back and smiled at her with undisguised gratitude. Despite the wet heat, the pale grey cloth stretched smoothly across his shoulders, his collars rose to his distinguished jaw line unwrinkled and stiff. Maria, conscious that this horrible climate had caused a dampness that appalled her at her waist and beneath her arms, straightened too, unfurled the handsome green parrot-handled umbrella she had bought in Bombay and brought it up smartly over her new hat, a hat of grey velvet roses tied on with a huge and becoming bow of green moire ribbon beneath her chin. As the umbrella went up, so did her chin and then she put a grey-gloved hand on her father's arm and stepped ashore.

Grace Prior, so properly subdued in Bombay, seemed full of a new and wholly unattractive confidence.

'I do hope you will like Mandalay, Miss Beresford. It really is such an interesting place and so beautiful and Papa has done wonderful things at the mission school. The numbers have gone up to forty! It is such a pity it is raining so, people say the climate in the winter is quite perfect and when we came it was quite dry and the sun shone brilliantly, oh, for weeks and weeks! And I am learning Burmese, Miss Beresford, and the children are so charming and tease me so—'

'Indeed,' Maria said and moved smoothly forward to be greeted by Colonel Browne.

'My dear Miss Beresford! How very fine you are! Quite an ornament to Mandalay. Good journey, eh? Only eight days, you know, not bad at all. It sometimes takes nine or ten and if the steamer gets badly stuck, longer still. No trouble from the banks?'

'Trouble?'

'Dacoits. That's why they always moor the steamer in mid-stream at night. Ah, Beresford. Good to see you, welcome to Mandalay. Your fame is before you, Miss Beresford. The Queen has expressed a desire to meet the European lady who plays the pianoforte so well.' He lowered his voice. 'The ladies from the missions only play hymns you know. Evangelical music don't seem to suit the Burmese ear. Now then, I'll show you to your quarters. I haven't put you up in the Residency, it's hardly fit for pi-dogs let alone a lady. But there's a pleasant bungalow and I've given you half of the Residency guard. Ten Madras sepoys, Beresford, not much use but better than nothing.'

Dismay was beginning to creep lumpily up Maria's throat once more. Not stay at the Residency? Her vision of green lawns, flights of white steps, wide cool rooms – was that not to be? And Colonel Browne himself was wearing some dreadful tartan tam-o'shanter, not at all as she had remembered. But there was at least the invitation to the palace. The Queen with the outlandish name had asked to hear her play. If Maria did not think the bungalow Colonel Browne had found them suitable, she would of course ask the Queen to use her influence. Cheered at the thought, Maria did not even object when she discovered Colonel Browne had offered Grace Prior a lift back to the mission in the same carriage.

Carriage? On the other side of the bund, down its equally steep eastern bank, waited a row of bullock carts.

'Does the luggage go first?' Maria inquired of Grace.

'Oh no! We do.' Grace turned to smile at Maria, caught her look and said encouragingly,

'They really are not so bad, you know. You get used to them quite quickly. And the roads in Mandalay are so rutted that anything else would be broken to pieces.'

'Even in Rangoon,' Maria said with tightened lips, 'there were rickshaws.'

Grace shook her head.

'Not here. There aren't any rickshaws here. I expect we have to use bullock carts because we are *kalās*, foreigners, you know. The Burmese despise *kalās*, they really despise any foreigner except the Chinese. Sometimes I rather see why. We look so huge and clumsy beside them, we must seem like big children.'

Stiff with outrage, Maria descended the slope to the waiting carts. It was difficult to do, for mud clung stickily to her shoes and hem and her hands were quite preoccupied with her umbrella and her reticule. Little Burmese watched her impassively, their dark eyes taking in her height, her blondness, her strange and fantastic dress. They themselves wore pasos of checked cotton and tight fitting cotton jackets and only a few held umbrellas over their sleek black heads. A handful of children smiled shyly, filthy naked children with navels protruding like acorns from their swollen stomachs, inhabitants of the huts that clung to this slope of the bund, made of matting and broken lattices, indistinguishable in colour from the mud that surrounded them.

Poor Miss Beresford, Grace thought pityingly, poor Maria, in her lovely clothes, so used to everything being comfortable and elegant. So awkward, climbing into a bullock cart for the first time, before one gets used to the way Burmans stare so, before one realizes that ankles really don't matter a fig in Mandalay. And of course there is never anything to sit on in bullock carts, just the planks and that green silk will get horribly dirty. It must be awfully expensive silk, it is so thick and rustling. At least carts can't harm my mackintosh, though I can see Miss Beresford thinks I look a perfect fright. I always will beside her, though I look better in Burma, being small is more suitable somehow and they have thin wrists too—

'My dear,' Hubert murmured in Maria's ear. He had put his arm across her shoulders to protect her from the rough planking side of the cart.

She smiled at him bravely. 'The royal coach, Papa!'

Grace Prior leaned forward. 'This is such a beautiful place, Mr Beresford, even the *kalā* town is beautiful but, of course, today it is a bit difficult to see . . .' Her voice trailed away doubtfully.

Hubert Beresford looked about him. 'Quite,' he said.

The rain had almost ceased, but the air was thick with steaming dampness making it almost impossible to see anything at all. The *kalā* town, the city for foreigners, had been built inside a wide, western-swinging curve of the Irrawaddy, so that the river embraced it on almost three sides, and all the rutted lanes that passed for roads led down to the water. The lanes near the river were lined with the hovels of the poorer Burmese which, although squalid in themselves, were greatly improved in appearance by an enormous number of trees, mangoes, peepuls and feathery tamarinds, that grew everywhere in profusion.

As the carts jolted bone-shakingly away from the river to the east, the huts gave way to large compounds, low houses with verandahs and courtyards thick with mango trees, and every so often among these low bungalows an unmistakably oriental building appeared through the foliage, roofed in a double or triple layer of corrugated iron supported upon eaves of vermilion-painted timber.

Colonel Browne followed Hubert's gaze. 'We sold them tons of the stuff. Corrugated iron. There's an ancient custom in the orient that royalty must be roofed in silver or lead, but of course the Burmese are too practical to follow that to the letter. It was Mindoon, the last king, who hit upon the notion of corrugated iron. He could buy it very cheaply in Europe. He roofed the whole of the Gem City in it. It looks fine in the sunlight, too. Here we are, Miss Prior. Tell your father I'll be in to see him later today.'

The springless cart had crashed to a halt outside one of the oriental buildings, one with a triple roof. It was built high on pillars of teak, and a flight of worn steps led up to a wide covered verandah which surrounded it. Like the houses all around it, it was sunk in rampant foliage.

Grace climbed down neatly, turning when she was on the roadway to say to Maria, 'If you are not too tired to come at teatime, Miss Beresford, my father and I should be so pleased to see you.'

Maria nodded and smiled tightly. Presumably at some point she should have to call on Grace in that peculiar crooked, carved dwelling, but not until she had made of their own infinitely superior house a place to be envied.

Colonel Browne leaned out of the cart and patted Grace's wet hand. 'Course she'll come. I'll bring her myself.'

Under Hubert's arm, Maria's back stiffened with irritation.

'Triple roof you see,' Colonel Browne said as the cart jolted on. 'Mindoon built it for Doctor Marks, Prior's predecessor. They got on very well. Marks was even allowed to teach some of the princes. I remember seeing them when I first came up to Mandalay in fifty-nine, all processing off to the mission school on an elephant apiece under a pair of royal golden umbrellas. It was a great mark of favour to have a triple roof; Mindoon meant it as a compliment. Wait till you see the royal city, Miss Beresford. The King's own apartment has seven roofs. I've only had two audiences and I must say kicking my heels doesn't suit my temperament. I shall send you in,

Beresford, and you can sit about for a few days instead of me, and wait for Thibaw not to appear. Well, here we are, my dear, home sweet home.'

Hubert's hand tightened on Maria's shoulder. Together they looked across the backs of the bullocks towards a small, shabby compound with great unkempt mangoes flopping over the walls of matting. Between their pointed leaves was visible a modest timber bungalow with a narrow verandah – and a single roof. No lawns, no prospect, not even the dull gilded carving that had covered eaves and doors at the mission, just a squat, weathered, wooden building crouching warily under the thunderous drip of overhanging leaves.

'Has it been uninhabited long?' Maria said, her voice quite steady for Hubert's sake.

'Not more than a few months, my dear. There's more room than there looks. I expect, being an Englishwoman, you could make something of the compound.'

'I have never had anything to do with a garden,' Maria said and then, with as much dignity as possible, she clambered from the bullock cart into the mud of the lane.

4

Grace Prior, behind the teapot at the mission, looked at the room with less satisfaction than she had felt with it before. When she first came, she had liked the simplicity of it, the way the windows and doors were the same thing – long shutters of carved wood, faintly gilded – and the great soaring roof had seemed to her noble, almost spiritual, like a cathedral, arching over all the little rooms that were clustered below it. Of course, as these rooms were divided from each other only by partitions, there was little privacy, but she and her father lived at either end of the building so she need fear no indelicacy . . . In any case, the screaming of ungreased axles from the lane and the ceaseless knocking of the coppersmith birds from the trees outside were enough to drown any other sound. Since school, and the agonizing sharing of a dormitory, Grace had always been afraid of snoring, utterly humiliated at the prospect of unconsciously causing other people to regard her with disgust. She was quite sure Maria Beresford never snored.

But then, Maria Beresford had this steely quality of success. She had been a month in that most undistinguished bungalow and already it was, Grace was sure, the most elegant house in the *kalā* town. Grace had gone down to it in a spirit of intense curiosity thinly veiled as helpfulness to assist in the unpacking of innumerable boxes and had watched the dull little wooden rooms brought to life and character with rugs and embroideries, little tables, pictures and ornaments. The simplicity of the mission that had seemed to her so beautiful, almost holy, now only looked raw and bare.

Colonel Browne had laughed about the Beresford's bungalow, but then you couldn't expect a middle-aged bachelor to admire that charming sitting room littered with pretty things.

'I said to him,' the Colonel had said to Tom Prior, 'I said to Beresford, bring as little as you can, we shall only be here a matter of months – and they turn up with enough knick-knacks to fill a mansion! Game girl, Miss Beresford, though, I'll hand her that at least. I imagine she's had to get used to making silk purses out of sows' ears.'

Tom Prior was a great liability in Maria's house. Smiling and kindly, frequently abstracted, he blundered into frail objects like an amiable bullock while Grace fluttered round him, all at once terrified at what he might break and mortified, yet again, by her own clothes when seen against Maria's.

Clothes don't matter, she told herself regularly and resolutely before the little freckled glass that hung on the wooden wall of her bedroom. Not outward clothes, just the clothes of one's personality, one's soul. Even if I had some silk as delicious as that yellow afternoon dress of Maria's, I should only spoil it in the making up and anyway I am too pale for yellow. I really am very pleased with my new pink, very pleased, even if it is a little harsher in colour than I meant, in any case, it doesn't matter at all, it isn't what God minds about—

Now presiding over her tea table, she began again, dismissing and despairing over the simple furniture at the mission, the absence of ornaments, the fact that the only pictures were badly drawn prints of martyred saints. Her father liked them. He teased her and said she liked them too really, only she would not admit to a taste for the melodramatic.

'Do you have more tea in that pot of yours, Mademoiselle?'

Grace blushed at once. This was the third time the young French engineer Bonvilain had come to tea, and she blushed every time he spoke to her. He was handsome too, which meant she could not look at him because of being afraid of looking too much. She poured tea silently into his cup and with relief and disappointment watched him go back to the group of men around Colonel Browne.

They met like this three or four times a week, her father, the colonel, Mr Beresford, sometimes the intriguing Italian consul, Signor Andreino, sometimes the French engineer, very occasionally a peculiar and disconcerting man called Denzil Blount. Grace had noticed, pouring tea and slicing the cakes she had taught the Burmese cook to make, that if Monsieur Bonvilain or Mr Blount were there, the conversation was always more stilted, no-one seemed so relaxed, the talk was always more general. She wondered if Monsieur Bonvilain's being a Roman Catholic or Mr Blount's being, shockingly, an unashamed atheist had anything to do with the constraint, but her father had laughed at her. He never, Grace reflected, took any of her opinions quite seriously.

'If I don't get any satisfaction from the palace soon,' Colonel Browne said, 'I shall call it a day. I shall have to anyway, because the Residency is about to fall down, quite literally, and Thibaw won't produce a farthing for repairs. I am not received at court, we are not properly housed or guarded—'

Bonvilain said smiling, 'You should be prepared to remove your shoes.'

A disapproving silence followed this remark. After savouring it for a while, Bonvilain drained his cup, stood up in a leisured manner and then came to bow alarmingly over Grace's hand and take his leave.

'Mademoiselle,' he said and looked at her directly and for a second she looked back and was quite overwhelmed. Then he turned and bowed easily to the men, and Grace saw Hubert Beresford give him a more than cordial nod of farewell. Then his footsteps rang out on the verandah and down the steps to the road.

The Italian consul, his fingertips lightly together, surveyed Colonel Browne with amusement. 'Too much said, my dear Colonel. It was you who first told me that the French were to be watched up here, oh, nearly twenty years ago, and now you slip up yourself. That young man is only supposed to be building bridges but he looks too clever for that. And he has taken off his shoes several times and been granted audiences. Thibaw seems to be as much taken by his moustaches as Signorina Prior—'

Grace, mortified, bent her head.

'Of course,' her father said, gazing upward into the dark peak of the roof, 'we are all on a knife-edge here, all we foreigners. Only money or God keeps us here, and for the money to flow we need the favour of the King. And the Queen.'

Grace came out from behind the table, drawn by the mention of Supayalat. 'I saw the sisters from the convent today. They were summoned to see the Queen yesterday and had to sit in an apartment while some women were beaten in the room next door. They said Supayalat and her ladies laughed at the cries, and afterwards she made them translate a very vulgar French novel and ordered them to send to Paris for heaps of things, watches and photograph albums and French silks, expensive things. The sisters are worried about payment because the Queen keeps ordering things and never pays for them.'

'I imagine,' Andreino said, smiling at Grace, 'that the handsome Frenchman will find himself soon in much the same case. Supayalat is assuming more power each day and although she likes to spend, she does not like to pay. Her own troops are short of money, and foreigners in the royal service will be next. I am grateful for the agency of the Bombay-Burmah Trading Corporation for without their interests to guard in the teak forests, I should be penniless too. I am afraid my country does not think a consul in Mandalay necessary to pay for.'

'And mine,' Colonel Browne said abruptly, standing up, 'will not have such a necessity to pay for much longer. My position is absurd. I have been here two months and done nothing and every time I complain to Rangoon, Aitchison says he quite understands but the governments in London and Calcutta are far too preoccupied with trouble in South Africa and Afghanistan to be bothered with Mandalay at all. I fail to see the point of going on. Beresford, I'm going back to the Residency. Will you walk with me?'

Hubert Beresford declined with perfect courtesy. He wanted to walk towards the royal city, he said, it had almost become a habit with him in the early evening.

'My regards to Miss Beresford,' the colonel said.

When he too had gone loudly down the wooden steps to the lane, the Italian looked across at Hubert Beresford. 'And if the colonel withdraws from Mandalay, what shall you do, signore?'

Hubert, who seemed to have been dreaming, turned his fine head and said calmly, 'I think there will be plenty to keep us here, Signor Andreino. Plenty. We are a resourceful pair, my daughter and I, and although there would of course be absolutely no difficulty in my going back to Bombay, my old position being always open to me naturally, we are disinclined to retrace our steps so soon.'

'I must warn you,' Andreino said smiling, 'Mandalay is full of strange people, people who cannot live anywhere else, people who are not welcome any longer in Lower Burma, British Burma. Tom says we are on a knife-edge here. We are indeed. We must be very careful not to fall nor to get sliced in two.'

Hubert, regarding him, made no reply.

Andreino went on, 'There is much to be gained here, especially with royal patronage. But royal patronage is as fickle as it is heady. There is also much to be lost.'

'Not,' Tom Prior said smiling, 'if you come for God. Only if you come for money. Forgive me, gentlemen, I am going down to the chapel for a while. Grace will look after you—'

'I will come,' Andreino said, 'I will come with you.'

Grace, afraid of being left alone with Hubert, was relieved to see him rise too, look at his watch and declare that it was now time for his stroll towards the palace.

'Of course,' Grace said, too eagerly, 'it is very beautiful, isn't it? I don't wonder you go every evening, it is so lovely.'

Hubert, looking at her abstractedly, thought what a pity it was that the only girl of Maria's age in the *kalā* town should be this unremarkable little thing with her anxious eyes and terrible homemade clothes. He said goodbye to her with the gracious kindliness he reserved for the very young and the very old, took up his beautiful silver topped cane, and went down the verandah steps.

As he reached the lane, Grace saw to her consternation that Mr Blount appeared to be approaching the mission. She keenly did not wish to have to entertain him alone, but observed with relief that Mr Beresford seemed to have diverted him from his purpose for the two men, having exchanged a word or two, set off together in the direction of the palace. Grace stood and watched them for a while, tall formally clad Europeans among the scattering of little brown Burmese in the lane wrapped only in their lengths of bright checked cotton, and then her gaze wandered up among the damp green trees to where the sun, exhausted by the effort of trying to penetrate the monsoon steams all day, was about to slide thankfully to rest in the Irrawaddy.

★　　★　　★

Denzil Blount, negotiating the puddles that made the roadway more lake than lane, observed how very much better polished Hubert's boots were than his own. It was also extremely obvious to anyone interested in such discrepancies that Hubert's suit was better pressed, his linen better laundered, his hat better brushed. Denzil's clothes had begun their lives superbly in St James's entirely on credit, and were now, after years of neglect in punishing climates, both travel-weary and still unpaid for. If Denzil were ever unwise enough to go back to London, he doubted St James's would provide him with so much as a new necktie.

Of course, Hubert had a helpmeet in his splendid daughter. Miss Beresford had been seated in her pretty drawing room, immaculate in yellow silk, when he had met her the day before and she had made him, for all the confidence he felt in his charm, feel crumpled and not in charge of the situation at all. She had given him tea with distaste and had then proceeded to manage her father with such affectionate adroitness that any resentment Denzil felt at being treated high-handedly vanished quickly into a mounting admiration. Hubert's connections with the British establishment, his vanity, his need for money, the credentials of his manners and appearance, coupled with his daughter's shrewdness, strength of mind and devotion to her father – all these things, Denzil felt, accepting a second cup of tea humbly, boded very well for the future.

After tea he had boldly expressed his admiration for the bungalow and all Maria had done to make it so charming. Maria had bowed stiffly but her eyes had gleamed for a second.

'Shall I have the pleasure of seeing you at the mission tomorrow?' Hubert had inquired in his incurious drawl.

'No. No, you won't. I seldom go there. I believe I shock good little Miss Prior.'

Maria had looked up then with a real smile, made brilliant with a touch of malice. 'Then we have something in common, Mr Blount. I seldom go to the mission either. I am always asked but am always deeply depressed by going. I prefer boredom here with pretty things to look at than boredom there in the company of St Stephen being stoned without proper perspective.'

Denzil smiled back at her with the lazy, intimate smile that had proved so invaluable with women all his life. 'Since we are in such perfect agreement, Miss Beresford, perhaps you will allow me to waylay your father after his visit to the mission tomorrow. We could stroll by the palace walls and I might amuse him with tales of Mandalay.'

She nodded assent but withdrew her smile, deepening his admiration. Now glancing at Hubert as they made their way towards the palace, Denzil envied him not only for his clothes, but also for his daughter. She would prove, Denzil had no doubt of it, an admirable asset in all the plans he was revolving in his mind.

They did not speak much, being too occupied with keeping their feet dry and when the palace walls and the moat came in view, they fell instinctively into complete silence, standing and gazing as all Europeans were wont to do, however familiar they were with the spectacle of the City of Gems, the golden city of Mandalay. Before them rose walls of coral-red brick, the top crenellated into shapes like spear heads, running away to the east and north for more than a mile towards the blue Shan hills. They marched for more than a square mile, those coral-red walls, broken only once in each flank, to the north and south, to the east and west, by the blinding white structures of the massive gateways each crowned with a spire of five-tiered roofs, winged delicate roofs, edged with carved wooden eaves painted in scarlet and gold.

Between the walls and the muddy roadway where Denzil and Hubert now stood stretched the moat, more than two hundred feet of still and shining water, its gleaming surface broken only by the brilliant green pads of the water lilies and the pink lotus. Some distance away, by the southern gate, just visible from the south-western corner where they were, floated two golden royal barges, delicate winged boats like gondolas, with prow and stern upswept into pennants of wood which looked as if they might lift the barge right out of the water and bear it away to Mandalay Hill which rose, blue and misty, to the north-east of the palace walls.

Despite the thick damp air, the prospect was very brilliant, the red walls, the white gateway, the blue shining water, the green lily leaves, the glittering golden boats basking in their reflections in the moat beside the white bridges. And if one raised one's eyes, and looked beyond, inside the walls, it was almost dazzling to contemplate the strange loveliness of the Gem City. The square mile inside the walls was packed with roofs, glittering tiered roofs of pagoda and palace, all edged with winged eaves in red and gold, all soaring into spires between the feathery fronds of the tamarind trees. The whole palace complex, temple, bedrooms, audience hall, kitchen, every single building was of wood, teak wood from the forests to the south-east of the city, carved and fretted and painted vermilion. Here and there a watchtower rose, a red column up which a gilded staircase wound in a spiral, up, up to the lookout at the top. It was magical but somehow, to a European eye, unnerving, so much red and gold, so many shining tiered roofs, so many spires, everything so brilliant, so winged that only the trees seemed natural, the frothy pale green of the tamarinds and the dark drooping branches of the mangoes.

Hubert said, a faint note of regret in his voice, 'My daughter does not much care for it. She thinks it showy.'

Denzil laughed. 'It is. Decidedly. I should not expect a lady to enjoy it.'

Hubert had been disappointed at Maria's

disgust. They had come on a relatively fine evening, soon after their arrival, and he had felt himself frankly overwhelmed, responding to the sinister splendour with a wholeheartedness that surprised him. Maria had not descended from the bullock cart, but merely surveyed the view from beneath her parrot-handled umbrella, pronounced it vulgar, flashy and ostentatious, and had then suggested returning home. He sighed faintly now, remembering.

'Have you had audience?' Denzil said casually, moving to lean against one of the mangoes that fringed the moat.

Hubert looked shocked. 'Naturally not. The shoe question—'

'Ah,' Denzil said, 'the shoe question. Representatives of Her Imperial Majesty Queen Victoria, etcetera. Well, Beresford, nothing venture, nothing gain. And there is much to be gained, much, so much. But,' he said with careful nonchalance, 'I doubt Horace Browne will gain it. It needs a man of – a different mettle altogether. A man of the world, of assurance, of polish, a man understanding in the ways of men.'

Hubert drew his gaze reluctantly from the pinnacles of the palace. 'I believe,' he said, 'that Colonel Browne was glad to have me here. I can only suppose he felt I should have a better chance of an audience than he. Being, you understand, rather less martial in my approach.'

'Precisely.'

Encouraged, Hubert said, 'It seems to me a

little strange that we have made no progress in seeing the King. I have no vaulting ambition myself, but I cannot help feeling that if the matter were in my hands, we should be farther forward than we are.'

'If Colonel Browne,' Denzil said, his eyes fixed on the moat, 'were to withdraw to Rangoon, wash his hands of the whole affair, what should you do?'

'My position in Bombay is always open to me—'

'But should you like to resume it?'

Hubert studied his gloves and considered a reply.

Denzil ceased to look at the moat and regarded his companion instead. 'You see, Beresford, if the British withdraw, the field will be open to the French. You cannot imagine that young Bonvilain is only here to make roads and bridges. The French will move into the teak forests and drive out the Bombay-Burmah and our consular friend Signor Andreino. And they will work upon Thibaw. They will not hesitate to take *their* shoes off. He is a weak young man; he was a monk before he was King. He isn't much more than twenty and the French have already wooed him with wine and champagne for which he has developed a violent fondness. He may be weak but he has much power, and that power could be of real use to you and me, Beresford, could we tap it. Thibaw holds the great royal monopolies in his drunken hands, the monopolies of timber and earth oil and precious stones. Would you wish, Beresford, to see the concessions to those monopolies fall into French hands?'

'But the British government, the government of India, they would never allow—'

Denzil laughed and snapped his fingers in Hubert's face. 'My dear fellow! They don't care *that* much for Burma! Their hands are quite full with trouble from the Afghans and trouble from the Zulus; they have not a moment to spare for Mandalay.'

Hubert drew himself up. 'Colonel Browne assured me that a post in Mandalay was of very real significance to the government of India.'

Denzil said nothing in immediate reply but anger flared for a second in his eyes. When he spoke, his voice was tightly controlled. 'Try not to be an ass, my dear Beresford. A diplomatic post up here is not worth an anna. Burma is a backwater to England, a disagreeable steaming place which usefully provides us with timber. It is not a place of consequence, not to governments. But it could be to *us*. It could be to you and me, Beresford, if we play our cards right, if you listen to me, if you stick by me when Browne goes down to Rangoon as he surely will do before the monsoon ends. Don't look mortified, dear fellow. Don't sulk on me. You *know* this is a hole. You *know* assistant to the Resident carries as much weight as his bootblack. I am offering you more than Browne ever did. I am offering you a position with the King, wealth, status, *real* wealth and status. You can help me. I can help you.'

Hubert seemed to consider for a moment. Then he said slowly, 'Monsieur Bonvilain and I – have spoken, only very generally you understand, on the matter of the royal monopolies. He is as you say, a clever young man, but not an experienced one. He cannot, of course, offer me anything except the fruits of his observations and it is perhaps fortunate that he is sharp-eyed. I should, of course, be only too pleased to help you, Blount, should my influence be required—'

'It is,' Denzil said shortly.

'In that case—'

'Listen to me, Beresford. Those concessions to the royal monopolies are ours for the taking if we go the right way about it. We, Beresford, you and I, Bonvilain even, on the right terms, though I am reluctant to put a farthing in a French pocket – we could win the right to work the ruby mines, to cut down the forests. You, with your manners, can work upon Thibaw for me. I will do the sums, I will arrange the business but *you* will smooth the way with the King. And the beautiful Miss Beresford—'

Hubert looked up sharply. 'My daughter?'

'Your daughter. Your lovely and admirable daughter will be covered with rubies from head to foot if I have my way. She will be of inestimable value to us, because she will be our path to Supayalat.'

Hubert said, 'When we arrived, we were told

that the Queen wished to see Maria, to hear her play on the pianoforte. But the invitation has never come. I find it most surprising.'

'I can make sure it is renewed.'

Hubert regarded him. 'You can?'

Denzil smiled. 'I have a *petite amie*. Among the maids-in-waiting. She will remind the Queen. You must never underestimate the Queen, Beresford. She is young, but she is worth a dozen of Thibaw. She has allowed him only one other wife, her plain and pious elder sister, and she rules him completely. He is enslaved by her. She will soon be the power in this country, the only power that counts. It was she who ordered the massacre of the royal rivals. She will stop at nothing to achieve her ends, nothing at all. And your daughter will become her companion. She will like Miss Beresford, she likes all things that are striking, dramatic. Miss Beresford will tell her in carefully chosen words of our plans and she, in turn, will tell the King.'

Hubert was visibly gratified. 'There could be no more fit setting for my daughter than a palace.'

'Even if she does regard it as hopelessly vulgar.'

'The chosen companion of the Queen – that puts quite another complexion upon it.'

'And does it,' Denzil said, leaving his mango tree at last and coming close to his companion, 'does it also put any kind of complexion upon my offer to you?'

Hubert said superbly, 'I shall be happy to help you.'

Denzil's hand came up involuntarily, as if it wished to strike Hubert of its own accord, but it was restrained and returned to a pocket.

'We must work fast, Beresford. We must get ourselves locked tight in with the palace before the Residency is closed and all the British have a bad name. The Burmese will not take Browne's departure kindly; we will all be tarred with the same brush. But if Miss Beresford has made herself indispensable to the Queen, and you have made yourself wholly agreeable to the King and not, repeat not, initially asked for any favours, we will prove the exceptions to the rule. I will obtain an invitation for Miss Beresford at once and you – you will present yourself at the Hall of Audiences tomorrow. Without your shoes.'

'No,' Hubert said. 'That cannot be done.'

'Then neither can our fortunes be made.'

Hubert regarded his boots for a moment almost regretfully. 'Very well.'

'And Miss Beresford? Will you permit me to see Miss Beresford?'

'Tomorrow,' Hubert said, 'you may come for tea tomorrow.'

'And you will also ask Bonvilain?'

'No,' Hubert said. 'I will speak to Bonvilain. In due course. It will be more satisfactory that way.'

When he had bowed and moved away along the western road that led back into the *kalā* town, Denzil realized that there was perhaps a compensation for dealing with a man so inordinately vain. There had been moments in their interview when vanity had quite obscured Hubert's wits, but that same vanity had happily rendered him totally incurious about Denzil's past, his reputation or his soundness as a partner in such an adventurous scheme as this.

5

Grace Prior was in Maria's drawing room when the royal summons came. She had arrived half an hour before accompanied by Hosannah Manook, an Armenian whose father was the *Kalawun*, or minister for foreigners. Hosannah was plump and dark and lively, with brilliant black eyes and startlingly colourful clothes and Maria had, from the moment they met, and despite Hosannah's father's position at court, regarded her in much the same light as she did Burmese architecture.

Grace, no longer even fractionally confident of her new pink, had come with another purpose than simply introducing Maria to the cheerful Hosannah.

'Miss Beresford, you must come with us! We are going to the Denigrés, the French weavers, you know. They weave velvet for the court, all those apricot velvet robes the ministers wear on feast days. They are father and daughter, Miss Beresford, just as you and Mr Beresford are, and father and me. Do come!'

Maria laughed a little. 'My dear Miss Prior! I have no need of any velvet. One hardly would in this climate. And I am sure that if I did need any,

Mademoiselle Denigré would come to me.'

'Oh, *no*, Miss Beresford, not like that at all. Not a business visit. A social call! They are so charming, both of them, and the daughter is so dignified and amusing and she is very well received at court. The house is delightful, just like a house in southern France, not Burmese in the least and Julie bakes the most delicious cakes you ever ate. Oh do come, Miss Beresford. I have promised I will bring you and told them so much about your lovely dresses!'

'No doubt you have,' Maria said without a hint of gratitude at this compliment, 'but you should not presume on my time in this manner. Living here may be quite extraordinary in all sorts of ways and compel one to do all kinds of things one would not ordinarily do, but there is a limit to one's eccentricities all the same. And calling socially upon a weaver's daughter is definitely beyond that limit.'

Grace, goaded by this supercilious ungraciousness and inspired by the knowledge that Maria had never left India before coming to Mandalay, retorted bravely, 'Oh, of course, one would not do it in *England*, I am sure, unless it was a pastoral call, but Mandalay is so very different from England.' She paused and then said, 'Is it not, Miss Beresford?'

Maria, outraged, looked past her into the compound where the mango trees dripped drops the size of marbles onto the soaked earth. Hosannah Manook, quite unperturbed by the barbed exchange, burst into a flood of enthusiastic praise for Mademoiselle Denigré and the taste she displayed both in her work and in her house.

'It could not interest me less,' Maria said, her voice taut with fury.

'Of course not!' Hosannah cried gaily. 'How could it until you have seen it, and observed how charming it all is! And when we have taken you there, we shall take you to the little cigar house by the western gate and you shall see the Burmese women rolling cigars with their little brown fingers and then you shall choose cigars for your revered father! And probably Julie will send one of her special *gâteaux au chocolat* home with you for Mr Beresford too and when he eats it he will be happy! And you will be happy too, for the Denigré house is always full of sunshine and pleasant people, all the charming French people in Mandalay, such as that delightful Monsieur Bonvilain!'

Grace coloured so quickly that Hosannah never noticed the brief gleam in Maria's eye.

'Oh, my dear Grace! Pink as your English rose! I don't blame you, my dear, he is so very amusing. Now, Miss Beresford, why do you not run and fetch one of the pretty hats I have heard so much about and let us take you there with no more objections?'

The door opened and a black Madrassee bearer – taken from the guard by Maria, who was used to Madrassees in the house and preferred them to the little Bengali Colonel Browne had brought from Calcutta and spared, at great cost to his own comfort, for her use – came in with a folded paper on the silver tray that used to wait in the hall at Tirimbatore for the calling cards that never came.

Maria, still flushed a little with temper, took the paper in her most haughty manner and, without begging pardon of her companions, proceeded to read it. She read it very thoroughly, several times, and as she did so her proud and disagreeable expression changed to one of open exaltation.

'I fear I cannot come with you this afternoon, Grace – Miss Manook. I have been summoned to court. Queen Supayalat has requested me to attend her.'

Hosannah laughed heartily. 'But not now, my dear Miss Beresford! Not in the afternoon! The King and Queen sleep now and then they will lie all afternoon in the gardens and watch the king-fishers! And then the Queen will change again for she changes three times a day, fresh tamein, fresh jacket, fresh pawa, different jewels. Never never does the Queen hold audience in the afternoons!'

It was too much that this dreadful vulgarly dressed person with her loud, jolly laugh should know more about palace life than she did. She rose, signifying that the visit was at an end.

'I am well aware, Miss Manook, that I am not required until the morning. But I wish to make sure that everything is in perfect order for tomorrow and also I do not wish to be tired out and shaken to pieces by bouncing about in a bullock cart. I will bid you both good day.'

When they had gone, Maria read the note over and over again, as greedily as if it had been a longed-for love letter. She had entertained Mr Blount to tea two days before – at Papa's request – and had been pleasurably surprised to see how much improved he was in appearance. His suit now looked worthy of its origins and his hair and moustaches had been neatly trimmed. Maria took all these significant changes in him as a compliment to herself and allowed herself to own that he was an extremely pleasing-looking man and one who clearly admired her more than any man had done since Murray Shaw had so nearly declared himself in Bombay. Murray Shaw had been an attractive proposition, it was true, but a callow and unformed one beside the practised ease of Denzil Blount. Of course, Mr Blount was hopelessly disadvantaged by having no money, but then, as he revealed his schemes to her in an irresistibly humble and self-deprecating manner, it appeared that his embarrassment in this matter was likely to be only temporary.

'So you see, Miss Beresford,' he said to her in conclusion, 'I am about to discover what your fortunate father has known for years. Namely, that we cannot do without you. It is only by your intercession with the Queen that we have any chance at all.'

Later that night as they dined together, Maria, using her little-girl voice to disguise a question she felt might be naive, said to her father, 'But Papa, there is nothing wicked in these schemes for the royal monopolies, is there? There is nothing naughty in our trying to gain the concessions?'

Hubert put down his soup spoon to stretch his hand across the table – it was a pitifully small table, they had only used it as a tea table at Tirimbatore – and clasp hers warmly.

'My darling girl! As if Papa would ever stoop to such a thing whatever the gain! It is as open a scheme as I ever saw! The King has a monopoly of these mines and forests but he does not always have the engineers to work them, so he will allow someone else to work them for him and to benefit from the results. That is all! All, my dearest. Mr Blount is simply anxious to secure the concession to at least one of these monopolies before, for example, the French do. And he needs my advice, my influence and your brilliant way with people to achieve his ends.'

Maria smiled and lowered her eyes, releasing Hubert's hand after giving it a grateful squeeze. The blue silk she wore, a strong soft blue, would be wonderfully set off by some sapphires . . .

Now, having slipped the note into her pocket, and abandoned the drawing room for her bedroom and a little sartorial deliberation, she acknowledged that it was not only the prospect of sapphires that excited her, but equally that of action. The idea of having something to dress for, somewhere to go, someone to meet – all these things aroused her as nothing had done since she left Bombay. And the fact that the somewhere was a palace and the someone a queen brought an animation to her whole being quite spontaneously, an animation she had had to force for the last few months whenever her father crossed the threshold.

They had been, for Maria, months of the acutest disappointment and almost intolerable boredom. There was no-one in Mandalay to see her clothes, to dine with, to play music to, to be admired by, no-one at all. Apart from Colonel Browne – and Maria had long since ceased to be grateful to him for bringing them to Burma, indeed she now regarded him with powerful resentment – there was no-one in Mandalay whom she could begin to countenance. The visions of the Residency and its life that had sustained her as she journeyed up the Irrawaddy had been dashed by the reality of the people who lived here, the rogues and ruffians of a dozen nationalities all hoping for the fruits to be gained from royal patronage, all unacceptable either in British Burma or in their own countries. They were ill spoken, badly dressed and worse behaved. Many of them even kept native women in their houses, a notion almost too disgusting to contemplate. Maria really felt that most of the *kalās* in Mandalay were worse even than the Burmese themselves, and she was not capable of a more insulting thought than that.

She chose a dress of rose pink, its skirt looped

up to show underskirts of cream embroidered in pink, and laid it on her bed to contemplate. It was the best of the new dresses from Bombay, dresses she knew with a pang of guilt had cost far more than they should have and which she had had no chance to wear at all for anyone of any consequence except her father. Hubert had intimated, very gently and with a regret that broke her heart, that the Bombay dresses must be the last for the moment and Maria knew that they had not been paid for before they came away, that money must be sent from Mandalay. Of course it would be sent, Papa was so honourable, but she regretted her extravagance bitterly. Perhaps when Mr Blount's schemes bore fruit, there never need be any worries of that kind again; money would be as unthinkingly plentiful as it had been in her childhood. Such a happy prospect was worth every effort, indeed it was, and Supayalat must be impressed at first glance. Even if she had nothing finer to wear than the rose pink, it would remain in the Queen's mind that Maria always dressed as magnificently, because she had first seen her thus. As Papa said, people only took one at one's own valuation and therefore one must put a high price on oneself.

With her dress decided, there was little else to worry about. It was the custom to take Supayalat presents, European presents for which she had an insatiable appetite. Mr Blount had said anything would do, any frippery she had no use for and that mirrors were particularly popular. That was easy. Maria would take her mother's hideous old-fashioned silver-gilt looking glass, its handle shaped like a fish, a dreadful object that had come from that happy childhood in the big, new, vulgar red brick house in Burslem. The fish on the handle had red glass eyes and the rim of the mirror was studded with imitation stones. Maria, not disclosing its origins of course, had shown the looking glass to Mr Blount with a deprecating laugh, saying she could not think how such a thing came into her possession and Denzil Blount had laughed too and said it was the very thing for the Burmese Queen. Supayalat might be a queen but she was, after all, only Burmese.

The present was chosen, the dress, the hat, the parasol. Maria surveyed herself piece by piece in her glass and decided that the elements that the Almighty had chosen would do very well also. It was a pity she had grown thinner in the last weeks but her blondness and elegance were undiminished, even though she had been so starved recently of the admiration that was life blood to her. Even if they had shown it, she would have despised admiration from the extraordinary handful of nonentities gathered in Mandalay. Tom Prior was amiable enough but, being a missionary, hardly counted, of course, as a human being socially speaking. Grace ditto, and she was not even so amiable; the Frenchman was handsome but quite evidently bourgeois; the Italian was as good as bourgeois and horribly casual over clean linen and fingernails; Colonel

Browne had proved a bitter disappointment; and Denzil Blount – not quite to be relied upon somehow . . . That was her audience, she reflected bitterly, that was what she had had to substitute for her visions of Residency elegance and a full social life of which she was to be queen.

She looked down at her mother's looking-glass. Tomorrow it would be in other hands, royal hands. Perhaps tomorrow would bring something else also, a life more like the one she had hoped for. She picked up the silver bell on her dressing table and rang sharply for her maid.

The following morning, she was kept waiting two hours. She rose very early, poured tea for her father at breakfast, saw him off through the rain to the Residency and then was dressed with the utmost care and slowness on account of the heat and the wet which seemed to fill the little house with a sticky steam. Once attired in the rose-pink silk, she sat down to wait for a carriage from the palace, arms carefully akimbo in that awful temperature to avoid the horrid possibility of staining her dress.

She sat and sat. In the lane outside wheels screamed past and the Burmese shouted to their bullocks and two coppersmith birds in the nearest mango knocked maddeningly, not quite together. Tuneless singing and an intermittent clatter came from the servants' quarters across the compound, but no royal messenger, no sound of trumpets. Maria sighed impatiently and stayed motionless, watching with distaste a pair of geckos flickering across the walls behind the pictures and a stout blood-red cockroach which, supposing the room to be empty, had come trundling out of the damp woodwork in search of crumbs.

She consulted her pocket watch as seldom as she could bear to and told herself that if no word had come by eleven she should ring for her maid to help her change. At twenty past eleven, when her impatience had flared into fury, a dark-skinned little person in white muslin with an absurd straw hat bobbing with cherries came tripping into the compound accompanied by a Burman holding an umbrella over her head. Maria remained where she was, only taking up a book from a side table and opening it at random.

'Miss Beresford?'

Maria started admirably and made a pretty show of almost dropping the book.

'Oh, did I disturb you? Forgive me, do. Miss Beresford, I am Mattie Calogreedy, I am European maid of honour to Queen Supayalat. I am come to take you to the palace.'

Maria rose and surveyed Miss Calogreedy. She had Eastern blood there was no doubt of it, with that dusky skin and slightly slanting dark eyes. She would also in a few years be extremely stout, although pretty and soft enough at the moment. She was smiling up at Maria from beneath her ribbons and cherries, showing teeth as small and even as a child's.

'You will wonder at my name, Miss Beresford! My father is Greek and much in favour at court. That is one reason why I am maid of honour. Come, Miss Beresford. We must not keep the Queen waiting. She is so anxious to see you and asked most particularly that you should wear your jewels.'

Maria's chin went up and her pearl earrings swung against her cheeks.

'Miss Calogreedy, I am wearing such jewellery as is appropriate to my dress.'

The royal carriage was yet another bullock cart, although the floor had been covered with a particularly hideous carpet of pink and yellow roses on a ground of emerald green.

'French!' Mattie said, patting it proudly.

Maria seated herself with as much dignity as she could and was disconcerted to find that two Burmese bearers sprang in after her and held umbrellas above her and Miss Calogreedy. The cart squealed atrociously and what with the axle and the rain and the wheels hitting ruts in the lane, conversation was hardly possible. Mattie Calogreedy sat and smiled at her or looked about her with an enjoyment that seemed to Maria both incomprehensible and distasteful. For her own part, she stared straight before her and let the wet trees and low buildings slide past her gaze, looked at but unseen.

It was only when the cart halted on the bridge to the royal city that Maria allowed her eyes to take in what was before her. Even her outrage at being kept waiting half a morning must give way to curiosity when actually about to enter the royal Gem City of Mandalay, and she leaned forward and observed that a guard of soldiers was coming forward to meet them, soldiers dressed in long red cloth coats over baggy white breeches, and wearing on their heads little winged red velvet caps embroidered in gold and surmounted by tin hats. At the head of the group was one who was evidently an officer, to judge from the coil of gold tinsel that adorned his hat and the embroidered velvet coat, bordered in gold, that almost obscured his balloon-like breeches. He spoke to Mattie Calogreedy in Burmese and, to Maria's disgust, Mattie dimpled and giggled in reply. When the bullock cart lurched forward, she actually waved her plump little hand to him coquettishly.

'Of course, we have permission to go in!' she cried to Maria. 'I can come and go as I please! I run in and out of the city all day, to see my mother and father and my friends, in the *kalā* town! Did you meet my friend Julie Denigré, Miss Beresford? Or Hosannah Manook? Or that dear, sweet thing at the mission who wouldn't say boo to a goose? There now, Miss Beresford, look about you, do!'

The rain had almost ceased and a milky sun was beginning to burn fiercely through the pearly vapours of steam. In the strange misty light, Maria saw the City of Gems for the first time, rising like a fairy city from the clouds, a dim magical spectacle of spires and wings and pinnacles, red and gold and glittering silver set in spaces of brilliant green grass and cushioned among trees.

'It is a square mile!' Mattie Calogreedy said. 'And almost a quarter of it was given over, in the late King's day, to housing the lesser queens. Look. There, over there in the middle, the seven-roofed building, that's the Glass Palace, that's where we are going. And the little one next to it is the royal kitchen and then there is the theatre. They are all on platforms, Miss Beresford, that is why they are so high. Perhaps I may show you the Lily Throne Room, it is quite lined with mirrors!'

The street along which they rumbled was packed with people, all Burmese, all prosperous looking and dressed in the slender tameins that they wound so deftly about themselves from waist to ankle. The tameins in the royal city seemed all to be of silk too, a rough gleaming silk in brilliant clear colours, jade and pink and sky blue, apricot, yellow, purple and grass green. Above the tameins were neat white muslin jackets, long-sleeved, close-fitting and at the neck little scarves of yet more brilliant silk. The oily black hair of this busy crowd was for the most part done up in a sleek cone on top of their heads and ornamented with flowers.

'We must walk now, Miss Beresford.'

They had halted at another gateway, almost as massive and quite as blindingly white as the one they had passed through at the bridge.

'You see,' Mattie said, sliding a confidential and unwanted hand beneath Maria's elbow, 'the outer part of the city, where we have just been, is for shopkeepers and merchants and lesser courtiers, but now we are going into the inner enclosure reserved only for the great ministers, the Prime Minister and such like, and in the heart of that, we shall find the palace itself!'

More soldiers in their strange uniform of scarlet and white escorted them through, and into another area of straight streets and wooden buildings and green grass mown as close and smooth as velvet. Before them rose a massive building supported on red and gold pillars and roofed in iron decorated with a wealth of curious carved animals and plants.

'The palace?' Maria said, startled out of her disagreeable silence by curiosity.

Mattie Calogreedy squinted up at the huge building. The gold on its pillars was beginning to dazzle in the strengthening sun.

'No. No, that is the *Hlutdaw*, the parliament. There, over there is the palace.'

There was another gate to be negotiated first, a little postern in a wall, and Maria was reminded of a Russian doll she had been given as a child – and despised – which had come apart at the waist to reveal a second doll and the second doll held a third and on and on until she was left with a tiny solid doll no bigger than half her thumb. But the sight through the last door was infinitely more rewarding than the last doll. The streets ended, the bustle of people vanished and instead Maria found herself in a vast, park-like place, a space of gardens, of lawns, fountains and trees and, here and there, the palace buildings on their great platforms. They were of teak too, like everything else in that extraordinary place, oiled dark teak, but the pillars that supported the entrances were lacquered in red and gold and set with mirrors, and the roofs, the glittering winged tin roofs, balanced on wooden eaves carved and painted to resemble scarlet flames, soared up into the sky.

There were some people about, after all, Maria realized, staring round her, unable to help herself, but only women – women and children. The grass was brilliant in itself after the rains, but the little bright figures that ran about on it were more brilliant still in their silks, like butterflies, like flowers, like scraps of coloured paper.

'Who are they?' she said, gazing. 'What are they doing?'

At the sound of her voice, many of the little creatures turned to stare at her so tall, so fair, so stately in her strange and elaborate clothes. Mattie laughed and called out to them in Burmese.

'They are the maids in waiting, Miss Beresford! The maids of honour. And the children of the court. We play all day, Miss Beresford. You cannot imagine what a delightful time we have! The King and Queen love the gardens as much as we do, they use the summerhouse over there, you see? The little one with the five roofs. Come, Miss Beresford, come.'

Outside the central hall, Mattie Calogreedy kicked off her slippers and indicated Maria should do the same. There was a moment of rebellion, a memory of the Shway Dagon pagoda in Rangoon, and then Maria recalled that her father had taken his shoes off, that Mr Blount had said success depended upon her friendship with the Queen. Slowly and stiffly she stooped and eased off her shoes, not best pleased to observe how large they were beside Mattie's little velvet slippers.

After the steam and the glare outside, the dim splendour of the central hall was a cooling relief. The doors were all thrown open, but they were low and narrow and only admitted enough light to see where one was going.

'Sit,' Mattie whispered, 'like me.'

The room was quite silent, carpeted in layers of rugs, some old and oriental, some new and European. There were maids of honour here and there, but no-one spoke. Mattie had dropped flexibly into the required sitting position with her feet tucked under her and Maria, attempting to imitate her, thought crossly that if Mattie's father was a Greek, her mother must certainly be Burmese, which would account for her catlike suppleness as well as the darkness of her skin.

It was agonizing, sitting like that. The bones of her corset dug viciously into her sides and it was impossible to breathe comfortably. The impression of coolness one received coming in from the outside proved only an impression and the heavy wet heat began to oppress Maria dizzily in her discomfort. She could feel a sliding finger of sweat running down her backbone and her upper lip was wet. Desperately she began to count objects in the room as a distraction, pillars, girls, mirrors—

At the far end of the hall, a golden door was opened. Instinctively, Maria attempted to rise.

'Sit,' Mattie hissed, seizing her. 'It is polite. It is the most humble.'

The girl who came into the room seemed to dart rather than walk. She stepped in quickly and lightly, her head turning this way and that, the diamonds in the tall cone of the hair catching the faint light, like cold fire.

'Down,' Mattie whispered and bringing her joined hands up to her forehead, bowed to the ground. Maria, uncomfortably impeded by her corset, followed suit as best she might.

In the silence, the girl spoke. Her voice was harsh and clear. Maria waited, head bent still, the blood thudding in her cheeks, and heard Mattie reply.

'We are to follow her,' Mattie said urgently. 'She wishes to see you in her own apartments. Come quickly, Miss Beresford.'

Stumbling over her flounces, clutching her hat and skirts, Maria followed Mattie up the hall and through the gilded door onto the scorching palace platform once more. Then Mattie went running down the platform and Maria hurried to follow her, through a doorway, across a small chamber, through a further doorway and into an empty room full of light where the small, imperious figure of Queen Supayalat waited in the centre of a rug that was almost a twin to the one that had lined the bullock cart.

Maria knelt.

'She wants you to rise,' Mattie said. 'The Queen wishes to look at your clothes.'

The Queen was very small and very supple and, Maria noticed with a shock, heavily pregnant. She prowled round Maria like a little brown snake that has swallowed a coconut, reaching out with her flickering fingers to touch the silk and velvet, talking all the time in her clear, harsh voice. She was not beautiful, not pretty even, but she had an allure, a power that Maria could feel as an almost physical influence, and when she raised her magnificent dark eyes to Maria's face and smiled, Maria felt herself for a second ready to faint.

'The Queen admires your earrings,' Mattie said. 'She asks if you have rubies for that gown.'

Maria smiled with difficulty down at the little glowing creature. 'I have no rubies, Your Majesty.'

Supayalat clapped her hands and called something sharply. She wore a tamein of the most lustrous silk, pink and green, embroidered in gold, and the muslin of her jacket was stretched tight over her silk bodice and the smooth high mound of her belly. Her small brown feet were thrust into red velvet sandals whose soles were edged with rubies, and the diamonds Maria had seen in her hair were echoed in her ears and hung in glittering strands around her neck.

Two maids of honour came running in with lacquer boxes which they placed on the carpet before the Queen. Supayalat took Maria's wrist in her thin tight grasp and drew her down to her knees, flinging open the lids of the boxes and revealing a heap of jewellery in each, a dazzling tangle of red and green and white and blue necklaces, bracelets, earrings, all thrust pell-mell in together. Supayalat laughed and pushed Maria's hand into the jewels; it was intoxicating, her fingers deep in such a pile, deep among the cold smooth smallness of the gems.

Supayalat pulled out a bracelet of pale pinkish rubies set in gold and held it against Maria's dress. Then she nodded and said something to Mattie and pushed the bracelet onto Maria's wrist.

'The Queen asks what you have brought her.'

Maria took the looking glass from her reticule and offered it to the Queen. Supayalat took it in silence, sitting on her heels, studying her fascinating, vivid little face in the glass and then she looked up at Maria and laughed again and began scattering jewellery all over the carpet, diamonds and emeralds and rubies rolling like marbles into the corners.

'The Queen is very pleased with your present,

Miss Beresford. She wishes you to keep the bangle.'

Supayalat stopped throwing jewellery and began to speak quickly and without smiling, her eyes fixed upon Maria's face.

'The Queen wishes to know why you are in Mandalay. There are few European women in the Kingdom of Ava.'

Maria looked steadily back at Supayalat. 'I am here because of my father. The Queen will know he is assistant to the British Resident. I go wherever my father goes. I am his chief companion.'

Supayalat smiled at her.

'Do you have a husband, the Queen wishes to know?'

'No,' Maria said, 'my father is all I need.'

A young man appeared in the doorway, a plump young man with deep sunk eyes in a faintly puffy yellow face, dressed in a green silk paso with a spray of diamonds in his top knot. Supayalat and Mattie instantly bowed upon their clasped hands and Maria, startled but entranced to find that she was almost alone in a room that held both King and Queen of Upper Burma, followed them.

Thibaw's voice was soft, almost hesitant. He glanced at Maria nervously once or twice, then crossed the room to sit cross-legged on the low gilded couch, a *salun-daw*, that was the only furniture. Supayalat, answering him in her rapid way, moved to sit beside him. Maria remained where she was upon the floor.

'The King says he has given audience to your father,' Mattie said. 'He says he wishes you to play music for the Queen. He has a German pianoforte that he would like you to play on. The Queen wishes you to rise in order that the King may see how tall you are.'

In silence the royal couple surveyed her and, despite the fact that her silk was now crumpled with so much getting up and down Maria looked back at them serenely.

'The Queen wishes you to learn Burmese so that you may speak together. She asks if you draw.'

'I do.'

'Could you draw Their Majesties?'

'Most certainly.'

Supayalat and Thibaw turned to each other in delight. Then Thibaw spoke once more, not to Maria, but to the carpet and her feet.

'His Majesty wishes to impress some things upon you. He wishes you to repeat them to your father. There are very few royal monopolies left. His father, the late King Mindoon, abolished almost all of them, leaving only those in teak and earth oil and precious stones. The teak is leased to the Bombay-Burmah Trading Corporation but, that lease aside, His Majesty wishes to establish a relatively free market. He wishes you to tell your father this.'

Maria bowed a little and looked at Thibaw. His face was quite expressionless but Supayalat was regarding Maria with a look at once determined and encouraging. She smiled quickly and spoke to Mattie.

'We should go, Miss Beresford. The Queen is tired. You will return in the morning.'

Maria subsided to the floor once more, her forehead bent upon her hands. When she looked up again, Thibaw was walking from the room, Supayalat behind him. Almost at the door the Queen spun round and darted to Maria's side, seizing her hand and saying something to her with rapid eagerness before running back to Thibaw who waited for her like a dog under orders.

Mattie Calogreedy put her plump little hand on Maria's arm and smiled knowingly up at her. 'Oh, Miss Beresford, you have been a success! The Queen tells you that your father must not be disappointed, that he must persevere, that the notion of free trade is only an idea so far. And when you come tomorrow, Miss Beresford, the Queen wishes you to bring your sketchbook.'

6

The colonel, waiting for Hubert in the Residency, was occupying his time in pondering. Before him on his desk lay a letter from the Chief Commissioner in Rangoon which had arrived on that morning's steamer, and which indicated that London and Calcutta had roused themselves sufficiently from their anxious contemplation of Afghanistan and South Africa to decide to close the Residency at Mandalay.

'It seems nothing can be gained by your remaining,' Aitchison had written, 'and you have endured enough indifference and humiliation. I have begged the Viceroy to reflect upon the indignity of your situation and at last he has listened. All British subjects in Mandalay should be informed of our withdrawal, naturally, although I suppose those who insist upon remaining might trust themselves in times of trouble to the ingenious Signor Andreino.'

Outside his study windows creamy frangipani and the blood-red blooms of a gold mohur tree were shuddering under thunderous raindrops. Two Indian servants, crossing the compound, had adopted the Burmese custom of wearing palm leaf hats a yard wide and they moved into the colonel's view like a couple of mobile umbrellas. Within a fortnight perhaps he would be gazing out, not at the unkempt and exasperating splendours of Mandalay, but at the ordered grounds – equally wet to be sure but ordered – of the British High Commission in Rangoon. Oh the wet! The ceaseless, exhausting monsoon season of Burma, rain and heat and rampant mildew from June to October, day in, day out. Turning back to his letters, Horace Browne promised himself a month in Simla.

His reply to Aitchison was written and sealed. The Residency would be left in the care of one of his junior assistants for a few weeks more, but he assured the Chief Commissioner that he and his staff should board a steamer for Rangoon within days. He agreed there was nothing for him to stay for. Thibaw seemed inclined to see anyone, everyone, and appeared unimpressed by a history of cordial Anglo-Burmese relations in the last twenty years. He had as yet ceded the royal monopolies to no-one, but Andreino had ferreted out the fact that he was in correspondence with the Czar of Russia and in any case the matter was not so much in his hands as in those of his Queen. If Supayalat went on in the way she seemed to be going, Colonel Browne doubted that even the Italian consul would be a match for her. That was what worried him. If Supayalat became obsessed with the notion that Burma was for the Burmese, that Ava could do without the *kalās*, or at least, those *kalās* with whom her father-in-law had had such steady and mutually profitable relations . . .

Hubert was announced, as impeccable and unruffled as if he had never heard of either bullock carts or monsoons. Colonel Browne rose to greet him in profound embarrassment, sore with the knowledge he should never have encouraged him to come to Burma in the first place and also uncomfortable under the sharp consciousness that his future was now something of a liability as well as a responsibility. Hubert seated himself, folded his hands upon the top of his cane and waited with composure.

The colonel picked up the Chief Commissioner's letter as a talisman to give himself courage. 'Bad news, Beresford. At least, bad for you and not so good for me, though it's all that can be done in the circumstances. The Residency is to close down. I'm to go down to Rangoon with my staff and the sepoys as soon as possible, perhaps even tomorrow. I'm sure you'll understand why. Thibaw won't see us without our shoes off and of course the alternative is not to be thought of. I've always been grateful that you are a staunch supporter of me in this. So he doesn't see us and therefore we can't achieve anything. It's inevitable. I'm – I'm damned sorry Beresford, I feel badly about it all, bringing you up here and then dragging you back almost at once, but affairs of state, you know—'

Hubert, whose face had not moved throughout

this speech, merely said, 'And is the closure of the Residency permanent?'

The colonel brandished his letter. 'Good heavens, no! At least, I should hope not. But it's the only way to teach these people that they are not the centre of the universe, that they cannot treat us like this. They'll miss us, mark my words, they'll come to see what an influence for the good we were.'

'And you, Colonel? Shall you go to India?'

The colonel's discomfort increased visibly. 'I – I had thought so. A spell in the hills, you know – But you, Beresford. Shall you go back to – to Bombay?'

Hubert smiled. 'Indeed no. I shall remain here.'

'You can't,' the colonel said flatly.

'Oh?'

'It would be madness. It is extremely unsafe. You cannot remain here. The Residency will be almost under siege, I am instructed to leave no sepoys. The mood at the court is extremely dangerous.'

Carefully Hubert said, 'I do not think so.'

'You know nothing about it!' the colonel shouted. 'Don't be a dolt, Beresford. Your daughter playing the piano at court every morning means nothing, nothing at all. If the Queen decides to take any revenge for our going, you will be the first victims. Do you understand me? It is imperative, absolutely imperative that you and Miss Beresford accompany me to Rangoon.'

Hubert rose and came to stand close to the colonel.

'You underestimate my daughter's relationship with the Queen. We shall not be harmed—'

Horace Browne threw the Chief Commissioner's letter to the floor in exasperation.

'Listen, Beresford. Listen to me. I know you haven't much to go back to in Bombay – no don't flannel me, I know – but I got you into this hole and I – I'll find some way—'

'I am not returning to Bombay, Colonel. I am not prepared to discuss the matter beyond telling you that my daughter and I are in no danger, we are not afraid and we have plenty to keep us here. You need have no regrets about bringing us to Mandalay and no doubts about leaving us—'

An accented voice from the doorway said pleasantly, 'And who is leaving?'

Colonel Browne said angrily, 'I am, Andreino, and so should Beresford here be.'

Signor Andreino came forward into the room, bringing with him his usual aroma of hair oil and garlic. 'Calcutta says withdraw, Colonel?'

'Yes. Lord Lytton has taken his telescope off Kabul long enough to order us down to Rangoon.'

'All of you?'

The colonel shrugged. 'I shall leave one of the juniors to close things up. There's nothing to stay for. This absurd shoe question. Beresford and I have sat for hours waiting for an audience.'

'And Thibaw won't see you,' Andreino said

softly, his eyes on Hubert, 'because you will not remove your shoes. Will you, Signor Beresford?'

'Naturally not,' Hubert said blandly.

Andreino smiled. 'Precisely, signore. Naturally not. So now you must go down to Rangoon.'

The colonel groaned faintly and Hubert said, 'We shall stay. My daughter and I.'

'Look,' Andreino said, 'look, Beresford. You make the poor Colonel ill at such a suggestion. You should not torment him so.'

'I wish you would assist me in reassuring Colonel Browne that my daughter and I are not his responsibility. He is under no obligation to ensure our safe conduct out of Mandalay. It is our choice to stay.'

'It's lunacy!' the colonel shouted. 'All the British here will be in the gravest danger. You might as well put your head in a noose—'

'Nonsense,' Hubert said sharply. 'I want no more of this. I appreciate your concern, Colonel, but I do not need it. We are well established, Maria and I.'

Horace Browne passed his hands over his face. 'Very well. You must do as you wish. Of course, you realize that your salary from the government must cease if you remain—' Here Hubert gave a small dismissive wave of his hand. '—and that you will no longer be regarded as having any kind of official capacity. If you are in any kind of difficulty, I am sure Signor Andreino will do his best to assist you. In fact that is the Chief Commissioner's wish.'

Andreino said smiling, 'I shall be happy to oblige him. I will, of course—' He glanced quickly round the room and said in a lowered voice, 'I will, of course, be happy to be, shall we say, news collector for the government of India? Lord Lytton's ear in Mandalay?'

'You would be of inestimable value.'

Andreino spread his hands, displaying the grimy fingernails that offended Maria so. 'I think it would be mutually valuable. It will be only one more little duty to add to my other little duties. So, Colonel, you are to leave us. There was a rumour on the wind this morning, that is why I came with such dispatch. Shall you take the steamer on Thursday?'

'May I,' Colonel Browne said in one last desperate attempt, 'may I not even take Miss Beresford down to the safety of British Burma?'

Hubert shook his head. 'You may not, Colonel. Thank you for your solicitude. But she would not wish to go. Her life is much occupied here in the last few weeks.'

Andreino smiled to himself. 'So it is, Signor Beresford. So it is. Now, we must leave the good Colonel to sort out his papers and pack his trunks. You will accompany me?'

Only Hubert's bullock cart waited in the dripping lane. Andreino had clearly, from the state of his boots, adopted his usual habit, and walked.

'May I give you a lift?'

Andreino shook his head. 'Thank you, no. I have business down on the bund. I wish only to say one word to you, signore, one word of warning. I know you have been most – most assiduous in your attempts to see the King, properly shod as a representative of Her Majesty should always be. I also know that you have made some of those attempts in, shall we say, another guise, a guise that does not require such formality of dress. Do not walk away, Signor Beresford, do not ignore me. All I say to you is that you must be careful. I can guess why you remain here; I know what the prize is as well as you. I know also Bonvilain and Blount. There is little in this steaming spot I do not know. And I tell you, you must be careful.'

Hubert, seated now in his bullock cart, merely touched his stick to the brim of his hat. 'I will bid you good day, Signor Andreino.'

Smiling under his moustaches, Andreino bowed elaborately and then, when the cart had jolted round a curve in the lane, turned his steps towards the bund and the river.

Maria did not go down to the bund to bid the colonel farewell. The steamer's departure time would have conflicted with her preparations for her daily visit to the palace and in any case, she wished the colonel to feel himself snubbed. So Grace Prior, enveloped in her green rubber costume, found herself the only English person by the river.

Tom had wished to come, but the colonel, striding, booming into the mission the afternoon before, had said he wanted no ceremony. 'Life

125

must go on, Prior, just as usual. I know you are occupied with the school in the mornings and I don't want lessons broken up for me. No, no, my dear fellow. I shall see you in Rangoon one of these days, who knows—'

Grace too was occupied with lessons in the morning, but they were sewing lessons – *only* sewing, she told herself – and therefore it was perfectly possible to put strips of white cotton into all those deft little dark hands and promise a great reward upon her return for the smallest hemstitching. She had then, guiltily, gone back to the mission to change out of the grey cotton she always wore at the school, into her pink, telling herself that it was not on Maria Beresford's account that she was changing – for Maria would surely wish to bid the colonel goodbye – but on Colonel Browne's.

She gazed dismally at her small blanched face in the spotted glass on her bedroom wall. Colonel Browne once said he liked me in pink, that it became me and I look terrible in grey, quite washed out, but it is practical and Maria doesn't have to do anything so practical so she can wear yellow silk and not worry all day if she wants to. Imagine rustling round the palace, talking to the Queen, a real royal queen covered in diamonds, even if she is a wicked murderess. And I'm sure Maria isn't frightened of her, not one bit, not like I should be. I should shake and tremble and not know what to say. There now. I've gone to all this trouble and put on my pink and I look awful in it because I am particularly pale today for some reason and I have mosquito bites on my nose and anyway I am going to cover it all up with my mackintosh which I know she despises—

Half an hour later, standing ankle deep in the pale yellow mud beside the Irrawaddy, Grace reflected that she had, in the event, put on her pink dress to no effect at all. Maria was not there, nor was Mr Beresford, nor Mr Blount, nor, to her mingled relief and disappointment, Monsieur Bonvilain. The only European besides herself was Signor Andreino, whose eyes were horribly bloodshot today and who had kissed her hand with a flourish that made her feel unaccountably silly. She stood for a long, long time it seemed, steaming inside her green rubber and watching while near-naked Burmese coolies carried all the bundles and boxes from the British Residency on board the steamer. Every so often, Colonel Browne's tam-o' shanter could be seen here or there on one of the steamer's three decks and his sepoys, white smiles of relief at leaving breaking their black Madrassee faces, stood lining the gangplank until the last piece of luggage had been carried aboard.

It wasn't only the colonel's going that made Grace miserable, though, goodness knows, it was a dreary enough spectacle in that never-ending rain, with the Irrawaddy the colour of milky coffee, streaked with long, evil-looking smears of scum. She knew perfectly well that both her father and the colonel had supposed her out of earshot the day before when Colonel Browne had confided his anxiety about the safety of the remaining British in Mandalay. She had said she was going down into the garden, but something had made her linger on the verandah and she had been well repaid for her dishonesty by what she heard.

It wasn't simply that what the colonel had said had frightened her. It had, of course. Who, she asked herself wretchedly in bed later, who really relishes the thought of dying at the hands of furious natives? And then it came to her that her father almost – yes, he almost did. He certainly didn't shrink from it, he'd said – and she could tell he was smiling from the warmth of his voice – he'd said, 'Colonel, you must remember that I am a *soldier* for Christ. A soldier.' That was what really dismayed her. Not that her father felt like that, but that she, Grace, *couldn't*. And neither could she tell him she couldn't. She was sure he believed she had his heart and stomach for Christ. Well, she did have the heart, she did, she *did*, but the courage, the physical courage, that was something else altogether.

And funnily enough, she thought Colonel Browne understood it. He had suggested, with a touching and awkward diffidence, that he should take her down to Rangoon and confide her to the care of Doctor Marks at the Anglican mission there until Tom could join her, and her heart had leaped at the thought and been outraged all at once. And her father had laughed gently and said, 'God bless you, Colonel, but there is no need of that. She is at one with me, my Gracie. You'd break her heart to take her.' Then the colonel had asked if he might ask her directly, and Tom had refused, smilingly, and Grace had suddenly felt that the colonel saw more than she thought, that he wasn't so bluff and straight-forward as he seemed . . .

Now he was going away, taking with him this newly appreciated sympathy, and she was to stay in Mandalay, with her father, whom she loved with all her being, and the Beresfords, whom she feared, and all these odds and ends of people and they *all* had something in common, something she didn't have; they were all brave, properly, truly, physically brave. She was the only one who feared for her skin and the only one to bear the bitter shame of such cowardice, bitter because anyone who had grown up hand in hand with God as she had done was the last person to be so utterly, despicably weak.

Colonel Browne, standing in front of her and holding out his hands, 'My dear child! If you look so woebegone at my going, I shall be discouraged all the way to Rangoon. I can't express my delight at your coming, my dear. The only one! The only one to take the trouble.' He leaned forward, showering Grace with heavy drops from his tam-o' shanter, and said confidentially, 'It won't be too long before I see you in Rangoon, I think. The Queen may decide it all for us, you know. I can't see that a continuing mission school is quite in her line.'

'I – I couldn't leave Papa—'

'I know, my dear. No more you should. I only meant that he will probably come down to Rangoon soon himself.'

Grace's eyes were filling with tears. 'Will you write, Colonel Browne?'

He looked visibly startled. 'Will – I – why – yes, yes, of course, my dear. If you'd like me to. Not much of a hand at letter-writing—'

The steamer trumpeted in a melancholy way from the river. Colonel Browne took Grace's wet hands and squeezed them painfully.

'Goodbye then, my dear. God bless—'

She nodded, her throat swollen with tears. He stumped down the last few feet of the bund, turned to wave once more and then disappeared across the gangplank into the steamer. A small detachment of Burmese soldiers in their absurd tin hats were ordered nearer the water's edge, but made no further move and simply waited there, in slightly ragged formation, while the steamer churned its way into the deeper channel in the centre of the river.

'Miss Prior, you pleased our old friend,' Andreino said at Grace's elbow. He peered to see her face, observed that it was pinkly blotched with crying and insect bites, and put a firm hand on her arm.

'I need two favours from you, Signorina. First I should be very grateful for a ride in your horrible cart. And second I want your help, with a girl. A Burmese girl.'

Grace, mindful of what rumour said about Signor Andreino's domestic arrangements, shrank visibly. Her own little maid, recruited from the mission school as being too intellectually idle to benefit from instruction and therefore better practically employed, had told her in a delighted whisper, that Signor Andreino had at least two *bo-kadaw*, possibly three. Grace's Burmese was now sufficient for her to realize, with a sensation she took for shock, that *bo-kadaw* meant white man's wife . . .

Andreino laughed and gripped her elbow more firmly. 'Ah, you English misses! I will do nothing to offend you, Signorina, nothing at all. I wish only that you should see a girl who deserves a better fate than the one she has been reduced to in a cigar factory. She is a girl unlike the other native girls. All Burmese are intelligent, but she is particularly so, sympathetic. I wondered, Miss Prior, if perhaps there is a place for her in your household?'

Grace struggled to explain that the mission was in the first place always straitened for want of money and, in the second place, heavily exploited already by Burmese in whom Tom Prior genuinely thought he saw Christian possibilities.

'Come all the same,' Andreino said.

'I have been,' Grace said, a little desperately, longing now to get back to the safe familiarity of her sewing class. 'I am sure you mean the cigar

131

factory by the western gate. I have been. Hosannah Manook took me. She goes often to buy cigars for her father.'

'Then it will be no surprise to you,' Andreino said, steering her firmly through the Burmese gathered on the bund. 'You will know what to expect.'

Grace, with a flash of temper, pulled her arm free. 'No, Signor Andreino! I don't wish to go and I can't help you. Nor can I see why you should – should—'

'Take an interest in this particular girl? I am trying not to offend you, Signorina, but perhaps the truth is more important. She has – shall we say been misused by an acquaintance of mine?'

Grace blushed hotly beneath her hat-cover and bending her head muttered that she did not know Signor Andreino saw himself in the role of knight in shining armour. He laughed at this and then gave her a great deal of alarm and a fair amount of pleasure by picking her up in his arms and lifting her easily into the bullock cart.

'You are as light as a child!'

Grace, confused and excited, said nothing. Andreino climbed in after her and seated himself so close that the smell of garlic and coconut oil was almost overwhelming.

'Miss Prior, I see you are astute as well as feather-light. You want to know what advantage there would be to you in taking such a girl in. Is that not it? I will tell you, Signorina, I will explain. Colonel Browne is not wrong to think these dangerous times. It is well for us Europeans to take all the precautions we can, and one of the best precautions, Miss Prior, is to have Burmese who are in some way indebted and thus more likely to be loyal in our households. It would be wise for you to have in the mission an intelligent girl who would, as you say in English, keep her ear to the ground. I have found you just such a girl. I do you a favour and also one to the man I spoke of, the man of my acquaintance. He has given me some information I needed and it is now my turn to do him a little service. The girl has behaved with great dignity since – since she left his house, but her mother and sisters give him no peace. They say they are disgraced by his being a *kalā*, a foreigner. They will not take the girl back, she is an outcast. She has been put to the lowest work in the factory, she is almost a beggar. The man in question – Miss Prior, you do not ask me who he is?'

Grace turned her face away. 'No,' she said stonily.

'I will give you a clue,' Andreino said, enjoying himself hugely. 'I will tell you that mine are not the only moustaches you admire. I have undertaken to help the girl because my friend is not experienced enough in Burma to know what to do. And he is trying, Miss Prior, to behave like a gentleman but, of course, as you English know, we Europeans are not so skilled at it.' He paused. 'Will you try to help me?'

'I – I don't know.'

Andreino waited a moment and then he said softly. 'The girl is fifteen. Fifteen only.'

The cigar factory was a low brown wooden house in the usual matting-walled compound some hundred yards short of the moat and the western gate to the royal city. The house was used mainly as a shop, the biggest room being furnished with a few crude European armchairs upholstered in red velvet and the walls were lined with shelves stacked with cigars in neat bundles. Each bundle was wrapped in newspaper – Grace could make out the familiar columns of the *Rangoon Gazette* here and there – and bore a band of coloured paper to denote the quality of the cigars. There was a smell of dust and mould and the sweet pervasive vegetable smell of tobacco.

The proprietress, an implacable-faced Burmese woman in her fifties, dressed in a tamein of wine-coloured silk and smoking a green cheroot, came forward to fawn upon Andreino. He smiled, pointing out various packets he wished taken down and sent to his house, while Grace stood by him and felt both bewildered and discomfited.

'And now, Hnin Si,' Andreino said. 'We wish to see Hnin Si.'

The proprietress shrugged, her usual impenetrable expression blotting out the brief eagerness of the saleswoman. Stumbling in Andreino's wake, Grace followed him out of the dusty room and down into a muddy courtyard in which a few bedraggled hens pecked moodily. The courtyard was lined with open sheds upon whose tin roofs the overhanging trees dripped in a dull tattoo. Women crouched in the damp dimness all along the earth floor of the sheds, thin, bent women in filthy ragged cotton tameins. Grace, who had never penetrated beyond the shop before, was horrified to see how old some of them were, old and crooked and almost toothless.

At one end of the sheds great piles of yellow-brown tobacco leaves hung in hammocks suspended from the ceiling. What the women squatting below them were doing Grace could not imagine but the women close to her, the ones she could see, were spreading a smooth leaf on a little board before them, laying upon it a handful of leaves and then, using a metal spike for shaping which was withdrawn at the last moment, were rolling the leaf up into a smooth and symmetrical cigar. None of them looked up.

'This way,' Andreino said.

Grace followed him dumbly, picking her way between the crouching figures on the floor and the piles of tobacco.

'Hnin Si,' she heard Andreino say, 'I have brought the English *thakin-ma*.'

Beneath the hammocks of dried tobacco, four or five women were sorting leaves, pressing out smooth the big unblemished ones that would serve to wrap a cigar, and heaping up the pieces that would stuff it. They were even, if it were possible, older and more ragged than the women who rolled cigars, for the job of sorting was less skilled and therefore more poorly paid. But among the grizzled and wispy heads was one sleek black one, decked with flowers.

'Hnin Si,' Andreino said again.

The girl raised a face that was not exactly pretty, though so delicate and fine-skinned that it almost passed for such. Her eyes were too slanting, her nose too snub for beauty, but her skin had a faint pinkness along the cheekbones uncommon among the Burmese and the bones of her face were beautifully moulded. She wore a checked tamein of poor cotton whose hem was splashed with mud, her feet were filthy and her torn cotton jacket revealed collar bones like wings and arms like brown sticks.

'You see,' Andreino said to Grace in English, 'she needs help.'

Hnin Si, after an anxious glance at the proprietress, raised her thin brown hands to her forehead and shikoed to Grace on the earthen floor of the shed. Grace knelt at once beside her.

'Oh don't!' she cried in distress, 'don't do that! Please don't do that!'

'We will speak in French,' Andreino said. 'The proprietress does not understand it but, as you may imagine, Hnin Si has learned a little in the last months. And you, Miss Prior?'

'Schoolgirl French,' Grace said, getting to her feet and feeling that what little grasp she had of the situation was slipping from her fingers. The girl was pathetic, and had such a sweet face, but how was one to cope with the responsibility of such a human being, recommended by Signor Andreino and cast off by . . . by . . . It did not bear thinking of.

Hnin Si was saying softly, 'I would work. I do not fear work. It is the shame I fear. I do not fear foreigners.'

Andreino stooped and said something in almost unrecognizable French, of which Grace caught only her own name and the words 'Christian' and the Burmese word for priest, *poongyi*.

Hnin Si turned her slanting gaze upon Grace and repeated, 'I will work,' and the sudden look of childlike pleading that came into her face made Grace burst out, 'But how could he, how could he be so cruel, so wickedly cruel—'

Andreino shrugged.

'These things pass, signorina. You cannot expect miracles. He has moved on, chosen elsewhere. You know his new companion, Miss Prior. She escorts the elegant Miss Beresford to the palace each morning.'

Grace exclaimed, truly shocked. 'Mattie! Mattie Calogreedy!' She took a step backwards, away from the Italian with his operatic moustaches and gusts of garlic, away from the silently pleading figure on the mud floor of the shed. 'I must go, I must go home! Don't make me stay, don't ask me any more. I must go—'

Andreino reached out and took her arm. 'If you insist—'

'I do, I do! I am so sorry, so sorry for – for that

poor girl, truly I am, but I can't – I can't bear –
Where is the way out? Where is the cart? You
should not have told me, why did you—'

Briskly, Andreino propelled her across the
courtyard and up the steps into the musty, cigar-
lined room. In the lane outside, the bullock
waited between the shafts and the four mission
servants, without whom Grace was not allowed
now to stir outside the compound, lounged
against the wheels, a reassuring reminder of
home. Without speaking, Andreino swung Grace
into his arms as he had done before and set her in
the cart, and when she glanced agitatedly at him,
she was astounded to see that he was smiling.

'How can you smile? How can you? If you are
laughing at me, you should at least have the
courtesy to do so behind my back, but I hope you
are not laughing at the – the situation this morning. I think – I think,' she cried out, gathering
courage, 'I think your conduct is despicable,
Signor Andreino! Despicable! You pretend
friendship with the English and yet from what
you have said to me this morning, you are plainly
on very cordial terms with the French also. I see
it – it is not only the Burmese we have to be
suspicious of in Mandalay!'

And then she burst into tears. Andreino continued to smile and offered her a disgusting
handkerchief she was too confused to reject.
After a while, when her sobs had subsided, he
leaned into the cart and said gently, 'Miss Prior,
you are perfectly right. I do ride, as you say, two

horses. I should ride three if I could. But you forget two things. One, I will ensure that the best horse wins. And two, I am an excellent horseman.'

He shouted to the driver and the cart lurched forward among the ruts away from the western gate. Grace did not look back but sat and stared stiffly before her, trying to keep her mind as blank as possible. When they were almost in the *kalā* town, a bullock cart came splashing past at a great rate, heading for the royal city. As it lumbered by, the tall graceful figure in the back, an unmistakable figure in yellow silk with pearls in her ears, raised a single gloved hand in brief salute to Grace, but the person next to her, a plump laughing little person in pink muslin, waved and blew kisses in a way Grace found utterly repugnant.

It was almost two weeks before Grace saw Maria again. During those two weeks, since the lanes in the *kalā* town were considered dangerous and her going out was discouraged, she immersed herself in the school in the daylight hours and prayed long and desperately in the black clammy nights for peace of mind. At the end of the first week of September, she arrived back at the mission at teatime one day to find her father already there, in company with Signor Andreino. She attempted to smile and murmur some excuse and slip past them to her room, but her father caught her sleeve.

'My dear Gracie, you must not run away, you must listen. What Signor Andreino has to say most nearly concerns yourself.'

Grace could not look at Andreino. She simply stood silently by her father and heard the Italian say, 'The British Ambassador in Kabul, Sir Louis Cavagnari, has been assassinated. The Viceroy in Calcutta has decreed that no unnecessary risk shall be taken with British lives further and that the Residency and mission in Mandalay are to close forthwith. Miss Prior, you are to go, for your own protection, by the next mail steamer to Rangoon. All the British colony will go, even the Chinese and the Indians.'

Grace clutched her father.

'But Papa! You must come! I can't go al – I mean to say, you must not stay if the danger will be worse—'

Tom Prior's face wore the expression of crusading zeal she had come to dread.

'Dearest child, of course I will come. In time. But I cannot let all our precious souls slip back. God is not accountable to Lord Lytton and in His service no more am I. You shall go down to Rangoon and be the invaluable handmaiden to Doctor Marks that you have always been to me. The nuns at the Convent of the Good Shepherd will take you in. And when things are quieter again, back you shall come.'

Andreino said, smiling beneath his moustaches, 'You must not weep on me again, Signorina. Come, dry your eyes. I have a task for you, Miss Prior, a task I think you will enjoy. The news of Afghanistan reached me but an hour since and Miss Beresford and her excellent father are still in ignorance. Will you go to her and tell her for me and then you may both make your preparations for the journey to Rangoon together? My own servants will escort you. You will have nothing to fear.'

So Grace, still in her regrettable grey cotton schoolroom gown, her feelings in a perfect turmoil, found herself being ushered into Maria's drawing room and confronting not only Maria, resplendent in rose pink, but the terrifying Mr Blount. He reminded Grace of nothing so much as the ferret that the school gardener in Brighton had kept to put down drains after the rats.

Grace sat down unhappily, accepted tea and cake she had no appetite for and waited an interminable ten minutes – during which time Maria and Mr Blount talked with perfect ease and a good deal of laughter across her before an opportunity arose for her to speak. At last Maria turned and observed that as Grace had very evidently run straight from her little pupils, she must have some quite urgent errand. Grace stammered a little, forgot the name of Afghanistan's capital, confused the name of the luckless ambassador and had, scarlet with shame, to begin her story twice over before she could tell it coherently.

When she had finished, Mr Blount and Maria exchanged glances.

'Signor Andreino,' Grace added diffidently, 'and – and my father, they say we must go down to Rangoon. At once. They think we should take the next steamer! There is a mail steamer waiting up river a little, ready to take all the British colony to safety. They think everything will become dreadfully dangerous here.'

Maria said to Mr Blount, 'They do?' and laughed. Then she turned to Grace and said, 'Miss Prior, I wish you godspeed upon your travels. However, I shall not be joining you. I am sure you will appreciate that my position now with the Queen means that I have nothing to fear here, nothing that is, one-hundredth part as unpleasant as the dreadful tedium of Rangoon. And in any case, my father and I – and Mr Blount – are much needed here now. Much needed. I am sure you have heard that the Queen gave birth to a son but a few days ago. I believe I am the only European to have seen the child. But that is not all.' She paused and then added in a voice of undisguised triumph, 'My father – and Mr Blount – cannot possibly leave Mandalay. Queen Supayalat has been gracious enough to award them the concession to work the ruby mines at Minhla. She gave me the news today.'

Grace rose unsteadily to her feet. 'Yes, yes, of course, I quite understand. I hope – I hope you will be very – very successful. I will say goodbye then, Miss Beresford, that is, until things are calmer, until I come back—'

When the door had closed behind her, even as

she hurried through the tiny hall, she could hear them laughing together in the drawing room and it seemed to her that she had never heard any sound so triumphant, so satisfied, so entirely self-congratulatory.

PART TWO

7

On a brilliant October morning in 1884, Archie
Tennant, aboard the SS *Nimrod*, entered the
mouths of the Irrawaddy. He had been at sea
for a total of thirty-seven days since leaving
Liverpool, not counting the week he had spent in
Bombay at the offices of the Bombay-Burmah
Trading Corporation at number 1 Nesbit Road, a
mere three doors away from the now departed
Indian headquarters of Tennant Phillipson.

He had been received cordially by a Mr
Richardson, the senior representative of the corporation in India, and had been informed that his
salary would be one hundred and fifty rupees to
begin with and that he would be provided with a
house, servants, transport and most importantly,
water, while in Upper Burma. Mr Richardson
had then shown him into a small panelled room,
an identical copy of the room in which he had
been interviewed in Austin Friars the previous
summer, except for the stifling heat, and had left
him with a high sloping desk, a clerk's stool
and copies of the corporation's annual report to
divert himself with.

He had started by taking off his jacket,

waistcoat and cravat. Five years had hardened the lines of his face to good advantage, but also deposited extra girth, which he detested but seemed unable to control, beneath that same waistcoat. Old Phillipson had warned him ceaselessly about the dangers of obesity until Archie grew to dread the powerful allure of the excellent food on his patron's table. He hoped that the East would simply, with its heat, melt him back to the size he had been when at Oxford and hunting four days a week.

The corporation's reports, satisfactory though they were to the directors, were not what Archie wanted of his week in Bombay. He learned painfully and with cavernous yawns that the present year had been a good one even though the rains in Upper Burma had not been sufficient to float down the Rangoon all the teak that had been cut in the Ningyan forests to the south-east of Mandalay. Despite this drawback, the directors could report an overall profit of more than five thousand rupees and reserves of above forty thousand. The corporation, Archie read with slightly more interest, possessed five thousand rupees worth of elephants and sixty-four thousand rupees worth of unsold timber. A twenty-five per cent dividend had been paid to all shareholders, the capital stood at – Archie yawned widely enough to crack his jaw and closed his eyes once or twice in an attempt to force his wits to cohere and concentrate, but they were disobliging. He put his forehead down upon the report balanced in front of him and felt his skin adhere damply to the paper. Figures in this temperature were intolerable; everything was a struggle, a battle against mental sloth. The only thing he really wanted to do was sleep and sleep or perhaps, he thought drowsily, feeling that there was something a little ignoble in wishing only for slumber, to try his hand at polo before the week was up—

The door opened and Archie peeled his face away from the annual report. An Indian clerk, beneath a pile of ledgers large enough to crush him, padded softly to Archie's side.

'Mr Richardson says you will be needing these now, Mr Tennant. These are the detailed accounts in which you will be seeing quite clearly the pattern of the annual finances, the debts and liabilities, the reserves, the needs for insurance, particularly against fire, the progress in ship building, the losses sustained by mortality among the elephants, the rise in dividends paid upon both shares in the original and in the second issue—'

'Go away.'

'Mr Tennant?'

'Go away. And take every scrap of paper in the room with you.'

A pause.

'But Mr Richardson is wishing—'

'And I am *not* wishing.'

Another pause.

'What shall I be saying to Mr Richardson?'

'That I am too hot, too weary and too stupid to take any of this in. And that I should like to play polo.'

'Hot, weary, stupid, polo—'

'Yes! Yes, all those! Now go away.'

Later that day, dining with Mr Richardson off mulligatawny soup and innumerable tough little roasted fowls, Archie found himself sitting next to a blandly good-looking young man in uniform.

'Digby Shaw,' the young man said, shaking red pepper into soup which had already filled Archie's eyes with scalding tears. 'Gather you're off to Burma. Hellish hot. Know my brother?'

Archie closed his eyes and swallowed one more spoonful of soup as if it were medicine. 'No. I'm afraid I don't. Should I?'

'No reason really, except that when the lid blows off in Mandalay, Murray will be in the thick of it. He's with the Hampshires and they are stationed in the Madras Residency so, when the call comes, they will be one of the closest regiments to Burma and the first to go and teach those—'

'I'm afraid I don't understand you at all.'

Digby Shaw looked up from his soup to give Archie's civilian clothes a pitying glance.

'No. Well, I suppose you wouldn't, fresh out from England . . .' He sighed, took a huge swallow of wine and said with the patience of someone speaking to the very simple, 'There is going to be trouble in Burma. Over the teak. Your outfit, you know. And the King is rotten through and through and drinks like a fish. He's quite willing to sell anything and everything to the highest bidder. If he tries any funny business with us, we'll send the redcoats in. And my brother Murray will be in the front line. White's his commanding officer. Know him?'

'Of course not,' Archie said irritably. 'How could I? I was a lawyer in London until two months ago, and on a ship until the day before yesterday.'

'I've an uncle who's a judge,' young Shaw said unperturbed. 'Sir Barnet Shaw. Know him?'

'Yes,' Archie said, 'I do.'

Young Shaw lost interest at once and fell upon the wizened little fowl that had been placed before him with an enthusiasm Archie found incomprehensible. The huge dusty fringe of the punkah swung relentlessly back and forth over the table, creating an unpleasant draught about his head and ears and not getting to the heart of the matter at all. A boiling yellow-brown sauce had been spooned over the poor little burnt bird on his plate and an array of chutneys, livid yellow, olive green, burnt sienna and shining brown was being held out for his choice. He waved them away. The only thing on that table laden with steaming dishes of terrifyingly coloured food that Archie could feel any affection for was a lonely pineapple in a silver dish shaped like a vine leaf.

Digby Shaw, having discovered that his other

neighbour ran a shipping business out of Bombay and knew nobody of interest either, swung back to Archie and said, 'Pig sticking?'

'Hardly,' Archie said, 'in England. But I'd love to have a try at polo. Do you play?'

'Rather! Most evenings except when it's too damned hot to do anything but die. Made up a team with Bruce Gardiner and his brother and Miles Lumsden. Know them?'

Archie ignored him. 'Could you help me, then? I know it's an awful lot to ask to borrow a pony but I can't tell you how grateful I'd be.'

'Absolutely,' young Shaw said, waving a hand airily. 'Be pleased to help,' and promptly forgot all about it.

The only advantage of that week in Bombay, Archie thought, boarding the *Nimrod* in relief, was that if he were not actually any thinner, he was certainly no fatter. He had spent every day at Nesbit Road and every evening in company with tea brokers, rice shippers and silk merchants. The notion of playing polo died as it was born and Archie steamed away into the Indian Ocean with not a single glance of affectionate regret behind him.

The mood of slight despair lasted him into the Bay of Bengal. There were a number of English and German merchants aboard the *Nimrod*, but no one of his own age or tastes, and in the intervals between meals he sat mostly alone on deck, trying to accustom himself by force to the

sunshine and to think of old Phillipson with all
the unstinted gratitude he knew was due him.
Old Phillipson had, indeed, been better than his
word. Archie had come down from Oxford in
the summer of 1881 with a perfectly respectable
second and, thanks to his patron's enormous
generosity in the matter of horseflesh, with two
splendid hunting seasons behind him.

He fully expected to be sent straight to Austin
Friars, and thence, equally straight to the Far
East, but old Phillipson, while beating him
soundly at billiards, said that he had changed his
mind.

'Or shall we say, postponed it a while. Don't
want all this law to go to waste, no indeed. You
eat your dinners my boy, and get called to the
Bar and then we'll see about the East. And I've a
cousin in Northamptonshire who'll let you have
his lodge to use for hunting. How old are you?
Twenty-one? Let us say in three years, three
years from now.'

They had been wonderful years to Archie. He
found the law a very different matter in practice
and hunting in the Midlands a glorious improve-
ment on the southern country. Old Phillipson
gave him a gig and a splendidly matched pair of
bays and he pursued a happy triangle around
London, Northamptonshire and Riverdene.
Once a year he went home to Suffolk for his
mother's birthday and after a day or so of being
ignored or gazed at in virulent reproach, left
again hastily.

'You should go more,' old Phillipson said. 'Once a year and a jeweller's box ain't enough. Not that I like to spare you, mind you—'

Frederick had survived quite comfortably from the dissolution of the company. What he did precisely Archie could not tell and refused to find out, but it involved a good deal of time in Newmarket and the entire refurbishment of the stables at Hasham. He brought his dubious friends home with him, who made great inroads upon the excellent port his father had left for both his sons, and Mrs Tennant, who now had real cause for distress, wept almost all the time so that the atmosphere about her was always damp like the air above a marsh. Archie did not know what to do about her and could not bear the situation in general, so he stayed away.

When his three years were up he went obediently to Wallace Brothers. He had half expected to be greeted as rather a catch by them, but was treated in a brisk and businesslike manner, informed that he should be posted to up-country Burma and that he should board the SS *Nimrod* from Liverpool in the second week of September. He had only agreed to pause in Bombay to please old Phillipson, because he might very well have been briefed about his duties in Rangoon, but old Phillipson wanted to know at first hand how Bombay did without him. Archie had attempted, not at all successfully, to write a letter that was both truthful and which said Bombay was splendid and that he was sure he should find absolute satisfaction as a recruit for the Bombay-Burmah. He felt, steaming down the Indian coastline in the shimmering heat, that Bombay was as exciting as an English suburb peopled with clerks and that the only thing that had ever given him absolute satisfaction in his life was to come first of the field over a particularly difficult fence and gain an appreciative nod from the master of the Pytchley.

Subtly, as Burma drew nearer, his reluctance began to disperse. He could not tell why, except that he was approaching a country of which only half was regimented by British bureaucracy and that half not the one he was destined for. It was difficult to visualize precisely how life would go on in a teak forest, with himself the only white man for miles and miles and his companions Burmese foresters and elephants. He could not, come to think of it, visualize Burma at all. People in Bombay had said, slightly disparagingly, that it was where the Orient began, rather as if civilization as known to the British, and therefore the only kind worth having, stopped abruptly at India. And then all of a sudden, after days of glittering sea and the thudding of the engines and the remorseless boredom of confined life on board, Burma had come and was slipping past the *Nimrod*, and the blue waters of the Bay of Bengal were changed to the milky-greenish ones of a great river.

The mouths of the Irrawaddy were many, he discovered, and the low-lying fingers of land which divided them were emerald green with young rice. Here and there among the paddies rose the gold-tipped white spires of pagodas and along the raised paths of beaten earth that crossed the rice fields plodded bullocks in wooden yokes drawing flat carts, small Burmese wrapped in checked cotton and occasionally the saffron-draped form of a priest.

Archie's spirits rose as the steamer churned onwards through the increasingly coffee-coloured river waters. Beside him on the taffrail, the Englishmen and Germans began to grumble about the climate, the awful Burmese climate that soaked you and roasted you and wrung you out entirely. Archie, his eyes smarting from the glare of the green and white and gold and the sun bouncing blindingly off the water, felt abruptly that none of that mattered, that his discomfort was nothing beside the sudden buoyancy that filled him, lifted him up with elation and expectation, making him peer ahead for his first glimpse of Rangoon.

The first glimpse did not fail him either. Up the pale brown breadth of the river they steamed to a shore lined with trees and low white buildings. Far away to left and right, Archie could see the bulk of godowns and shipbuilding yards, but ahead it was only delightful, a green and white contrast to the choking urbanity of Bombay, crowned with something that made Archie clutch his neighbour's arm in amazement. Above the city, some way to the north, a glittering gold pinnacle sprang hundreds of feet into the hot blue sky like some divine finger.

'The Shway Dagon,' Archie's neighbour said. 'Over two thousand years old.'

'Yes,' Archie said, 'yes.'

The pinnacle had a smooth dome-shaped base out of which it rose with the grace of a swan's neck. Its goldenness was a miracle, all at once blazing and glowing, breaking out at the tip into a shower of little bells they were too far away to hear.

Archie's neighbour removed his sleeve from Archie's grasp. 'It's four miles away, but a clear day like this makes it seem closer. It's a perfect forest of pagodas up there, all round the base, there must be over fifty. If you ask me, it's better than anything they've got in Siam but then it's all they *have* got. First time?'

'Yes,' Archie said from far away, 'first time.'

'Rangoon?'

Archie shook his head, his eyes still fastened on the soaring golden spectacle to the north. 'No. To Mandalay. In a day or two.'

The man looked at him admiringly. 'That so? Well, well. You are in luck though. Best week of all the year to be in Rangoon. It's the autumn meeting. Rangoon races, you know.'

Archie's gaze left the Shway Dagon for a moment. 'Local races?'

'Some local riders, a few boys from Rangoon, always some Bengalis from Calcutta. But mostly Englishmen. You a horseman?'

'Yes.'

His neighbour surveyed his bulk. 'They're only ponies, you know.'

Archie sighed. 'I don't suppose a newcomer could ride in any case.'

'Why not? If he's good enough. Race secretary is a great friend of mine. Would you like me to have a word?'

Archie, full of the frustration of his dashed hopes over polo and his eagerness to seize life in Burma with both hands, said with fervour, 'I'd be so grateful, you cannot imagine—'

'Who are you joining?'

'The Bombay-Burmah.'

'Ah,' the man said, 'a teak boy. Look. Here's my card. Got anywhere to stay? Good. Now come round to that address the day after tomorrow, after dinner, and I'll take you to the assembly rooms. That's where they have the lottery the day before the big race, and we'll see what can be done.'

Archie indicated the card. 'I'm an Archibald, too. You are very kind, Mr MacGregor.'

'But you're no Scot?'

'By family, not by birth.'

The steamer slid competently into her berth by the dockside. Down below on the wooden quay was a solid mass of Burmese, their gleaming black hair coiled in top knots, almost all of them, even the children, Archie noticed with surprise, smoking green cheroots.

'Every man jack of them,' Archibald MacGregor

said, 'puffing like trains, day in, day out. There, look down there, the man in light grey, that's your man in Rangoon, the Bombay-Burmah fellow. Come to meet you. That's decent, isn't it, young man? Well, here we are, and although I can think of places I'd rather be, one of them certainly isn't Aberdeen. I'll be seeing you then. Day after tomorrow.' He paused and put out a freckled hand to shake Archie's. 'Welcome to Burma, young man.'

8

The atmosphere in the assembly rooms was like a steam bath. Archie, sweating freely in evening dress, joined a crowd of civilians dressed likewise, officers in mess dress and a vast number of Chinese, Burmese and Indians who were comfortably and intelligently wrapped in loose lengths of cotton. Among the civilians Archie, as he pushed behind Archibald MacGregor's back through the crowd, heard Greek spoken as well as German and English and he felt his face being minutely examined from all sides as a newcomer about whom nothing was known today, but everything doubtless would be tomorrow.

The race secretary, a small spare man with the wiry look of an ex-jockey, was standing below the stage at one end of the room beside a table which bore a thick coating of dust and the lottery box. He held a large yellow handkerchief in one hand and a wooden hammer in the other and the sweat was gleaming on his forehead just as Archie could feel it shining on his own. MacGregor made introductions and Archie shook hands damply.

The secretary eyed him critically. 'I've found

you a mount. Not up to much but MacGregor here said you'd need a weight carrier. We've three classes of horse here, Indian Arabs and country breds, pure Burmans and half-breeds. I've got you a half-breed. Sluggish fellow, but you might get something out of him. Give you a ride in any case.'

'I'm awfully grateful, sir—'

The secretary waved his hammer and handkerchief. 'Think nothing of it. Only too pleased to have boys from home riding. These local johnnies ride like the very devil. It'll amuse you. Point-to-point, do you?'

'Yes.'

'You'll stand a fair chance then. Look, I have to start, nearly nine thirty. Infernal hot tonight. I don't advise betting myself, but if you must, stick to your own kind. The Chinese are very devils, gambling is like mother's milk to them—'

MacGregor drew Archie to the side of the room where a group of young officers were eyeing him speculatively. 'Gentlemen, a rival,' MacGregor said.

One of them, his shoulders to the wall, said, 'What have you drawn?'

'Jack Tar.'

'Wish you luck. Ugly beast.'

'To look at or by temperament?'

'Both, I'm afraid.'

The hammer crashed for silence. When the voices fell, the mosquitoes could be heard plainly wheeling and droning in the thick, hot air. One landed on Archie's wrist and before he dashed it off, he observed that it was as large as a wasp and speckled in dun and black.

'Who'll bid for The Parson?' the secretary was saying, his hammer poised. 'Great pony. Winner of – I don't know how many—'

The Chinese and Burmans on the floor had stopped their indolent squatting and smoking and had crowded to the front. The secretary fixed his fierce blue eyes on a huge stout Burmese like a swollen brown fruit, wrapped in a paso of pink silk.

'Wake up, Maung Hpo! Ain't you listening? Now, a hundred rupees at a time. Bid up now. Who'll start me off? Fifty rupees for The Parson, sixty, seventy, eighty – one hundred. One hundred to Ah Sin. One hundred and fifty? And fifty, Maung Hpo. Come on, gentlemen, bid up, bid up. Fine pony. Don't keep me here all night—'

'Worth six hundred,' one of the officers near Archie said. 'Rode him in the Grand National here myself last year. Slow starter but stays like anything.'

'If you have the winning horse,' Archie said, 'what might you win from the lottery?'

The officer shrugged. 'Three thousand, perhaps.'

'Three *thousand*!'

'Ah, but if your horse loses, you must pay out the lottery and the man with the losing ticket on your horse. You see, they all buy lottery tickets to get a horse in the race. There'll be seventeen runners tomorrow, therefore seventeen lottery tickets out of perhaps, twenty thousand applicants for those seventeen tickets. They gamble like fury here, even the women. Jack Tar is owned by a woman.'

Archie took his eyes off the flailing yellow handkerchief.

'A woman?'

The officer grinned. 'A little Jill Burman. There's a number of women owners. There are women in everything in Burma. You'll see.'

The following day seemed, if it were possible, even hotter than the one before. Archie lay for hours in a large tin tub while a bearer poured can after can of cold water carefully over his shoulders and he waited with each canful to see steam rising as the water hit his burning skin. The tub stood in a small stone cell, almost windowless but for a square cut high in one wall, adjoining the bedroom in which he had battled with mosquitoes his first two nights in Rangoon. His host, the corporation's representative in Lower Burma, had been meticulous in describing the precise operation of the mosquito net, but Archie, covered in agonizingly itching bumps, was convinced that the mosquitoes crawled into his bed in the daylight and lay in wait there, licking their lips, until both they and their victim were safely tucked in together at night.

He was, despite sleeplessness, highly elated

both by Rangoon and by the prospect of steeplechasing. He had spent two happy days ambling among the corporation's godowns and admiring the seemingly endless stores of long, dark teak logs that lay there in the dusty, timber-scented gloom. He had seen the first consignment of logs lying in the river after being floated down from the northern forests after the rains and had watched the nimble Burmese skipping from log to log with their spiked implements, deftly keeping this vast and unwieldy flotilla in unified movement. He had also spent a sunset hour at the Shway Dagon and had felt himself ready to faint at the splendour of it. There had been moments in Oxford, summer moments when the setting sun lay golden on Christ Church meadows or lit up the spires and bell towers clustering round Radcliffe Square, when he had felt his soul filled with a sweet contentment. But that was gentle soothing stuff. This soaring stupa, at once barbaric in its magnificence of gold and size and civilized beyond anything in its grace, almost prostrated him with a mixture of awe and rapture. He had stood at the base and flung his head back to the heavens and gazed and gazed until his throat ached and his eyes were dazzled.

The bearer, Ah Chun, stepped back and said, 'Dressing, *thakin*.'

Archie shut his eyes and slid beneath the water, blowing bubbles like a hippopotamus. When he surfaced, Ah Chun was smiling, showing teeth blood-red from betel juice. He was from Mandalay, recruited there by some mysterious Italian who seemed to combine being both Italian consul and agent for the corporation, and he was anxious to get Archie, his *thakin*, back to territory he knew. He held out a vast rough towel and waited for Archie to heave his bulk out of the tub and spray the air and floor with flying drops of water.

'*Thakin* will be winning.'

'I doubt it,' Archie said, succumbing to the pleasure of being rubbed dry by other hands than his own. 'I'm overweight and out of practice.'

'In Mandalay, no racing.'

Fresh sweat was beginning to run down him with the water drops. Ah Chun knotted the towel deftly round Archie's waist and stood back for him to pass into the bedroom. The silks of his owner lay upon the bed, a thoroughly Burmese combination of pink and lime-green.

'I shall look like a sherbet.'

The breeches he had not worn since England felt pleasurably loose at the waist but the light-weight borrowed boots were, whatever the number stamped on the sole, too small.

'Must bear, *thakin*,' Ah Chun said from knee level, pulling and tugging. Even with such exertion his even brown skin remained smooth and dry. He was a Shan, he had told Archie, born in the blue mountains to the east of Mandalay and he had lifted his high cheekboned, slant-eyed Chinese face to Archie to prove it. Shan food was

165

the best in Burma, he said, delicate and delicious, smoked duck in ginger, spiced chicken cooked with half-raw sprigs of cauliflower and watercress, pure white rice, slightly sticky, better than any rice, even the rice of the Rangoon delta.

'Winning,' he said now firmly to Archie, surveying his pink and green quartered master.

'Have you money on me?'

Ah Chun shrugged.

'Not much, I hope,' Archie said. 'You'll surely lose it.'

'My *thakin* win, I am much respected.'

Archie grinned at him. 'Your *thakin* win, I am much surprised.'

Down in the drawing room furnished with oak from England and brass from Benares, two people were waiting in the gloom caused by the drawn-down shades. Wates, the representative of the corporation, stood by the unnecessary fireplace and jingled coins in his pockets, and the nearest chair, a giant affair with wings upholstered in burgundy leather, completely dominated a small young woman in white who sat unhappily on its extreme edge.

'Ah,' Wates said, 'Ah. Archie. Dressed for the fray, I see. This is Miss Prior. Miss Grace Prior.'

Archie stooped and held out his hand, smiling. Grace forgot to be taken aback by his size or his clothes and smiled back at him rapturously. She was sure she had never seen so large a young man, nor one with so peculiarly sweet a smile.

'Are you coming to watch me make a fool of myself, Miss Prior?'

'She is, indeed, Archie. And then she needs a favour in return.'

Archie and Grace gazed at each other in embarrassment.

'Of – of course—' both said together.

'Fact is,' Wates said, taking his hands out of his pockets, 'fact is, Archie, Miss Prior needs an escort up the river to Mandalay. Her father is – is—'

'My father,' Grace said with difficulty, wishing suddenly and to her horror, that Tom were not what he was, 'my father is the Anglican missionary in Mandalay. He has been there four years. He sent me down here when the British Residency closed in Mandalay in seventy-nine. But I must go back to him. I must.'

'Is he ill?' Archie asked helpfully.

'Oh no! Not that kind of need, Mr Tennant. He needs me as – as a helpmeet you see. The nuns have been so kind to me here but I want to go back. I loved Mandalay and there doesn't seem to be any danger any more. It was just the journey, you see. I mean, the steamers are perfectly safe and the captains are such kind fatherly men, but Papa felt, I mean, I wasn't sure—'

Archie said, smiling, 'I think the escorting will be the other way about, Miss Prior. I'm a babe unborn in Burma. It will be wonderful for me to have a guide.'

In order to express her gratitude at this

gallantry better, Grace rose eagerly from her chair and Archie found that her head barely reached his shoulder. She was wearing some extraordinary garment, goodness knows, he had little opinion and no knowledge of women's clothes, but this strange draped affair reminded him strongly of the choristers in Christ Church Cathedral and gave no indication at all of the outlines underneath. Looking amiably down at her while she thanked him breathlessly for his kindness, he thought that perhaps missionary's daughters *had* no outlines out of sheer godliness, and even if they had, one certainly should not be thinking of them.

She was quite pretty really, in a pale and unspectacular way. Her wide, light eyes, turned with childish warmth up to him, were fringed with soft, brown lashes that matched her hair; her nose was small and straight; her teeth even. But she was a watercolour girl, a faint and delicately tinted thing, and Archie had the sensation that if he stretched out his lime-green right arm and laid his hand upon her head, he could crumple her up as easily as if she were made of paper.

'Walked the course, have you?' Wates said, tiring of Grace's effusiveness.

'Early this morning. It doesn't look too alarming except I don't much like the look of the stone wall at the fourth and of course the ground is like iron.'

'I think it's so awfully brave of you, Mr Tennant. I do hope—'

'You shouldn't have much trouble,' Wates said. 'At least you know what you are doing. You will find three or four professionals from Calcutta but the others are either local boys from Rangoon or chaps who've done no more than follow the Rangoon beagles. Of course, the soldiers think they can do it backwards—'

'They probably can.'

'Are you nervous, Mr Tennant? I am awfully nervous for you. I wasn't before we met, but you have been so kind that I, that I—'

Wates looked at his watch. 'We should be going.'

Grace picked up her parasol and moved ahead of them into the hallway which was furnished with stuffed heads and oak chests just as it might have been in Perthshire. Behind her, Wates said in a low voice, 'Nice little thing. Hope the chattering won't be a burden. It's a real kindness, Archie. Andreino asked me that the next recruit I sent up, you know—'

Archie nodded. 'No trouble at all.'

In the hall, Grace was counting. There was today, and the races, and then tomorrow and then the next day the steamer would leave and she would have at least eight days with him, eight or maybe nine or even ten if, by great good luck, the steamer got stuck on a mudbank, and she would be able to tell him so much, all she knew about Burma, maybe even the language. Including today, there would be ten days at least. Ten days of being very happy. She turned as

Archie and Wates came out to join her.

'Oh, Mr Tennant, I do hope you will be careful!'

Jack Tar had a short neck, small eyes and ears, and feet like soup plates. He glanced contemptuously at Archie and curled his lip, showing huge yellow teeth. Then he laid his ears back and braced his powerful shoulders as if prepared to resist any attempt to mount him.

Archie said to the grinning syce at his head, 'Hold his head up. *Up*. As high as you can.'

Jack Tar's sneer vanished as he felt Archie's weight and his expression became startled for a moment and then sullenly resigned.

Archie leaned down. 'The whip.'

The syce handed it up, still grinning.

'I'm going to ride longer,' Archie said, pulling up the saddle flap. 'I have to, there's too much of me to ride as short as they all are—'

Around him several dark little Indians and Burmans crouched on their ponies. The officers of last night were mounting in a leisurely manner amid a good deal of laughter and chaffing from fellow officers who had gathered round to make a crowd. The heat was terrific and the earth under Jack Tar's great hooves was baked as hard as a rock. Behind Archie rose the skeleton of what would be the grandstand, a distinctly oriental-looking structure in teak, with wide verandahs and up-winging roofs. The space of grass between this and the white-painted rails that edged the flat course was entirely jammed with people, thousands upon thousands of people, mostly Burmese in their bright silks and cottons, the air above them quivering and slightly blue from the smoke of innumerable green cigars.

Archie's owner had been pointed out to him. If he won, they would meet; if not, not. She was small and perfectly finished, like some little piece of enamel work, and there were diamonds blazing away around her throat and in the black tower of her hair. Her husband, gross with prosperity, trod softly behind her, his small eyes bright with intelligence in the smooth yellow moon of his face. Archie watched them for some time. She so small and contained and cylindrical, he so vast and sleek, like a great swollen yellow candle, how did they ever—

'Starter's orders, Mr Tennant.'

The starter was flustered. All the horses were milling and wheeling about him and he shook his flag at them as if it were an angry fist.

'In line, gentlemen, in line, if you please.'

Jack Tar felt wooden and reluctant in Archie's hands. He planted his hooves firmly as if setting himself against Archie's weight and then dropped his ugly head dispiritedly.

'In line, damn you, get in line!'

A local boy, frail and brown in blue and scarlet silks, jostled clumsily into Archie. Jack Tar affected not to notice and hung his head still farther. The starter's flag went up. Archie pulled at Jack Tar's head, but the horse appeared to ignore him, merely shifting the bit to a tougher and more comfortable place in his mouth.

The flag went down and Jack Tar leaped forward almost taking Archie's breath with him. The pace was tremendous immediately, accentuated by the hard ground which made each drumming stride shudder and jar. Around Archie, pressed close, several native boys clung to their ponies, not riding, he could see, but simply hanging on limpet-like, their slight bodies arched over their mounts' necks. The first fence, a hurdle, seemed to flash by with Jack Tar hardly altering his stride, then came a nasty double, flanked by ditches, and Jack Tar pecked on landing, forcing Archie to collect him and his own scattered wits at once.

The third fence came wheeling up, a low mud wall with a ditch on take off, then the three-foot stone wall which Jack Tar took with surprising ease, only grunting as he landed, and then the course swept round and it was the water jump by the grandstand and all those little butterfly ladies and a blur of brilliant colours. Ahead of Archie, The Parson, a bay, and a lean chestnut were going with comfortable competence. A quick glance over his shoulder told him that the water jump had checked a large part of the field, although a couple of good-looking little Arabs he had admired in the paddock were gaining ground on him. Jack Tar's ears were flat back and it felt to Archie as if he had the bit clamped between his teeth.

At the sixth, an in-and-out about ten paces

apart, he stumbled and the little Arabs sailed by. Archie's blood rushed up. The seventh, a teak post and rails of terrifying solidity, loomed ahead and Archie shortened the reins more savagely than he would have dared to do on an obliging and delicately brought-up English hunter.

'Get *on* with it, you clumsy—!'

Jack Tar took it like a bird but his ears didn't move. Five of the fences to take again, the last one being the water and a grand finale in front of the ladies . . . Archie took out his whip. If Jack Tar could have slotted his ears into his skull he would have done so, but his heavy shoulders, flecked now with foam, moved as steadily and powerfully as pistons. He gained on the Arabs steadily, took the double beautifully and left them behind. Archie let him have his head a little and he stretched his neck in pursuit of the bay and the chestnut, still stride for stride ahead of him. At the stone wall the chestnut swerved abruptly flinging his rider over the rails into the rough dry grass beyond and the bay, unnerved, jumped too late, lost the rhythm of his stride and allowed Jack Tar to thunder by. Only the water jump now and the crowd roaring at him like the sea coming in and The Parson's sweat-dark rump nearer and nearer, and then the collecting under him and the leap and The Parson's nose passing his knee, backwards and backwards and the roar of the crowd turning to thunder and the white disc of the winning post fifty yards ahead, forty, thirty . . .

Jack Tar slackened. Archie took the whip to him, shouting, but the great muscles which had served him so well were now entirely directed against him, not for him. The thudding gallop broke down to a canter, Jack Tar let his head go down, bunched his neck. Slowly, inevitably, The Parson drew level again, more than level, half a length ahead, a length . . . At a ragged and surly trot, Jack Tar passed the winning post in second place.

Grace, hoarse with screaming, was now in tears. Wates and MacGregor, who had failed to find alternative escorts to themselves for her, passed her their handkerchiefs in silence and turned their backs discreetly.

'He should have won, he should have, that horrible horse. Oh, what happened? It's all wrong. Poor Mr Tennant, he should have won. It isn't fair—'

'Told you he was a bastard,' The Parson's rider said cheerfully to Archie as they unsaddled.

'Does he always do that?'

'Not exactly that. New trick every year. But he's always in the frame. Madame May will smile upon you, never fear. She'll be at least four thousand to the good so she can afford to smile.'

'Madame—?'

'Daw Kyn May. Your owner. I say, watch out!'

One of Jack Tar's huge hooves lashed out and missed Archie by an inch.

'You *are* a bastard,' Archie said in amazement, 'a real, through and through *bastard*.'

Jack Tar swung his ugly head round and regarded Archie with his small malevolent eyes.
Then for a fleeting moment his ears went up and
he drew his lips back over his ochre teeth in the
grotesque semblance of a smile.

'Five thousand rupees!' Grace said in genuine
admiration.

Archie nodded. Madame Kyn May had not
thought it necessary to see him, send him a
message even, but just as he was boarding the
steamer, not ten minutes before it churned out
into midstream, a boy had come up, running,
with a packet and a message.

'Look!' Archie said. 'Look at that! And will
I ride him in the spring meeting! I *say*, oh I
say, five hundred, over three years' salary, five
hundred—'

Grace said, meaning it, 'Oh, Mr Tennant, I am
so awfully pleased for you!'

There was everything, today, to be pleased
about. She looked down at her blue muslin lap
and was particularly pleased about that and full
of gratitude for dear Hosannah Manook, who
had been in Rangoon for a month or two and had
said that if Grace were to charm a young man all
the way to Mandalay, she must do it properly
dressed. And then, because there was so little
time, she had taken two of her own dresses – they
were slightly over-flounced, Grace felt, and
they made her go in and out in a way she didn't
at all naturally and was perhaps not quite decent

– and reefed them in to fit Grace and here she
was, blue muslin frills and parasol, and a tiny
straw hat with daisies and blue ribbons, and then
Mr Tennant all to herself and the journey ahead
and now the money and him so excited . . .
Everything looked so lovely, the blue sky and
the green banks far away across the glittering
stretches of water and the golden finger of the
Shway Dagon dwindling in the distance, fiery in
the sunlight.

'I wish she'd done it sooner,' Archie said. 'I
could have bought a horse. Yesterday, I mean.
Or a couple. And brought them with me.'

'Can't you do that in Mandalay?'

He turned to look at her. She looked quite
changed today, even a different shape somehow.
He wondered how it was done.

'I doubt it. There aren't enough Englishmen
up there to ensure good horses. Never mind. I'll
save it to buy myself a beauty on my first leave.
Five hundred! I say, Miss Prior, what shall we do
to celebrate?'

'Oh, we can't, there's nothing!' she cried,
despairing at once. 'Oh, you should have, I
don't know, champagne or something or make a
speech, but there's nobody, just me. Oh poor Mr
Tennant!'

Looking at her, smiling and thinking of the
money, he said, 'I don't think I am poor at all,'
and Grace, understanding him as she wished to,
fell at once from admiration into love.

'It will be – eight days, you know,' she said,

'at least. Eight days of just this steamer and – and—'

'And then Mandalay.'

'Yes,' she said sadly, 'then Mandalay.'

'Don't you want to get there? And see your father?'

'Oh, yes, yes, of course, I do! But I love this kind of journey, so peaceful and safe and nothing mattering. I love Mandalay. You will too, it's so beautiful, so strange. Some of the people are, well disconcerting I suppose, not like they are when they are in England—'

'Men like me? Teak boys?'

Grace raised her eyes for the luxury of looking at him.

'Oh no. Not like you. Odd sorts of people. Papa said they were speculators. I am not sure whether that necessarily means that they are wicked or just that they are ready to take a great gamble to be rich, but they used to hang about the court and fawn upon that terrible Queen to try and get permission to work the forests and the mines. There was one—' she stopped. This golden day, this golden time ahead could all be spoiled entirely if she began to think about Maria Beresford.

'Go on,' Archie said. 'Please. I want to know all I can about Mandalay.'

'There was a girl,' Grace said carefully, wanting very much to put her hand in Archie's for reassurance, 'a girl I knew in India, before Mandalay, and her father was some sort of – of administrator, I think. At least he was a tea-planter first but he lost his money. And she was very – very handsome,' Grace said, forcing herself to be honest, 'and she became a great favourite with the Queen and the Queen gave her father and – and, oh, Mr Tennant, an awful man, a sinister sort of man called Mr Blount, well, the Queen gave them permission to work the ruby mines at Minhla. And there was a Frenchman involved too, a *Frenchman* and they are English. And Papa tells me they are so rich now and the Queen has built them a house with a triple roof, just like Papa's mission, and Maria can do anything she likes and she has lovely jewels and they call her the Queen of the *kalā* town—'

Archie passed her his handkerchief. 'Please don't look so distressed, Miss Prior. What is the matter? Did this person upset you, do you an injury?'

'Oh, no!' Grace said vehemently, clutching the handkerchief with fervour. 'She didn't upset me, well, not much, by what she *did*, but by what she *was*. She always dressed so wonderfully and knew what to say and didn't mind at all what people thought of her. I'm so sorry to talk to you like this, Mr Tennant. I really am. I never meant to. It is simply that you have been so kind and I feel you are a friend.'

'Oh, yes,' Archie said, 'I hope so.' Then he stood up and held out his arm. 'We are going to walk three times round each deck, otherwise we shan't deserve our luncheon, and you can begin

178

teaching me Burmese. The only phrase Ah Chun has taught me is "Give me the money!" ' '

Grace stood up laughing. 'Oh yes! *Pike-san pay-like*, they all say that a great deal! Don't expect too much of luncheon, Mr Tennant, the food on these steamers isn't good at all. One can never look forward to it. I find the only thing I do look forward to very much is the evenings, when they moor near the villages and the people come out in their little boats. That is lovely.'

It was indeed. The steamer lay like a great whale in mid-stream while the boats of the villagers jostled round her in the fawn-coloured waters. Above them the sky was rose and apricot and thin, clear faded blue, and here and there from the banks a pagoda caught the last light, its whiteness flushing pink and amber. In the boats the villagers shrieked for custom, holding up chickens in wicker baskets, necklaces of persimmon seeds, chunks of sugar cane, trays of heart-shaped betel leaves, green coconuts, melons, fans of little bananas. Archie bought a bundle of green cheroots tied neatly with a plait of grasses and leaned on the rail, smoking and gazing, while item after item was held up for his inspection. And then the moon came up, white and brilliant, and the river waters became like polished jet and a velvety softness fell upon the banks out of the deep hot darkness of the Burmese night.

9

Afternoon sun fell golden on the heavy leaves of the mangoes and the blood-red blooms of the mohur trees. Between their leaves, Maria could see the creamy sweeps of frangipani and the delicate pink of Chinese roses and the brilliant purple – a colour she detested even in flowers – of the bougainvillea climbing like wildfire over anything to hand. That sunlit spectacle was framed by the blue-shadowed posts of the verandah and again by the wide-flung doors of her drawing room, doors lacquered vermilion inside and hung upon wonderful brass hinges fashioned like dragons. Between herself and the doors stretched a satisfying sweep of teak floorboards, gleaming with oil and scattered here and there with silk rugs from China in duck-egg blue and pink and cream, rugs that had been carried by coolies over the Shan hills to be sold in Mandalay.

The little table upon which they had been forced to dine five years ago now stood at Maria's elbow and bore a crystal bowl of water in which three perfect white hibiscus floated – and the tea things. Maria herself, almost as perfect, wore a dress European in cut but made of rough gleaming Burmese silk and in her ears and round her wrists shone rubies as dark as good claret. The chair she sat in was French, gilded and upholstered in rose brocade, and its companion stood opposite her, across the best of the Chinese rugs. On the teak walls hung French looking glasses and the watercolours that had dictated the colours of all Beresford drawing rooms since the days of Tirimbatore, interspersed here and there with groups of eighteenth-century French miniatures that Supayalat had demanded from adventurers seeking to win her favour, and then laughed at as soon as she had them and handed them directly to Maria. In corners stood exquisite old Chinese lacquer cabinets, pieces that had also found their way over the eastern hills to the bazaars of Mandalay and on them were delicate old blue and white bowls which Maria had filled with glimmering, quartz-like pieces of rock from the mines, valueless but highly decorative.

The room was her domain. When the house was built two years ago she had begged that one room might be much larger than most Burmese rooms, at least thirty feet in one direction, because, she explained laughingly to the Queen, when one was so tall, one needed space to move. Supayalat had been in high good humour that day. She was wearing a watch Maria had given her, a watch made like a tiny enamelled beetle whose jewelled wings flew open to reveal the face – it was a watch that Maria had no business to give to anyone, being Hubert's wedding present to his wife, but Hubert knew better than to remonstrate with Maria in any way these days – and it was always a good sign when the little beetle adorned the white starched muslin of the royal jacket. Yes, Maria should have her great room, as great as she wished, two perhaps . . .

Now she sat in it and waited. The teatray was level with her elbow, laid with English silver and bone china and a plate of almond biscuits made from Chinese almonds as sweet as honey. Her gaze wandered round the room in self-congratulation but her thoughts drowsed in the heavy warmth of late afternoon. The morning had been spent at the palace, as usual, a morning like almost every morning in the past five years, attending Supayalat's ritual bath and first dressing of the day, helping to oil that silky brown skin or stitching the lining of soft muslin that had to be put in, fresh at each wearing, as the tamein's only undergarment. The Queen was pregnant again, smoothly swollen, and she was sullen and dangerous for Thibaw had been caught with a mistress and the court was waiting in trepidation to see what would happen next. Maria knew what would happen, she now knew the Queen too well. The little mistress would be summoned to play a game with all the other little maids of honour and then gradually the game would become a scuffle and then the scuffle would become a battle and the little mistress would limp disgraced from court, her teeth broken, her face a livid mass of bruises, her hair pulled out in handfuls, her hands and feet stamped on, twisted. And the Queen would watch, laughing. But that had not happened yet, nothing had happened but that Supayalat had smouldered in her garden pavilion and would, as usual, only allow near her the tall *kalā*, the Englishwoman in her sweeping silks.

Unfortunately, there had been little to divert her with that morning. Maria had been meticulous in showing the Queen every drawing, every plan to do with the ruby mines and they had spent many hours poring over Bonvilain's diagrams and charts. The Queen was in many ways a frustrated businesswoman and her sharp little brain was easily diverted from domestic upsets by the prospect of new and improved schemes to work the mines. But today there had been nothing to give her, not even a selection of rubies from which she could choose the best as the terms of the concession dictated. She had shrieked for music to be played louder and louder and had sat upon her cushion, smoking furiously, exuding sparks of danger and temper.

Five years of that now. Five years of that red and gold palace, the gardens with their grottos and waterfalls and summerhouses, the little maids of honour in their butterfly silks, who came and went as if they were as disposable as paper kites. Five years too of Supayalat, of her fascination, her power, her passionate possessiveness of the King, her conviction that she was the centre of the universe, her beastliness and cruelty and charm. Five years of a tinsel world, where a king and queen above the earth played all day like children while royal prisoners starved beneath it in dungeons of unspeakable squalor; where one trod upon precious carpets and lay upon soft silks and threw the empty food tins of asparagus and artichoke hearts imported from Europe to stink beneath the palace platform in the rat-infested gloom. Five years of intrigue and spying and an uncertainty at once heady and terrifying. Five years which had given Maria position and admiration and jewels – and dulled her hair a little and drawn fine lines beside her eyes and mouth. Five years—

A fifth of her lifetime, no less – of a chance for queenliness, the chance that she had, since those arrogant childhood days in South India, felt she was not so much lucky to have, as entitled to. Her first great public moment in Burma, a year after her arrival, had satisfied her absolutely and had given her proof that this was the kind of position which should be hers by right. In the late autumn of 1880, that most lovely of the Burmese seasons when the stifling, drenching rains had given way to clear, strong sunlight, Maria, attended by her father and Denzil Blount, had gone down to Minhla to inspect the ruby mines. In addition to her father and Denzil she had full royal escort, particularly ordered by the Queen as a mark of most especial favour, and she rode out of Mandalay upon an elephant, preceded by yelling lictors in royal livery, followed by a detachment of the Queen's own bodyguard and surrounded, for every step of the way, by a surging and fascinated crowd of Burmese.

She did not observe, swaying down towards the river where a royal steamer had been put at her disposal for the journey down the Irrawaddy to Minhla, that in contrast to the magnificence of the elephant trappings and the scarlet and gold of the soldiers, the crowd that gaped at her magical progress were barefoot, filthy and ragged. She did not look down at them but gazed superbly before her, only conscious that she was the focus of all attention and that both Hubert and Denzil rode some way behind her, on inferior animals, attended only by a handful of soldiers attired in the uniform of the guard of the Gem City, not the Queen's own livery.

The journey had lived up to its beginning. She was allotted two staterooms aboard the steamer, even if they were furnished with a Burmese disregard for European lack of suppleness, and four of the little maids of honour from the court knelt reverently in corners awaiting her pleasure.

'One might say,' Denzil said, looking about him at her borrowed splendour, 'that you have, my dear, arrived—'

Maria regarded him without smiling. 'And not, I may say, before time.'

More elephants awaited them at Minhla and huge tents, carpeted and with gilded guy ropes, had been put up a little distance from the mines.

It was an unprepossessing area, a flat plainlike stretch of dun country, its surface scarred and pitted with the mine workings, baking beneath the relentless sun. Robed in a flowing white dustcoat over her silks, Maria arrived to inspect the site and found a delegation awaiting her with garlands of jasmine and a canopy of cheap English umbrellas obtained, no doubt with enormous difficulty, as a compliment. The manager of the mine, a scrawny and scarred individual with the keenly intelligent look of a practised exploiter, offered to show her the mines themselves.

'On no account!' Hubert cried, horrified.

Maria turned to him. 'Papa! Why not?'

Denzil said, 'You have no conception of how rubies are mined. It's an appalling business. The tunnels in which they work are improperly shored up, the heat is terrible, not to mention the smells. And the depth—' He paused and looked over her shoulder. 'Take a look for yourself. Those are the men that work here.'

At the mouth of the main entrance to the mine, a square hole cut in a shallow mound and lined with teak trunks, a small band of men was being marshalled into order for inspection. They were, for the most part, almost deformed in appearance, with grossly enlarged joints, humped shoulders and thrust-forward necks. They were also naked, apart from filthy loincloths and turbans.

Maria looked at them swiftly and turned back.

186

'But I should be escorted. I am under royal protection. There is nothing to be alarmed about.'

'There is no question of it,' Denzil said shortly. 'Pierre has been down, merely to satisfy us that the gem-bearing seams are as rich as we think. You are here merely as a figurehead. Choose some stones for the Queen and then we shall go.'

Maria said furiously, 'You treat this as if it were a charade—'

'It is.'

'Dearest,' Hubert said, 'do not upset yourself. Come—'

'We would not have this concession if it were not for me! If it were not for my intercession with the Queen, almost a year of paying court, of daily attendance, of presents and flattery—'

'Forgive me,' Denzil said, 'I apologize. You are too precious to risk in a Burmese mine, believe me. Out of kindness to myself and your father, don't think of it. Do as the Queen would do, choose jewels, let them gaze at you and come back to Mandalay.'

With four magnificent rubies, two cabuchon and two brilliant cut, in a gilded lacquer casket lined in velvet, Maria made her stately progress back to Mandalay. A detachment of soldiers waited on the bund to escort her back to the palace for Supayalat was impatient to see her, eager for trophies. She was entranced with the jewels, holding them up to the light, putting them between her small, strong teeth and then selecting one, a cabuchon, and holding it out to Maria, laughing, as a gift. It was memorable, that day, the Queen's narrow little hand in hers, the smooth small egg-shape of the jewel falling into her palm, the sense of triumph, of power. Four years ago now and, had she but known it, only a beginning—

A voice from the doorway said, 'I disturb you, Mademoiselle.'

'Pierre, you are late.'

'Five, it is only five—'

'I did not say five.'

Bonvilain came into the room, grinning and shaking his finger. 'Don't scold. You must not scold. I bring excellent news.'

She held out her hand. 'I know perfectly well you do. That is why I am impatient.'

'And Denzil? Him also? Is he coming?'

Maria rang for hot water. 'Later,' she said, 'Later. When you have told me.'

He settled himself in the empty chair opposite her. 'Ouf. This chair is terrible. Our French chairs are to look at but your English ones are to sit in. You would not give me whisky instead of tea?'

'I would not.'

'So beautiful and so severe—'

'Don't flirt with me, Pierre,' she said, not meaning it, turning her head a little.

'I can't help it. And you like it.'

Maria's Madrassee bearer, now in a sort of livery she had devised for her servants out of yellow Burmese silk – the only thing she had ever done which Denzil Blount had dared to tell her was utterly ludicrous – came in with hot water and green Chinese tea and Maria busied herself with the pretty ritual of tea-making, delighted to have Bonvilain's eyes upon her.

'When I am married,' he said, putting his sunburned hands fingertip to fingertip under his chin, 'I shall still flirt with you.'

She looked up, the teapot poised.

'Marry! Are you to be married? But not, surely not, Pierre you could not—'

'Marry Mattie Calogreedy? Naturally not. She feels herself to be married in the Burmese sense, which is sufficient for her self-esteem, but she knows that as a Frenchman I cannot marry her in the European manner. I doubt she would expect it and in any case, she is growing stout and yellow—'

'She does expect it.'

'Then I shall not tell her.'

Maria shrugged. 'It is your affair.'

'I wish you could be *mon affaire*. I am going home to marry a sweet child my parents have chosen, blonde *comme une ange* and good as gold. I have only been waiting for her seventeenth birthday.'

Maria said nothing. Five years in Burma had not increased the liberality of her views in any way, notably those she held about the free-living behaviour of Europeans in Mandalay. Mattie had been undeniably useful to Maria, but being half

Burmese, could not expect to count as a full human being in her consideration and although Pierre's liaison with her was in the first place disgusting, his planned abuse of her was certainly not more so. It was rumoured too that Pierre had once had some little native thing from the cigar factory in his protection and Mattie had behaved just as you would expect someone like her to do and screamed and wailed. She had tried to tell Maria about it one day in the palace and Maria had turned her back.

'I will send Mattie a dress from Paris.'

'I expect that will seem to her as good as a marriage.'

'I have drunk my tea. Now will you give me some whisky?'

'When you have told me what I want to know.'

'Ah,' Bonvilain said and leaned back, stretching his legs. 'My information. My information is no less than that Thibaw has sent a mission to Paris. I have not been idle at court either, you see. A full-blown Burmese government mission has left Mandalay for France, ostensibly to assemble information about arts and sciences, industrial progress, that sort of thing. They all speak French and English and it is being put about that they will go first to Paris and then to London. But the *atwinwun*, the officer of the royal household, who leads them tells me that they mean to go no further than Paris. And while they are in Paris, they mean to offer to the French at the King's, and therefore the Queen's, instructions, concessions to work mines of coal, of lead, of sulphur, of silver, of rubies, the ruby mines at Mogok—'

'Pierre!' Maria said, her eyes shining, 'Oh Pierre!'

'It annoys me a little that my charm cannot make you smile at me as such information does. It piques me. I am not used to this. Now you see why I must go home. Just for a while. I shall follow the mission and make sure that nothing happens on the Quai d'Orsay that is not to our advantage and, of course, while I am there, I shall marry my little Marie-Thérèse and everyone will say Bonvilain has gone home to fetch a wife.'

'Mogok,' Maria said, 'Where is Mogok?'

'East of the Irrawaddy, high. The Shweli, the tributary of the Irrawaddy, goes almost all about it.'

Maria rose and paced slowly towards the open doors. A coppersmith bird beat in the trees outside and the late sunlight was as thick as syrup.

'When the present business has passed,' she said, 'the business between the King and Queen, I shall speak to her.'

Footsteps sounded on the verandah. Denzil Blount, not supposing for one moment that Maria was in the doorway because she had risen to greet him, took off his hat and remarked that she looked like a cat with cream.

'Not cream. Rubies.'

'More! But my dear Maria, you are stiff with rubies. There cannot be one single item of jewellery in which rubies can be used that you do not possess already—'

'Mogok,' she said, and laughed and went back to her chair to pour tea for him.

Denzil followed her, nodded briefly to Bonvilain and said, 'Ah, Mogok. Pierre, you are before me. I had promised myself the pleasure of telling Maria.'

He took his tea and went to stand against the shining wall between the chairs, the space that in European houses was given over to a fireplace. 'I don't think I'm altogether pleased, Pierre. And I hear you are going to Paris too.'

Bonvilain shrugged and smiled. 'My dear fellow, if it was not for me, for my being French and an engineer, we should never have got the concession to work the mines at Minhla—'

'Nonsense,' Denzil said crisply. 'Your nationality has nothing to do with it. I may not be much of a patriot but even I would rather you were not French. It is your engineering skills we prize you for, as well you know. Just as you could not do without our diplomacy and standing at court. Not to mention our ability to borrow money. And this delegation of Thibaw's is going to London after Paris, therefore English links with Mandalay will be just as much strengthened as those the court has with France.'

'No,' Maria said, 'it is not.'

Denzil glanced at them both, gestured defeat with his teacup and said, 'Then I suppose the die is truly cast. We must choose between Queen

Victoria and Mogok. How do you know the Burmese will not go to London?'

'The *atwinwun*, the officer who leads it, he told me. He says they will put about that they will go but they will not go.'

Denzil put down his teacup. 'Is this your doing?'

Bonvilain looked amused. 'Not entirely.'

'What is being offered to work the mines at Mogok?'

Maria leaned forward a little. Bonvilain, on the other hand, leaned back and put his hands, fingertip to fingertip, beneath his handsome chin.

'Three lakhs of rupees annually. No parties other than ourselves admitted. The King to have first choice of all rubies but to pay full value for any he chooses. The rest ours to sell as we will, where we will.'

Denzil let out a breath. 'Three lakhs! We don't pay half that for Minhla. But then on the other hand the King does not pay full value for the best stones either. And no hindrance to our taking all the rest out of the country!'

Maria said, 'The royal coffers are empty. Thibaw and Supayalat know that. They are monstrously extravagant, they always have been. Three lakhs will be a drop in the ocean. I lend the Queen a little here and there – at least I give it for there is little chance of seeing it back and it is a good investment. She is really pressed for money, ready money.'

Denzil smiled down at her. 'Does the Queen know of Mogok?'

'No,' Bonvilain said, 'not yet. But our charming ambassadress here—'

'You mean you have worked out these terms with the King alone?'

'And his adviser, Prince Yanaung. Yes.'

'Then we cannot rely upon them.'

Maria rose and swept rustling to the open doors. 'Oh, yes, we can. I shall speak to the Queen and Pierre will accompany the Burmese mission to make sure no higher bidders win Mogok.'

Denzil said, 'I don't underestimate your power in any way.'

'Don't flatter me.'

Bonvilain got up, smiling. 'I will leave you, Denzil, to see if you may soften her heart any better than I. She refused to let *me* flirt with her either.'

'Ah, but you are French and therefore not to be trusted. When do you leave?'

'At once.'

'I am a little envious of your going to Paris. I have not seen Paris in sixteen years. Paris—' he stopped. Maria's back, suddenly stiffening in the doorway, reminded him that she did not care to hear Europe spoken of so. She had never seen it. Piere, glancing at him and understanding, moved to Maria's side and took her hand to kiss it.

'Shall you come and wave me farewell with tears in your eyes?'

'I only ever have tears in my eyes on account of the dust.'

'The man who wins you will be a conqueror beside whom Alexander will pale. You will speak to the Queen? Tomorrow? And send me word before I go?'

'If I think fit. Naturally.'

When Bonvilain's footsteps had resounded down the verandah and he could be heard shouting for his servant in the lane, Denzil said, 'I do not really flatter you, you know.'

'Of course I know. That is why I won't allow you to pretend to.'

'Will you come and sit down?'

The room was growing dim as the sun sank lower. The Irrawaddy would be copper in the early evening now, its farther banks violet, the trees along the bund smudges of indigo and the dying sun, poised above it, would be veiled in dust. Denzil, seated opposite Maria with his back to the open doors, was almost invisible apart from the white of his shirt front and the sudden gleam of his teeth.

'You know why I do not flatter you. If I did, it would prove that I was hiding my disappointment in you. As it is, I admire you more than any woman I have ever encountered and I would not dare to flatter you. So I will do the opposite. I will warn you.'

Her chin went up. 'Oh?'

'Yes. Mogok is by no means a certainty. What-ever,' he said emphatically, gesturing her to silence, 'you may say to the Queen. I tell you why. This is not simply a trade mission going to Paris nor is Pierre merely going to collect his child bride. It is a political mission as well. Pierre will see Jules Ferry, the French Foreign Minister. That means one thing only and that is that the French mean to cut out the British here, the Bombay-Burmah, all that teak—'

'Cut out the British? Why do you say it so lightly? Don't you care?'

Denzil smiled at her. 'Don't be queenly with *me*. You know I don't. I may have been born English but that I regard as a sort of accident. Don't misunderstand me. I don't mean that the remoteness of my feelings for England makes me in the least partisan towards the French. I care nothing for either. I care only, as you know, for myself. But you are not the same. Whatever the circumstances of your life, you are English. I only wish to make it clear to you that if Bonvilain brings back all the prizes you hope for from the Quai d'Orsay, you will be throwing your lot in with the French. It will not be the same as with Minhla. There the concession was to a group of us, two Englishmen, one Frenchman; patriotism, for want of a better word, was not involved. But Mogok – with Mogok, it will be. It does not bother *me*. *I* want you to speak to the Queen. But it is sufficient proof of my real admiration for you that I ask you to consider whether your own feelings will permit you to help the French so much.'

She stared at him with her cold blue stare. 'Why has this come about? Why has it all become a French affair? Why does it not stay as it was with Minhla?'

'Your friend, Pierre Bonvilain.'

'And you, presumably. You to encourage him.'

'A little. I am prepared to help the French because in so doing I help myself. I would help Germans, Greeks, Italians in just the same way if I saw in their dealings an advantage for myself. But would – could you?'

Maria wanted to ask, 'And Papa?' and would not let herself. Hubert spent a good deal of time at court, strolling through the audience halls, advising newcomers, being enigmatic with acquaintances, persuaded always of his own usefulness. Maria knew quite well where his usefulness lay. His clothes, his air, his manner, all these had been invaluable in persuading the Indian and Chinese merchants of Mandalay to lend them all sufficient money to pay the first enormous instalment to the Burmese government for the right to work the mines at Minhla. In two weeks only, Hubert, languid and self-confident, had borrowed the rupees that were necessary for the project even to begin. It was a talent the others could not do without. On the other hand, Maria knew but would not acknowledge, it was his only talent. Pierre and Denzil would not tell him of Mogok until they had a task for him. Maria's spirits soared and sank at once at the knowledge that she was told in full and that he would not be.

'I must, of course, tell Papa.'

'It is unlike you to be unable to make a decision on your own.'

'That would not be the reason!' she said angrily.

'Why must you build up his self-esteem so?' Denzil said, leaning forward in his chair. 'Why always present him to himself as greater than he is—'

'Stop it!' she said. She was almost shouting. 'Stop it! I – I *order* you not to speak so!'

She saw his smile glimmer maddeningly in the gloom.

'Let me tell you some news, then. Tomorrow's steamer brings an old friend of yours to Mandalay. Little Miss Prior.'

'Grace! But I thought she was in a convent. In Rangoon.'

'She was. I saw Tom today. She has decided to rejoin him. He is, of course, enraptured. She is landing tomorrow. Tom said she was in the care, would you believe it, of one of those over-educated schoolboys the Bombay-Burmah sends out to die in the jungle. What possesses a young man to take such a job? This one is to go down to the Ningyan forests it seems, not up the Chindwin like so many others. Of course, if Pierre does his job properly, there will be no jobs for these boys at all and the teak forests will be full of Frenchmen.'

'So Grace has not married.'

There was a pause.

'No more, my dear, have you.'

Maria said smoothly, 'My choice has been severely limited.'

'Certainly. A situation intensified by the fact that you would not have *me* if I asked you.'

'You would not ask me.'

He laughed easily. 'Quite right. I would not. And yet I come closer to it with you than with any woman before. No, Miss Prior is not married. Her father claims proudly she is quite unchanged.'

Maria looked about the room with its lovely objects and colours, at her dress, at the jewels on her wrists. She said with complacency, 'I wonder if she will find me much changed,' certain of his agreement.

He laughed again.

'Oh, no, my dear Maria, she won't. She will find you much the same only, if you understand me, very much more so.'

10

Archie, leaning on the taffrail, felt he had been in Burma for weeks. He also felt – guiltily because it was not an entirely satisfactory sensation – that he had known Grace Prior all his life. They had been together nine days, one day of which had been spent motionless and blisteringly hot upon a sandbank (the leadsman who had thus failed in his duty had been flogged by the captain and Grace had cried and cried and needed hours of comforting), and all that time Grace, in her blue and pink borrowed muslins, had been at his side, chattering and laughing and gazing earnestly up into his face. In many respects, he told himself sternly, he had been very glad to have such a companion, a pretty girl who had lived in Burma for four years and who had a tolerable command of the language, but their being such an obvious couple and the only white people on board had segregated them from many other passengers Archie would have liked to talk to. He leaned heavily forward on the taffrail now so that she could not possibly take his arm.

'Look!' she was saying. 'There's Papa! Oh, dear, *dear* Papa! I can see his clothes need mending from here, and his beard – Oh, and there is Signor Andreino! He isn't a bit changed! And little Ma Zan, Papa has brought her too. She used to be my maid, you know, because she wouldn't work in the school so we took her into the house. I wonder where you will live? I expect Signor Andreino will have found you a bunga-low—'

The day was brilliant. The wide sluggish breadth of the Irrawaddy glittered with points of sunlight and the hard blue sky rose like a shell behind the heavy trees along the bund. The bund itself was hardly visible under a crowd of Burmese, some dressed in their bright cottons, some entirely naked or almost so but for a strip of dingy cloth around their hips.

'Mandalay,' Archie said to himself, 'Man-dalay.'

Little houses had been built out into the river on stilts with crude boats moored to the posts and lines of washing from house to house like coloured flags. There were children in the water too and a good deal of rubbish and, along the river's edge, women slapped and banged their laundry against stones. Voices came floating to Archie above the chug of the steamer, shrill Burmese voices like the dawn chorus in England, echoing and dancing on the water. He straight-ened up, feeling his clothes peeling damply away from the skin of his back and smiled delightedly at it all.

'Papa has seen me!' Grace cried, forgetting her

parasol in her rapture so that it swung danger-
ously close to Archie's eyes. 'Oh, how wonderful!
I do so want you to meet him, he will be so
pleased you have come and so grateful to you for
looking after me!'

Beside the bearded missionary, who was now
waving in huge wide sweeps like a windmill,
stood another European with tremendous black
moustaches and extravagant linen. He was talking with a great deal of gesturing to Tom Prior
and some stone on his finger caught the light
with every movement and flashed like fire. At
Archie's elbow, Ah Chun said, '*Thakin* Andreino.
He was finding me.'

Archie nodded. The deck was becoming
crowded as all the passengers pushed towards the
rail, eager to land. Ah Chun started shouting and
waving, vigorously clearing a space around Grace
and Archie with his knees and elbows.

'I wish the journey wasn't ending! I cannot
thank you enough, you have been so kind, you
have amused me so well. I do hope we won't lose
touch – when do you go into the forests?'

Passengers, despite Ah Chun, were beginning
to push between them, barging through with
bundles and baskets and chickens in wicker
cages. Across the stream of people, Archie
shouted, 'I – I don't know! It's been a great
pleasure, I've enjoyed it too, can't really believe
I'm in Mandalay—'

They seemed almost to be washed over the
gangplank on a river of people. Grace was terri-

fied to see that the gangplank had no sides and that the Irrawaddy, ten feet below, was choked with children and refuse, so she clung to Archie like a limpet and said she must close her eyes, he would have to guide her. Archie saw Andreino watch them as they came unsteadily towards him and wished he did not look so wonderfully amused.

'A good journey, I am sure, Mr Tennant.'

'Excellent,' Archie said, attempting as gently as possible to disengage his arm.

'And the boy? Ah Chun? You are satisfied?'

'First class.'

A voice behind Archie said, 'How good you have been to my Grace! She could not have come without you. I cannot thank you enough.'

Archie turned with difficulty. Grace let go of his arm and sprang into her father's embrace. Over her head Tom said to Archie, on a note of amusement, 'Still a most affectionate child.'

Archie grinned in relief.

'Have you clung to Mr Tennant like a creeper all the way from Rangoon?'

'Almost,' Grace said happily.

'Then I give you your freedom, Mr Tennant. And when you have savoured it a little, come to us in the mission. Come and see us. The cooking has fallen off a little since my daughter went away – apart from a brief spell when a young American Baptist was here, a Miss Newman, an excellent cook – but I hope the welcome hasn't.'

'He should not be here,' Andreino said,

looking after him, 'nor should Miss Prior. I fear you have not come to a safe nor a comfortable place, Mr Tennant. We Europeans are a dwindling band. I expect you were warned of all this in London.'

'No. No, I wasn't. Warned of what?'

A crowd of children was gathering round them, drawn like magnets to gaze at Archie's fair skin.

'Ah!' Andreino said with annoyance, 'typical! Always, *always*, the British ostrich has its head in the sand when it comes to Burma. It drives me mad. Still, all the British government, all the Viceroy can think of, still it is only Africa, Afghanistan. The Transvaal is their great obsession at the moment. And much though I bless the Bombay-Burmah for the use they make of me, they are not much better. The teak is so important they will not heed the dangers. Mr Tennant, life will not be very comfortable here.' He took Archie's arm and began to steer him down the far side of the bund, the knot of children keeping pace with them, their circle unbroken.

'I didn't suppose it would be,' Archie said, his mind filled with schoolboy images of jungles, images he had been trying to replace with something more realistic ever since he left Liverpool.

'When you are in the forests,' Andreino said as if reading his thoughts, 'then you will be safer, I think. Even with dacoits. The boys who work on the elephants are peasants, far from court influence, quite reliable in their way. But

Mandalay is not good, now. Only a few *kalās* are safe. I suppose the Queen would hesitate actually to kill a British subject but, of course, accidents can be arranged here so easily. You will be sharing quite a comfortable bungalow. No small matter to have such a place, I can tell you.'

Archie stopped. Several children cannoned into him from behind and there was an explosion of giggling. Andreino spoke to them sharply.

'I don't mind them,' Archie said, 'it would take more than a few children to knock me over. But I thought I was to go out into the forests straight away. I didn't really imagine needing a bungalow.'

Andreino stood aside with a flourish by the bullock cart for Archie to climb in ahead of him.

'You will go in a couple of weeks, when you have the feel of the place. Mostly they fell from November to March and float from March until October. It was a poor floating season this year, there's far too much timber still lying. Not enough rain, though on a daily basis it seemed hard to understand how that could be.'

Archie settled himself with discomfort in the cart. The trees and huts around him were obscured with dust which he could see rising in soft choking clouds and feel gritty on his lips and tongue.

'How old are you, Mr Tennant?'

'Twenty-four.'

'Then you have an excellent chance of

becoming a forest manager. How many other Bombay-Burmah recruits have you met?'

'None,' Archie said.

'There are plenty here, but mostly up the Chindwin. All sorts but very well educated. I sometimes wonder what use an intimate acquaintance with the ancient languages is in a remote Burmese forest. There – that is the Anglican mission.'

An ancient-looking, weathered building of carved wood could be glimpsed among the dense foliage.

'Did you say I should be sharing a bungalow?'

'Indeed yes. You will find Frederick Winser there. He knows a lot about your forests, he came from the Burma Police. And a couple of others. You won't be lonely. I don't think that in Burma you will be bored either. I just ask you to be careful.'

Archie lifted his face to the sky and felt the sun smite it like a scalding iron. He was full of a most peculiar contentment, peculiar because he had expected to feel the keenest apprehension at all that lay ahead of him, and he felt nothing of the sort. He felt instead a great and comfortable happiness, despite the tremendous heat, despite the springless cart with its gaping sides like wooden ribs, despite the dust and his sweat-soaked shirt and the utter unknown of the next few weeks. He closed his eyes and let the sun burn into his skin like a brand. The air smelt of heat and dust and dung and various fruit and vegetable smells, slightly sweet with an edge of decay. He breathed in deeply.

'Mr Tennant,' Andreino said, 'look.'

Reluctantly, Archie straightened his neck and opened his eyes. The world swam in a dazzle of sunlight.

'Look.'

Before him was a fairytale. A shining moat filled with lilies and dotted with golden boats and white bridges encircled a magical city apparently made of gold and silver and scarlet lacquer. Great walls of russet brick, edged in white, rose out of the waters of the moat and above them soared the towers and spires and pinnacles, the tiers of roofs like winged saucers, everything shining, glittering, glowing, a shimmering fantasy place—

'My God,' Archie said, 'my God. I never, I mean, nobody ever – nobody said – it must be the palace. Is it? The royal city? Is it? I can't believe it—'

'It is.'

'The City of Gems.'

'The same.'

'I – I saw the Shway Dagon. In Rangoon. But this – this—'

'It is extraordinary. Some Europeans hate it.'

'I can't believe that I see such a thing—'

'No. Sometimes nor can I. But I have known it so long now that those times are only when I am a little drunk.'

'It makes me feel drunk.'

A tiny breeze blew from somewhere and a ripple of sunlight ran down the moat like a tinsel ribbon.

'What is that hill?' Archie said, pointing to the north-east.

'Mandalay Hill. There is a gigantic gold Buddha at the top, pointing down upon the city King Mindoon built. And those, to the right, those are the Shan hills. And there,' he said, his pointing finger swinging to the south-east, 'over there are your forests. Ningyan and the Pyinmana forests. Trees and elephants, elephants and trees.' He looked at Archie. 'You must make the most of Mandalay.'

Archie nodded in silence, still gazing.

'You must call at the mission,' Andreino said after a while, smiling, 'just once, perhaps. But you must go. Tom Prior is a brave and interesting man, he will intrigue you. And the little signorina—'

'Yes,' Archie said, not listening really, 'yes,' and then he took his eyes from the blue line of the hills that hid China and feasted them again on the gold and scarlet glory of the royal city.

It was a week before he got to the mission and even then, it was only because Andreino prompted him. The delights of a bachelor chummery were too strong for Archie to remember much else, his days, after the weeks of inactivity on board ship, too headily filled with games and exploration, and the nights, blue with cigar smoke, too absorbing with tales of the forests, discussions on the habits of elephants, reflections on the mysterious and powerful allure of being alone in such places for weeks on end. Frederick Winser seemed to know an encyclopedic amount and preferred to instruct Archie while occupied, so that his first days in Mandalay were spent in happy pursuit of snipe accompanied by Frederick's running commentary on Burma.

'The Kingdom of Ava,' he said, waist high in the grasses of the foothills to the east of Mandalay, 'is about five hundred miles from north to south, three hundred east to west. The population,' he brought his gun up sharply to his shoulder and squinted along the barrels, 'is about three million. I suppose the most revolting aspect of Thibaw's reign—' a short pause while a snipe rose and began its darting, zigzagging flight away from them, followed by the sharp report of Frederick's gun, '—is that the sovereign has a right to whatever adult labour he chooses. A vile slavery, that's what it amounts to.' He then waited while the bird was brought back to him, examined his shot without comment and resumed. 'Quite a substantial army, though none of them but the Palace Guard are much use. Must be ten thousand, all told, but they lack horses and guns shockingly and the officers! *We* know more about things military than they do.' His gun swung up again. 'Good at river fighting though. Thibaw is utterly improvident. They say he is going to import plates from France to print his own money. Fondly imagines that's how you have enough. How are you doing? Fine, fine. Want to call it a day and wait for some geese this evening? Best geese and duck shooting I've ever had. Can't fish though. Coarse, bony fish, like all tropical rivers. I say, good shot. Nothing like snipe, eh?'

When they paused for a moment or two out of the blistering heat and Frederick had time to look at other things than snipe, the sight of distant hills and forests would remind him of Archie's future.

'Of course, it's a roughish life. You'll be superintending the felling and dragging of the timber. Mind you, the forests are far too full, some places we won't have to fell for years, the ground is simply solid with fallen timber. Want a cheroot? We pay the King a royalty on each log and about four and a half lakhs of rupees annually for the concession to fell in the area I'm taking you to. That's a pretty fine gun you have. Present, eh? We pay the foresters in silver, terrible stuff to carry about, weighs a ton. I suppose there are about three hundred foresters in all down in Ningyan, each with his own elephant. We have to give them an advance each season before they'll lift a finger, it's the custom here. And, of course, you'll be doing a bit of exploring. There are no maps, we make 'em. Right then. On your feet. Any good at languages? Won't get far without a bit of dialect here. I say, don't forget your topee. Shouldn't stir an inch without it in day-light.'

In the late afternoons, before the sun sank low enough for the heavy flights of ducks to come winging across the sky, Frederick and the two Chatsworth brothers, who shared the bungalow, would take Archie lime-cutting. Deprived of polo, he was in his element. Mounted on an amazingly game Burmese pony – 'Ought to take one home with you,' Frederick said. 'They'd be perfect for hunting' – and armed with a Burmese *dah*, he rode full gallop at a stick planted in the ground and crowned with a lime. The aim was to slice the lime as cleanly as possible from the stake as one thundered by. Archie's skill was such that even Ah Chun almost forgave him for his failure steeplechasing in Rangoon. After these bouts, he would return to the bungalow and stand naked in his brick cubicle of a bathroom while Ah Chun hurled bucket after bucket of water over him with as much force as he could muster.

It was during the exertions of one of these improvised showers that Ah Chun's impeccably folded garment parted a little to reveal the skin of his thighs darkly and horribly mottled in deep blue, like a matted tracery of veins. Archie pointed, gasping, his face and hair running with water and trails of soapy bubbles. Ah Chun put down the bucket and parted the cotton that wrapped him with pride. Archie, squatting before him, blowing soap and water out of his mouth and nose, saw that Ah Chun was tattooed, closely and evenly, all over his skin from his waist to his knees, every inch. Since Ah Chun wore an expression of extreme satisfaction, Archie did not quite know what to say and contented himself with, 'Did it hurt?'

'Much, *thakin*. But me, I take no opium. Many boys, they take opium for tattoo.'

'Good Lord,' Archie said and stood up. He surveyed his own thighs and found that, despite the heat, he was goose-pimpled at the mere notion.

'They all do it,' Frederick said later at dinner, his mouth full of mutton. 'It's a sign of manhood. Must be agony.'

The tablecloth that stretched between the four men was linen, made in Manchester, the laundry label told Archie. On it, apart from the heavy paraphernalia of knives, forks and glasses, stood a huge pot of yellow mustard and a blue glass bowl – doubtless also from Manchester – which held custard apples, greenish yellow and covered in spikes, mangoes and small sweet bananas like little yellow fingers. They had eaten a thick brown soup, an extremely dull fish full of peculiar wedge-shaped bones, and were now contemplating a dish of tough chops. Archie, replete with air and exercise, found himself enthusiastic about every mouthful.

'Of course,' Frederick went on with one of the abrupt changes of subject Archie was becoming used to, 'you should have had a squint at Moulmein. That's where most of our teak is exported from. Rangoon is nothing much yet. It's Indian railways that will do it. Teak, teak and more teak. Thousands of tons, can't get enough. Don't be put off by the smell of those things,' waving his fork at the custard apples, 'they are pretty good. What do you think of Andreino?'

The Chatsworth brothers, due to go up river to the Chindwin forests, said they couldn't see why a company as prosperous as the Bombay-Burmah needed a greasy little foreigner to look after their affairs in Mandalay at all.

'What d'you think?' Frederick asked of Archie.

'I supposed,' Archie said carefully, much pre-occupied with the prickles on his fruit, 'that it was because of his relations at court. With the King. But that was only what I supposed.'

'Quite right,' Frederick said, 'quite right. Don't like him much myself.'

Archie looked up. 'I do.'

'He is an Italian,' the elder Chatsworth said reprovingly. His nose had burned and peeled to a brilliant rose pink.

Archie grinned at him. 'Yes,' he said.

Frederick finished his last chop and threw the bone onto his plate. 'Hundred thousand people in Mandalay. Four of us. Next week in the forests, it will be one of us and fifty natives or so apiece. I'll keep you with me a while until you know what you are doing. Show you how to measure the logs, what to look for in terms of quality. You'll need a bit of help with negotiations over money too, I should think. Throw me a mango, Archie, would you? Bridge?'

The next morning Andreino was there on the verandah when Archie got back from an early ride. The temperature was fierce already, but the light was clear and lovely and the cartwheels had not yet had time to fill the air with clouds of dust.

'You see,' he said to Archie, smiling beneath his moustaches, redolent of hair oil and garlic, 'I told you that you would need some time to settle. You enjoy yourself, I think. You Englishmen are never happy without a horse. I am come to widen your horizons a little, to interrupt your bachelor games. You should meet the other Europeans in Mandalay before you go. There is not so much time.'

Frederick had promised Archie guinea fowl that day. Andreino laughed and shrugged.

'As you wish. I will return this afternoon. English teatime still happens in Mandalay.'

Ah Chun came out and handed Archie a towel. He rubbed his face and neck vigorously, saying as he did so in tones occasionally muffled by terry cloth, 'It's no time to ask you and in a way none of my business, but I have been wondering a little why – I mean what made you – rather why you should choose the Bombay-Burmah—'

Andreino leaned smiling against the verandah rail. 'It chose me. Most fortunately. I am a creature of no place, born an Italian, adopted by nowhere. My early career does not matter except that it was quite respectable and somehow –

perhaps it was the respectableness – I came up here and found myself consul for Italy. I don't think Italy really wants or needs a consul here, we have so few interests to protect, but she has one and I am he. It was William Wallace of the Bombay-Burmah, the Wallace who gained the first big teak contracts here, he asked me if I would be agent. You can do nothing without the King up here and I was close to the King's father. He was remarkable, Mindoon, the best and wisest of these kings. I have not lost my touch, I know almost all that goes on. A young lady of your acquaintance once told me I had no principles. She felt I, as you English say, rode too many horses. I told her and I tell you, that I do, I ride as many as I can, it is my survival. But in the end, I will always ride the winner.'

'Even if it is Burmese?'

Andreino leaned forward and said softly, 'The Burmese winners? With this king? Young man, there will be changes. You will see them. If you keep your head and take no foolish risks, you will find you are here at a golden time.' He straightened up and took a long green cigar from his pocket. He turned the end up and with a none too clean thumbnail, neatly skewered out a small plug. 'Keep close to me, young man. Tell me anything you see. You will not regret it.' He put the cut end of the cigar into his mouth and Ah Chun, whom Archie had supposed inside, came forward with a match. 'Look at this!' Andreino said. 'Matches from Sweden in Upper Burma!

Absurd.' He spoke sharply to Ah Chun who retreated at once. 'The French must have an eye kept upon them. These teak forests are worth thousands of lakhs and the French are well into the Far East, Cochin China, Tonkin, why not Burma. There is a mission—' He stopped and smiled. 'But I can tell you all this later. I shall come for you at four. I wish you a good bag.'

He was late, which was just as well since Archie, tumbling dust and sweat covered off his pony that afternoon, was late also. He had shot better than ever before in his life and had, with the deepest reluctance, left Frederick and the Chatsworths waiting for the twilight and the geese. He thundered into the bungalow, shouting for Ah Chun, and saw formal clothes laid out upon his bed with a sinking heart. But the ex-hilaration of his success that day uplifted him to such an extent, despite the prospect of a tea party, that he became aware as Ah Chun doused him and he sang lustily, but flat, well-known opera choruses, that he had become thoroughly aroused. This confused him at once and, not sure whether Ah Chun had noticed, he turned his back and endeavoured to fill his mind with thoughts of the most unstimulating kind. His efforts were partially successful, sufficiently so at least for him to leave the bathroom only a little stooped and to climb hurriedly into his under-clothes while in his wake Ah Chun protested at such independence. When at last he clambered into the bullock cart with Andreino, he felt that the Italian, with his amused black glance, knew exactly what had happened and understood precisely the disconcerted but elated state the incident had left behind.

Grace Prior, all in white with a sash of pale blue, was the only woman present at the mission house. Besides Archie and Andreino there was a man of perhaps sixty immaculately dressed in white, a garrulous Armenian called Manook with some position at court, and an Anglo-Indian with responsibility for the mails up from British Burma, a duty of which he was inordinately proud. Grace sat behind a tea table which reminded Archie very much of the ladies' bazaars his mother used to hold complainingly at Hasham in aid of converting little heathen souls in some outpost of the Empire – and then he realized, taking a cup of tea, that he was in just such an outpost and indeed in a mission, and he laughed outright so that Grace, who had ventured some mild remark about the enduring quality of English habits even abroad, felt that Archie was quite as pleased to see her as she was to see him, and gave him a smile of purest adoration.

Archie observed the smile but not its implication, and grinned amiably back before going to seek his host and apologize for not calling before as invited. Grace watched him walk across the room with a possessive delight that rendered her immune even to the daunting prospect of Maria's imminent arrival.

'But I agree with you,' Tom was saying earnestly to Manook. 'I don't disallow at all the liberality and generosity of Buddhism. But I cannot regret too bitterly the principle of annihilation which Buddhists covet so, it is so negative, so low spirited, it can only destroy the soul by weakening it – Mr Tennant. How enormously glad I am to see you. Mr Tennant escorted my Grace up river ten days ago. Without him I think the journey would have been unthinkable.'

'In Rangoon, were you?' Manook said, his plump sallow face creased with friendliness. 'And did you see my daughter Hosannah? And my wife? I sent them to Rangoon for safe keeping, you know. I thought it only wise—'

'I am afraid I did not,' Archie said, straining to be back with Buddhism. 'I was only there a few days. I saw all the corporation's godowns and offices and I failed to win the Grand National, but that was all. Do the priests believe in this annihilation principle too?'

Tom, not in the least disconcerted by the leap from race course to religion, put his hand on Archie's arm. 'More than anyone. The *poongyis* are men who have renounced their lives in order to work towards the principle more fully. Mendicants, ascetics—'

'*Professed* mendicants,' Manook said with smiling emphasis, '*Ostensible* ascetics.'

'And every man must pass through a monastery at some time?'

From outside in the lane a woman's clear voice rose above the creaking of passing carts. 'You may tell him to wait, Denzil. I shall only be a quarter of an hour. I mean simply to say what is necessary, remove Papa and come away.'

Archie looked inquiringly at his companions. Manook was laughing, Tom had glanced towards his daughter. Grace was pouring tea for Andreino and appeared to have heard nothing.

'Who was that?'

'Miss Beresford, Miss Maria Beresford. That is her father in white.'

Archie said, 'Grace told me about her. She is a favourite with the Queen and has some connection with ruby mines?'

'Yes,' Tom said sadly, 'yes. I fear that she and my Grace were not destined to be companions. The only Englishwomen here too—'

Sweeping along the verandah in her silks with Denzil reluctantly at her heels, Maria was at her most imperious. The morning had been a great success, during the course of which Supayalat had said, 'The mission to Paris can do nothing without my orders. I shall give no orders that do not please me. You know what pleases me. Bring me the plans for Mogok.'

Maria, kneeling before her in the garden pavilion, had bowed her head. Thibaw was present too, but cowed and silent after the dismissal of his mistress and slightly fuddled with the wine he had taken in consolation. Maria knew she need not do more for Thibaw than observe the formalities.

'The English and the French are great nations, Majesty. They have powerful armies. They want the riches of your kingdom.'

Supayalat drew on her cheroot. Her brilliant eyes flickered with amusement. 'Bah! Great! No nation can touch us, they must beg for what they want, *beg*, not take. They cannot take. Cannot. We will consider all these mines, coal, lead, silver, all of them, and our orders will go to Paris.'

She had given Maria, then, a box like a golden bird, its wings outlined with emeralds and rubies, a box that her father-in-law had used for his betel nuts. With this proof of supreme royal favour clasped to her bosom, Maria had first prostrated herself before the Queen and had then risen to withdraw, observing as she did so that Thibaw had fallen asleep, slumped upon his *salun-daw* like a stout and sulky boy.

Supayalat's manner had remained with Maria as it frequently did, and she bore with her into the mission house an impossible haughtiness. Her glance swept around the room, took in nothing new beyond a large, loosely made young man with rumpled brown hair and no distinction, and then, without so much as a nod of greeting to either Grace or Tom, she moved swiftly over to her father.

'Papa! I thought I should find you here. It is quite time you came home, do you not think?'

Tom's immensely kind face tautened with displeasure. Archie, quite bowled over by the splendour of Maria's appearance, was rooted to the spot and could take in nothing properly except that tall, long-necked figure in its wonderful clothes.

'Miss Beresford,' Tom said, his voice quite unnatural with self-control, 'how good of you to come.'

She turned slowly, with a small smile. 'I heard that your daughter was back in Mandalay, Mr Prior.'

Hubert's hand came out and lightly touched Maria's sleeve. She drew her arm away at once, but smiled at him as she did it.

'Grace, Miss Beresford, has been home a full ten days.'

Grace rose from behind the tea table. Beside Maria she seemed hardly to exist at all but became as insubstantial as a shadow, her pale face and smooth hair seeming as gauzy as her dress.

'Good afternoon, Maria.'

Her voice was almost steady. She had achieved this by gazing relentlessly at Archie since the moment Maria had entered and drawing courage from his solid and comforting presence.

In silence, Maria turned slowly towards her. Colour rose in Grace's cheeks like a pink tide, suffusing even her forehead.

'I trust,' Maria said, 'that you had a pleasant journey.'

'Oh yes!' Grace said, too eagerly, 'Mr T – Tennant was so kind—'

'Mr Tennant. Of course.'

Behind her, Hubert said, 'Dearest, may I present Mr Tennant to you?'

She was, without doubt, the most wonderful and disagreeable creature Archie had ever seen. He stepped forward, forbidding himself to smile until she did, and bowed very slightly but did not offer his hand. She remained holding hers out, imperious.

'Mr Tennant,' she said, with more than a hint of command.

Archie's hands remained by his side. 'Miss Beresford.'

Behind her, Denzil Blount gave a snort of laughter. Archie inclined his head a little once more, retrieved his teacup from the table where he had left it and went purposefully across the room to Grace.

'Would I be allowed another cup? I was shooting all day and I feel I could drink a river.'

Grace, with a heart that was almost bursting, seized his cup. 'Oh, Mr Tennant, of course, of course, as many as you like!'

'Snipe?' Denzil asked, his eyes still upon Maria, 'You were shooting snipe?'

'Guinea fowl.'

'Not quite such sport but plenty of them.'

Hubert said, 'Better game here than I ever saw in India.'

'I think it's splendid, sir,' Archie said, 'the whole place.'

Grace said, 'Will you have some tea, Maria?'

'Thank you,' Maria said furiously, not moving. Grace poured out a cup and placed it carefully on the edge of the table, keeping her hand upon the saucer to prevent any of the men picking it up in helpless gallantry.

'There,' she said, 'your tea.'

In silence, Maria stalked to the table. Across her Denzil said to Archie, 'I wonder how splendid you will think Burma when you have been out in the forests for weeks.'

Archie grinned. 'I'll tell you. When I come back.'

Maria, her cup rattling in its saucer, said, 'Papa, we should not be long.'

'Up the Chindwin?' Hubert said to Archie.

'No, sir. The other direction. I shall be working with Frederick Winser under Eisenhauer. He is the manager of the Pyinmana forests, I believe.'

'I would not know,' Hubert said.

'Papa, when you have finished—'

'Have you any experience of dacoits?' Denzil said.

Grace gasped.

'No. But I imagine I soon will have.'

'Andreino has been telling me,' Tom said from the other side of the room, a spot he had not moved from since Maria's entrance, 'that now the Bombay-Burmah extract all their own timber,

223

now they no longer use contractors, that they plan to build a hill station for all you young men, somewhere for you to recuperate.'

'Papa! I am waiting!'

'Yes,' Archie said, 'a place called Maymyo, I believe. It has a lovely climate, you need a fire at night in the winter.'

Denzil put down his teacup. 'Forty degrees not uncommon. You should go and see it. It isn't more than forty miles or so though, of course, the road is hardly more than a track. Poinsettias grow there like rhododendrons in England.'

A small spasm crossed Maria's face.

Archie said, 'Do you know Maymyo, Miss Beresford?'

She did not look at him. 'No. No, I do not. I have been too much preoccupied with court affairs during my time in Mandalay to go on excursions. Papa, we must go.'

'Court affairs?'

Maria did not like the tone of Archie's voice. Her own was at its most haughty as she replied, 'I have daily audience with Her Majesty Queen Supayalat.' She turned to Grace. 'I hope you will find it – pleasant to be back in Mandalay.' Then she nodded to the men present, paused fractionally before Archie as if she might say something but changed her mind, and swept, head high, out onto the verandah.

Hubert paused long enough to say to Archie, 'Of course, having been here so long, we are reasonably experienced and you should not hesitate to ask us if there is anything you wish to know,' before following her.

'Not,' Tom said quietly to Grace, bending over her, 'a success, my dear.'

She looked up, smiling. 'I don't mind. Not any more.'

'Ah! The comforts of growing older.'

Grace dared not look at Archie.

'Well?' Andreino said, 'Mr Tennant. What do you think of our self-appointed first lady?'

'Very, very handsome.'

Denzil laughed. 'Oh yes. Undeniably that.'

'Come,' Manook said, 'come. We must talk of serious things. Are you not perturbed, you British. The French—'

'No,' Andreino said smoothly, his eyes flickering towards Denzil, 'we are not perturbed in the least. I speak as agent for the corporation, you understand, not in any way as a mock Englishman.'

'Signor Andreino, I wish I had your confidence.'

'You must keep it,' Denzil said. 'It might sustain you in time of trial.'

Andreino glanced at him again. 'It will also prove justified, Signor Blount.'

Grace had left her post to stand as close to Archie as she dared. 'Will you go soon? Will you go to the forests soon? And will you stay there all winter, will I – will Papa and I not see you until the rains begin?'

He looked down at her. She wore an

expression he had been used to see on the liver and white face of the springer spaniel he had reluctantly left at Riverdene with old Phillipson. His response to the dog had always been to put a brief but grateful hand upon her head. Grace's head was the perfect height for such a caress and her hair as fine and smooth as silk. Archie thought what a stir he would create if he touched her thus. He smiled down at her.

'Oh, you should pity me, Miss Prior! I go next week into the forests where I shall probably catch a fever from the night dews and if I don't die of that, die of the frustration of not being able to make myself understood by the fifty elephants and foresters in my charge. There are leeches and probably snakes and any books I take will go mouldy and goodness knows what I will eat—'

'I know you are teasing but there's too much truth in it for me to bear. Are you really to be so wretched?'

'I shall be as happy as a king.'

Grace looked down. 'I shall not, thinking of you there.'

Unaccountably, Archie's heart sank a little. Too heartily he said, 'Then don't think of me. Four months will go by very fast, you'll see. And you have the school here and your father—'

'Yes,' she said, 'yes.'

Andreino was bowing before her. 'I must take your escort away, Signorina. It is a great pleasure to have you back with us in Mandalay. We were sadly deprived of pretty faces.'

'Come again,' Grace said to Archie, 'before you go. I am always here in the afternoons. Please come.'

A minute later, clattering down the verandah steps to the lane, Archie had the sensation that Andreino, for the second time that afternoon, knew precisely his state of mind. He was even laughing softly.

'Well? What would you do?'

Andreino put a hand on his shoulder. 'Just what you are about to do, my friend. Go to the forests.'

11

Ah Chun was squatting, waiting, in a corner of
Archie's bedroom.

'*Thakin* Winser. Has fever.'

'Good God!' Archie said. 'But he was fine! I
left him this afternoon absolutely fine—'

'Fever here so sudden. *Thakin* Winser coming
home on pony, lying so, on pony, arms hang.'

A mosquito net shrouded Frederick's bed so
thickly that he was scarcely visible within its
folds. The drill trousers and tunic he should have
worn that evening lay neatly across the only chair,
and his bearer, a fly whisk in one hand and a
palm leaf fan in the other, crouched on the floor,
swatting and waving, with an expression of the
most intense gloom.

'Frederick!'

A muffled oath came from within the white
folds, followed by a sharp command. The bearer
leaped to his feet and pulling up the net, revealed
Frederick, stark naked and pouring with sweat,
his eyes closed. His fists were clenched and he
was shaking uncontrollably. Archie put a hand on
his shoulder and almost leaped back at contact
with that scalding skin.

'Don't worry,' Frederick said without opening his eyes or unclenching his teeth. 'Over soon. Always is. Got some stuff to take but it needs time to work. Quinine mostly.'

'Can I get you anything? Or do anything for you?'

'No. Nothing thanks. Doesn't usually hit me until I'm in the jungle. Still work then. Takes my mind off it. Always pounces on me. Never know it's coming.'

'Shouldn't you have a doctor?'

Frederick gave a short yelp Archie took for laughter. 'Might as well ask for the moon here! Europeans don't know any more than I do and the Burmese a good deal less. Remind me to tell you what they do to women after childbirth if you want a taste of Burmese medicine. I say, Archie—'

'Yes.'

'It shouldn't take long. This, I mean. I usually sweat for a couple of days and then stagger about finding my legs for three to four. We won't have to postpone departure for more than a day or so. D'you want to go ahead of me?'

'Not particularly.'

A spasm shook Frederick so violently that his teeth chattered. When it was over, Archie said, 'Shouldn't Ba Sein be sponging you? To bring the fever down a bit?'

'Good idea. I'd rather you didn't go ahead. You are perfectly capable I know, but I'd like to show you the ropes. Especially as you don't speak the language much yet. Mind?'

'Of course not.'

'Tell that idle brute to get water and a sponge. Thanks, Archie. I say. Say good luck to the Chatsworths for me will you? Off tomorrow. Shan't make dinner.'

Dinner was dull without him. The Chatsworths were understandably preoccupied with the following day's journey and either ate with dedication or muttered remarks to each other in the telegrammatic manner of family familiarity. The younger one, tilting his chair back at the end of the meal, eyed Archie across the debris of crumbled bread and banana skins.

'What about your tea party, then? Pretty girls?'

'Two.'

'Ah!' young Chatsworth said knowledgeably. 'The two. Miss Prior and Miss Beresford.' He looked at his brother. 'The corporation don't mind, you know. There's no policy. About Burmese girls.'

Archie tried to subdue the eagerness in his voice. 'Really?'

'No. They are pretty open minded. One of the managers down in Rangoon said to me, "I have neither attitude nor rules." Of course, the Burmese regard it as an honour.'

Archie leaned forward. 'To – to be an Englishman's mistress?'

'Surely. *Bo-kadaw*. White man's wife, they say. Doesn't spoil their chances of marrying a Burman later either.' He looked at his brother again and grinned. 'You can take them into the forests with you. If you like. They regard themselves as married to you as long as you want them. Marriage here is purely civil. You can get rid of them the moment you are tired of them. No trouble.'

The other Chatsworth said with elder brotherly tolerance, 'Oh, of course, he knows all about it. One whole forest season behind him and I don't remember we saw a woman in months.'

'Does Frederick—?'

The elder brother shrugged. 'I don't know. I'm not interested really, not like young Robert here. To tell you the truth, I don't like the idea of native women much, never have. Now, Miss Beresford—'

'Yes,' Archie said, remembering.

'*She* wouldn't have any of us if we were the last men on earth,' young Chatsworth said. 'Give me a Burmese girl any time. Eh, Archie?'

Archie said, 'And they will come with you into the forests? They don't mind?'

'They are proud to.'

The elder Chatsworth stood up. 'Bed, Bob. We're to be off by sunrise. We go in one of the Irrawaddy Flotilla Company steamers with one of their managers from Rangoon. He wants to see how far up the river is navigable for him. We have got a pretty unchartered area this season, Bob and I. Should be amusing. These infernal insects!'

He gave wild slap on the side of his neck and

231

a huge speckled mosquito went singing off into the shadows of the room.

'Worse in the forests,' he said. 'Well, goodbye, Tennant. And the best of luck. See you in March.'

'Frederick said to say good luck to you.'

'Poor devil. Never known him ill before. Come on Bob, chop, chop.'

When they had left the room, Archie became aware that he and the mosquito were not the only living things in it. He turned in his chair and observed Ah Chun squatting by the doorway.

'You devil! Were you listening?'

'No, *thakin*.'

Archie strode over to him and pulled him to his feet. 'Not only an eavesdropper but a liar! Either stand behind my chair so that I know you are there or keep away! Don't sneak in corners.' He gave him a rough shake. 'All right, then, Ah Chun. You heard what you heard. And this afternoon you saw what you saw. Do something about it then. Now go and let my net down. I'm going to bed.'

The bungalow was strangely empty the following day. The servants went on padding about their duties in house and garden, wheels screamed as usual outside and the coppersmith birds knocked as relentlessly as ever, but there was no-one to breakfast with, no-one to shoot with, no Frederick shouting at his bearer. He was no better. His skin was greyish in the morning light and Archie, putting a hand on his forehead, doubted that his temperature was any less. Archie decided he would order Ah Chun to take turns with Ba Sein in sponging him and that, if necessary, he would himself sit up with him the following night.

He wandered from room to room, aimlessly. There was a pile of old copies of the *Rangoon Gazette* – always at least ten days old on account of coming up river with the mails – but these were as unalluring as they had ever been, partly because events had overtaken all the news and partly because there was so little mention of anything to do with Mandalay in them. Archie did a clue here and there at random in the crosswords but soon gave up and allowed himself the pleasure of flinging the newspapers all over the floor in the comfortable knowledge that within minutes someone would have picked them up and reassembled them in their neat stack.

He thought of shooting and decided he was not in the mood to do it without a companion. He thought of riding and maybe practising his lime-cutting and then came to the conclusion that it was the one thing he seemed to be able to do without practice and, in any case, he liked an audience. He remembered what Andreino had said about the corporation's plans to build a hill station for its forest employees at this place called Maymyo, and he was half out of his chair at the thought that he might go up into the hills and see it, when he remembered that a forty-mile journey up a rough road and back could not be accomplished in a day and that he should not leave Frederick overnight. He slumped back in his chair and bit his nails and sighed.

Andreino's voice, calling for Ah Chun from the verandah, was unbelievably welcome. Archie leaped up and went out to meet him.

'Ah, my friend! I hear poor Winser has the fever. So you are all alone. I saw the brothers Chatsworth off on their travels three hours ago. What are you doing with yourself today?'

'I thought of riding up to Maymyo. But it would take too long.'

'Three days, to do it comfortably, there and back. But you should go, it is a most lovely place—'

'I don't want to leave Frederick.'

'No. No, of course not. But you may leave him for a few hours? Take off those clothes and dress properly. I shall take you to the palace.'

'The palace!'

Andreino shrugged. 'I fear it won't be very amusing. I have to do this at the beginning of each season. We will squat for hours on some floor in the palace while we negotiate the price of the leases, the price the King must pay for any timber he wants, the wages of the foresters. But I should be glad of your company.'

'Do we negotiate with the King himself?'

'Ah, no. Only with ministers. It is a very lengthy business. But you will like to see the palace and the royal city. Wear shoes, not boots, they are easier to remove.'

Archie looked both astounded and indignant. 'Remove them!'

'Of course. We must all do so. The old British Resident here, he managed to keep his shoes on and, of course, Miss Beresford is permitted to appear shod in the palace. Even I was allowed to keep my shoes on for the late King's funeral. But that was an especial favour. In the ordinary course of events, we must humble ourselves and appear barefoot.'

Archie nodded. 'Actually,' he said, 'I'd humble myself much further in order to get inside the palace.'

Once there, however, nothing was quite as he had expected. There was more space everywhere, the streets of the city were wider, straighter, cleaner than he had imagined. There were plots of grass scattered among the wooden houses with their winged and glittering roofs, the harshness of the scarlet and gold was softened by the frothy boughs of the tamarind trees. A procession came out of the palace as Archie and Andreino approached, a procession headed by a general dressed in scarlet velvet and copper, who held his reins high and wide in an extraordinary formal fashion and rode with two huge brass shields suspended from the saddle between his legs and the horse's sides. Over him a bearer held an umbrella on a long curving pole and behind him walked a column of attendants, barefoot but wearing turbans of gold-embroidered velvet. Behind them was a detachment of much more poorly dressed men, each carrying a rifle with a roll of cloth bound to one end and a cooking pot swinging from the other.

'Ah,' Andreino said, 'the Burmese army. That wadding on their rifles, that is a sleeping mat. And there is rice in those pouches at their waists. Each soldier is self-sufficient. This way, through this postern.'

Archie followed him through the low doorway and past the parliament building and a gilded and mirrored structure outside which a sickly looking elephant with a strangely mottled trunk stood glumly, head hanging.

'The sacred white elephant?'

'The same.'

'He looks the same as any other elephant to me. Only not so healthy. What is the matter with his trunk?'

'That's the whiteness,' Andreino stopped and regarded the elephant. 'He takes milk directly from the breasts of nursing women. They clamour for the privilege. It does not seem to do him much good, does it? They line up here, a dozen, twenty sometimes, and he goes along the line from breast to breast, his trunk—'

'Stop it,' Archie said, revolted.

'I shock you?'

'He does.'

Andreino laughed. 'You will get used to it. The East does not have the same regard for the flesh as the West. You will see. Now you must take off your shoes. We will climb onto the platform.'

The audience hall into which Andreino led him more than fulfilled his expectations of Eastern royalty. The huge teak pillars which marched down the length, on either side, had been lacquered in scarlet and studded with scraps of mirrors so that the room was filled with a winking, darting light as of a million fireflies. The floor was of teak, huge, wide, gleaming boards, down the centre of which ran a strip of vermilion carpet bordered with capering yellow dragons. The walls were panelled with mirrors edged in dull gold and the ceiling, high and dim above their heads, was intricately painted and carved. There was no furniture beyond a low *salun-daw* on a platform at one end, but the room was lined with people, some Burmese, some Europeans, all squatting in groups in such privacy as the spaces between the pillars afforded.

'We wait,' Andreino said. He chose a corner at some distance from everybody else and lowered himself onto the floor. 'Those two there are Greeks, engineers, and the big one, he is a German, a railway specialist, and the two Indians are British subjects – which reminds me. Some other Indians, British subjects also, whom Mindoon gave land to for building themselves houses, they have been turned out, no compensation, nothing, and their property given to Burmese. And what is worse, two traders from Madras, British subjects again, have been murdered in prison. No-one knows why they went to prison in the first place. I have managed to get their wives and children places on a steamer for Rangoon, but what they will do there, I don't know, poor creatures. I don't keep warning you for nothing.'

Archie, shifting uncomfortably in an attempt to find a bearable arrangement for his legs, said, 'But would we be touched? We white men?'

'Three, four years ago, I would have said no. Today I only say maybe not.'

'But there are white people in high favour at court, Miss Beresford, her father, the Frenchman everyone speaks of who has recently left—'

Andreino shrugged. 'This is such a fickle place. Like a firework. One match and it can all go up, very pretty, very spectacular, all gone in a moment.'

'I've seen nothing,' Archie said. 'I've been here a week and the nearest I have come to hostility is a sullen look or two in the roads, nothing more.'

'Even while we sit here, even beneath us, the violence is happening. The dungeons are full of royal prisoners, princesses, queens, anyone who might suggest that the present rule is in any way corrupt or ill-judged. Do you know how they live, those poor women? They are bricked up except for one small opening, their legs are ironed, the temperature must be always over a hundred. If the Burmese behave like that to their own people, what might they not – Bow, Archie, just a little. Our ministers are coming.'

Four men were advancing down the strip of red carpet. Despite the heat, which had reduced Archie's shirt to a clammy skin he was trying not to think about, they wore velvet robes to the floor with high tunic collars and surcoats of gold brocade. Huge winged over-collars stretched out to the edges of their shoulders and down to their breasts and on their heads they wore incredible hats, pinnacles of gold and scarlet rising from wide brims of beaten copper. Behind them attendants padded softly.

Andreino said something to them, in a tone of respectful formality. The smallest of the ministers replied in the same rhythms, and then all four seated themselves kneeling upon the floor, their hands folded in their brocaded laps, their slanting eyes fixed incuriously upon Archie.

He understood almost nothing. It seemed to him an interminable time while Andreino and the ministers talked in the strange yawning vowels of the Burmese court language. He dared not move, for no-one else had, and his limbs ached intolerably. The air, which had seemed so mysteriously dim when they first entered, he now perceived to be thick with dust and flies, and the humming of the latter and the muttering of the crouching groups among the glittering pillars filled him with a drowsiness so heavy that once or twice he caught himself swooning forwards onto the floor. He was rescued by a gecko which darted around the pillar nearest to him and began to move desperately back and forth on the mirrored surface, as if frantic to escape the jagged little fragments of its own reflection. Archie watched it with interest, as it quivered and flickered, its tiny hands clinging for a fraction of a second, now here, now there—

'We may go,' Andreino said softly.

Obediently and stiffly, Archie bowed. The four little brocaded figures in their absurd hats like temple roofs rose easily to their feet and retreated up the red carpet in precisely the formation they had come. Archie stood with difficulty, grimacing.

'Not what I had hoped,' Andreino said. 'The King is becoming more demanding each season and more intransigent. It is not what it was in the old days with Mindoon, with his father. There were difficulties then, but we adjusted them. This King is a spendthrift, the Queen is worse.' He spoke so softly, Archie had to crane to hear him and his eyes moved round the room ceaselessly, watchfully. 'It seems the King will soon require a loan from the corporation if he is to renew the leases. The figure mentioned is twenty-two lakhs of rupees. That is well over one hundred and thirty thousand pounds. His ministers say he is increasing the royal lotteries by the fantastic method of decreeing that each rupee shall be worth sixteen, not fourteen, annas so that every person shall have two more annas to put into the lottery and thus fill the royal coffers. If that fails—'

'It's mad!' Archie said. 'Can't he see?'

'No. You must understand the nature of royalty here. They are omnipotent. All powerful, quite literally. They do not see themselves as men among men, not in the smallest degree. Come, we should go. I have had to promise more to the foresters, I fear. It means that you will have even more rupees to carry, the coins are so bulky I am afraid. Ah, what a world, what a world.'

The sunlight and heat outside smote them like a blow in the face. They descended carefully from the palace platform, retrieved their shoes and retraced their steps past the despondent elephant and the parliament building to the gate that led into the city. As they stepped through, watched with disconcerting intentness by the guard in his velvet cap and tin hat, a bullock cart drew up outside containing a plump little woman, obviously part Burmese despite her European clothes, and Miss Beresford, cool and pale beneath a parasol of pale green silk.

The little woman leaned forward excitedly, grasping the ribs of the cart's sides. 'Why! Signor Andreino! Have you been having audience? We go each morning, you know, every day I come to fetch Miss Beresford. I don't suppose there are two Europeans who know the court so intimately—'

Maria, who had been gazing steadfastly ahead with no apparent consciousness that Archie and Andreino stood in the road below her, said coldly, 'We should not linger, Miss Calogreedy. The Queen does not like us to be late.'

Mattie gave a peal of laughter and put a smooth plump little brown hand out of the cart for Andreino to take and kiss. Her eyes, black like any Burmese, but lidded and fringed with thick lashes like those of the Mediterranean, flickered appraisingly over Archie. He bowed very slightly.

'Miss Calogreedy, may I present Mr Tennant to you. Miss Beresford, I believe you have already met Mr Tennant.'

Archie rested his elbows on the side of the cart. 'Good morning, Miss Beresford.'

The green parasol gave a small shake. 'Please do not attempt to delay us, Mr Tennant.'

'I do not suppose there is any frantic hurry, Miss Beresford. Signor Andreino and I have sat for two hours over a ten-minute bargaining point, having waited above an hour before that.'

'Audiences with the Queen are entirely another matter, Mr Tennant.'

'Am I to believe,' said Archie conversationally, aware that Andreino, though ostensibly flirting with Miss Calogreedy, was listening with amusement, 'that you have done nothing in all the last four years but go in and out of the palace at the whim of the Burmese Queen?'

The smooth line of Maria's throat bulged a little as she swallowed her temper. 'Can you imagine a greater or rarer distinction, Mr Tennant?'

'I wasn't thinking so much of distinction, more of amusement, of enlarging one's knowledge, one's sympathies. Have you not ventured outside Mandalay in five years?'

Maria, from the moment she had observed Archie climbing stooped through the palace postern, had resolved to remain as aloof as possible in order to impress upon him her superiority to and her disdain for people of his sort. But he seemed strangely impervious to the manner she used so successfully upon everyone else and, what was worse, he was even beginning to disconcert her with his comfortable persistence. The grey flannel that clothed his folded arms she observed to be only inches from her own skirts. In order to descend with proper dignity from the cart, she would have to ask him to move and, preferably, to move away altogether since, even after years of practice, it was not an operation that could be performed with reliable dexterity. The bullocks occasionally lurched forward or the cart tilted abruptly for no apparent reason, or one simply missed one's footing. She turned her head at last and looked down at him as chillingly as she could.

'The court has not thought it necessary to leave the royal palace and therefore any movement has been unnecessary for me also.'

'I thought of going up to Maymyo,' he said. 'A little mountain air, see the pineapples being harvested. My departure into the forest has been delayed a few days, Frederick Winser is unwell. If I were to make up a party, a sort of excursion, to go up into the hills, would you come? Would you forsake your duties at court, duties you must be heartily sick of, and come for just two or three days?'

Dignity or no dignity, Maria rose in the cart. 'It is an absurd idea. Most certainly not.'

Archie shrugged. He said to Andreino, 'Then it seems that in a few weeks I shall have the privilege of knowing more about Burma than Miss Beresford has known in five years.'

Mattie Calogreedy began to giggle and clapped her hand to her mouth. Andreino, bowing to hide his own smile, took a step away from the bullock cart.

'We must not detain you further, ladies. We must bid you farewell.'

Slowly, Archie took his arms off the cart and put his hands into his pockets. He walked a few deliberate steps from the cart and then turned to say his goodbyes. Maria had remained quite motionless, standing stiff and furious in the cart in the watery shadow of her parasol.

'Miss Calogreedy, Miss Beresford, good morning—'

'Mr Tennant!'

'Miss Beresford.'

There was a small pause. Archie waited, his eyes screwed up against the glare.

'Mr Tennant. Do you never smile?'

He shook his head. 'Very seldom, Miss Beresford. And then only – it is my strict rule – as a reflection of another's.'

Andreino took his arm as they walked away

and through it Archie could feel convulsions of laughter.

'You English! You English! Where do you find the courage? Ah, you have lightened my morning, more than you know. "Mr Tennant, do you never smile?" "Very seldom, Miss Beresford—" Magnificent! Wonderful! She is becoming absurd, our Miss Beresford. It is not before time she is mocked a little. She was always proud, now after these years at court, she is really intolerable, scarcely human. Her father dares say nothing. Signor Blount, who might, values her influence with Supayalat too much to chance a correction and, in any case, he does not care, she amuses him! I think you are like him, you too are amused.'

Archie looked over his shoulder. The palace postern was empty but for the guard, not so much as a flicker of green silk.

'Partly I am amused, partly—' he stopped.

'And the other partly? You find her handsome?'

'The other partly,' Archie said firmly, quickening his stride, 'the other partly does not matter in the least.'

He slept heavily that afternoon, a hot troubled sleep full of dreams that were lunatic but so powerful that their influence dogged him through an early evening ride and even his solitary dinner. He ate mechanically and without appetite, a mildewed copy of *Punch* from March 1880 laid out before him, and he chewed and gazed at the parliamentary report and saw and tasted nothing. Frederick was as hot as ever but had had sufficient strength to say between his clenched teeth that the last thing he wanted was Archie brooding over him like some damned old woman all night and, if Archie wanted to make himself useful, he could remove those two infernal blacks and their sponges before they soaked him, Frederick, into an early grave.

Huge blue flies crawled across the tablecloth towards the crumbled bread Archie had scattered. He watched their progress mindlessly, pushing crumbs in their path, making obstacles they maddeningly refused to acknowledge. One flew heavily into the water jug and floundered there, buzzing, knocking itself helplessly on the glass walls. Archie peeled a banana, took one bite and threw the rest across the table. He then occupied a full five minutes by making bread pellets and attempting to hit the banana target with them. When he had scored eleven out of sixteen attempts, Ah Chun padded into the room and put a port decanter at his elbow.

'No,' Archie said, 'not in this heat. Take it away.'

'*Thakin*.'

'Yes?'

'In two days we cannot be going. *Thakin* Winser more ill. Six, seven days maybe. Maybe eight.'

'Then we will go ahead.'

'Alone, *thakin*?'

'Alone. Even danger, Ah Chun, is preferable to sitting alone gazing at a whole lot of bluebottles.'

Ah Chun waited a moment. 'I have family in Maymyo. You are going to Maymyo, I tell them. They cook for you, make welcome.'

Archie shook his head. 'I don't know, Ah Chun. Ask me in the morning. I simply don't know. I feel too stupid tonight to think about anything.'

'*Thakin* need me, want—?'

Archie stood up. 'No. No, nothing. I shall sleep off my lethargy. I'll be better in the morning.'

His bedroom was ready for him as it was every evening, the folds of the mosquito net let down, the nightshirt he never used lay on a chair as a sort of ritual to please Ah Chun, and two oil lamps, giving off their sickly odour and dim yellow light either side of his bed. The floor was bare, the screened window curtainless, the walls empty but for a scattering of geckos. There had been a single picture when Archie arrived, a framed reproduction of Queen Victoria by Winterhalter, the infant Prince of Wales cradled in her arms, but Ah Chun, dismissing the significance of any queen but his own, had said that the picture would attract ghosts and had taken it away.

'He'll sell it of course,' Frederick said, 'in the bazaar.'

Archie did not mind much. The romantic and

sentimental image of motherhood, swathed in white frills and flowers, had only seemed to him extraordinary. He would have liked some hunting prints, the hand-coloured Jorrocks with their balloons of comic conversation that had decorated his bedroom at Hasham perhaps, but failing those, the geckos would do very well. He sat down in the cane-bottomed armchair, unbuttoned his collar and began to pull off his shoes. Ah Chun had initially been most put out at Archie's insistence on undressing alone but had been forced to give way. Archie did not understand it himself but only knew that whereas for the whole of the rest of the day he liked to have Ah Chun at his elbow in case he should need him in any way, last thing at night he needed his solitude. He would sit down to take off his shoes and socks, then wander about the room, dropping his clothes on the floor as he removed them before climbing naked into what always seemed to him the ridiculously bridal folds of his mosquito net.

He let one shoe fall onto the floor.

The laces of the second one twisted, knotted and when he jerked at them irritably, broke. He swore.

In French, a girl's voice said softly, 'May I help you? My fingers are smaller than yours.'

In the darkest shadows by the doorway leading to the bathroom, a small figure was kneeling, small enough to have been a child, but for the silhouetted cylinder of hair upon her head.

'Who are you?' Archie said. 'What are you doing here, who let you in?'

The girl rose and came silently forward to kneel at his feet. She wore a cheap tamein of pink cotton, a jacket of coarse muslin over a band of patterned stuff bound tight across her breasts and tassels of jasmine flowers in her hair. She brought her hands up, palm to palm, the fingertips touching her forehead, and shikoed low before Archie who still sat, gazing at her, one foot bare, his shirt open, his fingers clutching the broken shoelace.

'Don't do that,' he said. 'Who are you?'

'I don't please you?'

He blushed. He said quickly, 'Yes, yes, of course, I do not – I do not know anything about you. Why are you here?'

She leaned forward and began to pick at the broken shoelace with slender brown fingers. 'My name is Hnin Si. Signor Andreino has been very kind to me. For years I must work in the cigar factory, now I am one of the best, the quickest. Ah Chun brought me here tonight. He put me in your room, to wait for you. He bought new clothes for me, these clothes. He says you will give me money for these clothes. There. There is your shoe. Tomorrow Ah Chun will find you new ribbons.'

'Laces. Why do you speak French?'

'During one year I am the lover of a Frenchman. Five years since. You will know him. He is named Pierre Bonvilain. He has just gone back to Paris with the King's mission.'

Barefoot, Archie stood up. She knelt still, staring up at him, her flat oriental face enlivened by the character in it and the rosy colour that spread along her high cheekbones.

'I don't please you, *thakin*?'

'Ah Chun brought you?'

'Yes. You are angry? You did not tell him to?'

Archie stooped and took hold of her elbows, fragile as bird bones in his grasp, and lifted her to her feet.

'I – I almost told him to. I am not angry, no, nor displeased. Just – just – Tell me. Bonvilain, Andreino, many others? Many other white men?'

She shook her head. He did not know if she were lying and discovered that he did not seem to care. He bent down to peer closely at her, at the tight smooth cone of her hair, her finely textured skin, and caught the mingled scent of jasmine and coconut oil and garlic that floated from her. Her body was tiny, as straight and featureless as a sapling, showing no curve of breast or hip and her wide brow, smooth as brown satin, was barely level with his chest.

She said, 'Ah Chun say you are a good man.'

'A good *master*, perhaps. I don't beat him.'

'You can beat me. If you like.'

He gripped her elbows more tightly. 'I do *not* like.'

She smiled then, her eyes vanishing into dark

slits of delight. She brought her hands up and laid them lightly, flat against his chest. He swallowed hard.

'Do you know any English?'

She said in English, with a heavy accent, 'I love you.'

'That is a silly thing to say. Is that all you know?'

She nodded.

'I will teach you some more.'

'Then I may stay?'

He did not seem able to let go of her elbows. He said, 'Yes. Please stay.'

She leaned forward and put her cheek on his chest between her two hands for a moment, then straightened up to smile at him again. 'Let go of my arms, *thakin*.'

Reluctantly his hands dropped to his sides. She reached up and began to unbutton his shirt, picking up first one arm and then the other to undo the cuffs. Archie watched her, mesmerized, entirely absorbed in her and the boiling turmoil that was going on within.

'Have – have you ever been in the forests?'

She shook her head. 'Not before.'

'Before?'

'Before this time. Come,' she said, taking his hand, '*thakin*, come,' and she put her hand on the buttons of his trousers.

'No,' Archie said, 'don't—'

'I don't please you?'

He shouted, 'Don't keep saying that! Of course

you do! You know you do! It's simply that I want
– I have wanted – it's so long—'

'*Thakin*,' she said, 'I have not come to talk.
Now take my hand.'

Huge and naked beside her, he said, 'But I am
so big, I will hurt you, you are small, so small—'

She shook her head. 'Not hurt. I am small but
not weak. You will see. Come. Come and I will
show you,' and gripping his hand in her small
calloused fingers, she towed him across the room
behind her towards the waiting bed.

12

In the dim greenish light of her bedroom, Grace
stooped before her little speckled looking glass.
Since the day before, when Tom, confessing
himself at last to be weary and sadly in need of a
change, had said that after all they should both
go up to Maymyo on Archie's expedition, she
had been in raptures of happiness. If Tom
wouldn't go, she couldn't and she had been in
the depths of misery at his obstinacy, his insistence that his task must keep him in Mandalay,
day in, day out, kings and queens and politics
notwithstanding, until the mission school was
thriving, packed to the doors with eager little
Burmese Christians. Grace had been afraid to
beg too hard, afraid that she might suddenly say
that she didn't care where they went as long as
she might have three days with Archie, so she had
sat and prayed, with her eyes tight shut as they
had been during childhood prayers, and chastised
herself for praying such a selfish prayer, and then
Tom had said suddenly, framed in the doorway
on his way down to the school, 'Gracie, we shall
go with Mr Tennant. It can't hurt to be away
only for a few days and I think I am tired, though

I don't like to think it. Perhaps I shall come back a lion refreshed—'

That was yesterday. That was before she had discovered that all her muslins were like limp rags after two weeks in the steam heat of Mandalay and before Mr Blount, coming by at teatime for some undisclosed reason, had said that he and Mr and Miss Beresford had been invited too. Grace had handed him his tea and, muttering hastily about having some dust in her eye, had fled to her room and its scanty privacy.

It is not fair, she said wretchedly to God, I don't ask you for much. I try not to bother you with little things, with details, but this is not a little thing, this is desperately important to me. It is the last chance I shall have of seeing him before the rains because he will leave on Saturday. Mr Winser will be well enough then to travel and they will be in the forests all that time. I know you think that human love shouldn't matter beside divine love, and I do try, I *do*, but we have to live our life here, we have to get through the days and it can't be wrong for me to long for the days when he is part of them and find the ones I don't see him so long. And I shan't see him for, oh, more than a hundred and fifty days perhaps, so why can't I have these three, only three, to myself, why must she be there . . . ?

'My dear,' Tom said, outside her door, 'Grace. Are you unwell?'

'Oh, no,' she said, forgetting the excuse she

had made to Denzil, 'just a slight headache, nothing much.'

'Come back, then,' Tom said, 'come back. We have guests.'

It was only Manook who was there, rubbing his hands and smiling, and Mr Blount still, his cup half full, his eyes appraisingly on Grace. He rose as she came in and drew a chair up close to her tea table.

'Tell me, Miss Prior, your friend Mr Tennant. He has been to the palace. You are great friends, are you not, after that long and intimate journey? You will know why Mr Tennant has been seeking an audience?'

She blushed a little and shook her head. 'No. I know nothing. I – I have not seen Mr Tennant since you have, not since you were both here—'

'But you will go up to Maymyo?'

'Yes,' Grace said carefully, pouring more hot water into the pot, 'I believe we will. If Papa can get away.'

'He intends to. He has just said so.' Denzil took his cup from her. 'I am not sure that I will go and you know Miss Beresford does not like to leave Mandalay. So I imagine you will be quite a small party. Perhaps you would do a little favour for me?'

Grace, aglow with sudden gratitude, beamed upon him. 'But of course, Mr Blount! I should be happy to. I am so sorry Miss Beresford has decided not to come. Maymyo is reputed to be so lovely and the air of course is so much superior to anything one breathes down here in Mandalay. What can I do for you?'

'It isn't much,' Denzil said, 'but I should be most interested to know what Archie Tennant thought of the palace, which ministers he saw and so forth. Don't mention my name, of course, because if I can help him – and I might well be able to if I know, through you, what it is he was seeking – I had rather not be burdened with gratitude. You understand me, Miss Prior?'

'Perfectly,' she said. 'And if he cannot be grateful to you, I can.'

He stood up. 'Please don't,' he said. 'I never know what to do with gratitude. When will you return? Friday? I look forward to it, Miss Prior. And a *bon voyage* in the meantime.'

Since that conversation, her every waking moment had been devoted to thoughts about or preparations for the journey. Most of those thoughts and preparations had been – to her despair and inability to do otherwise – concerned with her appearance. She had a new straw hat with a deep crown smothered in marguerites. It had come by steamer from Selah in Rangoon with a note to say that it was Parisian and a little present and that they missed her sorely at the convent and were very dull. Grace sat up half the night changing the pink ribbons on her muslin for yellow, too excited to sleep and terrified of having circles under her eyes the following day through not having slept enough. When she heard Archie on the verandah the next morning, talking to her father, she had dropped on her knees by her bed, for once careless of crushing all those flounces, and said a heartfelt prayer of thankfulness.

Archie was dressed as usual in the khaki drill trousers and tunic that were to be his uniform in Burma. He was swinging his topee by its strap in one hand and listening to her father with the intentness that made him such a flattering companion.

'You should not be surprised that the Beresfords will not come,' Tom was saying earnestly, forgetting the cup of tea he held so that his own clothes were becoming liberally sprinkled as he gestured, 'but I am disappointed for you. Indeed I am. Of course, Miss Beresford's head has been a little turned, but she has sterling qualities and it is a pity you should not have a chance to see them, a great pity she only appears to you at her worst. Her father is indeed a vain man, pitifully so, but the love and loyalty she gives him are unstinted, she would do anything to protect him, promote him. It is a great misfortune for her to be motherless. A mother would have a balancing influence—'

Grace tripped along the verandah and put her arm through her father's. 'Papa will forgive anyone for anything. He simply does not have the capacity to see ill for more than two seconds together. Mr Tennant this is such a lovely plan! It will be – I mean, it will do Papa so much good!'

'We will not be very many,' Archie said. 'Only

four in fact, yourselves, Signor Andreino and me – but we have an army of servants, all armed to the teeth.' He smiled down at Grace. 'Frederick insisted, so did Andreino. Neither of them supposes we shall have the smallest interference but they want us to be prepared. Prepared! Two elephants, four ponies, a bullock cart, enough provisions to feed an army – it's astonishing. The Burmese—' he checked himself. Hnin Si, pressed close to him in the hot heavy blackness of the previous night, had said that if he permitted her to come into the forests with him, she would be no trouble, get in no one's way, bring nothing that she could not carry in a Shan bag slung over one shoulder. He had been about to contrast this economy of luggage with their own extravagance and had suddenly realized the impossibility of his remark and blushed hotly.

Grace gazed at him with earnest sympathy, hoping that she might relieve whatever discomfiture he was suddenly afflicted with, but he did not look at her, only regarded his boots for a while, very intently, and then announced that if the Priors were ready, they should be off.

The elephants had departed some hours before in darkness, shuffling on their huge dry feet away towards the east and the first rosy streaks of dawn. They carried a cooking stove, an immense quantity of rations, bedding, mosquito nets, folding tables and chairs, brass lamps and the oil to fill them, canteens of water and a considerable number of green rubber groundsheets. The bullock cart, canopied against the sun, was for Grace, and the gentlemen were to ride, a syce leading the fourth pony should Grace become weary of her springless conveyance and need a change. The entire caravan would set off, leaving the statutory quarter of a mile between each group to allow the dust to settle, the gentlemen going ahead, the cart and the bulk of the servants following.

The ponies and the cart and all the servants who could be spared from the corporation bungalow and Andreino's house had been assembled in a dusty space under some tamarind trees at the south-east corner of the palace walls.

'Rifle to each man,' Frederick had said the previous day, sitting on the bungalow verandah with an abacus and a series of much-altered account books. 'Any trouble, don't stand any nonsense, shoot for their feet. Tie 'em up, tie 'em to a tree and leave 'em to sweat until you come down the hills again.'

Archie, feeling that it all sounded as improbable as a story in a boy's adventure book, grinned and said wasn't he supposed to hold his fire until he could see the whites of their eyes?

'Don't be an ass,' Frederick said shortly, and returned to his checking and muttering.

Grace was settled in the bullock cart and cushioned with the ponies' haybags, the gentlemen were mounted, and had already begun to move off eastwards when rapid hooves were heard from the city and a voice was heard calling in commanding English, 'Don't move yet! Don't go! We are come to join you after all!'

Maria did not quite understand the powerful impulse that had woken her at dawn and driven her to persuade Hubert to accompany her up into the Shan hills. There were plenty of excellent outward reasons and she had advanced all these to her father; Supayalat was to be confined within a day or so and, of course, at such a time, could not let even so favoured a foreigner as Maria near her; also she, Maria, considered her father to be looking a little fatigued and in need of a change and – she put this argument most forcibly of all – the waiting for news from France was already irksome and likely to become more so and a diversion could only be beneficial. As for the expedition itself, Maria said scornfully, pouring tea for Hubert at an extremely early breakfast, that of course held very little charm for either of them, in the company of that mousy little Grace and the raw boy from the Bombay-Burmah who had fewer manners than any man she had ever come across. Signor Andreino had manners to be sure, but of an unpleasantly oily kind that made one wonder if Archie Tennant's boorishness were not in some ways preferable.

Hubert, deep now in an indolence of five years' standing, drank his tea and smiled at her fondly. He loved to see her animated, absorbed in some scheme; it reminded him of those far off days in Tirimbatore, days when he had seemed consumed by energy himself, driven on ceaselessly by it, days that seemed so distant and strange to him in his present, almost drugged condition, that he could hardly believe himself to be the same man. Perhaps, he reflected, Maria had taken over from him; perhaps Maria had drawn so greedily on the life force they shared as father and daughter that there was nothing left for him now. This notion, surging unbidden into his brain, was not particularly comfortable for a second or two, and when he looked up at Maria her face was to him, for a moment only, that of a hard and calculating stranger.

Breakfast had been followed by the usual whirl of activity that accompanied Maria's dedication to some purpose. Hubert's customary white linen suit was taken away and replaced by a grey one – 'More practical, dearest Papa, on account of the dust' – bags were packed, orders and counter-orders were given to servants and syces, Maria's jewels were packed in chamois leather and hung in a pouch at her waist, messages were sent to Denzil, to Mattie, to the corporation bungalow, to the mission—

'Good Lord!' Archie said, turning in his saddle, quite forgetting Tom's presence. 'Good Lord! Look!'

Maria felt it unnecessary to make any explanation at all. Never mind that she had first refused to come on any terms, then exercised her own unassailable privilege of changing her mind – she now sailed into the small company's midst without the slightest consciousness of doing anything other than granting the most immense favour. Everybody stared to be sure, Tom and Archie in amazement, Andreino smiling and Grace in horror, but she was used to stares, took them as her due. She bowed slightly to them all in turn and, riding to the head so that her pony's nose was clearly in front of Archie's, said over her shoulder, 'Should we not be off?'

Dumbly in their appointed order, they followed her. Early though it still was, the heat was terrific and the white dust of the road, laid briefly at night by the light dew, began to rise in soft puffs and clouds about their hooves. The road was built on a kind of embankment between paddies of young rice which stretched away bright, clear green to the blue hills ahead, the even greenness broken only by the occasional white stupa or clump of darker trees or peasant's hut built of grey weathered teak and tottering on unsteady stilts. It was all very quiet and still except for the shuffle of hooves and bare feet and the grinding squeal of the ungreased axle of Grace's cart in the distance behind, and the silence was made worse by the tension. Only Hubert seemed not to feel it, riding with a faint smile upon his handsome face and his eyes fixed upon the hills ahead or upon his daughter's upright back in her blue-grey habit.

After three or four miles, Archie could bear it no longer. He was about to expostulate to Tom but found he did not wish to be talked out of his anger and into a more Christian and forgiving frame of mind, so he merely muttered that he was going forward a moment and kicked his mount to a trot.

'Miss Beresford.'

She did not turn her head but continued to look ahead, presenting him with her elegant profile under a charming small bowler hat trimmed with grey feathers.

'I may not have had the distinction, the *doubtful* distinction, of knowing you long, but I think one hour's worth of acquaintance would justify me, in the present circumstances, in saying that I find your behaviour perfectly intolerable.'

A small lurch took place somewhere deep in Maria but she gave no outward sign of it. She continued to ride forward, looking fixedly ahead.

'It is one thing,' Archie continued furiously, riding so close to her that their knees almost touched, 'to refuse an invitation with the utmost lack of grace. It is quite another to change your mind with no reference whatsoever to the convenience or feelings of anyone else and to arrive, unannounced, with an air of the most intolerable queenliness and proceed, without a word of explanation or apology, to lead the expedition you spurned contemptuously a few days ago. What made you change your mind I neither know nor care about, but I do know that you have upset everyone here and I do care that their pleasure should be spoiled.'

Sweat had broken out unaccountably on Maria's upper lip and in her armpits and down her spine. It was indeed a blessing that she did not seem to know how to blush, but unfortunately she did not appear to have the same immunity to trembling. She clenched her hands upon the reins and stared rigidly before her, taking deep breaths and holding her smarting eyes forcibly wide open.

She said, 'I will not be spoken to so!'

'And I,' Archie said, in a more normal tone, 'will not be used so. You will oblige me by reining in and dropping back to ride with your father.'

She opened her mouth to overwhelm him with all the imperiousness that had rendered her untouchable in the last few years, all the biting haughtiness that had kept people at bay, and made them afraid to cross her in the smallest degree – and found that she could not trust herself to utter. There seemed to be an obstruction, partly caused by the most blinding fury and outrage, partly by something less manageable and familiar, which made her distrust her ability to be even halfway articulate. Almost choking in her angry confusion, she uttered an unintentional almost pitiful sound, a sort of low moan, and pulled fiercely at her horse's head.

'Dearest!' Hubert said anxiously as he drew level and observed her bent head. 'Dearest! What is the matter? Are you unwell? Come, look at me, you frighten me!'

There was a short pause and then Archie heard her say in a voice of almost steady cheerfulness,

'Dear Papa, how you do fret! Of course, it is nothing. I merely received a whole cloud of dust in my eyes and they are smarting terribly. May I ride with you, Papa? I should so much enjoy it, we never seem to have enough time together, do we, and if I ride with Mr Tennant, we shall only argue about the best route as we did just now and that would hardly be profitable, would it, since neither of us has been this way before!'

At the back of the procession, Grace's teeth were being almost shaken from her head. She had at one moment tried to cry out to her father, riding far ahead with Signor Andreino and deep in conversation, that she should like to get out and ride herself. But he was too far away, too absorbed in what he was saying – indeed it was a good thing Archie had found him a docile and sensible pony for he frequently dropped the reins altogether in order to gesture more eloquently towards his companion – to hear her and, in any case, she supposed miserably that as she did not possess a beautiful habit like Maria's she would only, in her crumpled muslins, look like a bag of laundry on horseback. In any case an unfamiliarly violent headache, brought on no doubt by this horrible cart, was beginning to grip her skull in iron pincers, and if she exposed herself to the sun, as she must do on horseback, she would only make it worse. She concentrated her energies on praying that Archie might drop back and ride beside her, but he appeared, after a few words to Maria, to have taken a decisive lead and was farther away from her than ever.

At last the flat white road between the paddies began to climb a little and the trees of the hills ahead came creeping down the slopes and sheltered them all a little from the now burning sun. Archie had promised that they should stop every eight or ten miles and rest, but Grace was sure he had forgotten this for he was now so far ahead that curves of the road sometimes entirely hid him from her view. Then Mr Beresford stopped for a moment and dismounted while a syce took a stone from his horse's shoe and Tom and Signor Andreino went arguing on past him and his daughter, so that now the only people Grace could call out to were the Beresfords and she would rather die from the heat and her headache and the jolting than address one syllable to them. She watched the trees jerk past, the dappled patterns of light and shade, and tried not to feel that the bumping and the squealing and the disappointment of her hopes might at any moment reduce her to hysterical crying.

So determined were her efforts at self-control that she hardly noticed the moment at which they fell upon her. It seemed that she was, at one second, sitting swaying and wretched and pricked maddeningly by little ends of hay which pro-truded from the nets, and the next that the hysteria she had supposed she was fighting from inside had fallen upon her from the outside. The bullock driver seemed to tumble abruptly from his perch, the bullocks themselves began to lurch about, bellowing awfully, and the cart, which had held only herself and the hay, was suddenly full of writhing, filthy brown bodies clad only in disgusting rags and screaming heathenishly. She heard her own screams coming high and shrill from far away and felt the crucifix that had been her mother's wrenched from her neck, the chain slicing cruelly into her flesh, and the canopy of the cart was ripped away to reveal a dizzying world of trees and savages and panic whirling round her in an incomprehensible nightmare.

When the shot rang out and the cart emptied as abruptly as it had filled, she was past noticing. Maria, handing her small revolver, still smoking, to her father, with a quelling and decided look to him as if to forestall any argument, swung herself down from her pony, stepped with distaste over the man whose knee she had wounded and climbed into the cart. When the gentlemen and the servants, clattering back down the road in an agony of alarm, arrived at the cart, they found Hubert standing beside it with a look of understandable confusion and Maria kneeling beside Grace, smelling salts in one hand, while she pushed Grace's head down between her knees with the other in a manner that was by no means ungentle.

'They must have thought the cart held our possessions,' she said, cutting short their breathless inquiries and indicating the slashed haynets and the hay scattered everywhere. 'I don't suppose they bargained for poor Miss Prior. There's one of them in the road.'

Archie stooped over the man. His hair was done up in the typical topknot, slipping now to one side of his head, and he wore nothing but a filthy loincloth around his tough little body.

'There,' Andreino said on a note of unnecessary triumph. 'One of the dacoits about which I have warned you all so often.' He stooped and slid a short knife out of the man's loincloth, holding it out as if it were some sort of proof.

Archie looked up. 'Who shot him?'

Maria said clearly, her back to him as she bent over Grace, 'My father.'

'Good shot, sir,' Archie said admiringly.

Hubert with a slight start bowed a little. In the cart, slumped against Maria's shoulder, Grace began to cry. Tom climbed in beside her and put his arms about her, taking her from Maria and cradling her against him, crooning and soothing.

It was clearly impossible for them all to go on. The dacoits, having attacked in error, would not do so again at once but might well spring upon the elephants some miles ahead. This possibility meant that some of the party must go on until the elephants were found and that some must escort Grace home at once to the relative safety of the mission. It was hardly mid-morning, they had not come twelve miles and the expedition was in ruins.

'I shall return,' Andreino said. 'And if you are

wise, you will all accompany me. I shall turn this rogue over to the authorities, of course.'

'Papa?' Maria said, but her tone made the query rhetorical.

Hubert appeared to be dreaming. He said, from far away, a little coldly, 'Whatever *you* choose, dearest. I am not afraid.'

'Mr Tennant?'

Archie looked a little guiltily at Tom. 'I – I do not wish to appear unfeeling but I should quite like to go on. That is, if no-one objects. I don't need anyone but Ah Chun. I should like all the rest to go with Miss Prior.' He leaned over the cart side and took Grace's hand. 'I would not have had this happen for the world.'

She said shakily, smiling at him, 'Not – not your fault, how could you know? Please go on and – and forgive me for wanting to go back.'

'But *I* want you to go back. I want to know you are safe.'

Behind him, Maria, who had descended from the cart when Tom took his daughter from her, said, 'May we accompany you, Mr Tennant?'

He looked round. She was not smiling but her voice was quite altered.

'Of course.'

Tom called from the cart. 'Miss Beresford!'

She went over to him, placing her hands on the wooden sides.

'I do thank you, Miss Beresford. I do thank you most sincerely.'

She said, 'But it is my father—'

'Yes,' Tom said, his eyes full of discerning kindness, 'Yes. But all the same I thank you,' and then he looked up briefly, caught Archie's glance and stooped over Grace again.

They did not find the elephants until mid-afternoon. Some time had been spent at the spot where the cart was attacked ferreting about in the undergrowth but nothing had been found. Grace had been sure there had been twenty dacoits, Andreino of the opinion, after questioning his prisoner, that there were only three or four. However many there were, they had vanished among the trees taking Grace's crucifix with them. The party separated, the bulk of the servants accompanying the Priors and Andreino back across the paddyfields to Mandalay.

Archie and his companions rode on in silence. They were preceded and followed by servants and they rode three abreast, Maria in the middle, up the rough track which deteriorated sharply at intervals or vanished altogether in a pile of boulders. The hillside was growing considerably steeper and once or twice they emerged out of the trees and could look down upon the plain below them and the winking, glittering roofs of the royal city, set within its square mile of walls. It was not a comfortable silence that enveloped them and it was made worse by their inability to break it and so there was nothing for them to do but ride steadily on while crickets chirped in the grasses beside them and, every so often, a clearing appeared beside the track planted with orderly rows of pineapple. They passed few people, only a labourer or two with broad calloused feet and faces of brown leather, and the only village they encountered was a dilapidated shuttered place, seemingly quite asleep in the midday heat.

Maria, her spine still straight beneath the now burning cloth of her habit, determined that she would not complain, nor ask to stop. She had ridden endlessly as a child but had had very little occasion to since coming to Mandalay and could feel her legs beginning to ache violently at this unaccustomed time in the sidesaddle. Hubert seemed still to be in a dream, only emerging from it now and then to glance at his daughter, and Archie, thrown into confusion by the collapse of what had seemed to him a pleasant, mildly exploratory excursion, was too preoccupied to think of anything very much but that they must find the elephants. Of all the peculiar things he had done in his few short weeks in Burma, this hot ride up a stony track to look at a place which hardly existed in the company of two people whom he scarcely knew and barely liked seemed to him by far the most fantastic.

With the elephants, luncheon also waited. A huge repast of curries, bowls of rice, dried prawns and sliced green mangoes lay spread out upon the folding tables in the shade of some trees. A field kitchen had been set up at some distance away, the whole spot having been chosen because of the view across the falling wooded hillsides to Mandalay, no more than a blur some twenty miles distant. They sat down in the chairs provided and were handed plates and bowls with as much formality as if they had been in a dining room while the elephants, tethered in the bushes below, tore off whole branches at once and crushed them noisily into their mouths.

Conversation even with food was only desultory. Hubert observed how extremely unlucky it was that the most timid member of the party should have been the victim and Maria said with unexpected charity that, whatever one's constitution, it must be terrifying to be fallen upon when trapped in a bullock cart and unable to escape, as one might on horseback.

'How far ahead were you?' Archie said, his fork poised.

'A hundred yards perhaps. Perhaps a little more.'

'My daughter has extraordinarily swift reactions.'

'You too, sir, if I may say so.'

'No,' Hubert said, looking down, 'Not so quick.'

Maria stretched out a hand and took her father's.

Archie said, 'Do you feel you are quite in another world up here? Do you feel everything is entirely different?'

Maria looked at him oddly. 'I do not know,' she said.

They reached Maymyo the following day, stiff
and saddlesore. Ah Chun had been as good as his
word and his relations had prepared what would
in India have been a dak-bungalow in which they
slept in tolerable comfort, apart from regiments
of cockroaches which swarmed across the floors
in a blood-red river. Conversation at dinner,
eaten by the yellow light of the oil lamps, flowed
no more easily than it had at luncheon, and
Archie flung himself under his mosquito net
profoundly thankful that in two days he would
be back in Frederick's idiosyncratic but easy
company. At the other end of the bungalow
Maria was disgusted to discover the state of her
clothes and berated her maid as sharply as if the
climate and nearly six hours in the saddle had
been her fault alone. Hubert, taking Maria's
revolver out of his pocket, looked at it for a long
time with a kind of resentment, and then placed
it under his pillow. He imagined, staring up into
the thick blackness above him as he lay in bed,
that he was a young man again, the pioneer of
Tirimbatore, riding about the neatly planted hills
below that palatial bungalow with an imperious
little thing in a sunbonnet demanding that he go
faster, that he race her. He had used the revolver
he kept in his belt only once, to prevent the flight
of the only dishonest overseer he had ever had.
He had shot him in the leg, below the knee, or
was it in the knee itself . . . ?

★ ★ ★

They slept badly despite the sharp night air of the hills and the complete silence. All three were pervaded with a sense of oddness, of improbability, which made them restless and uneasy, despite the fatigue induced by long unaccustomed hours on horseback. They came to breakfast each with a profound desire to return to Mandalay and an absolute determination not to suggest it. It was the third meal over which silence had hung oppressively, a silence broken only by the self-conscious clatter of plates and knives. Maria ate almost nothing, but watched her father relentlessly, leaning forward when breakfast was almost over, to say in a voice which had more of command than cajolery in it, 'But you have not drunk your tea!'

And Hubert, looking up from his plate, said in a tone of irritation he had never used before to her in all her twenty-five years, a tone sharp with resentment, 'Do not treat me like a child.'

Archie, expecting this to be a common sort of exchange between a father and daughter thrown always together, was astonished to see all the colour drain at once from Maria's face and her eyes and mouth widen in an expression at once horrified and vulnerable. He said, 'I should be grateful for more tea myself' as a diversion, but she did not hear him and went on gazing at her father with that stricken look, her lips trembling very slightly. Then she rose abruptly and left the room and they could hear her outside on the bungalow verandah calling for her maid.

Hubert seemed not to observe her going and merely said calmly to Archie, 'I think we should be mounted soon. It would be preferable to ride before midday.'

'Yes,' Archie said, 'Yes, it would.'

'Then, if you will excuse me—'

'Of course, sir.'

Hubert rose slowly and left Archie alone with the teapot. His cup of tea, Archie noticed, had remained untouched.

In the tiny cabin of a room in which he had tossed all night, Hubert stood for a moment to compose himself, his eyes closed upon his clamouring thoughts. He was thirsty still, but nothing would have induced him to drink his tea after such an instruction, and so bear his thirst he must. It was, after all, a distraction from his state of mind.

He could not recall ever having suffered so from a state of mind in all his life as he had that previous night, pressing his cheek into the hard pillow of cotton wadding and feeling the revolver there, like a probe in a wound. He had believed – fondly, now he told himself, foolishly – that Maria had always wished to see him appear well in public for the best of reasons, merely that she admired him, was proud of him and wished others to love him and respect him as she did. Now it seemed otherwise, subtly, disturbingly otherwise, and a conviction was worming itself into Hubert's brain that she only saw his good public performance as a necessary appendage to her own reputation, an extension of her own success, window dressing for her image in other eyes.

So that, he told himself, if it seems to her that I might fail in any way, she quickly takes over the action to avoid the possibility of failure. I may still get the credit publicly but she and I know I do not deserve it. I might have shot the bandit – I might – but she would not risk being seen as a successful woman whose father might, even in the smallest measure, be a shame to her. She protects me, but only for her own ends, and because she protects me, she has come to think she has a right to control me.

He opened his eyes with an effort. A bright square of sunlight fell on the rough disordered sheets of the narrow bed. Hubert put his hand beneath the pillow and drew out the revolver. It was small and elegant, the barrel finely inlaid with brass. When he had given it to Maria it had seemed to him then such a dashing present, a gallant gesture with a flavour of intrigue to it, from a worldly father to a beautiful daughter. It was a symbol of their companionship, their unique association. Now – Hubert tossed it onto the bed for the bearer to find. He would not look at it again. Lying there gleaming blue-grey against the white bedclothes it seemed to tell him, as plainly as words might have done, that Maria, for a quarter of a century such an ineffable delight and satisfaction to him, had ceased to love him.

The main street of Maymyo was quite unlike Mandalay, being lined in part with timber buildings, but also with houses and shops of carved grey stone on which clumps of bright green ferns had settled here and there in cracks between the blocks. It was only a small place as yet, and an exclusively Burmese one at that, but there was an air of solidity and dignity about it that Mandalay, for all its splendour, conspicuously lacked. The air was glorious, warm in the sunlight but with a sharp clarity to it that was a wonderful relief after the humid heat of the plain, and even the light seemed sharper and clearer, all objects more brilliantly defined.

Hills rose all around, spreading away to north and east and south and falling to Mandalay in the west, blue still but now clearly seen to be thickly wooded. Maymyo itself was wooded, not in the dense, heavy jungle manner of Mandalay, but with tall and graceful trees around whose slender trunks poinsettias grew in green and scarlet profusion. It was easy to see where houses might be built on the level ground around the village, houses which would have wonderful views to the west while the Shan hills would rise up on all other sides to shelter them.

'Look,' Archie said, as much to break the silence between them all as anything, 'that would do wonderfully as a cricket pitch.' He pointed with his whip to a smooth oval clearing among the trees edged with rocks that would make a natural grandstand.

Hubert said, 'I have never much cared for cricket.'

Maria said nothing.

It was, in view of the constraint now added to incompatibility, as endless a morning as the previous afternoon had been. For the look of the thing as much as to satisfy his own determination not to call the expedition a failure, Archie rode determinedly all around the village and all over the gentle hillsides immediately to the north and north-east which were the obvious sites for a European community. He was, to his incomprehension and mounting irritation, followed, and in silence. He tried humming to show of what little consequence the Beresfords' presence was to him but found he could not seem to hold any tune and relapsed into silence himself.

Luncheon was spread out with the same meticulous care and superabundance of food as the day before and eaten with as little animation. Maria watched her father with an expression of both bewilderment and alarm, but said nothing to him, and he ate placidly and did not return her glance once. Archie ate voraciously to give himself some occupation and wished both Beresfords at the bottom of the ocean.

When the fruit had been removed, Hubert announced his intention of sleeping before they returned to the bungalow. Archie most powerfully did not wish to be left alone with Maria but could see no way to avoid it without adding to the wretchedness she was already and most evidently suffering from. When Hubert and his servant had gone in search of a suitable spot among some neighbouring bushes, Archie remained slumped in his chair, enervated beyond all ability to make either conversation or decision.

Maria said abruptly, 'I am afraid we have been an intrusion, Mr Tennant.'

'Oh – oh, no – Miss Beresford, of course you haven't – only too pleased—'

She said, 'I must apologize.'

Archie ducked his head and groaned inwardly. He wanted no reference at all made to the day before, nor to his reprimand to her.

'You did not want us to come up to Maymyo with you, Mr Tennant. I forced our company upon you. It has been very awkward for all of us – ' She stopped, her voice shaking a little, took a breath and went on, 'I had rather you were not polite, Mr Tennant. I had rather you told me the truth. I find – I find I prefer it. From you, at least.'

He risked looking up. She sat in a camp chair, bolt upright, but looking at him with an expression of determined candour. He said bravely, 'Very well, Miss Beresford. I *have* found the last two days difficult. We have, none of us, anything to say to each other. It makes such an expedition, as you say, very awkward.'

She said unexpectedly, 'I am not used to conversation, you see. I do not have any here. There is no-one to talk to. I discuss things, of course, plans and schemes, but that is not the same as conversation.'

'Perhaps you are not much interested,' Archie ventured.

'I thought I was not. I thought it a waste of time. But I have had some hours to ponder on – on everything while we rode about this morning. I do not seem to feel sure about anything up here, I seem to feel – almost another person—'

She stopped and then she said, with extraordinary deliberateness, 'It was not my father who shot the dacoit yesterday. I did it. There is no particular merit in that since my father taught me to shoot when I was only a child and I showed great aptitude at once. I hit the bandit exactly where I intended to and then I handed the revolver to my father. I feel that I should apologize for not telling the precise truth, for misleading you—'

Archie said hurriedly, 'Please do not feel you have to confess anything to me, Miss Beresford. You hardly know me. I do assure you that what is done is done and forgotten. You will only embarrass me by apologizing.'

'I have already apologized,' she said calmly. 'I shouldn't do so again. I am merely making the truth clear – and perhaps thinking aloud. You see,' she said with a sudden rush and in quite an altered tone, a tone he found inexplicably touching, 'you see, I am English and I have never seen England. I know only India and now Burma. I have no roots, only my father—' She paused for a moment and a look of pain passed swiftly across her face, 'my father. We have been inseparable – all my life. All of it. First in India and now in Mandalay, and Mandalay, as you said to me, has been my world. My only world. Coming up here has made me think, Mr Tennant. It has made me remember that there is another world, the world of everything outside Mandalay. And I thought, riding about after you this morning among the trees, what will become of us after Mandalay, what will we do next? Or will we do nothing, will it be Mandalay for ever and ever? Papa and me and the Queen and the mines, on and on.' She stopped again and then she said, 'What do you think?'

He put his elbows on the table between them and leaned towards her. 'Why do you ask me?'

'Because you are the only person I have met here who is here for a conventional reason. Your coming makes me see what strange and improbable people I live amongst – or at least I have seen it this morning.'

He grinned at her. 'If I am the most conventional person in Mandalay, Miss Beresford, you must be one of the most unconventional.'

'It is not in the least remarkable to be unconventional here. As I said, we are two a penny. I begin to see that when everyone around has to some extent lost their heads, it seems perfectly commonplace to lose one's own. What is your background, Mr Tennant?'

Startled by her directness, he told her. She listened to him most intently, regarding him with great seriousness and, because of the compliment of having her attention so absolutely, he found himself telling her far more than she had asked for, even so far as to describe the birth and death of Tennant Phillipson.

When he had at last finished, she said, 'Thank you, Mr Tennant. Thank you very much.' And then she paused and looked away among the trees for a moment. 'So you see, I was perfectly right to ask you how you see the future of someone such as myself. We are both English, but our growing up has been as different as it possibly could be. Yours, I perceive, has been a proper education in the most solid and full sense. I really am – today – at a loss to describe mine at all—' She looked back at him and gave him a smile of startling brilliance. 'Do you see me as an adventuress?'

Overwhelmed by the smile, he stammered a little and said, 'Of – of a sort.'

'And I shall come to a disgraceful end?'

'I hope not.'

'You say that as if you really meant it, Mr Tennant.'

He stood up and stretched, looking down at her. She seemed to him extremely beautiful at that moment. 'I find I do.'

'You are my junior by two years, yet I do not seem to feel that you are younger. I think perhaps you are a great deal more worldly than I am—'

'Oh no,' he said hurriedly, 'not at all.'

She smiled again. 'We shall see,' she said and rose also.

'Miss Beresford—'

'Yes?' she said.

'Miss Beresford – why did you insist it was your father's shot that wounded the dacoit yesterday? Why did you not admit to it as your own?'

She came close to Archie, so close that he could see her fine, pale skin had an irreverent dusting of freckles across the bridge of the nose.

'My father's self-esteem is of the utmost importance.'

Archie said, blushing a little, 'Heaven knows, Miss Beresford, I'm no student of human nature, I've no business to point out anyone's mistakes but – but might your father not see such an action as condescension? Might – I mean suppose he saw it as more a blow to his self-esteem than, well, than a boost?'

'Oh, no,' she said with certainty, 'he would never do that.'

'You are a cracking good shot, Miss Beresford, in any case. And I haven't seen many women who sit a horse as well as you do. It's a pity you haven't been to England. I think hunting would suit you.'

Her eyes clouded for a moment and then she moved away from him and said in her old hard way, as if the spell were broken, as if the mood of Maymyo were slipping from her, 'No doubt I should, Mr Tennant. I am accustomed to excel.'

Archie began to laugh. She watched him for a moment and he thought she was about to be very angry, he could see her knuckles white around her riding crop. But then her face relaxed abruptly and she gave him another of those rare and brilliant smiles. She shook her crop at him.

'One day I shall prove it to you, Mr Tennant, and then it will be my turn to laugh. Now I must go and rouse Papa. We should be getting back to the bungalow.'

If Hubert had not been present, Archie reflected, conversation during that day and the following one as they descended the hills to Mandalay once more might have been as easy and surprising as that short half hour in the sunshine at Maymyo. But Hubert seemed content – or even, Archie began to suspect, determined – to be silent, so none of them spoke much and when Archie tried, as he frequently did, to catch Maria's eye, she seemed always to be looking ahead or at her father. What was more disconcerting was that, as they approached Mandalay, her old habit of imperiousness seemed to settle back upon her, like a miasma rising from the city itself and enveloping her as she came closer. Archie began to think he had imagined the brief softness and breadth of mind that had mellowed her during their conversation and when at last the rose-red city walls came into view once more and he said to her, daringly, 'The end of an adventure, Miss Beresford?' and received in reply only a look of the most chilling reproof, he hardly felt surprised.

As their roads parted by the city walls, she held out a hand to him.

'Mr Tennant, goodbye. And I trust that your first season in the forests will not be too unpleasant.'

He held her hand firmly.

'Then I shall not see you until the spring?'

'My duties at court resume the moment the royal child is born. You must realize that my time is fully taken up.'

He smiled at her, hoping to elicit even a flicker of what she had responded with at Maymyo, but she regarded him stonily. He released her hand.

'Goodbye, Miss Beresford. Goodbye, Sir.'

Neither Maria nor Hubert looked back as they rode away. In fact, they did not even mention Archie beyond Maria's saying, in a tone that had an edge of supplication to it, 'Well, Papa? And what did you make of our escort?'

Hubert did not smile. He simply gave a small sigh, as if the matter were utterly without interest and said, 'A most undistinguished companion, my dear.'

Maria looked at him quickly, her mouth open to reply, but something in his face daunted her and she merely urged her pony homeward in silence.

13

Grace lay in her dim and shuttered bedroom and felt the fever ebb and flow from her like a scorching tide. It seemed so silly to be ill; she was sure it had no connection with her fright three days before. In fact she could remember, in odd lucid moments, that the headache which had now clamped itself upon her skull relentlessly had begun even as they left Mandalay, long before she was attacked. Lots of people had a fever in Mandalay; Europeans were always taking to their beds; it seemed almost a matter of course, but she had never been really ill, not all those five years in Burma. There had been times in Rangoon when she suffered from the results of the rather haphazard kitchen arrangements at the convent – the nuns, being so little interested in food, were quite content to leave it to zealous but unfastidious Burmese converts – but that sort of affliction was part of life in the East, everyone knew that no-one was immune.

But this, Grace thought, pushing vainly against the thudding waves of fever, this is quite different. I can't seem to control my thoughts and my arms and legs go wandering off and I wish everything didn't throb and pound so. How can I think when I am all scattered and pulsing like this? The nights are horrible. I know when it is night because my brain goes screaming off into nightmares and of course I believe them when I am in them, I believe that they are real. Where is Archie, she thought, struggling to raise her head and look for him, he should be here, he should be, I have asked and asked—

Tom sat with her during the nights, administering himself the quinine Frederick Winser had sent to the mission. A terse note had come with the medicine to the effect that these jungle fevers came and went, but reliably went with rest and regular dosing. Tom, who had never known a day's illness himself – chiefly, other people had always supposed, because he forgot for nine-tenths of his live that he was possessed of a body – felt curiously adrift sitting by Grace's bed watching her mutter and toss, her smooth hair plastered damply to her cheeks and forehead and her skin alternatively burning or clammy. It wasn't that the ability to pray had deserted him but the form of prayer he needed now was foreign to him. He had always begged for direction and inspiration, never for any worldly thing; the blessing of a good wife and child had been, he considered, a sign of divine bounty; he had never consciously asked for any benefit for himself. He had asked, day in, day out, over nearly fifty years for the chance to serve, that the way of best service be made plain to him, that such talents as he had be used only and fully in the life he had chosen. And now he needed a favour. Now he wanted a direct gift from God, a selfish gift to himself alone – and he did not know how to ask for it. It seemed to him that some bargain should perhaps be made, but felt that there was nothing he possessed of any value that he had not surrendered long ago as a curate of twenty-two. So he prayed shyly and with difficulty, like a novice uncertain of being heard.

Denzil brought Maria the news of Grace's illness. She was surprised to find how much it disquieted her so in order to disguise this from him she said brutally, 'Hardly a surprise, I think. One would expect her to succumb to the slightest thing.'

He said, 'I think it is serious.'

A pair of slippers being embroidered for Hubert had lain unfinished by her chair for weeks. Maria now snatched them up as if their completion was a matter of the utmost urgency. She bent her head and sent her needle stabbing in and out of the velvet almost viciously, hardly looking to judge the accuracy of her stitches. Supayalat had been delivered of a daughter that morning and no one in the palace had been in a high good humour except for Thibaw, who, for all his indolence and sulky weakness, was truly attached to his children. Also, there was still no news from Pierre, not so much as a letter to say he had reached Paris. Now Grace. Maria was not in the least superstitious – at least she told herself so – but she could not help observing that Grace's illness made the third preoccupying fact in her life, all three of them facts that hardly made for reassurance or stability. There was still no direct heir to the Burmese throne; there was no certainty that the future would bring the position and security of the last five years; and Grace, insignificant, unremarkable as she might be, represented some kind of order and continuity in this strange life in Mandalay. Maria shook herself resolutely and pricked her finger deeply in the process.

Denzil held out his handkerchief. 'You will put blood on the slipper.'

She took his handkerchief in silence and pressed it to her forefinger.

'How is the mood in the palace?'

'The King is pleased,' she said, 'but he was drunk this morning. Those *pwes* – those *pwes*—' she put her hand briefly to her forehead, remembering a ceaseless banging of gongs that had beaten, like a headache, all morning. 'Denzil, they go on almost day and night now. The palace theatre is never quiet, there are musicians and dancers everywhere. The King shouts for more, louder and louder, if they so much as stop for a moment.'

'It's to distract his mind. Just as the champagne is. He is no more fit to govern than the sacred white elephant and his conscience smites him at all the deeds of cruelty done in his name. You look tired.'

'I am perfectly well.'

'Something is the matter.'

'No,' she said, 'nothing.'

He got up and began to walk about the room. He said, with a certain hardness, 'It is difficult for all of us, this waiting. I know no more of Pierre than you do. I am just as helpless. But you and your father – Maria, it is of no assistance to our cause, our standing in Mandalay, our morale, if you and Hubert quarrel—'

'We have never quarrelled in our lives,' she said sharply, looking down at her lap.

'You are beginning to behave very stupidly,' Denzil said. 'I begin to think you are losing your head. Or if not, it has been so turned for you it is abandoning all commonsense. True, we could not do without you and your influence with the Queen, but by the same token, you would not be laden with those jewels if it were not for the rest of us and our various talents. May I remind you that it was I who secured that very first audience your father had with Thibaw. Without me the entire scheme would not exist; without Pierre we should not know how to go about the technicalities; without Hubert we might not so easily be able to raise the money. Don't forget that, Maria, not for a moment.'

She said nothing, but went on sewing, jabbing at the velvet with her needle. He came close to her chair and stood looking down at her bent head.

'Sulk if you will, my dear. But don't imagine yourself indispensable. And don't be fool enough to think that any of us, *any* of us, your father included, would have the smallest scruple in doing without you should we need to, should you become impossible to deal with. It is utter folly to alienate yourself from your father—'

She glanced up, her eyes hard with fury, and said, 'Please go.'

'In a moment. When you have heard me out I shall leave you to reflect upon what I have said. Listen, Maria—' He stooped close to her. 'Do not, for your own sake entertain the smallest delusion of grandeur. I don't know what you have done to offend your father – I don't wish to know – but I know you have done something from his own changed behaviour and I must deduce that you are acting towards him as you are now to all of us. If you wish to stay here my dear, if you wish to keep the position you so enjoy, you must give as much as you take. I don't care one iota if your heart is in it or not, I only care for appearances.'

'Oh, yes,' she said savagely, jerking her thread, breaking it, 'that is perfectly evident. You have no more heart than a stone.'

Denzil said, laughing, 'And you do, my dear, you do?'

She thrust the needle into the slipper and pushed it off her lap to fall onto the floor. 'You should go.'

He bowed. 'If I may be assured that you have both heard and comprehended what I came to say.'

She rose and stood regarding him. 'I understand you perfectly. My opinion of what you say will remain my own affair—'

'Naturally.'

'—but you must know that I am extremely resentful that you should suppose me in any way careless of the future.'

He moved towards the open double doors. 'Maria my dear, how could you be careless? Hardly, I feel, with this – this new-found heart of yours.'

When his step had gone lightly down the verandah, Maria found that she wanted very much to sit in one of her rose-pink chairs and cry her eyes out. Instead, she kicked the slipper spinning across the polished floor and then rang violently for a servant to retrieve it.

'Are you there?' Grace said, 'Did you come?'

Archie tried to loosen the burning fingers a little from his own.

'Yes,' he said. 'Two hours ago.'

Her eyes opened briefly, regarding him in puzzlement, and closed again.

'I asked for you. I asked and asked. I wanted you to save me from the dreams.' Her head rolled fretfully on the pillow, damp strands of hair peeling from her cheeks as she moved. 'I'm so hot. My head is terrible, you can't think how much it hurts. I don't want to be brave, I don't want to be ill—'

With his free hand Archie took up a sponge that floated in a basin of water beside him and squeezed it to dampness. He began clumsily – for it was his right hand she clung to so desperately – to wipe her forehead and cheeks, but she rolled her head faster and faster as if trying to escape his ministrations, and trickles of water ran down into her ears and the dark moistness of her hair.

She said, 'I didn't want Maria to come, I didn't ask her. Why did she come?'

'She isn't here. You are thinking of the expedition. That is all past, forgotten. You must not think of it, you must only think of getting well.'

'I can't be well,' she said peevishly, opening her eyes to show him that they were filled with tears, 'I am only ill, I hate being ill, it tires me, it tires me right out. Send Maria away. Say I don't want anyone, just you, just you and Papa. Don't go!' she cried suddenly, although he had never moved. 'You mustn't leave me! You mustn't go!'

He checked a small sigh. 'I am not going. I am staying by you. As long as you want me.'

The room itself made him uncomfortable. It was not simply the overpowering heat or the sickroom smell or the pathetic and defenceless sight of Grace, shrunk with fever, but the warring components of the room itself. A crucifix hung above the bed, symbolically enshrined in clouds of folded mosquito net, a small porcelain virgin and child stood tranquilly on the bedside table among the bottles and glasses and the walls were hung with slightly sentimental pictures of Christ surrounded by improbably plump Jewish children and St Francis liberally loaded with wild birds. But besides these things were a looking glass, several hats on pegs, bunches of ribbons hung on nails – one even on the corner of St Francis – stools and chairs laden with piles of crumpled gauzy stuffs no-one had seen fit to put away, scattered slippers, brushes, combs, a fat pink satin pillow bristling with what Archie took for hairpins. The sheer economy of Hnin Si struck him again – guiltily in such a situation – the spare neatness of her gestures, the small tidy pile of her discarded clothes, the single prong with which she skewered her glossy hair. Except for her physical self, she often left no other trace at all of her presence in a room. But this clutter, this disorder, this conflict of piety and self-indulgence—

Grace gave a little cry from the pillow. Her closed lids were pulsing with the misery of some inward image and her mouth was puckering childishly as if she would cry.

'Don't,' Archie said, 'dear Grace, don't—'

Tears slid from beneath her closed lids.

'I can't bear to watch you,' Archie said, 'you poor little thing, poor little Grace—'

From the doorway, Tom said, 'How good you are to stay, I know how distressing it is. But school is finished now and I can relieve you.'

'It's all right sir. I'll stay. I – I think she wants me to. She keeps waking just for a moment and I wouldn't like her to think I had deserted her.'

Heavily, Tom took the chair on the opposite side of the bed. He reached to take Grace's free hand, but she tore it from him, flailing about wildly with it.

'Archie! Archie! Oh, why don't you come?'

Archie took the roaming hand and held both hers between his own. Her skin was as dry and hot as burning paper. She opened her eyes briefly and then closed them and sighed and muttered a little.

'Of course—' Tom said, 'and this is something I should not have known how to say to you had she not been ill – of course, you know how devoted she is to you. I shouldn't want you to feel her affection a burden on you, you know, but if – if it were to make a difference to her – her recovery, you know, if you were to – if you could, in some way, reciprocate just – just a little, enough to give her hope, enough to give her something to recover for—'

He stopped. Archie, overcome with the most horrible confusion, looked down at his hands holding Grace's. Very carefully he laid Grace's hands on the sheet.

'Don't misunderstand me,' Tom said hurriedly. 'I can't expect any promises. I don't look for any commitment. I don't know what else to do, I don't know who else to turn to. I just thought perhaps as you were, are, a little fond of her—'

'Oh yes,' Archie said, 'yes, I am. Fond—'

Grace opened her eyes, looked at him with great clarity and firmly retrieved his right hand with her own. 'Of course – of course, I want her to recover. More than anything. You must know that. And – and I'd do anything I could to help. But – but not that sort of promise. It would not be true, not fair—'

'No promises! I don't ask for promises! Just a word of encouragement, of affection, just a word, you know.'

'Even that would be unfair. I couldn't do it.'

Tom shut his eyes and gave a sound like a stifled cry. He said, 'No. No, of course not,' and then he opened his eyes and smiled and said, 'I shall fetch you something to eat. You must be very hungry.'

Archie said too heartily, 'I am afraid so, sir. I always am you know.'

'Stay,' Grace said to him sternly from her pillow. 'Don't leave me. Stay.'

Tom stood up and remained for a while looking down at her. 'Only jungle fever,' he said after a moment, 'that's all.'

'You should see Winser,' Archie said, 'straining at the leash to be off in the forests and he was like this only a few days ago.'

'Yes,' Tom said, 'yes.'

When he had gone, Archie looked down to find Grace staring at him intently. He smiled.

She said earnestly, 'You must send Maria away. You will, won't you?'

Grace died before dawn the following day. She died in her father's arms quite silently while Archie slept on a cotton quilt on the floor of the living room. The fever had climbed steadily all the previous evening and her room had become an inferno of darkness, and pain and wild cries. Several times Archie felt ready to promise anything if only the delirium would calm, but he doubted, even in the most frenzied moments, that he possessed any magic potion in any case. Tom knelt and gazed at Grace and shot Archie glances of terrifying beseechingness. After midnight the fever suddenly seemed to subside and Tom sent Archie for a few hours' rest, promising he would call if he needed help. When Archie had gone, he put his arms about Grace and she lay so tranquilly in them, so limp and quiet and still, that she must have been dead some time before he observed it. Even then he could not release her at once but continued to cradle her and gaze down at her, devastated by such a sense of absolute desolation and abandonment that he wondered if he himself were still alive.

He could not speak to Archie, he could only touch and point. He let himself be led to a chair and be fed sips of sweetened tea as if he were an invalid. He heard Archie's voice in other parts of the mission, and then cries and wailings and after a long time in which his thoughts stumbled helplessly about in no direction at all, Archie saying, 'I'm awfully sorry, sir, but I don't think all the servants will stay. I've tried to persuade them but they say there will be ghosts now. It isn't more than three or four but they are packing now—'

'Christians,' Tom said softly. 'I taught them to love Christ.'

'Can I get you anything? They are preparing breakfast.'

'No. Nothing. Absolutely nothing. Nothing, nothing at all—'

'Could you sleep? You should you know, you have been up for nights.'

'I want to sleep,' Tom said a little petulantly, 'I want to—'

Archie put pillows behind his head. 'Don't worry about anything. I will arrange it. I will see to things.'

'But you are going! To the forests. You must, you said so.'

'A day or so will make no difference. Please lie still.'

Tom caught Archie's hand. 'She knew how to love, Archie. She knew about people. I wonder – I begin to wonder – if I know nothing, if my idea of love bears no relation to humankind at all—'

Gently, Archie freed his hand. 'Don't think about it. Not now, just sleep.'

Tom watched him leave the room, his clothes like rags after the ordeal of being slept in. He wanted to call him back, to see that tired, kind young face turned towards him again, to ask if he, Archie, thought that perhaps this was not the end but the beginning after all, that the lessons of this world were the only ones that really schooled you for divine service, that heaven was in fact bought on earth. He said, very faintly, 'Archie,' but he said it to empty air.

He woke to find oblongs of midday sunlight on the floorboards at his feet since the double doors had not been shuttered while he slept. He turned his head a little in the first bewilderment of waking, then remembered Grace in an onrush of wretchedness and saw that Maria Beresford was sitting near him, watching him with an expression of uncharacteristic uncertainty.

'Mr Prior, I hope I did not wake you.'

He struggled free of his pillows. 'No, not at all. I have slept for several hours.'

'I have watched you the last one,' she said surprisingly. 'The news was brought to me at breakfast. I postponed my visit to the palace.'

He inclined his head in silence.

'You are very good to come so soon,' he said after a while.

She spread her hands.

'I can think of nothing else I can do. If I could, I would do it. Sitting here is of no use to you, I know, but I do not know how else to show you what I feel.'

He smiled at her. 'It does me a great deal of good to see you here, to hear you speak so.'

Maria said, 'I was not always – gracious to your daughter. We did not have sympathetic temperaments I think, but that is no excuse. I know – I know—' she stopped, and then said in a great rush. 'I know what you have lost.'

Tom leaned forward. 'I think I hardly know myself yet. But I value your sympathy and your courage immeasurably.'

She snorted. 'Courage! Courage is of no value. It only means you have not the imagination to fear the right things.'

Tom rubbed his hands over his forehead tiredly. 'No, my dear, no. Courage is most assuredly not that. Courage is seeing what there is to fear and going on bravely all the same.'

'That is real courage. Your kind of courage.' He heard her catch her breath a little. She said, 'Mr Tennant!' and Archie came into the room with a tray of toast and fruit which he put beside Tom.

'The servants would have brought it—'

'They are busy,' Archie said awkwardly, averting his thoughts as best he could from the deft activity in Grace's bedroom.

'Then I am not the first caller,' Maria said.

'Yes, you are, Miss Beresford. I was here all night.' He indicated his clothes. 'As is all too evident.'

'Did you send the message to me this morning, Mr Tennant?'

'Yes,' he said.

She looked at him for a long moment with her

wonderful directness and then she said, 'Thank you.'

'Eat,' Archie urged Tom, 'just a little.'

Maria rose. 'I believe you go into the forests any day, Mr Tennant?'

'Yes,' he said, 'as soon as—'

'You should go,' she said. 'Life must go on. If there is any help of any kind that Mr Prior needs, I shall be happy to give it. More than that, it would be a kind – a kind of relief. That is, if you will let me help.'

Tom rose also and held out his hands to her. 'Whenever you wish, my dear Miss Beresford. Any hour, any time.'

Maria held out her hand to Archie. 'And we shall look forward to seeing you back in Mandalay in the spring, Mr Tennant.'

He wanted to hold her hand a moment longer but she disengaged herself firmly. Then, without looking back, she went, head high, down the verandah steps to the bullock cart waiting in the lane.

PART THREE

14

Isolation, Archie discovered, had little to do with merely being on one's own. Before two months in the forest were out, he could feel a sense of the most piercing – and exhilarating – isolation in the midst of a clearing full of trampling elephants and shouting *mahouts*, a knowledge as sharp as a physical sensation of his aloneness, his alienation from the dank forest trails and the huge beasts and brown men who worked them. It was a knowledge he relished, just as much as he relished being beholden to no-one, expected to conform to no social rules, and it had come upon him almost the day Frederick Winser had left him to his own devices.

'Pretty uncomplicated, your duties,' Frederick had said their first night in the chill darkness of the forests. 'The elephant men will show you how to work the timber. We work from them, they work from their forefathers. Your main responsibility will be the transport and safeguarding of all those damned silver rupees. You give each forester an advance and pay him off finally at the end of the season. The negotiation of the advance is up to you and, I'll tell you, bad debts are not looked kindly upon by the company. In the morning I'll show you which trees to select for girdling.'

Waking to his first forest morning had been unforgettable. The mutterings of darkness had given way to a rowdy bright green world full of movement and chatter, and in the bamboo clump only feet from his tent door a group of pigeons with backs the colour of jade sat droning companionably. They breakfasted under a handy acacia tree, Frederick more absorbed in maps than food, and then set off down a series of, to Archie, eerie and indistinguishable trails towards the faint cries and shouts that led them to the elephant men.

That day he watched trees being selected and girdled. And the next and the next. Day after day, acre after acre, until teak trunks danced in his sleep like a vision of eternity, he watched the long saw cut being made deep into the heartwood of the tree, girdling it entirely, to stop the circulation of the sap.

'Dries it out,' Frederick said, 'In a couple of years. Not only makes it lighter for the elephants but a dead tree will float. Living ones sink.'

After two weeks he was marking trees of his own accord; after three, standing on the river bank, he could see that measuring by eye was going to be a rapidly acquired accomplishment. After four, Frederick left him, to chart new land to the east.

With Frederick went all chance to speak

English except for the limited amount possible with Ah Chun. To Hnin Si, who had made herself an inconspicuous part of his baggage without any direct request on his part that she should do so, he spoke French; to the *mahouts* he attempted stumbling sentences in Burmese. He had a group of thirty-nine in his charge, thirty-nine working elephants, thirty-nine men and seven elephant calves. The advances he had to pay them had been settled by Frederick before he left, and the store of silver coins necessary for the final payment at the end of the dry season was the only thing that weighed at all heavily upon his mind. He was reduced to carrying a good deal of it about with him on the elephant that became as familiar a mount to him as horses had once been.

Time took on a different, more elastic dimension. Days were spent in swaying elephant rides to reach particular clearings and, if night overtook him, he slept tentless on a groundsheet under a dense rug to protect him from the dew that fell as thick as snow in the cold forest nights. If he was in camp, Ah Chun cooked for him with pointless punctuality; if he were not, he hardly seemed to notice hunger for the first time in his life. His day was measured by the chattering brilliance of early morning, the thick and stifling heat of midday, where mud and dust vied with each other for supremacy, and the cold sudden nightfalls lit by the flames of his camp fire.

Ah Chun roused him at daybreak to shout

hoarsely for the *mahouts*. Invariably one or two were missing – the excuses Archie neither understood, nor cared much about. In his green and strange kingdom his concern, apart from a perpetual and fascinated examination of his own state of mind, was to get a sufficient number of good trees girdled and the required number of logs, carefully selected and measured, dragged to the river banks and lowered into the water on the first stage of the journey to Rangoon.

'Forest officers,' Frederick had said in parting. 'Loneliest fellows in Asia.'

If he was lonely, he hardly felt it as such. Monotony had not eaten into him; he only felt the days to have a seductive and languorous rhythm. The evenings were long it was true, with little to fill them but the solitary gulping of Ah Chun's curry and then reading or mapwork by the dim yellow glow of the oil lamp, but sleep came swiftly and heavily to him, speeded on by Hnin Si's fingers soothing his neck and shoulders into perfect relaxation. She was there each night he was in camp, kneeling waiting for him in the darkness, small and strong and amenable. Every so often he gave her money which she took with perfect composure.

One night about the turn of the year, he said to her, 'And what will you do in the spring? Will you go back to the cigar factory?'

'No,' she said, 'I stay with you, *thakin*.'

'Suppose – suppose we tire of each other—'

She glanced at him calmly. She was kneeling

beside him, smooth and pale brown, no bigger than a tall child.

'Then I stay with Ah Chun,' she said, 'for you are, as he told me, a good master,' and Archie saw, as he supposed he had always suspected, that she was Ah Chun's mistress too, perhaps even, in the Burmese sense, his wife. He put his hand on her shoulder.

'Ah Chun by day, me by night.'

'You always, if you order it.'

He laughed. He was astounded to find how little he was outraged. He said aloud, thoughtfully, 'Do you suppose I have no pride?'

She did not understand him.

He turned to look at her. 'I should beat you for sleeping with another man.'

'If you please. But that I only do when you are not in need of me. If you need me I am ready. Ah Chun also.'

A sudden unattractive and grimy image of rooms in the Jericho slums of Oxford rose before him. He rolled away from Hnin Si and lay staring at the rough walls of his hut.

'You are angry, *thakin*?'

'No,' he said, suddenly tired.

'You are weary of always the elephants.'

'No,' he said, again, 'not that, something I can't explain to you.'

'I go?'

He did not want her to go to Ah Chun. He said, 'Stay until I sleep,' and before he slept, while her fingers moved round and round the muscles at the base of his neck, he saw Maria in his mind's eye, as clearly as if she were before him, saying, 'I do not seem to feel sure of anything up here, I seem to feel almost another person,' and he thought that's how I am too, really, here in the forest. I wonder where I have got to? Then he plunged into sleep and in his dreams Hnin Si followed him among the teak trees, flitting persistently behind him, from one to another, beseeching, 'I don't please you, *thakin*? I don't please you?' and because it was a dream, he didn't care about it at all one way or the other.

After that, things changed a little, not so much in themselves but more in the emphasis he put upon them. The long repetitive days in the forests became each a separate and comparable challenge – a certain number and standard of trees to be marked and dragged, a tightening of discipline among the *mahouts* – and the dream world of the nights, the fantasies he wove in the darkness, became a luxury he treasured and longed for. The half-dream, half-reality of Hnin Si – half-dream to Archie because nothing in his upbringing had led him to suppose one could possess a girl for one's pleasure so simply – lost the astounding enchantment of the early weeks. She became for him one of the few comforts of his life in the forest, but without the romance she had first filled him with. He pondered for a long time on his feelings for her after her revelation of her relationship to Ah Chun and was forced to admit that he could not, deep down, resent Ah Chun being either Burmese or a servant but merely another man. A small, smooth-skinned, almost, to Western eyes, girlish-looking man, but a man none the less. Archie saw that he had seen in Hnin Si an image of submissive devotion that was entirely of his own romantic making; the master–slave relationship had seduced him as much as the girl herself. She, on the other hand, had been entirely practical throughout and he must now imitate her.

So his dreams took over. He worked harder, physically, than he had ever worked in his life, often, if away from camp, spending thirty-six hours in the same sweat-soaked collarless shirt. He had always, because they were so universally the fashion, spurned either moustache or beard, but now he let both grow luxuriantly. If Ah Chun had not fallen upon his hair and nails with such vigour, he would, by January, have been a veritable old man of the woods. He wished he had brought more books with him – the Gibbon he had instructed Ah Chun to pack in a sort of romantic ambitiousness had already been re-duced to pulp by the forest damps – for there was a limit to the amount of re-reading he could do. Dreaming, on the other hand, he could always repeat, even embellish, and the long monotonous miles on elephant back, or evenings when the tedium of a day prevented him from sleeping with his customary suddenness, he beguiled with fantasies. Fantasies of Mandalay and the gilded palace and the hidden royal couple, no bigger than his own servants but dressed and jewelled like idols exuding their irresistible power, their barbaric and beastly charm; fantasies of his imagined influence with them, his exposure of that tawdry collection of gambling Europeans who clawed at the coat tails of the palace; fantasies of his achieving a second Tennant Phillipson, a teak company to rival the Bombay-Burmah, born out of his unique relationship with Thibaw and Supayalat, the French wiped out of Burma, as well as the Greeks and the Italians and the Germans, Burma British throughout perhaps, with Thibaw a puppet king . . . Sometimes the fantasies even involved Maria, though hardly in a clearly defined role. Her ability to be both admirable and despicable, alluring and repellent, provided splendid fuel for his imagination. He scarcely knew her, yet he told himself he knew a great deal about her. Her image remained more clearly upon his mind's eye than any other and the fleeting look of beseeching that he had caught on her face once in Maymyo, once in the mission, remained powerfully with him and worked upon his romantic self just as Hnin Si had done, quite unconsciously, when she first led him to bed in Mandalay.

A month before the rains began, an elephant went berserk. It was a cow elephant in the early stages of pregnancy whose previous calf had been born dead, Archie was told, and she suddenly cast aside the log she was carrying – the twentieth such log she had moved impeccably that day – crushing the near forefoot of the elephant working beside her, scraped her *mahout* off savagely against a tree and turned, bellowing and trampling, upon the team behind her.

Archie was perhaps two hundred yards away. It sounded to him as if the world were being torn apart. Men came tearing through the undergrowth towards him, screaming in panic, clutching at his arms and hands, and then he saw the beast, among the trees, flailing and trumpeting like some monstrous machine of destruction. His rifle was strapped to his own elephant who, though normally as docile as a lamb, was displaying distinct and understandable signs of unease, shifting and grunting, swinging its great head. He shouted to the *mahout* to make it kneel.

Behind him the din was fearful. The maddened elephant was going round and round in circles while before her trees crashed and splintered and the terrified *mahouts* tried to urge their own beasts out of her path.

'Boy's adventure book,' Archie said in English to the *mahout*. 'Schoolboy hero stuff.'

The *mahout* said the *thakin* did not make himself plain.

'I am not trying to. I am keeping my own courage up.' He said in Burmese, 'Will the elephant go close?'

'No,' the *mahout* said, 'no!'

The rifle was slippery in his sweating hands

313

and he was glad there were no witnesses of his shaky loading of it.

'Send my belongings to my mother,' he said to the *mahout*, smiling. 'In England it is customary.'

The *mahout* said that if the *thakin* wished to give orders he must do so not in English.

'No orders,' Archie said. 'But I shall tell you, in English, how terrified I am because you won't understand me but it will relieve my own feelings.'

He grasped the rifle and began to walk away. The *mahout* shouted. Ahead of him, he could make out very little. Which elephant was which? It was madness to be on foot, he was bound to be crushed, but at this moment he could see no other form of mobility that was any use—

The frantic elephant whirled into view. He raised his rifle, took clumsy aim, fired and missed her. The scream that rose from the clearing was deafening. He pinned himself against a tree and swore. Twenty yards away a huddled body lay in the undergrowth and an elephant calf with a raw wound in one leg in which splinters of bone gleamed like teeth was circling wretchedly round and round, howling, on three legs. All round the clearing, shouts and bellowings echoed from among the denser clumps of trees, and occasionally a high wild scream charted the progress of the demented elephant.

He dared not move. He waited perhaps ten minutes before she appeared again and this time managed to graze her in the shoulder, enough to halt her in her charge. She swung round towards him, blood streaming from her where she had dashed herself into trees and he raised his rifle, shaking so hard he could hear the rhythm of his teeth chattering and echoing in his skull, and fired, blind and wild, hitting her in the base of her throat. She sank, huge and flailing, to her knees and then, like a ship tilting into the sea, heaved over onto her vast grey side. In the ecstasy of mingled relief and misery at not having acted sooner, Archie fired twice into her skull.

She had maimed seven elephants and two men lay dead, one her own *mahout*. Nobody would work further that day. Back in camp that night, Archie met Ah Chun in a highly excited state for dacoits had, for the first time that winter, set upon the camp and, though they had stolen nothing, the boy whom Ah Chun had used as his own servant in the kitchen had been taken with them and all Archie's possessions had been thrown about in search of valuables. Hnin Si had been washing her hair in a nearby stream or she would undoubtedly have been raped.

Archie slept badly, for the first time in the forest. What recompense – if any – the corporation made to the elephant men customarily he did not know, but if he was to return next winter, he felt some kind of payment must be made before he struggled back to Mandalay. One thing was certain and that was that in the weeks to come neither rupees nor rifle should leave his side for a moment. When Ah Chun came to him at dawn as was his custom, he brought the news that another of the elephants, one not involved in yesterday's catastrophe, had anthrax.

'I suppose,' Archie said, 'that this is really what I came for.'

Ah Chun performed the sketchy shiko from which he always contrived to eliminate all respect.

'*Thakin*,' he said, 'that is so.'

15

No-one told Maria of Bonvilain's return. She had taken to spending far more time in the palace than before, though the din of the ceaseless *pwes*, the gongs and the singing and the drums, made it a far from peaceful place to be. Noisy though it was, far changed though it was from the first day when Maria had seen the gardens full of waterfalls and birds and children and the pretty little maids of honour in their rainbow silks, something held Maria to it, something quite as powerful as Supayalat herself. Fear had always been part of life in Mandalay, inseparable from the unpredictability of any way of life that hung upon savage royal whim, but that fear now seemed to stalk visibly in the palace itself, seemed to pursue even the King and Queen, so that Maria, to whom fear was largely a hysterical ailment only indulged in by those with nothing better to do, even she felt that the sands were stirring uncomfortably beneath her feet and she was reluctant to be away too long, afraid only of missing something vital.

People were dying in the palace, and being violently dismissed. Favourites, like vulgar little Hosannah Manook summoned back from

Rangoon to teach the court photography, was thrown out summarily with screams.

'A traitor!' Supayalat howled. 'A traitor! A *kalā* who cares nothing for us! If I think you have betrayed me I shall get permission from Calcutta, from the Governor General, to kill you, kill you!'

Thibaw's old mother died from blood poisoning in a welter of extravagant accusations. She had taken a lover, Supayalat insisted, a young lover from among her own attendants, she should die alone, like a dog; no-one should wait upon her.

'And you!' the Queen cried to Maria. 'You! Do you have a lover?'

Maria drew herself up, her court manners swamped by outrage.

'Naturally not.'

The Queen laughed and clapped her hands.

'You!' she said. 'You! If all the English were like you, perhaps we could not drive them out so easily.'

'*Ashin-nammadaw-paya*,' Maria said, using the formal court manner of addressing the Queen. '*Have* you driven all the English out?'

Supayalat leaned forward, her small face as flickering as a snake's. 'Not all, but soon will be all. Soon. If a bird has a wing long enough ready to fly, cut the wing. Cut it! There shall be no power here but our power. The English shall fear us.'

'And after the English? What then?'

'Ah!' Supayalat smiled. 'Ah! After them a great

Burmese nation where the only *kalās* will work for us, bow to us, bring tribute to us.' Her brow darkened suddenly and, snatching off her slipper, she hurled it across the room to catch the cheek of one of the young Shan maids in the King's service. It was a commonplace. Thibaw's glance had only to rest upon a pretty face for more than a moment for the Queen to take revenge. She stood up.

'Traitors!' she shrieked, 'All traitors! All traitors will die—'

Thibaw, from his couch, gestured feebly. Supayalat ran towards him, seating herself beside him, taking his hand and stroking and crooning over it.

'You make all people fear you,' she insisted to him. 'All those who would betray you are in fear of their lives, their lives—'

For such scenes, Maria stayed. In any case, nothing held her now at home. Hubert had withdrawn from her to such an extent that she felt her presence at meals was only to satisfy her own sense of propriety, not for his pleasure at all. The dull and leaden ache of misery with which his behaviour left her she dealt with by hardening herself to it, surmounting it, subduing it with the imperiousness with which all her life she had crushed all things she did not understand or like. He smiled at her absently at meals sometimes and she returned his smiles, but her own were more the carefully contrived ones she had once given to Horace Browne, to Murray Shaw, not the spontaneous expressions of love. Once, and only once, she had caught Hubert's sleeve as he left her drawing room and had said in a voice of pleading which sounded as strange to her as if it had belonged to someone else, 'Papa – dearest Papa – why have I displeased you so?'

And he, gazing down at her with the mild, indolent, withdrawn look that was now habitual with him, took his sleeve away gently and replied, 'I do not understand you, my dear. I do not understand you at all. When has such a word as displeasure had any significance between us?'

And for a moment her heart had leaped up and she lifted her face smiling for him to kiss, but he had stared blankly down at her as if that proffered cheek were nothing to him at all, nothing, and then he had bowed a little and smiled and had left the room.

After that, she had taken her cue from him. She knew that his days were spent chiefly among the halls of audience in the palace and that his nights – unnaturally long nights which engulfed most evenings as well – were passed behind the closed door of his bedroom. Their conversation was mostly palace gossip of an entirely trivial kind, since Maria did not feel she could convey the unease that filled her days with Supayalat to a father whose responses to her had dwindled to those of a courteous stranger. So when Bonvilain came back, although Andreino, because he knew most things, knew of his arrival, and so did Denzil Blount and Hubert and the rival engineers who had squatted on the palace floors all the months of the Frenchman's absence, hoping to advance themselves behind his back, Maria knew nothing. She went into the palace as she had always done, to assist at the ritual dressing of the morning, and left it, as she had become accustomed to do, after the ritual dressing of the evening, before the King and the Queen processed in their diamonds and gold-shot silks to the ceaseless din of the royal theatre. Then Maria returned, dressed for dinner, ate it more or less in silence across the table from Hubert, and withdrew to the lamplit solitude of her drawing room while he, after a short ceremony with a cigar, went to his room.

Without Mattie Calogreedy, her ignorance might have been extended from days into weeks. Mattie had lived all the period of Bonvilain's absence in the security of her own conviction that he would return, rich enough on account of the concession to work Mogok to defy his parents and marry her. He had told her, she confided to an uncaring Maria as they jolted into the palace, that in his country, in France, a man might not marry without parental consent before he was twenty-five. Well, she had pouted, soon he would be rich enough to cock a snook at parents and in any case, he and she were married already. This notion, this peasant belief that cohabitation made a marriage, seemed to Maria no less than one would expect of the Burmese. She drew her skirts away from Mattie Calogreedy in distaste. What the Queen saw in her could not be imagined but there she was, European maid of honour, though she was getting so plump, so coarse, that she lolled about in Burmese dress mostly now, presumably to avoid the discomfort and discipline of corsets. Bonvilain had sent Mattie a dress from Paris and Mattie had offered to show it to Maria who, burning to see it, had laughed and said she thought it would hardly be to her taste.

Mattie, who had shown surprising resilience to Maria's disagreeableness throughout the five years of their acquaintance, had suddenly looked crestfallen, more than that, almost wounded at Maria's scorn of her Paris dress. She had not the capacity to see that to have a bourgeois Frenchman as a lover was, in Maria's eyes, beneath contempt, and so she was dismayed and disconcerted at Maria's refusal and put the dress away in the room she used in the palace and said no more about it. It was such a forgotten subject that when she came stumbling into Maria's house late one afternoon, dressed in a profoundly unbecoming European dress which strained hideously over her plumpness and was unforgivably blotched with sweat, Maria did not at first recognize her.

'He is married!' she wailed, her hat awry over one eye. 'Married! He has brought back a French wife to whom he has given a ring! He never gave me a ring – She is a pale little thing, I saw her, but he was so stern with me, he said I should never have expected marriage—'

She fell into one of Maria's French chairs and burst into noisy tears.

Maria said, standing quite still in the doorway onto the verandah, 'Then Monsieur Bonvilain is back in Mandalay?'

Mattie screamed, 'Married! Married! He is married!' and rocked herself about.

'I know,' Maria said.

'He promised.' Mattie sobbed, not listening. 'He promised me! I was his wife, he my husband, he cannot leave me, he cannot! He must be making a joke—'

'No,' Maria said, 'no. European men marry their own kind. You must know that.'

'I am half-Greek,' Mattie said, rolling her handkerchief into a damp ball. 'Half-Greek. And my mother has light skin, very light. Oh, speak to him for me, Miss Beresford, speak to him, I implore you, I beg you, speak to him!'

Maria said nothing but looked out into the heavy gold and green of the garden, gold and green soon to be deluged with the rains, those awful ceaseless rains.

Behind her Mattie said, in tears again, 'I believed him, Miss Beresford, I believed him. I believed his promises. What shall I do without him, oh, whatever, *ever* shall I do?'

Maria did not mean to be touched. Mattie was so absurd, ugly even, with her grief-mottled face and her hair coming down, her body straining away at the dress like too much sausage inside a too tight skin, and her dreadful peasant credulity and vulnerability. Almost against her will, Maria moved to sit opposite her, to hold out a clean, dry handkerchief, to say, 'There is nothing I can do. If speaking to him would help you, I would do it. But it will not. You must make your life in the palace now. You must not have dreams of Europe, you must turn your back on them.'

Mattie looked back at her for a moment, submissive and subdued. Then her face contorted and she screamed, 'He will pay for it! He will, he will! And so shall you all, all you *kalās*, all you people who take what you want, using us as your slaves, your toys!' She got up hastily, gathering up her bag, her gloves, her parasol, jumbled in her arms like a carelessly held baby. 'He had his pleasure with me, he thought he could take, take, take and not give. I will show him! I will teach him! I am not a mistress. I am a wife! His wife! He will live to regret treating me as a woman of the street. You'll see, you'll see!'

At dinner that night Maria attempted to be particularly charming and animated so that she might have a hope of a full response to her question when the moment came to put it.

'And Papa! Guess what happened today! I heard – quite by chance – that Pierre Bonvilain has returned!'

Hubert said easily, 'Oh yes. Yes, I do believe that he has.'

'I heard it from Mattie Calogreedy. She was dreadfully distressed because she believed he meant to marry her and then, of course, to go down to the bund and meet him off the steamer today and find that he had brought a wife, well, that, even for her—'

'Oh, not today,' Hubert said calmly, laying down his fruit knife. 'His steamer did not come today. He arrived a week ago, a week ago precisely. With the mails.'

Maria held the edge of the table. 'A week ago? A *week*? And you knew and said nothing of it to me?'

Hubert rose. 'No, my dear,' he said and smiled down at her, 'No. Nothing at all. After all of what possible interest to you could Monsieur Bonvilain's return be?'

He turned and was about to leave the room, but she rose rapidly and hurried after him, reaching his side just as the doors began to open for him.

'Papa! Papa, what can you mean? Of no interest to me? Who told the Queen of Mogok, who showed her all the plans, who gained the chance of the concession almost alone? Do you know what you are saying?'

'Perfectly,' Hubert said, still smiling. 'And we are very grateful to you for the charming manner in which you have interested the Queen in our project but, my dear, things must now – as I am sure you see yourself – go beyond that. It is the affairs of men, my dear Maria. You need trouble yourself about it no more, it is no concern of yours at all,' and then, with a steady determination she could only have broken by casting herself physically in his path, he moved out of the room and, within seconds, she heard the quiet click of his own door closing behind him.

In the morning, before her departure for the palace, Maria wrote a letter to Denzil Blount. She would be glad, she wrote, to see him at teatime, that day, after her return from the palace. It was, she added, quite like old times to have Pierre Bonvilain back in Mandalay and perhaps Denzil would bring him so that she might have the chance of asking what day would be suitable for her to call upon Madame Bonvilain and welcome her to Mandalay.

At the palace, Maria knelt and touched her forehead to the floor. '*Ashin-nammadaw-paya*, the Frenchman has returned.'

'Oh, yes,' Supayalat said, leaning forward for one of her little maids to light her cheroot. 'He brought me carpets, and a looking glass framed in gold lilies, and a camera. A good camera with a tripod. Perhaps you will learn to use it better than that fool Manook.'

Maria took a deep breath. 'And Your Majesty, did you give him what he asked for?'

In the doorway, one of the ministers hovered, the old *Taingda Mingyi*, with his carved merciless face. Supayalat waved her maids away.

'Go, go! Go, all of you. And you!' She gestured at Maria, her free hand held out to the old man. 'Go too! Your Frenchman has his rubies, you have what you wanted. Go!'

In the antechamber the little maids were crouched, whispering. They looked over their shoulders at Maria but did not beckon her to join them. She stood by one of the long openings that served both for window and door and looked out at the empty palace platform, the deserted gardens, the shining tin roofs between their wings of red and gold, and heard the wailing throbbing of the music of the *pwes* pulsing from the theatre. Her sleeve was plucked. The girl at whom Supayalat had thrown her slipper stood looking up at her.

'We wish to know, because you are so much in the confidence of the *Ashin-nammadaw-paya*, if the *Taingda Mingyi* has often had audience just recently?'

'Yes,' Maria said, thinking of nothing much but her own bewildering position. 'Yes. Every day that Her Majesty has been in the pavilion by the waterfall. He comes to her there.'

'And you hear them?' the maid said, scarcely audibly while the others crept closer. 'You hear what they say?'

'Naturally I wait outside the pavilion. Her Majesty has assured me that their conversations concern solely the best interests of the King.'

Supayalat was closeted with the *Taingda Mingyi* for above an hour and afterwards was remote and thoughtful, smoking furiously and spinning the diamond bracelets on her wrist in a glittering circle of white fire. She spoke to no-one, not even to Maria, and the King kept to his own rooms and came nowhere near her. Her dinner was brought in in the customary jewelled lacquer urns, and she pushed the curry and rice about her plate for a while but ate nothing, merely smoked and drank water, glass after glass, her eyes fixed upon the view outside but not seeing it, seeing nothing.

Maria was afraid to leave her, but afraid, too, of not being at home. She ordered the bullock driver to go quickly and arrived at home shaken almost to pieces and smothered in dust. Within twenty minutes, changed and outwardly composed, she was waiting in the drawing room with tea, as was her custom, at her elbow. For two hours she waited, while the light thickened and the coppersmith bird beat out his relentless knocking and then a message was brought from Denzil saying how much he regretted being unable to come. Another day perhaps, when Madame Bonvilain was over the fatigues of the journey . . .

Hubert did not appear at dinner. Long after midnight, wakeful and restless, she heard his steps pass her door without pausing and go on down the verandah to his own room. I will go to Tom Prior, she thought, I will go and ask him what I have done, what is happening. I will tell him what I have seen in the palace. And then she thought, I cannot, I cannot tell him, I cannot tell anyone that I am afraid of failing. And he would not know what is going on, he would not care about the palace. The only thing he would understand about is my – my losing Papa and that I do not want to admit to anyone, anyone at all.

When Denzil finally came, he found Maria unprepared for him and he brought Bonvilain and his wife. Marie-Thérèse Bonvilain was slight and blonde, dressed in dove-grey silk. She had perfect poise and eyes for no-one in the room but her husband.

Maria said to Bonvilain, dispensing tea as she spoke, 'And France? Did you amuse yourself well in France?'

'Admirably,' he said, smiling at her and then with an intimacy which exasperated her, at his wife.

'And profitably too, I trust,' she said directly to him, her eyes fixed upon him.

He grimaced faintly at his wife. 'We have promised not to speak of that, heh? A weekend of wickedness at Deauville, Mademoiselle, among bachelor friends was not, as my wife will tell you, profitable in any way. *Les diamants, chérie*,' he said to his wife. 'Show Miss Beresford your ring.'

Marie-Thérèse held out an impeccably kept pale hand and displayed a marquise of diamonds of an impressive size.

Maria said coldly, 'Charming.' She looked across at Denzil. 'And you seem to have been much occupied of late, Mr Blount,' she said. 'I have not seen you in weeks.'

'Times change, my dear Maria. And so do habits. I cannot always do what once I did. But I know you are well. I have seen your equipage going in and out of the palace with a punctuality that would do credit to a railway timetable.'

Maria said as lightly as she could, 'You have seen me but have not seen fit to speak.'

He laughed and shrugged. 'My dear, you know how it is in such communities as ours. So little happens there is so little to say. We amuse each other far better if we see as little of each other as we can. Think how much you saw of Grace Prior when she was alive!'

Maria fought back sudden hot tears that sprang to her eyes. Head high, she said with an attempt at playfulness, 'Since, by your own account, this is the last I shall see of you for some while, I must make the most of it. Tell me how plans for Mogok are going.'

Bonvilain stretched out his long legs and took his wife's right hand. 'Well enough, I think, to promise *ma chère femme* – and you also, Miss Beresford – a companion ring for this charming but unadorned hand.' He kissed it and smiled, replacing it in her lap. 'Do you know, Miss Beresford, that this bad little girl of mine says she does not care for rubies?'

There were, as was her habit, rubies in Maria's ears and round her neck and wrists. She said to Denzil, ignoring Bonvilain, 'I don't wish to speak of jewels. I wish to speak of the concession, the concession to work Mogok. Do we have it? There are rumours in the palace, but I wish to know what the facts are—'

'Madame,' Denzil said to Marie-Thérèse across Maria, 'Madame, Englishwomen are intrepid beyond belief. I should not be at all surprised to see Miss Beresford mine a ruby for herself. Indeed, I almost had to prevent her forcibly, once, from plunging into the earth's depths to see for herself. I am sure you have heard what a favourite she is in the palace, and to spend much time around the Queen requires one to be very intrepid indeed.'

Madame Bonvilain smiled, showing perfect teeth, and resumed her contemplation of her husband. He said, 'What news from the palace, Miss Beresford? There are rumours that all those political prisoners they have confined down there, beneath the palace, are plotting against the King. But you, naturally, would know more of this than anyone else in Mandalay.'

'And equally naturally,' she said to him in revenge, 'I should tell you nothing I see or hear in confidence. Any information I may have I regard as my own.'

Denzil said quietly, 'In that case, my dear Maria, we understand each other perfectly.' He rose. 'We should detain Miss Beresford no longer—'

A step sounded on the verandah. Hubert came in, perfectly composed, kissed Madame Bonvilain's hand, with the appearance of having done so already several times, nodded cordially to the two men and brushed Maria's cheek lightly with his own.

He said to Marie-Thérèse, 'How good of you to call so soon upon my daughter. I know she wished to call upon you first, but pressing engagements at the palace take up so much of her time. There is a terrible noise up at the palace tonight; the *pwes* have become quite deafening.'

'We were just leaving,' Denzil said, his eyes upon Maria. She turned her head away and looked out into the garden.

'Let me come with you,' Hubert said. 'Let me take you down to the lane at least.' He offered his arm to Marie-Thérèse. 'How charming you look. My daughter's hair was as blonde as yours, you know, when she was a child—'

In the doorway Pierre and Denzil turned to bow farewell.

'It was delightful to see you,' Pierre said, smiling. 'I should have been disappointed to find you any less stern or beautiful. It would quite have changed Mandalay for me.'

She bowed. 'My congratulations on your marriage, Monsieur.'

Denzil said, 'Goodbye, my dear.' He paused a little and then said, 'When next you construct yourself a bed, my dear Maria, you must use your considerable intelligence to reflect upon the fact that one day you must lie upon it.'

She did not even incline her head to acknowledge that she had heard him.

That night in the palace a massacre took place, a far more savage massacre than that of five years

332

before. On the orders of the *Taingda Mingyi*, himself acting upon instructions from the Queen, the prisoners in their unspeakable pits below the palace had been told that they had a chance to escape, that their irons would be struck off. Disguises were left for them in their cells, words of encouragement that the plan came directly from the exiled princes who were poised to over-throw the King and his all-powerful Queen were passed to them from their gaolers, posing as allies. And then, as they struggled, dazed with weakness and hope, into the clothes provided for them, the prisons were set on fire and became at once an inferno of panic. Those who were not trapped to die in the flames fought their way out of the blazing holes to be hacked to death as they took their first breaths of free air.

The King, cringing in a corner of the palace, his head buried against his Queen in an agony of terror and horror, begged that no enemy should be left alive, that the insurrection in the prisons should be quelled, that all those who opposed him and had striven to rise up against him be-neath his own palace should be killed, every one. In silence Maria and Hubert stood on their verandah while flames and screams tore across the hot black sky and the throbbing of the *pwes* from the royal theatre went on and on, on and on.

In the morning, Maria set out as usual for the palace and, as usual, made her way towards the western gate, the only gateway to the city permitted to foreigners, because of its ill-omened associations with death. On that brilliant morning, she found the ground beyond the moat by the western gate was choked with bodies, pile upon pile of hideously mutilated corpses, between two and three hundred of them, men, women and children, naked and pitiful in the merciless light. The stench that rose from these butchered bodies was beyond description.

'Let them lie,' Thibaw had cried, his eyes hidden against his Queen. 'Let them lie unburied! Let all men see what a thing it is to offend the King.'

Convulsed with nausea, shaking and retching, Maria ordered the bullock cart turned about and made her way blindly home.

16

'And now,' Andreino said, 'now that you are rested, there is much to tell you. Much.'

'I might have been on the moon,' Archie said musingly, his legs stretched out before him in clean drill trousers whose ironed creases were a source of wonder and delight to him after months of Ah Chun's jungle laundry methods. He pulled his tunic up and slid his hands inside his waistband. 'Look at that. Just take a look, will you? I am inches thinner, *inches*—'

Andreino said, 'It won't last my boy, not if you eat as you have just done.'

Archie closed his eyes. 'It was wonderful. Wonderful. The mutton—'

'Listen to me.'

'I am.'

'Open your eyes. Otherwise you will be dreaming of food. Open them. Ever since you came to Mandalay I am warning you, warning and warning. Now we must do more than keep our eyes open, we must be prepared to take action. People are fleeing over the border into British Burma, hundreds of them, every day. For why? Because the royal purse is empty, the soldiers of the King are not paid so they have taken to the jungle and its laws. They terrorize the villages, they make the roads impassable, they massacre whom they please in the name of Thibaw. And in the royal city things are little better. That villainess of a Queen! She may be clever but she is not clever enough to see that you do not eradicate opposition by massacre. She reigns by terror and that is no secure basis for the future. And now she needs money. Where do you think she will turn?'

'To us?' Archie said. 'To the corporation?'

Andreino flung out his hands. 'To the English, my friend? The *English*? To the nation who shelter the exiled princes of Burma in India, the nation who already possess the lower half of her country? Never! Not in a thousand years, a million. I told you we should watch the French, I told everyone. For years and years I am telling people that they must never take their eyes off the French, never. But the British government and the government of India, they will not look at Burma, they will not regard it as important. What has happened now? Khartoum has fallen, the British are defeated again, your great General Gordon is dead and when I write to the Chief Commissioner in Rangoon and tell him of what the French do here, he says only Khartoum to me, Khartoum, Khartoum—'

Archie said, 'What about the French then?'

Andreino leaned forward, his black eyes fixed on Archie's face. 'I will tell you, my friend. I will tell you. Monsieur Bonvilain – that is a good name, ha? – has returned from Paris where he clung to the Burmese delegation like a shadow, with the concession to work the ruby mines at Mogok. It is a remarkable achievement for an adventurer like Bonvilain. But then, of course, we know who helped him to it.'

'Yes,' Archie said, unwillingly.

'Our handsome Miss Beresford begged for the Queen's favour and got it. And her father will assist in raising the three lakhs of rupees to pay the Burmese government, and Mr Blount will see that the scheme spreads to no-one further.'

Archie said, 'I don't believe Miss Beresford would do such a thing to help the French.'

Andreino smiled. 'Your months of solitude have made you gallant. But you are right also. She interceded with the Queen on behalf of herself and her father for their part in the scheme, just as she once did for the mines at Minhla. I think she did not believe – for she must have known – that Bonvilain might enlist the help of the French Foreign Minister. I tell you, Archie, that Jules Ferry has extracted from the Burmese delegation the right to take over almost every-thing in Mandalay but the throne. The French are to build a railway, found a bank, take charge of the army. And the others, the other *kalās*? My own country is a cauldron of political troubles and cannot spare a moment from Abyssinia for the outside world, and Germany's parliament has declared it no longer supports Bismarck's colonial policy, and the British – the British I told you of. So there is no-one to oppose the French, no-one. They will run arms through Burma to Tonkin, they will pillage the country of her natural resources, they will take the teak and the jewels from beneath our noses. I am afraid my friend, afraid that the Bombay-Burmah are in grave danger of being driven out of the forests. We have only to displease the palace in the smallest degree and pouf! our concession goes. So you see, you have not come back to much of a place. Mandalay is falling apart before our eyes. Sensible people are going to Rangoon. Even, I tell you, even Tom Prior is going down to Rangoon, even he.'

Archie got up and began to pace about the room. 'How is he?'

'He? Tom? Not so good. Something in him has broken, he does not burn with zeal now. He will be better in Rangoon back in the capable hands of Doctor Marks, shown where to go once more.'

Archie said, his back to Andreino. 'I want to see Miss Beresford. I don't understand all this, her connection with Bonvilain. It isn't like her, she is no traitor—'

'No,' Andreino said softly, 'she is an unhappy woman.'

'Her father?'

'Precisely so. Bonvilain is using the father. You will see. When the father has raised the money to pay for the first year's contract, the father will go. He does not know it, but he will. Miss Beresford is not needed already, matters are beyond pleading with the Queen, they involve the French Foreign Minister and the Burmese government these days. Her usefulness has gone. So, I think, has her father's love for her. He only resents her now.'

'What fools,' Archie said, furiously. 'What blind, duped fools.'

'So you agree with me? We must not let the French get away with it?'

'Absolutely not.'

'Then you will help me?'

'Of course. Only tell me how.'

Andreino came to stand close to Archie. 'I need proof, my friend, written proof. I need evidence of French undermining of British influence here, copies of contracts, letters, any reference we can find to the Bombay-Burmah in correspondence between Ferry and Mandalay. You can work upon Hubert Beresford, you can also work upon little Mattie Calogreedy, who has access to all sorts of things in the palace and who is burning for revenge upon Bonvilain.'

'Why are you doing all this? Who for? After all you are an Italian—'

Andreino shrugged. 'The British pay me.'

'And if someone else offered you more?'

Another shrug. 'Perhaps. Perhaps. Who knows? But only I think if that someone else had a chance of final victory. And I don't believe the French have that. They will give us all a bad fright, but I shall do everything in my power to see that that is all they do.'

In the comfortable bungalow that had been secured in the expectation of a French consul arriving shortly in Mandalay, Pierre Bonvilain lounged as Archie had been doing a mile away, his long legs stretched before him and his hands beneath his chin, pressed finger tip to finger tip. Beside him, on a low rattan table, lay a pile of papers weighted with a glimmering lump of ore such as Maria had filled the Chinese bowls in her drawing room with, and his gaze returned with satisfaction time and again to the topmost paper of the pile.

It was a letter, dated a month ago, and the address heavily embossed in the top right-hand corner was the Quai d'Orsay. It was, next to the written concession given to him by the Burmese delegation in Paris to work the Mogok mines – a copy of which, incidentally, he must retrieve from Hubert and that quickly, before Denzil discovered that vainglory had led him to do anything so unwise as to show it off – the most satisfactory and flattering letter of his life. It was, Jules Ferry wrote to him – to him, personally, Pierre Bonvilain by name – of great satisfaction to the French government to hear of his achievements in Burma and in particular his securing of sole rights to mine for rubies in Mogok. It had initially been thought that the money for the venture must be put up by Bonvilain himself on account of the adventurous nature of the scheme, but another complexion had been put upon the matter by the success in securing influential treaties with the Burmese that made France in Burmese eyes, the 'most favoured nation'. In view of this turn of events, Ferry was pleased to tell Monsieur Bonvilain that the necessary three lakhs of rupees would now be guaranteed by the French government and that Monsieur Bonvilain need look to no-one else for assistance.

Pierre smiled beneath the moustache that his Marie-Thérèse was not the first to admire so profoundly. His schemes were turning out far better than he had ever, arriving in Mandalay five years before as a penniless engineer, dreamed of. The Beresfords had been of inestimable use to him and, now that they were becoming a hindrance, he must extricate himself from all connection with them. This was facilitated by the disintegration of their own relationship, and Bonvilain had no doubt that he could in some way insinuate to Hubert that his no longer being necessary as a fund raiser was in some measure due to the impossibility of his daughter's temper nowadays which, coupled with her greed, made her an unpredictable and dangerous partner.

Denzil Blount was rather another matter because there was something in him of which Bonvilain, even in his most self-satisfied and cavalier moments, was a little afraid. Without Denzil, he might still be a penniless engineer and also have been unable to disentangle himself from the Beresfords as painlessly as he seemed to be doing. He resented the prospect of sharing the profits from Mogok with Denzil but, on the other hand, could think of no alternative that did not fill him with distinct alarm. Denzil, caring for nothing but himself, was without a single scruple and Pierre, the new darling of the Quai d'Orsay, found that for the first time in his life he had something to lose that he cared very much about. Things would, there was no doubt, have to remain as they were for the time being. If he antagonized Denzil there was a strong chance that Denzil, in revenge, would reveal to the Bombay-Burmah Trading Corporation the French plans to usurp the concessions to the teak forests, plans that Ferry had entrusted to Bonvilain and which Bonvilain's boastfulness had allowed to escape, just as it had permitted Hubert to see the copy of the concession to work Mogok. If Denzil ever went down in life, he would make sure he brought down as many with him as he could—

'Pierre,' Denzil said from the verandah, 'I received your note. I am delighted the mails brought you good news—'

Bonvilain laughed. A renewed sense of his own invincible success flooded through him and dispelled any doubts. He stood up and put his hands on Denzil's shoulders.

'My good friend, how glad I am to see you. Yes, indeed, I do have good news. Excellent news. Excellent, that is, for you and for myself, but bad I fear, very bad, for Monsieur Beresford.'

Denzil moved away as if he disliked to be touched. 'Am I to understand that your government will finance us?'

'Precisely so.'

'Guaranteed?'

Pierre drew the letter from beneath the lump of ore and handed it to Denzil. 'See for yourself.'

Denzil read it rapidly with intense concentration.

'Well?' Bonvilain said.

'You have done excellently.'

Bonvilain grinned. 'Rare praise—'

'Rarely deserved. But deserved this time.'

'You will inform Hubert?'

Denzil stared. 'I do it? Oh, no, my dear Pierre, not me. As a last task before they withdraw to lick their wounds in Rangoon – and withdraw they must now there is nothing to keep them in Mandalay – I shall ask Miss Beresford to tell her father for me. It will, as I am sure you will agree, be so very much better coming from her.'

Bonvilain began to laugh. 'Villain! My friend, you are a villain!'

'Yes,' Denzil said evenly, 'And don't you ever forget it.'

17

Tom Prior left Mandalay with only Maria Beresford to wave him away. He stood on the bund for a long time before boarding, his battered possessions in an untidy heap at his feet, a heap which seemed to have a life of its own, sliding and shifting and changing contour as if it were trying to adjust its contents more comfortably. Tom had breadcrumbs in his beard, two buttons missing on his coat and, Maria could not help but notice as he stooped absently to caress the dusty head of a nearby child, odd socks. He looked about him at intervals as if he expected someone, as if a ghostly horde of past familiars of Mandalay might come drifting through the trees along the top of the bund – Colonel Browne, Grace, old Manook rubbing his hands – and restore to him the spiritual vigour of his past.

'Andreino—' he said suddenly, 'Signor Andreino—'

Maria looked about her. There was no European in sight, nothing but a chattering and distasteful mass of Burmese. Tom looked at Maria.

'Archie,' he said in deep reproach.

'Perhaps he does not know you are leaving. At least, he does not know it is today.'

Tom lifted his face, screwing his eyes up against the sun. 'You should be coming with me, my dear. You should not be staying. What am I thinking of, going down to safety and allowing you, a woman, to remain here? Go and pack your things at once, at once, don't delay a moment, come with me, come down to Rangoon!'

He clutched her arm and she saw that his eyes were quite glazed with fatigue. 'Maria, come with me, I beg you, come with me, don't stay, don't let me—'

His fingernails digging into the stuff of her sleeve were far from clean and, close to, he emitted a frowsty smell of unwashed clothes. With an effort, she put her own hand on his.

'It would not help you if I came. In your heart you know that. At best I can only be a brief distraction. And I do not want to come. It sometimes seems to me that I have spent five years insisting to one man or another that I am not afraid to stay, that I want to stay.' She paused and took her hand away. 'In any case, I have nowhere else to go.'

'You are wrong, my dear, so wrong. We all, always, have a place to go. We are never alone in this world, never, when we have a Father who loves us in whom we trust—' he shut his eyes again, 'in whom we trust and trust—'

She eyed him sceptically. 'Do we?'

From the river the steamer hooted mournfully.

'You must go aboard, Mr Prior. Where are the mission coolies?'

Tom said, 'I sent them back. I can manage quite well, I have so little, nothing that matters—'

Maria made a sound of impatience. 'Of course you cannot carry your own baggage. It would be unthinkable. I begin to think I should come with you in order to ensure at the very least that you do not disgrace the name of England.' She turned and called sharply. Her own servants, lolling against the wheels of the bullock cart, grinning and spitting red jets of betel juice into the dust, came scampering up the bund. Maria indicated the collapsing canvas mound of Tom's possessions and ordered it aboard.

'I will see you again?' Tom said, his eyes upon her face.

'Of course,' she said briskly.

He looked over his shoulder at the dusty road that led back to Mandalay, back among the dispirited wooden houses of the *kalā* town to the dangerous glitter of the royal palace.

'The City of Gems.'

Maria touched her ears. 'So it seems.'

'Goodbye, my dear.'

Their hands touched. His eyes were full of tears. He said, 'God keep you.'

'Goodbye, Mr Prior.'

She watched him stumble down the steps towards the landing stage. One of her servants fielded him as he lost his footing among the broken stones and, with another, guided him along the gangplank, crabwise as they were too many to walk abreast. Once on the deck, Tom turned as if he were about to wave, but seemed to forget what he had turned for and went shuffling along holding the taffrail until the upper decks of the steamer hid him from her view.

Back in her drawing room, Archie was waiting. He had leapt up, hearing the rushing sweep of her dress along the verandah, and with this sudden movement had precipitated an avalanche of small silk cushions to the floor. She regarded him for a moment as he frantically chased the sliding cushions across the slippery surface of the polished boards.

'Mr Tennant.'

'Do forgive me, Miss Beresford. I am so sorry – I don't think anything is damaged—'

She stepped past him and rang the bell. 'Of course it isn't. Please leave them. The servants will pick them up. It is of no consequence at all.'

He straightened up in relief. 'I am so very glad to see you, Miss Beresford.'

'Are you?' she said, without coquettishness. 'And will you sit down? Somewhere less hazardous—'

A servant slipped in and retrieved the cushions deftly. Maria said, looking at Archie with her usual directness, 'You look extremely well, Mr Tennant. A beard becomes you.' It was the most intimate remark she had ever made to him.

Blushing helplessly, he said, 'If – if I had thought a beard might please you, I should have grown one earlier. Shaving arrangements in the forests were – a little rudimentary.'

'And you are in Mandalay now for the wet season?'

'Yes,' he said, glancing out into the garden, 'any day now.'

She said, 'I dread it.'

He turned to look at her. She had grown much thinner, thin to the point of gauntness around her face and neck, so that her eyes seemed much larger and her hair more luxuriant, heavier.

'I have to chastise you, Mr Tennant.'

'Oh,' he said, immediately repentant.

'Tom Prior left Mandalay this morning for Rangoon. He would most evidently have liked to see you before he left.'

Archie's face was flooded with contrition. 'Oh, my God – forgive me, Miss Beresford, but I would not have missed his going for worlds. But I knew nothing of it, I mean, I knew he was going, but not when, not that it was today—'

'He will be better in Rangoon. He is not really fit to look after himself.'

'Then he did not recover? He did not recover from – from Grace's death?'

'No,' she said, 'he did not.'

'Is – is this place a destroyer, Miss Beresford?'

She turned her head away from him. 'Only, I think, Mr Tennant, if you permit yourself to be a victim.'

He said, 'I was under the impression that your days were spent in the palace.'

He caught in her eyes a fleeting glance of unease.

'I regarded Mr Prior's departure as a priority.'

'How are things in the palace?'

In a low voice, her head bent towards her lap, she said, 'Unstable. Dangerous, perhaps.'

'That is what I heard myself. Acute shortage of money, savage repression of opposition, weakness and vacillation on the part of the King—'

'All those things.'

'Is it really safe for you to go there still?'

She looked at him. 'Safer than anywhere else.'

'Should you not have gone to Rangoon with Mr Prior?'

'No.'

'Because of other matters which keep you in Mandalay? Business matters?'

She got up abruptly. 'It is impertinent to crossquestion me, Mr Tennant. What I do is no affair of yours. My decisions are entirely of my own making.'

Archie rose too so that they faced each other across the beautiful faded Chinese rug. 'What you do may at the moment be no affair of mine, but I have to tell you, Miss Beresford, that I wish it were. I have thought about you so much in the forests, so much that in the last weeks thoughts of you have almost obsessed me. You may have done your utmost to discourage me in the past, as you seem to have done with all other human contact, but the effect of your behaviour upon me has merely been to arouse first my interest and secondly my admiration – and – and fascination, Miss Beresford. I don't really seem to care about your interest in me, indeed I should think it is minimal since you have not asked me one single question about my time in the forest, but that aspect is beside the point. The point is that I find I am in love, quite violently in love with you, and the only way I can appease my feelings is to ask you, however hopeless my chances, if you will consider marrying me.'

Maria's face betrayed nothing. 'I am sure you will quite appreciate that I must refuse you, Mr Tennant.'

'Must?' he shouted. 'Must? Why must?'

She folded her hands calmly before her. 'I am a woman of independence, Mr Tennant. I am not a woman who needs looking after, I am not a woman who needs a man—'

'I don't want to look after you necessarily – at least, I do, but not if you don't wish it. I want to have you, I need you even if you don't need me.'

'What you need, Mr Tennant,' she said, her lip curling, 'is any woman. It is common knowledge that you went into the forests with more than simply your manservant. How you can outrage me by such a proposal when your behaviour is so utterly – disgusting, *depraved*, is beyond my comprehension.'

Archie spread his hands. 'Oh Miss Beresford,

don't demean yourself by speaking so. What does a mistress mean in a place like this—'

'Get out,' she said, her hands over her ears.

He stepped forward and took her hands away, holding them hard in his own. 'I will go when I have been properly answered. Do you refuse me because you have no feeling for me at all, because you intend never to marry anyone, or because I have kept a Burmese mistress for a few months?'

She struggled a little in his grasp but found it was fruitless, so let her hands lie in his and said impatiently, 'All those things, Mr Tennant.'

He let her go. 'So it does not matter a whit to you whether or not I try again?'

'Not a whit.'

'And your father? Does he wish to see you die an old maid?'

An expression very like pain crossed her face. 'My father's views coincide entirely with my own.'

'I don't believe you, Miss Beresford.'

She gave a small, immediately suppressed gasp. 'Please – please go, Mr Tennant.'

He held out his hand to her. 'If you will shake my hand.'

She put hers into his. Hers was trembling very slightly.

Archie said, 'We are more alike than you will admit, Miss Beresford. We have so few human intimates. I suppose my closest relationship is with an old man in England who has no reason except for his loneliness and goodness of heart to love me, but love me he seems to.'

'Then you are most fortunate, Mr Tennant.'

'Yes,' he said, 'yes, I am. And you might have made me as fortunate as I ever hoped to be.'

She took her hand away abruptly. 'No,' she said, 'I could not. I could not do that for anybody.'

'May I ask you one small last favour?'

'You may *ask*—'

'I don't need to tell you how much we all live on the edge of a precipice here, nor how the danger level rises every day, nor how growing French influence here makes our own position more uncertain at every moment. All I do wish to tell you is that, given all these imponderables, I want you always to remember that I am there in time of need. After what I have said to you this morning, you will understand that I am not just prepared to help you if ever you are in difficulties, but hoping against hope that such an occasion might arise.'

She bowed her head very slightly but said nothing.

'Goodbye,' he said, 'Maria.'

She still did not speak and her face was turned away from him again so he sighed, involuntarily but loudly enough for her to be in no doubt as to his feelings, and clumped disconsolately down the verandah to his waiting cart in the lane.

★   ★   ★

It required for some reason all the self-discipline Maria possessed to dress herself for the palace later that day and to order herself driven there. Supayalat and Thibaw would have eaten in the fountain room as usual, Thibaw drinking steadily, Supayalat watching him with her intent, unblinking stare, and they would now have retired to their own apartments and be sleeping in the heavy afternoon heat, heavier now with the approaching rains than ever. Maria planned to be waiting for the Queen when she awoke. The afternoon would be like all other afternoons, spent in a pavilion in the gardens, lighting one after another of the Queen's cheroots, listening to story after story told by nervous maids of honour – nervous because of the increasing unpredictability of Supayalat's temper – watching scornfully while Mattie Calogreedy sought to oust her, Maria, from royal favour in revenge for her lack of sympathy over Pierre Bonvilain and his insipid little wife . . .

At the palace walls, just as she was about to cross the white bridge over the mirror-still moat, her cart was stopped.

'Miss Beresford,' Andreino said from the roadway.

She looked down at him with distaste. He wore a dreadful coat of figured velveteen and smelt strongly and sweetly, like some essence of overblown roses.

'Forgive me for halting you. I shall only take a moment of your time.'

The sun blazed down even through Maria's parasol, she could feel it like a brand on the base of her neck.

'I have some hard things to say to you, Miss Beresford, and I only say them out of respect for your intelligence. It is imperative that you leave at once for Rangoon. Even to travel the streets here as you now do will soon become impossible. The position of the English here becomes more perilous every hour—'

Maria glanced up at the shining roofs that flew above her. 'Not mine, Signor Andreino.'

He grasped the side of the cart. 'Even yours, Miss Beresford. That is precisely why I wish to speak to you. You have too good an intelligence as I said to be misled any longer by your father, by Monsieur Bonvilain or Mr Blount. The truth is, signorina, that your father has, for whatever reason, long decided that you shall have no further part in the concessions to any mines in Upper Burma. What is more, Bonvilain, as you know, has secured all he went to Paris to secure and he and Blount are in the process of divorcing your father from all their plans also. Your father was in touch with Bonvilain all the time he was away, but did not tell you, and furthermore – these are cruel things to say to any woman, signorina, but for your own safety they must be said – he agreed with the other two that your part in their business affairs must cease. He now finds himself in the same position – or at least, he will do very shortly. If you wish to warn him, that is a matter for your own discretion. But I cannot urge you too strongly to leave. Bonvilain is the favourite, a French consul is coming, the future for the English is very black. Mr Blount only stays because he has some hold on Bonvilain, but you will see, he too will go if the fire gets hotter.'

Maria looked steadily ahead all the time he was speaking, her back straight, her chin raised. 'Why should I believe you, Signor Andreino?'

'You will be gravely mistaken not to.'

'Please take your hands from the cart sides.'

He stepped back. 'Despite your ungraciousness, Miss Beresford, I will offer you any help I can. You must not hesitate to ask me. The next steamer leaves on Thursday and it is imperative that you are on it. If times get much worse, there may *be* no steamers.'

The bullock cart ground forward, missing his glossy boot toes by inches. He gazed after it for a while with a mixture of admiration and indignation and then, tucking his cane beneath his arm, set off briskly in the direction of Archie's bungalow.

Maria, creaking forward towards the palace, would not even allow herself to think. She rode as she had always done, bolt upright and looking resolutely before her, as if the butterfly crowd of little Burmese who thronged the royal city simply did not exist. At the outer postern, she climbed out of the cart, furled her parasol and stepped inside. The *Hlutdaw* soared before her as it had done hundreds of times before, scarlet and gold and massive, its great steps empty of any sign of life but the odd bird investigating corners for insects. At the postern to the palace platform she was stopped.

'Nonsense,' she said, 'I am Miss Beresford. I am never stopped.'

The guard was joined by another. 'Orders of the Queen.'

Maria looked at them in incredulity. Her first instinct was to ignore them and march forward as if they simply were not there. But some slight movement caught her eye and she stayed where she was, gazing across the green lawns and waterfalls where she had spent afternoons without number. Moving across the gardens, in the distance but unmistakable to Maria's clear vision, was Queen Supayalat, attended by her fluttering band of maids of honour and in their midst, her blond hair clearly visible beneath a charming hat of pale straw, walked Marie-Thérèse Bonvilain.

'I am so sorry,' Andreino said, 'I feel for you so. A father—'

'No,' Archie said, 'not my father. But like one. Better in some ways, I think.'

The letter lay between them where Andreino had laid it on a stool.

'But you are rich now, my friend. A great house, servants, money – There is no need for you to go back to the forests.'

Archie put his hands over his eyes.

'But I want to go back. He would want me to.

If it wasn't for him I should be idling about as some penniless and inky clerk in Chancery Lane. It's the least I can do—'

'My dear fellow. Believe me. I do feel for you.'

'Would you think me churlish if I asked you to go? I'm sorry but I – I can't seem to manage anything else today—'

Andreino stood up. 'Forgive me. I shall leave at once. I should just tell you that I saw Miss Beresford today and told her of her position here. I think you should consider yours, communicate with the manager in Rangoon—'

'Get out!' Archie shouted.

'Forgive me,' Andreino said again, 'forgive me.'

'Go. *Go.*'

When he had bowed himself out, Archie stumbled to his bedroom. It was as orderly as usual, evening clothes laid out, polished boots, mosquito net in symmetrical folds, water jug and upturned glass on a tray by the bed. With flailing arms, Archie crashed around the room, sweeping his clothes to the floor, kicking his boots wildly about, sending jug and glass flying in a hail of glittering splinters. Then he cast himself down across the bed and burst into noisy uncontrollable tears.

Two days later, the rains began, sweeping, blinding deluges of water surging in from the Bay of Bengal. Frederick Winser came back from the forests too in a strange and intractable frame of mind, curiously uncommunicative about his months of solitude. Archie could not even wring from him the smallest details of what he had achieved in his winter of map-making and after an awkward week in which Frederick answered Archie only in grunts he announced that he was taking the next steamer to Rangoon.

'Rangoon!'

'Yes. Coming?'

'But – but why?'

Frederick waved a letter with a nonchalance Archie did not trust. 'Company business. They want to see me.'

'Not – not trouble?'

'Oh, no!' Frederick said, avoiding Archie's eye and plunging with elaborate vigour into the dissection of a mango. 'Not that. Do assure you. Want to come?'

'No thanks. I want to see the action here.'

'Might be nasty. I've warned you.'

'Yes,' Archie said, 'everybody does. That's what I am staying to see.'

When Frederick had gone, lethargy stole upon Archie like a constant drowsiness. He began to eat too much and tried to rouse himself from a luxurious anticipation of the next meal by giving himself a strict timetable – beginning with being shaved once more each morning – and from which he lapsed inevitably at some point in each day. He ordered a pony brought round before the afternoon deluge drowned Mandalay with its appalling regularity but some days could not rouse himself to mount it. Ah Chun cleaned his gun faithfully each evening, whether it needed it or not, with a kind of steady reproachfulness. Andreino, calling at intervals in his busy round of inquiry and intrigue among the half-worlds of Mandalay, was the only European he now saw.

Until Hubert came. Archie had told himself that to sleep after luncheon was not only destructive to his willpower but also wasted one of the few dry moments of the day, but each afternoon was a battle against slumber that required superhuman efforts on his part. He came stumbling out of the dining room, Ah Chun padding in his wake with the cheroots he had taken to in the jungle, and found Hubert waiting for him, immaculate as ever in white linen, his handsome face now so expressionless that it was difficult to tell if he was aware of any other human being on earth but himself.

'Mr Beresford!'

'Mr Tennant.'

Archie fumbled hurriedly with the buttons of his tunic. From behind Ah Chun tugged and tweaked him surreptitiously into place.

'This is not a convenient time? You were lunching?'

'A little late—' Archie said shamefacedly.

'You could spare me a few moments?'

'Of course, of course—'

From the only comfortable chair, Ah Chun removed an untidy heap of *Rangoon Gazettes* and dusted the cushions obsequiously with the flat of his hand. Hubert handed him his hat and cane with no indication that he saw in him any more presence than that of a piece of furniture.

'We are quite alone, Mr Tennant?'

'Entirely, Mr Beresford.'

Archie turned and gave orders to Ah Chun who went out closing the door elaborately.

'I have no reason to doubt your manservant's discretion, but I cannot, in the present instance, be too careful. You would oblige me, Mr Tennant, by drawing your chair as close to mine as possible so that I may speak low.'

Intrigued entirely out of his drowsiness, Archie leaned forward, his elbows on his knees. 'How can I help you?'

Hubert put his hand over the right hand breast of his jacket.

'I have something here that I am anxious to entrust to you. I think you will by now be aware of the position which I have held in Mandalay since my arrival here in seventy-nine and I also assume that you will know that I and my partners gained the concession from the palace to work the ruby mines in Minhla soon after our arrival. Is all this known to you?'

Archie nodded.

'I am aware that as a forest officer you have been out of touch with affairs in Mandalay this last cold season, but I am certain that Signor Andreino has been most assiduous in putting you in possession of all details. You will therefore have heard rumours that the French wish to supersede British influence here in Upper Burma and that they are prepared to replenish the empty royal coffers in return for concessions in mining, banking, railways and so forth. Indeed, a French consul, a Monsieur Haas, disembarked from a steamer here only yesterday.'

'Yes,' Archie said, 'yes, I heard.'

Hubert drew a deep breath and leaned forward so that his fine, blank eyes were no more than a foot from Archie's.

'It was my understanding, Mr Tennant, that I was indispensable to the partners of whom I spoke to you earlier. I have, of course, on account of my background, no difficulty at all in raising for our partnership the vast sums of rupees necessary to pay the leases on the concessions. It seems, however, from an interview I had only yesterday with Mr Blount and Monsieur Bonvilain that they have no further desire to take advantage of the talents I can offer them.' He stopped and drew back and Archie saw that expression had crept into his glance for the first time, an expression of anger and – and of something else, something more dangerous. 'I do not care for speaking frankly, Mr Tennant, but in this instance I feel I must tell you that I am in no way prepared to bow to such treatment. Mr Blount and Monsieur Bonvilain entirely forget with whom they are dealing. More to the point, perhaps, Mr Blount does not know, and Monsieur Bonvilain has temporarily overlooked the fact, that in a moment of bravado inspired by the success of his time in Paris, Monsieur

Bonvilain lent me copies of the signed treaties between the French and Burmese governments.' He put his hand to his jacket again. 'He will live to regret both his boastfulness and his lack of discretion.'

Archie said, pointing, quite forgetting his manners in his eagerness, 'Do you mean, Mr Beresford, that you have proof, written proof that the French are in league with the Burmese and that the palace is being encouraged to oust the British?'

'I do,' Hubert said calmly. 'I have a copy of the signed concession for the French to manage and finance banks and a letter from the French foreign minister, Jules Ferry, to the *Kinwoon Mingyi* saying that the French will arrange for the Burmese to import arms through Tonkin. I have been able to use some influence at court and persuaded Miss Calogreedy to obtain copies of the Burmese reply to that letter and to others which are evidence of Burmese favour towards the French. Miss Calogreedy had an admirer in a clerk in the *Kinwoon Mingyi*'s office and the matter was easily arranged. I also possess the copy of a letter which will interest you in particular, Mr Tennant. It is from the new consul, Monsieur Haas, and it assures the palace that if an excuse can be found to cancel the Bombay-Burmah Trading Corporation's leases upon the teak forests, France will be more than ready to take them up.'

Archie was too excited to sit still. He got up

and began to pace about the room, his hands in his trouser pockets. Hubert watched him calmly. After a while, shaking his head, as if too bewildered to think coherently, Archie came back to his seat and said, 'But the French don't want war, do they? I mean, they are hardly powerful enough in this part of the world to defeat us—'

'Precisely. That is one reason why Haas has come. His mission is to persuade the Burmese government to make treaties with Germany and Italy by which they will join with France and declare Upper Burma neutral. England could not defy three such powerful nations as that. But the time is not yet ripe. France does not want to provoke England yet because, as things now stand, England is strong enough to drive out the French.'

'And you—' Archie said, almost in a whisper, 'you wish to precipitate things. You want those letters made public to London and Calcutta. You want an English army to march into Mandalay. You want revenge—'

'You take my point precisely, Mr Tennant.'

Hubert put his hand inside his jacket this time and drew out a flat packet of papers. He held them out to Archie. 'You will oblige me, Mr Tennant, by taking these papers to Signor Andreino. He is in private correspondence with Calcutta and, as you well know, with the Bombay-Burmah Corporation in Rangoon. I would be grateful if you would act with the utmost dispatch.'

'But why me, Mr Beresford? Why not take them to Andreino yourself? Of course, I will do it for you, for – for the corporation, for England, of course I will, but why choose me?'

Hubert stood up. 'No suspicion or intrigue attaches to you, Mr Tennant. Signor Andreino is surrounded by it and as I believe I am closely watched these days, I do not choose to run the risk of being seen in his company. The connections could be made so obviously. In your case, as a forest officer only out of the jungle a few weeks and also as one of the few Englishmen left in Mandalay, my calling upon you will seem a commonplace courtesy.'

Archie looked down at the packet in his hands. 'I can't believe it – I can't believe that you – Mr Beresford, what will you do now?'

'I leave for Rangoon this afternoon. The steamer is due to depart at four o'clock. At that hour precisely, when you hear the departing signal from the river, I would be obliged if you would deliver this packet to Signor Andreino.'

'And – your daughter? Miss Beresford?'

Hubert's face betrayed nothing. 'I believe she chooses to remain. I do not burden her with my plans.'

'And this?' Archie waved the papers. 'She knows nothing of this?'

'Naturally not.'

Archie shouted, 'So you intend to escape retribution by running away to Rangoon, but you don't mind leaving her to face it?'

'She has nothing to face. She is not in the least involved.'

'But what will she live upon? How will she live? What will she do?'

'Money is not a problem, Mr Tennant.'

'I wish,' Archie said furiously, 'I wish I could feel anything but contempt for you. I wish I could see anything remotely patriotic in your gesture, anything but a desire for personal revenge on Blount and Bonvilain. I wish I saw something in your behaviour to your daughter that savoured of anything but the most inhuman callousness.' He brandished the papers, 'I will run your errand, Mr Beresford, because greater things are at stake than your petty vengeance, but don't for one moment suppose that I am doing it for you.'

Hubert said blandly, 'Your motives do not concern me in the very least, Mr Tennant. I am only concerned that these papers reach Signor Andreino and in that matter, since as you say, great issues are at stake, I know you will not fail me.'

He moved towards the door. 'You would be so good as to ask for my hat and cane, Mr Tennant?'

'If you cannot look after your daughter, I can!'

Hubert turned at the doorway with the faintest of smiles. 'I am not a believer in advice, Mr Tennant. It is invariably inappropriate. But I feel it only fair to warn you that the outcome of any such chivalrous intent will only lead to the loss of your own self-esteem. You may assume, if you wish, that I speak from my own experience.' He paused and then said lightly, 'My own bitter experience.'

PART FOUR

18

On 2 November 1885 in Madras, the Burma
Field Force loaded its stores and weapons onto
steamers of the British India Company in delug-
ing rain. The night was spent in the greatest
possible misery under canvas at Fort St George
and the tent which Murray Shaw shared with
another adjutant was flooded to a depth of six
inches and had to be abandoned. If he spent the
night wretched and sodden, with his high spirits
at the prospect of the Burma campaign as damp-
ened as his clothes, so too did the ten thousand
other men of the force, gathered from the armies
of Bengal and Madras on the instructions of the
Secretary of State for Foreign Affairs in London
and Lord Dufferin, Viceroy of India.

To men jaded with hanging about the garrison
towns of India, the instructions to embark for
Burma had come as a welcome relief. Murray
Shaw himself saw it partly as a chance for pro-
motion to major and partly as an opportunity
to see if the 2nd battalion of the Hampshire
Regiment could actually put all the theories he
felt he had enriched them with in his small way
into practice. He had, like most officers in India,

felt very little interest in Burma during his seven or eight years in the East but the behaviour of that preposterous little savage of a king in Mandalay in recent months had aroused both his fascination and his fury.

His colonel, George White – a man he admired chiefly for the Victoria Cross he had won on the North-West Frontier – had been extremely helpful in explaining what seemed to Murray Shaw a pretty complex and tricky situation. Of course, old White had been military secretary to the previous Viceroy of India for a while and therefore you would expect him to have a better grasp of the things political johnnies got up to than many, but all the same, he did put the situation remarkably plainly, so plainly in fact that Murray felt himself able to repeat what he had heard to fellow junior officers without, for once, feeling he might have got hold of the wrong end of the stick.

'It's pretty simple, really. Somehow the news of what the French were up to leaked out to Calcutta and then to London and then, to cap that, this Thibaw fellow tried to throw out the Bombay-Burmah chaps by claiming that they had defaulted on payments for their leases. Apparently they are supposed to pay a royalty on each log they export, and Thibaw said they had smuggled some out without paying. White told me that the Burmese parliament – some rum name I can't remember – said the Bombay-Burmah had defrauded the King out of over seventy-three thousand pounds and the forest workers of thirty-three thousand. Can you believe it?'

'Just as well we are going,' someone said, beside him. 'Teach them a thing or two—'

'But you haven't heard the whole. Apparently the Burmese said that they would fine the Bombay-Burmah twice the amount owed and, if they refused to pay, they'd have all their timber seized. So, of course, we sent the Burmese an ultimatum.'

'Of course—'

'We said that the Burmese must allow the fine to go to proper arbitration, and then we said that they must receive and treat a British Resident properly – after all, they have some Frenchman up there having the time of his life – and that they should not enter into any foreign relations without consulting us. Apparently the Queen, who really rules the roost up there, wouldn't hear of it. They said they didn't mind having another British Resident and they would listen to the Bombay-Burmah's case, but they wouldn't on any account have their foreign affairs interfered with. So there you are. Old Thibaw wants a fight!'

'And that,' someone else said, 'makes two of us.'

Murray was to wonder later if his colonel had actually overheard his enlightening lecture on the background to the need to march on Mandalay. When 3 November dawned, thankfully bright and cloudless after the drenching night, and

Murray found himself on the quayside next to his commanding officer while the sepoys were embarked in the steamers, White said, 'Of course, we mustn't underestimate the Burmese. I don't want you or any other junior officer of mine to do that. We have made a lot of mistakes recently in this respect and suffered terribly. Between you and me, Shaw, I hope that Thibaw's answer will be defiant, so that we have a soldier's duty to perform, not a policeman's.'

The crossing to Rangoon took only three days, across sea like a millpond, but most of the sepoys were sick nevertheless. Rangoon, Murray considered, looked a low dull place, but the Burmese girls, clustered along the river banks with chattering immodesty, looked both pretty and approachable. Not for the first time, Murray was glad that the sudden excess of romanticism that had seized him at a regimental ball in Madras the previous winter had not led him, as for a moment or two he had feared it might, to propose to a very pretty Miss Purvis who had laughed so obligingly at everything he said. He knew the sudden headiness that seized him as they sat out in a shadowed corner between pillars had been partly champagne, partly sheer frustration and partly because Miss Purvis, being tall and fair, had summoned up the memory of a magnificent girl he had known briefly in Bombay in '79. Maria Beresford had remained in his memory long after she had followed her father on some extraordinary expedition to Burma, whence she was by now bound to have travelled on and was doubtless now queening it as the wife of some distinguished fellow in Government House in Calcutta. He had wondered once or twice if the powerful imprint of her personality had prevented him from finding any subsequent girl desirable enough to marry, but such speculation was usually quickly quenched by a hearty recognition of the advantages of bachelorhood. Murray was under no illusions about the catch he represented being heir to a baronetcy and now in possession, six years past his twenty-fifth birthday, of a handsome income. He could afford better polo ponies than anyone else in the regiment, old White included, higher gambling stakes and a vastly superior cellar. There were many moments – and this, steaming gently into Rangoon with the prospect of a fight and all those pretty little things lined up before him, was one – when he felt he had got life entirely measured up, tailor-made to fit him.

There was, he soon discovered, to be no hanging about in Rangoon. Within five days, the Field Force had moved north by rail from the capital to an undistinguished little hole called Thayetmyo on the Upper Burma border, where a vast convoy of steamers and flats from the Irrawaddy Flotilla Company lay on the great shining breadth of the Irrawaddy. The steamers, which for years had carried chiefly Burmese and their bundles and the mails and occasionally Europeans with their accompanying mountains of luggage, had been fitted out hastily with arms racks, water tanks and latrines and the flats they were to tow had been adapted to carry artillery. The convoy was to be escorted by steam launches equipped with machine guns to sweep the river banks as they moved northwards.

In common with all the other officers, Murray was issued with a ration list for his men which specified, among other things, an ounce of lime juice for each man per week, and in addition to that, a list which Murray himself found quite baffling. Not liking to ask any fellow officer for enlightenment, he sought out a journalist chap called Moylan, employed by *The Times* as Rangoon correspondent, who was accompanying the Field Force to Mandalay.

'That,' Moylan said, giving Murray one of his keen, sharp glances, 'that is a list of the most celebrated antiquities in Upper Burma, books and scripts and Buddha images, that sort of thing. So if you come to sack a monastery, Captain Shaw, you would be obliging the world infinitely if you safeguarded any library or shrine you find rather than permitting your sepoys to rampage through it.'

'And if the enemy rally in monasteries?'

'You must refer to your colonel. But in such a case, I should suppose unhappily that the soldier must precede the preserver of antiquities.'

'Rum language—' Murray said, gazing at the sheet in his hand.

'Now that,' Moylan said, following his glance

and pointing to a name on the list, 'that one you will be quite safe with. The Tripitaka commentaries. That is the world's greatest book on Buddhism, it says everything there is to say. But I am delighted to tell you that the pages are of marble, set into marble plinths. Not easy to damage, Captain Shaw.'

After a day at Thayetmyo, Murray was dispatched with a small force back to the railway terminus at Toungoo to assist in the safe embarkation of many employees of the Bombay-Burmah Trading Corporation who had come south when Thibaw had refused Lord Dufferin's ultimatum and were headed for Rangoon and temporary safety. Murray's brother Digby, when they had seen each other briefly before the Hampshires embarked for Rangoon, had said in his careless way that he had met a Bombay-Burmah fellow the year before in Bombay, destined for the forests of Upper Burma.

'Pleasantish chap,' Digby said. 'Big. Seemed not to know whether it was Christmas or Tuesday. Expect he's lost in some jungle now. Somebody Tennant – Archie, I think it was. Keen on polo.'

Having dispatched all the corporation's employees south and elicited all their names, Murray found no-one called Archie Tennant among them. As Digby had said, he was no doubt lost in some jungle which was, if Murray's martial ambitions were to be realized, the safest place for him.

He returned to Thayetmyo to find great excitement. It appeared that a steamer had arrived from Mandalay two days earlier with the news that the city was in a ferment and that some Italian fellow, a Signor Andreino, whose connection with the Bombay-Burmah Corporation Murray could not for the life of him make out, had gathered all the foreigners he could find into a single house and barricaded them in. The streets were no longer safe as roaming bands of dacoits prowled day and night and it was not possible even to move guarded about the *kalā* town, let alone attempt to enter the royal palace. The din of music and gongs and the Burmese notion of singing still reverberated from the royal theatre and it was reported that Thibaw, grasping his Queen's hand for reassurance and licking his lips nervously as he spoke, had told his ministers, 'It is only by war that I can save the honour of my kingdom. The trade and business of every subject of mine has suffered because of the English who have made improper demonstrations of war—'

And his Queen, pregnant again the report said, had risen and shrieked, 'Improper! Improper! What the English do is unlawful! Do you hear us? Unlawful!'

These stories had stirred up Murray's blood wonderfully but Moylan, always visible somewhere among the troops with his notebook, had been sceptical. 'There won't be a fight, Captain Shaw. I am sorry to disappoint you, but there'll only be a lot of noise. Shall I tell you something that came up to me by telegraph from Rangoon today and which you may disseminate among your fellow officers? The French are getting out as quickly as they can. They don't want to fight the English. The consul, Monsieur Haas, is being recalled at once and will be reprimanded for, as they say, acting without authority. End of his career, I shouldn't wonder. There's another Frenchman up in Mandalay, an engineer and his wife, but Andreino has them safe. Also, I am told, a bevy of intrepid American lady missionaries, one of the Bombay-Burmah's forest officers who was disinclined to miss the fun and an Englishwoman. What she is doing there, I could not say, but she appears to be quite without family. A Miss Beresford.'

'Maria Beresford?'

'I have no idea.'

'Must be,' Murray said, while quite a new anticipation took its place beside his eagerness to fight. 'There can't be two Miss Beresfords. Not in a place like Mandalay.'

Sixty miles above Thayetmyo lay the only place where the Field Force anticipated any difficulty. It bore the name of Minhla and was distinguished by being reasonably well fortified and also by possessing considerable ruby mines to the west of the river. On the way north towards Minhla, two Italian army engineers in the pay of King Thibaw were captured during their failure to blockade the river and the diary of one revealed the interesting information that they two alone had been entrusted by the royal palace in Mandalay with the task of closing the frontier.

'You see?' Moylan said to Murray Shaw. 'You won't get a battle. As the Burmese would say, it's a fish to fight a dog.'

'There's Minhla,' Murray said doggedly. 'They say there are eight thousand Burmese troops waiting for us across the river from Minhla.'

There were, but Captain Murray Shaw was fated hardly to see them. His brigade, led by White – now a general for the duration of the campaign – was ordered to follow as a reserve upon the brigade commanded to attack the great brick fort at Minhla, the strongest, Moylan said, in Burma. They disembarked from the steamers at dawn, watched with considerable envy the Royal Welch Fusiliers and two companies of Madras Infantry march off and then listened impatiently to the gunfire that resounded some hours later. By early afternoon when they reached the fort themselves, they found it in British hands, every Burman fled. There was nothing to do but march disconsolately back to the river and listen, with ill-concealed resentment, to tales of the lively fighting that had taken place all day in the thick jungle on the opposite bank of the river. The commander-in-chief, General Prendergast, was heard to say that not only had Jack Burman put up a lively fight but that he considered the infantry skirmishing over the hills at Minhla one of the prettiest sights he had ever seen.

After such bitter disappointment it was not even balm to Murray Shaw's feelings to see the wooden houses of Minhla ablaze that night, nor to watch Burmese soldiers driven from their hiding places to drown in the Irrawaddy. As the night wore on, thickening cloud began to obscure the brilliant stars and before dawn it began to rain, to the misery of the troops and the astonishment of any who knew Burma and declared it to be far too late in the year for such a downpour. When day broke, grey and chill and impossibly wet, news was brought to Murray that one of his sepoys had cholera. It was, as he said to a fellow officer from whom he borrowed a rubber cape, all he needed to hear.

19

'They are through Pagan,' Andreino said. 'They scuttled the royal steamers—'

It seemed almost impossible to imagine, the huge efficient steamers of the Irrawaddy Flotilla Company bristling with khaki coats and Manchester-made guns opposing the gilded steamers of Thibaw with their cargoes of soldiers in scarlet and white and purple-red, the officers in state beneath golden umbrellas, every head crowned with velvet and the curious tin helmets with upturned wings.

'Listen,' Maria said suddenly, commandingly.

A faint booming came on the hot wind from the south, a rumble like thunder.

Archie said, 'Guns—'

'Guns, English guns. They must have reached Myingyan, perhaps more. Maybe they are only forty miles away.'

Marie-Thérèse Bonvilain began to cry again. It not only irritated Maria that she should cry at all, but that she could manage to do so becomingly without so much as a hint of swollen eyes or a reddened nose. But she sobbed inevitably as she wept and the sound, shut up together as they were in the house that had belonged to the British political agent in Mandalay twenty years before, was sufficiently exasperating in itself.

Andreino had not ceased to marvel at the apparent docility with which Maria had finally agreed to leave her own house. All summer, after all, he had begged and cajoled her to leave Mandalay, to go down to Rangoon, to Madras, to Calcutta, anywhere, anything but remain. She had refused adamantly upon every occasion. What she did all day he could not imagine, living there in virtual seclusion, seeing almost no-one, no longer welcome at the palace. His quick ear caught the news that she was selling things, pieces of French furniture, Japanese lacquer, Chinese porcelain, but she appeared to him, on each occasion he called, as impeccably dressed as ever and her drawing room as charming as it had ever been. Rubies still clustered at her ears and round her neck and wrists, but she was absolutely, maddeningly uncommunicative about any single thing except her determination not to leave Mandalay.

In the last week of October he had almost despaired. It had become entirely apparent to him that there was no-one but himself to whom the foreigners left in the neighbourhood of Mandalay could look. On instructions from the corporation, Archie had not gone back to the forests for his second winter but had chosen – in defiance this time of the manager in Rangoon – to remain in Mandalay, and for that Andreino could only be thankful. Between them, they selected the most impregnable of the houses in the *kalā* town that had once had European occupation, and into this they induced any foreigner remaining in Mandalay and those who arrived daily from outlying missions, drawn by rumour, to take refuge. Miss Beresford remained adamant and, for some strange reason, Archie seemed reluctant to visit her. Only at what Andreino considered to be the last moment, when news came that the Burma Field Force had arrived in Rangoon, did Archie at last agree to go.

'I don't say I shall have any more luck than you. If I don't we shall have to go together and carry her away by force.'

Maria received him with perfect composure. She looked a little pale, her pallor thrown into relief by a dress of the same colour as her jewels, but he could at first detect no outward sign that her strange isolated summer since her father's departure had had any ill effect upon her.

'Please sit down, Mr Tennant.'

He lowered himself gingerly into one of the rose-pink French chairs.

'If you have come, Mr Tennant, to tell me all the things I am weary of hearing from Signor Andreino, I must tell you that you are wasting your time.'

'Then I will start with some other matters to divert you, Miss Beresford. The first is that Monsieur Haas has left Mandalay, recalled to

Paris in public disgrace. He will be, it seems, the scapegoat to save French face. The second is that I was witness three days ago to an interview between Signor Andreino and Denzil Blount, the upshot of which was Mr Blount's refusal to come under any kind of protection and his subsequent vanishing. Both Ah Chun and Andreino's servants have done a considerable amount of searching and inquiring and it seems Mr Blount has entirely disappeared. The third is that Monsieur and Madame Bonvilain have cast themselves upon our mercy since the contracts with which he hoped to make himself a fortune are now, of course, not worth the paper they are written on. I quite see that they are hardly an inducement for you to join us, but join us, Miss Beresford, you must.'

She did not speak, but looked out past his shoulder to the heavy green garden where the coppersmith bird still beat out his aggravating rhythms, and the pulsing gongs of the royal *pwes* throbbed in the sunlit air. After a while, in which he watched her intently and observed that there were dark circles under her eyes and that her hands shook however hard she clenched them together in her ruby silk lap, he said with all the gentleness he could summon. 'Won't you tell me why? Won't you trust me? Me, Maria, of all people?'

He was not at all sure what made him choose those words. He had scarcely seen her all summer and had determined not to examine his feelings at her rejection of his proposal, but rather to plunge with Andreino into the complexities and intrigues that followed the dispatch of those fateful papers to Rangoon. But she looked so vulnerable to him at this moment, a vulnerability made all the more poignant by her endeavours to overcome it.

'Maria,' he said again, coaxingly.

She said, without looking at him, 'I am so bitterly ashamed. I cannot hold my head up in any company.'

'But why? What have you done?'

'The world knows what my father did. And I did. The world knows we tried to line our pockets at the expense of British interests and that my father, for revenge, betrayed the people who were his partners. I saw the contracts in his bedroom – I was looking for evidence of quite another kind – and two days later they were not there.'

'No,' Archie said, 'the world does not know.'

'It must. It must—'

'I will tell you something. If your father chooses to say anything in Rangoon, it is only his own reputation he will destroy. Nobody but you and I know how I came by those papers. You know because you saw the papers in his bedroom. I know because your father came to me. And Mattie Calogreedy knows because she obtained copies of the Burmese replies ostensibly for your father but in truth for her own revenge. But she will say nothing. She is quite stricken enough by the consequences of her actions already and won't risk anything else. When I took the papers to Andreino, I did not tell him where I had obtained them and he, though he must have a shrewd idea, did not ask me. I suggested he send them to the Chief Commissioner in Rangoon as if he had come by them himself, which he was extremely pleased to do because his position is very precarious and he needs the good opinion of both the British government and the Bombay-Burmah. He is delighted to take all the credit. So you see, no one knows. They know your father left for Rangoon but it is generally supposed that – that relations between you both had become too strained to bear. Opinion condemns him as a bad father, but not as a traitor to boot.'

Maria was breathing very fast, her eyes fixed upon Archie's face. 'You have told no-one? No-one at all beside myself?'

'No-one.'

She gave a little gasp and stretched out her hand. He took it and found it unaccountably cold.

'Perhaps you think me mad, Mr Tennant. Perhaps I am a little. But all the time that I have suffered for feeling I have not been a good Englishwoman, I have suffered far more violently for feeling that my father had in some way betrayed Queen Supayalat, that he had delivered her, as indeed she will be delivered, into the rough hands of British soldiery. You may despise me for any allegiance that I have for her because I know she is violent and barbarous, but for me, Mr Tennant, she represented the first place I could belong to in my adult life, the first great lode star, the first chance to fulfil any ambition, the first society which I could feel, if I am to be honest, to be worthy of me. She is in a sense more than a queen to me, Mr Tennant, she is a country, a belief, a mother. She gave me chances I could never have hoped for elsewhere and even when she denied me audiences these last months, she has not forgotten me. Gifts come from the palace. I am allowed to remain here in the house she built for me when all other foreigners are driven from Mandalay. So when I realized my father had betrayed her, you may perhaps conceive of the agony and bitterness I suffered. I will not leave Mandalay because I must be near her even if I can give her no help. I cherish the hope that maybe at the end I can mediate with the English commanding officers for her – oh, anything, even light her cigar. It utterly broke my heart that the world should know what my father had done to her and I could not show my face. But you tell me, Mr Tennant, you tell me—'

'That nobody knows but we two. It will seem perfectly natural that Andreino should have sent the papers to Rangoon since the Bombay-Burmah was so closely involved and he is, after all, their agent. The secret is utterly safe.'

She said in a steadier voice, 'Thanks to you.'

He ducked his head.

'I owe you a great deal, Mr Tennant. I cannot repay you in any way except by the courtesy of more frankness than I feel comfortable in indulging in. I imagine you have had great satisfaction in being so entirely right about my father—'

'No!' he said, shocked, 'Not satisfaction, how could I—'

'You told me during that memorable conversation at Maymyo a year ago that I was destroying my father's image of himself. I disbelieved you entirely and have lived to regret my disbelief bitterly. I am mortified at my own cruelty, aiding and abetting my father into greater depths of folly and vanity until his eyes were suddenly opened and he saw himself as the puppet I had made of him. And I had gone on in my own way so long it hardly seemed that I knew how to change. He withdrew himself from me completely, first emotionally and then, finally, physically. I have heard nothing from him since he left, only a note from Hosannah Manook to whom he confided, during a chance meeting in the street in Rangoon, that he intended to return to India. He did not, apparently, in the few minutes they spoke together, mention me at all. I should not, of course, expect it.'

'Oh, Maria,' Archie said, 'Maria—'

She said, 'I am not afraid for myself, but what will they do to the Queen? Oh, Archie, what will they do to her?'

'Nothing violent. That I promise you. And try to remember that if your father betrayed the

Queen, she, in her turn, attempted to betray us, we English! The army is coming up the Irrawaddy with almost no opposition; in fact Andreino says they are losing more men through cholera than bloodshed. The aim of the British government is to annex Upper Burma, to run it like Lower Burma, not to conquer it like some invading medieval horde—'

'But it will all be gone, won't it? The City of Gems will be just another British-run Eastern place, like Bombay, like Rangoon. I know the cruelty is a bad thing and the savagery, but, oh, the pride of it all, the lovely arrogance, the way that the King and Queen are life and belief to their people, the beauty of everything here, the wonderful unconsciousness of anything else—'

She fumbled with uncharacteristic clumsiness for a handkerchief.

Archie rose and came and knelt by her chair, taking her free hand in his. 'Maria, you must come away with me, away to relative safety. If you stay here, in this house, there is an increasing chance that you will be harmed. Not by official Burmese soldiers, but by one of these marauding bands that are hardly particular about their victims. The army will be here in about a fortnight, we estimate, and if you wish to cling to any chance at all, however slender, of serving the Queen, you must make sure you are alive to do it. Everything you have said is safe with me. You know you can trust me. That – that I want you to. And you must trust me now to know what is best for you and to come with me.'

She blew her nose and said with something of her old briskness, 'What may I bring?'

'As little as possible. What we can carry in a bullock cart.'

'Can you wait one half hour?'

'If you can be quicker, I should be grateful.'

She was twenty minutes. A small trunk was carried down to the lane, a hatbox and another box tied with cord. She came back into her drawing room dressed for travelling, holding only a parasol and a reticule Archie supposed held her jewels and, after a businesslike look around the room that had been her heart's delight, she reached up and unhooked two water colours that hung on the gleaming teak walls. She handed them to Archie.

'These have been on the walls of every drawing room I have ever known, so I must keep them to grace the next one.'

When they were seated in the cart and it had jerked forward among the ruts on its journey towards the agent's old house, she said with a kind of diffidence, 'Would it be foolhardy to have one more glimpse of the palace walls? Could you ask the driver to go round that way?'

It was foolhardy and they went. For several minutes they sat alone and conspicuous, two Europeans in a bullock cart among the jostling Burmese, gazing at the glittering palace, silver and gold and scarlet roofs swooping like wings above its walls of rose-red brick, the barbaric splendour of it softened by the gauzy green of the tamarind trees and acacias, by the soft blue backdrop of the Shan hills, grave and lovely behind so much overwhelming gorgeousness. They sat spellbound, Archie as he had always done, Maria as she had never done before, and then a harsh cry rose from a group of men near them and a hail of stones spattered the cart, and the driver stood up and lashed the bullocks into a stumbling sickening canter among the ruts. Andreino, seeing Archie come in some ten minutes later with his prize upon his arm, felt that nothing now was too improbable to happen.

The mood of wonder could not last. Some seventeen adults shut up with each other in a stifling wooden house in uncertain circumstances was no breeding ground for a sense of the miraculous. Pierre Bonvilain was foolish enough to test the remnants of his charm upon Maria and found himself publicly humiliated; the lady missionaries – whose clothes and manners aroused in both Maria and Marie-Thérèse Bonvilain the only fellow-feeling they shared on any subject – sang rousing evangelical choruses at headache-inducing volume and smiled cheerfully with exasperating monotony; Andreino and Archie came and went with an unannounced suddenness that was wearing to everybody's nerves; and Maria, having made the supreme sacrifice of leaving her own house, was prepared to make absolutely no more. Marie-Thérèse's perpetual elegant tearfulness was a weak-willed luxury that Maria felt she should be prepared to forgo.

'I can only warn you, Madame, that the English private soldier has a very low opinion of poor-spirited women.'

At night the throbbing of the *pwes* that had disturbed the sleep of every inhabitant of Mandalay for almost six years was supplemented by bursts of gunfire. The black sky glowed scarlet at intervals and sometimes, lying in bed in a room she was forced to share with two young American missionaries who, shrouded in thick cream flannel, prayed loudly and relentlessly each night for twenty minutes before climbing into bed, Maria could detect the wild cries of human beings on the rampage. She kept her revolver under her pillow at night and in her pocket by day and her rubies with it. Both the weapon and the jewels represented far more to her than their intrinsic value.

Food was scarce and dull, the servants mostly terrified Indians from the Methodist missions, except for Ah Chun and two Burmese loyal to Andreino. Hnin Si was also inconspicuously about the place but her offer of acting as maid to Maria – upon Archie's suggestion – had been so violently rejected that she preferred to remain in the background. Maria dressed herself and her own hair, rousing everyone's reluctant admiration but endearing herself to no-one but Archie. He rejoiced to see her every day, lamenting to himself that it was always so publicly, but he watched her as much as was possible, so that when her glance did stray towards him and rested there, even for only a second, he might not miss the chance.

Even Andreino's habitual jauntiness could not disguise the perilousness they were all in. He might be a little irritated by Marie-Thérèse Bonvilain's tearfulness but he could well understand her fears. They were all, as he explained to Archie and Maria, in a blind alley.

'You will understand now why I wanted you to leave, Signorina, why I begged you to go down to Rangoon. We are now dwellers in a city where there is no law but that of the jungle; there is no-one to be in authority here any more. The King's power dies every day, the British are not yet here. And if the King's rule dies quite – before the British come—'

Maria looked at him steadily. 'Should we be the first victims?'

'Of the people of Mandalay? Most certainly. Many hate the King and Queen for their oppression with as much vigour as they love them for their royal omnipotence, but quite as many hate us *kalās*, whom they think have exploited them, grown fat on them—'

'We have,' Maria said.

Archie turned to look at her.

'If the money from all the ruby mines had gone to the people of Upper Burma, to feed and clothe them, they would be a very different race. Of course, that is a foolish dream since, even if we did not take the money, the palace would. The people never benefit.'

Archie began to laugh. 'Maria! Maria, what humanitarian feelings for such an iron-clad heart as yours—'

'I have had time to think recently. Months. And one cannot drive about Mandalay for six years and not see how people live. The squalor may disgust me, but I also find myself comparing it with the way of life of the palace.'

'Signorina—'

She turned to Andreino.

'Signorina, is it possible that you do not know fear?'

'I know it intimately, but it is not of the kind you suppose. I am not physically afraid.'

'Do you know what you may have to face? If, in the next few days, law and order break down utterly here and the crowd goes wild, like a horde of maddened beasts?'

'Of course I don't know. But I can well imagine.'

Andreino stood up. 'I admire you, but almost I find Madame Bonvilain a more natural woman.'

'Go then,' Maria said, 'and pay compliments to her.'

'You astound me,' Archie said when he had gone. 'How can you be so calm, when any day, any hour even, a band of drunken brutes may slash their way in here? How can you not be afraid?'

'I keep telling you. I am not afraid of that.'

'What then, what—'

She said softly, 'You know quite well, Archie. Of an obscure and empty life.'

However calm she might be, the tension in the house was a palpable thing. The three men, and the four manservants who could be trusted not to be reduced to gibbering incompetence by panic, took turns to patrol the house, moving from window to window, armed with rifles. At night they took it in turns to do sentry duty, Archie proving much the steadiest at this, claiming that forest life had made him sharp-eared and eyed in the dense nights. Even with his comforting presence moving softly across the wooden floors, sleep could only be fitful and unrefreshing, broken constantly by screams from neighbouring houses and lanes, and gunshots which echoed whining among the trees of the compound. Bullets were found once or twice, lodged in the balustrade of the verandah, or in the door frames, and one morning, before any of the men had observed and removed it, a body was found slumped upon the verandah steps, the body of a young Burman, his throat most thoroughly slit. Even the missionaries could not sing that day, but stayed near Madame Bonvilain, huddled all together in the centre of the house, as far from windows and doors as was possible.

Minutes passed like hours. Fear robbed most of them of appetite so there was not even the welcome diversion of mealtimes to break the monotony and the anxiety. They were afraid to talk too much for fear of attracting anyone's attention – and anyone might so easily be crouching among the mango trees which, with a flimsy wall of matting, was all that protected them from invasion – and in any case, no subject could hold any interest for them except their plight and that, somehow, seemed worse if discussed. So the endless daylight hours were passed mostly in silence, straining to hear any sounds closer than the distant jangle of Mandalay being taken over by the mob . . .

On 24 November, Mandalay erupted with delight at the news that the best of Thibaw's generals had defeated the British at Myingyan. There was singing and dancing in the streets and a procession went past the besieged house on its way to the river, bearing golden bowls and cups and medals for distribution among the victorious troops.

'It was nonsense,' Andreino said next morning. 'All the Burmese did was withdraw. They never so much as raised their rifles. The British artillery silenced the Burmese batteries before a Burmese soldier had fired so much as a shot—'

Later that day Archie, whom Andreino had warned against going about too freely in daylight, returned with his tunic slashed after a scuffle down by the river, but also with some dramatic news.

'The royal barge of state has just gone down the river. Forty golden oars – it was flying a white flag and there were two envoys, under hat umbrellas in the bows. It seems they are taking a letter from the *Hlutdaw* asking for an armistice, saying that the British government had not understood that Thibaw needed time to do all the things he promised.'

'And if Prendergast refuses?' Maria said, her face white. 'If he refuses an armistice? What will become of the palace?'

Archie said soothingly, 'He won't, you'll see. You'll see by tomorrow.'

On 26 November, General Prendergast replied to the envoys in the golden barge by saying that he could not grant an armistice.

'The Queen!' Maria said to Archie in a whisper of anguish. 'What will happen to the Queen?'

He touched her hand briefly. 'Prendergast has asked the King to surrender himself, his army and Mandalay. He says if he gets to Mandalay, finds that all these requests have been granted and that none of us have been harmed, he will spare Thibaw's life and that of his family.'

'Then don't endanger yourself,' Maria said. 'Don't keep going out and exposing yourself to harm. If anything happened to you, revenge would be taken upon the Queen.'

'And do you,' Archie said in half-mocking despair, 'not care what happens to me?'

She looked at him directly and then she said, in exactly the tone she used to admonish Madame

Bonvilain for weeping, 'Oh yes, Mr Tennant. I care.'

Two days later, Andreino roused the household at dawn. No-one had slept because the anti-*kalā* feelings in Mandalay, which rose as the British army came nearer, had culminated in a night of stone-throwing and hostile yelling outside the house which had reduced almost all the inmates, tense with long strain, to hysteria. An hour before dawn, the bands of Burmese had straggled off, spent by their own lawlessness, and the inhabitants had fallen into an exhausted slumber, only to be aroused almost at once by Andreino.

'You must rise all of you! The British army is come, the whole flotilla will be here by mid-morning. It takes up five miles of the river! We must be down on the bund to greet them, to show that we are safe!'

The lady missionaries declined to come, saying they would not add to the crowd, and as Andreino and Archie, Maria and the Bonvilains made their way towards the river, they could be heard on the first of their jolly morning choruses, praising the Lord for the day He had made. The Irrawaddy was choked all across its breadth with steamers and flats, both they and the bund seeming to swarm with red coats. General Prendergast, upon being presented to Maria and finding himself asked at once what he intended to do with the Queen, whom his troops referred to as Soup-plate, was quite taken aback and for a

397

moment felt himself not to be in charge of the situation at all.

'Miss – er, Miss Beresford. I – I have received no reply to my request for the King's surrender. It is my intention that we march to the palace and gain an answer directly.'

Maria's chin went up and she gave her parasol a little shake. 'General, I should be obliged if you would permit me to accompany you. For five years I was accustomed to have daily audience with Her Majesty and I am familiar with the ways of the palace and with court language. I believe I should be of assistance to you.'

From the deck of a steamer some distance away, Murray Shaw had his field glasses trained upon that elegant figure in blue. He saw her presented to General Prendergast and then he saw them exchange a few words and then, to his astonishment, he saw her accept the arm the general offered. As they moved away among the trees at the top of the bund, Moylan said at his elbow, 'Your Miss Beresford?'

'By jove, it is,' Murray said. 'My Miss Beresford!'

20

From the Lion Throne Room could be heard
the regular approaching tramp of marching men.
Supayalat, attended by a weeping Mattie
Calogreedy, had mounted one of the wooden
watchtowers that stood at the palace walls and
together they had watched the first columns
come into view up the four white roads that led
to the City of Gems. For some minutes they
had stood there together, the vibrant, pregnant
little Queen and the plump, coarsened maid of
honour, watching those steady ranks of red-faced
Englishmen and brown-faced Indians and then,
abruptly, Supayalat had rushed screaming down
the spiral stair of the watchtower and cast herself
howling to grovel in the white dust of the courtyard, tearing her hair down from its knot,
scattering the diamonds that had decorated it like
raindrops. The violence of her grief – maybe even
her remorse – had only lasted moments. Under
Mattie's bewildered, sorrowful gaze, she had
picked herself up, twisted her hair back onto her
head and, dusty but still magnificent, had gone
to the Lion Throne Room where Thibaw sat
motionless except for the restless shifting of his

eyes. Silently, Supayalat slipped onto the *salundaw* beside him and took his damp and trembling hand in hers.

'*Poon-dawgi-paya*,' she said. 'My Lord. The Lord of all the Universe.'

'They are coming,' Thibaw said. 'They are coming to execute us.'

She said, soothingly, 'No. No. Not that. Never that. Lord of the White Elephants, Lord of the Lion Throne—'

She left him briefly for the last ritual bathing and dressing of her time in Mandalay. Mattie stayed by her, but many of the little butterfly maids had gone, driven by a terror of the English soldiers back to their relations. They hardly spoke, she and Mattie, but simply went through the familiar motions of the bathing with scented water, the oiling of that smooth brown skin still as unlined as a girl's after half a dozen pregnancies, the brushing and arranging of her gleaming black hair, the richest tamein, the finest muslin jacket, the most impressive diamonds in her hair, at her neck and ears, weighting her thin supple brown wrists and fingers . . .

Back on the Lion Throne, Thibaw waited for her. Side by side they sat in their brilliant silks and diamonds, even their majesty dwarfed by the huge gilded and fretted screens of the throne that soared behind them, edged with flames of gold carved out of teak. Before them, descending some fifteen feet to the floor, fell steps to a red and golden balustrade that kept everyone at a distance. The room, lined now with ministers and court officials, was quite still except for that advancing, shuffling stamp, the army of the great white queen from the West, coming nearer and nearer at every moment through the white dust of Mandalay.

It seemed that despite the approaching tramp of marching men the British officers were in the Throne Room with startling suddenness, big and red-faced, their huge feet heavy-booted on the floor where only velvet slippers had been before, velvet slippers and submissive bare feet. Supayalat stretched out her hand to her husband and peered at the Englishmen. One she knew, a Colonel Sladen, chief political officer, a friend of Burma in the old days. But the others, all strangers, all of them. Thibaw's fingers tightened on hers. Her eye caught a flash of blue among the drill coats of the officers and as she watched it a voice she knew well from days and days of idleness among the fountains and lawns of the palace gardens said, 'Is it really necessary, General, to wear swords in the presence of Their Majesties?'

She gave Thibaw's hand a little jerk. 'Miss Beresford—'

He was not listening. He was very afraid, she could tell. Sweat had broken out gleaming upon his upper lip, his forehead.

'Great Lord of my life,' she said, 'Lord of the House of Alompra, the Kingdom of Ava. Eye of the Universe, Jewel among jewels of the City of Gems—'

Colonel Sladen and General Prendergast stood below them, armed and shod.

'Are you my executioner?' Thibaw asked.

Edward Sladen, who had known Burma for twenty years, shook his head in reassurance. He indicated Prendergast.

'This is the English general, Your Majesty. He has come to request you to keep your promise of yesterday and to surrender yourself to his charge.'

Supayalat could feel the bones of the King's fingers pressing painfully on hers. He cleared his throat and said in a voice that was much steadier, 'And will the general spare my life and the lives of my family?'

'Certainly, Your Majesty.'

Thibaw's fingers slackened their grip. He gave her hand a little squeeze and withdrew his own to his lap.

'Your Majesty,' Sladen said gently, 'the general will treat you with great respect and consideration and will allow you to take anyone with you that you please, together with your personal property.'

Thibaw licked his lips. 'And – and will the English soldiers protect me from my own people?'

Prendergast said something in English, his eyes fixed all the time upon the King.

'Your Majesty, the general wishes me to tell you that he will see that you are surrounded by soldiers on your way to the ships.'

Ships! Supayalat gave a startled, almost fearful, glance at her husband. Where were they going? Where were they to be taken? Where was there in all the world, but Mandalay?

Sladen said, as if reading her thoughts, 'We will escort you to India, Your Majesty. A house – a fitting house – has been prepared for you at Ratnagiri on the Kolkan, the southern coast of India, not far from Madras. The government of India will supply you with a pension, a generous pension.'

'But I am to be an exile?'

'Yes, Your Majesty. You must be an exile.'

Thibaw's gaze went slowly about the Lion Throne Room, travelling over the scarlet and gold lacquer, the mirrored pillars, the gleaming floorboards of polished teak where the sunlight fell as thick as syrup from the open doors onto the palace platform. He took a deep breath and spoke with a dignity that brought a glow to his wife's face.

'When I go into captivity, those who love me may follow me, but those who like themselves best will stay and look after their own property.' He paused and glanced briefly at the Queen. She was gazing at him, intent upon his every breath. 'I shall leave my palace now. I shall go into a summerhouse in the gardens and there, tomorrow, my formal surrender to the general may take place—'

Supayalat leaned towards him, whispering.

'You will grant my request that the Queen's

ladies may be permitted to use the western gate freely tonight.'

The Englishmen exchanged glances. They moved together and conferred in that strange, muted tongue of the English and only Maria, standing behind them, her eyes fixed upon the jewelled dolls on the Lion Throne heard Sladen say, 'Damn it! You can't refuse such a thing to the ladies! One night—'

Prendergast hesitated. 'Very well. I'll put White and the Hampshires on the western gate. Even if the King did attempt to escape, dressed as a woman, which is my fear, I don't think he would get past White—'

'There would be no question of such a thing,' Miss Beresford said sharply from behind them, 'no question at all. The King will remain entirely faithful to his Queen and she, as I am sure you will observe, is in no condition to ride anywhere upon an elephant.'

'Miss Beresford is very familiar with both King and Queen,' Sladen said. He turned to the King. 'The ladies of the court may go freely in and out, Your Majesty. You will understand the need for a guard for your own safety, but you have no need to be in any way alarmed by their presence.'

From her golden height, Supayalat leaned down a little. 'Miss Beresford, you will attend me this night.'

And Maria, in the presence of the English officers, knelt on the floor of the Throne Room amid the billowings of her skirts and touched her forehead on the ground in humble thankfulness.

'*Ashin-nammadaw-paya*. It will only be an honour.'

It was a strange and horrible night. Neither Supayalat nor Thibaw slept but sat upright and watchful, hand in hand upon the *salun-daw* in the little pavilion that had seen so many games and intrigues in the past, and listened to the howls and cries as Mandalay was looted. Thibaw's people, the citizens of Ava who had struggled for so long under the burden of corrupt and savage rule, had erupted into a screaming horde. Maria, stiff and cold, knelt by her Queen, the only servant remaining beyond the two old ministers who had helped to drive the monarchy into British arms, and the handful of court ladies left from the three hundred who had once surrounded the royal pair. In the shadows of the gardens, by the streams and waterfalls, at every flight of steps, in every doorway, at each corner of the palace platform, English sentries stood, uniformed, thick-booted men of the guard of the 67th Hampshires. No-one spoke, not one word in all those long and bitter hours, and the only movement in the sorrowful and dignified little group in the pavilion was Supayalat, leaning forward at intervals from the couch, for Maria to light a fresh cheroot for her.

21

'You must be the fellow my brother met. In
Bombay,' Murray Shaw said.

'Oh?' Archie said idly, not really listening, his
eyes fixed upon the little procession of women
that had been trotting past them, either in or out
of the palace, since dusk fell.

Murray shifted his feet. The recent unseasonal
rain had made a marsh of the outer palace compound and it was a pretty damned uncomfortable
place to be. Still, it was his men who were
on guard duty, even if standing ankle deep in
Burmese mud watching a crowd of rough-looking
peasant women was hardly a substitute for the
action they had all been hoping for – and endure
it they must.

'He said he met you at dinner somewhere. Said
you played polo—'

'I tried to. I say, I know I am not a soldier, and
therefore you probably won't listen to me, but
you know all these women are looters, don't
you?'

Murray gave him the pitying glance soldiers
reserve for unprofessional civilian misconcep-
tions. 'No, they are not, old fellow. They are the

Queen's ladies-in-waiting. Old Soup-plate's little lot, as my sergeant says. We gave them free access as a favour to the Queen.'

Archie said mildly, 'Take a look at them.'

By the light of the flares that had been lit on the massive white walls of the western gate and which threw jagged flames and shadows over the soldiers stationed either side of it, Murray peered at the women scuttling through.

'Not what I had expected, I grant you. Always thought the Burmese women would be finer looking—'

'They are,' Archie said. 'These are the wives of fishermen from the bund, from the river, whores from the town, peasants from the fields round Mandalay. And beneath your military noses, they are carrying away everything of small size and great value from the palace. If you don't inform your commanding officer, there won't be a diamond left to take home to Queen Victoria.'

Murray said, nettled, 'What do you know about it in any case?'

'Enough,' Archie said. 'Are you going?'

'Why did you come up here, Tennant? What are you doing in the palace in any case? Why aren't you with the other civilians and that Italian fellow? May I remind you that it is the Burma Field Force that have taken Mandalay—'

'Ah,' Archie said, 'so it was. Walked in and took it. I came up to the palace because there is someone here I want to be sure is safe. An English person. A lady.'

Murray said, with the air of someone whose job it is to know everything, 'I imagine you mean Miss Beresford. She is in the garden pavilion with the King and Queen.'

'I know.'

'Of course,' Murray said, 'I knew her years ago. In Bombay.'

'Busy place, Bombay.'

'I dined with them several times. I was a guest at her twenty-first birthday party in fact. She must have been the handsomest girl in Western India. And the most spirited. Knew her pretty well, to tell the truth.'

A soldier came up, stamped to attention in the mud, and presented Murray with a folded paper.

'Sorry, old chap,' Murray said to Archie with a grin. 'General's orders. All civilians to leave the palace. All, that is, except the ladies-in-waiting.'

Archie said, 'Will you inform him that these are no more court ladies than angels?'

'Theory of yours, old fellow. Nothing to do with me. Wilkes here will escort you out. Night, Tennant.'

When Archie had gone, Murray took out his notebook and after a considerable amount of thought and a false start or two, succeeded in scribbling a message. He summoned the returning Wilkes.

'Take this to the guard at the pavilion, would you? Where the King and Queen are. And see it is given to Miss Beresford there. Miss Maria Beresford.'

Dawn came at last, rising rosy over the long
blue lines of the Shan hills and behind the tall
cone of Mandalay Hill where the giant golden
Buddha, placed there by King Mindoon, stood
and pointed down to the city of the kings of Ava.
Soft plumes of mist rose from the wet gardens
around the summer pavilion, swathing the harsh
and brilliant outlines of the palace, the implac-
able forms of the English soldiers, the menace of
the day ahead. A small procession of ladies-in-
waiting, dressed in their customary brilliant silks
as if this day were no more irregular than any
other day, came across the misty spaces bearing
the lacquerwork urns that contained the royal
breakfast. It was spread before the King and
Queen, golden dishes of curry and rice, rice-flour
pancakes smeared with a paste of sesame seed,
mangoes sliced to translucent thinness and laid
on leaves, dried prawns arranged in a wheel on
a silver plate, a gilded basket of pineapples, a
jewelled goblet for Thibaw, French crystal for his
Queen, for his second Queen, for the Queen
Mother. Maria rose to attend them.

Supayalat said, 'Take it. Take it all away.'

'*Ashin-nammadaw-paya*—'

The Queen clapped her hands together and
raised her voice. 'At once! Take it away! Everything!'

Thibaw said nothing. His pale plump face was
slack in the dawn, his eyes dull and tired. His
second Queen, Supayalat's plain and older sister,

409

made some small move towards the dish nearest to her, caught her sister's commanding eye, and withdrew her hand. She had put on the apricot robes of a nun and sat behind her sister, apprehensive and suppressed, Thibaw's wife only in name. Supayalat leaned towards the King, her hard little brown fingers laid upon his plump soft hand.

'You must dress, my lord. You must dress for the English general.'

Thibaw looked down at his clothes in some surprise, at the gorgeous ripple-woven silk of his paso, silk woven on a loom of two hundred shuttles, the pattern done by eye. He had worn it since yesterday, since the afternoon of yesterday, he, who was accustomed to wear nothing for more than a few hours together. He glanced at his Queen and nodded faintly.

'For the English general of the great white Queen—'

For the last time, Supayalat's litter was carried across the gardens to her, the litter that had carried her about the palace for six pregnancies in as many years. It was a little pagoda-shaped cage, scarlet and gold, with gilded gauze windows, set in a golden boat and slung on poles covered in velvet. Maria rose to attend her as she had done for the unwanted breakfast and Supayalat said, 'You. Just you,' and bowed her sleek black head to step behind the doors of golden gauze.

Maria dressed her in silence. All around them, in other rooms of the great rambling palace, voices shouted and laughed and feet went stampeding by, the feet of the women of the town, their brawny arms straining round velvets and silks, cushions and stools, golden cups and looking glasses framed in gems, ivory combs, boxes of lacquer and scented woods, fans and bottles and gilded umbrellas. Maria looked about the little room where she knelt by the Queen, the room which had witnessed a hundred ritual dressings and which held only four great teak wardrobes inlaid with silver and mirrors and a huge looking glass swinging on a golden stand.

'There is nothing here to take,' Supayalat said.

She was wound into a tamein of cream, thickly embroidered in gold, and wore over it a jacket of a pattern only permitted to royalty, the hem wired up into stiff little points like wings, each wing edged with golden teardrops. Round her neck Maria clasped a diamond necklace of dazzling splendour – paid for, Archie might have told her, by the Bombay-Burmah Trading Corporation who had purchased it three years before, on royal orders – and then she knelt to slip onto those smooth brown feet golden slippers lined in red velvet, the edge of the sole studded with rubies.

'Nothing to take,' Supayalat repeated bitterly, 'only myself.'

'Your Majesty, I do assure you that you will be treated with the utmost deference.'

Supayalat spat. 'Exiles!'

Maria waited, watching the vehement little

figure struggle with itself before the looking glass.

'The letter!' Supayalat said suddenly, 'You received a letter! In the night!'

'It was from a gentleman I once met in India. Many years ago, Your Majesty. He is come up with the army. He simply wishes to be remembered to me.'

Supayalat's eyes gleamed. 'You must not waste your chances! You are a girl no more, you are old to be married. Of course—' She stopped and in the looking glass her brilliant dark eyes met Maria's blue ones, 'You might come with me to India.'

'*Ashin-nammadaw-paya*, Your Majesty, the honour you do me—'

'I shall not rest. Not in India. There are many scores to be paid. The English will feel me still, here in Mandalay, they will not be free of me.' She stopped and laid her hands either side of her swollen belly. 'Call the litter. The *Poon-dawgi-paya* needs me. Call it.'

'Your Majesty, are you asking me to come to India with you?'

'I would order,' Supayalat said, 'but now I ask.'

'And would you permit me a little time to reflect upon your request?'

'Yes,' Supayalat said, 'yes.' She went past Maria, smiling, tapping the pocket where she had thrust Murray Shaw's note. 'There are things to be seen to, heh? Gentlemen from Bombay—'

Maria drew herself up. 'Such consideration

412

would not influence my decision in the least, Your Majesty.'

Supayalat's smile faded. She looked at Maria with her hard searching gaze.

'They should, Miss Beresford,' she said, her tone sharp with reprimand, 'they should.'

On the open verandah of the pavilion, Thibaw waited, simply dressed in white, his head swathed in a turban of white and pink. Behind him, his second Queen still knelt, and beside him the old Queen Mother, mother to both Queens, crouched in meditation, her lips moving silently, her little old brown claws held out in supplication to some unseen source of strength. Thibaw sat cross-legged upon a carpet, quite without occupation apart from a betel box, shaped like a golden bird with emerald eyes, which had been his father's, which rested upon the floor within reach. The boards of the verandah were already splashed with blotches of betel juice, scarlet stains like blood. Supayalat was handed from her litter and went swiftly to seat herself by her husband, coiling herself beside him, supple and watchful, the teardrops on her winged jacket winking in the strengthening sun. Stiff and aching, sour-mouthed and sore-eyed from a sleepness night in the open air and the discomfort of the clothes of the previous day, Maria sank upon the verandah steps and waited with them, her thoughts a confused and exhausted jumble of a future in Ratnagiri and a past in Bombay.

At noon, General Prendergast came, complete with pith helmet and riding boots polished to a dazzling brilliance. Maria moved away from the verandah steps as the soldiers approached, but Thibaw made no attempt to rise, only glanced about him apprehensively and then, as the English general bowed and shook him firmly by the hand, looked much astonished. He remained for some time afterwards gazing down at his hand as if having such a liberty taken with it must surely have changed it out of all recognition.

'Your Majesty, you are asked to come to the ship with us now, at once.'

'Tomorrow,' Thibaw said, his eyes sliding past the soldiers, 'only tomorrow—'

'Today, Your Majesty. There can be no more delaying.'

'Two hours, one – one hour—'

'Ten minutes,' the general said inexorably.

Maria's vision was blurring. The Queen's voice, only a whisper, was repeating steadily, 'Lord of my life, Lord of the White Elephants, Lord of the Lion Throne, King of Ava, of the House of Alompra—'

The general said, 'I must order you, Your Majesty. It pains me but I must.'

'A little while,' Thibaw's gaze went swinging wildly round the gardens and grottoes, the fountains and groves of so many days of idle pleasure, 'a little while, a little—'

He stopped, his eyes sinking to the ground. 'We have two children alive. Three are buried in the northern garden here. Let—' He paused again and then said with gathering resolution, 'Let Sladen govern the country for five years and when he has everything in good order then I will come back and be guided by him.' He lifted his eyes and looked at Prendergast with diffidence. 'You English think I killed all my relations, but it is not so. I was under guard myself and they were murdered. I only ordered that they should be imprisoned to avoid a disturbance in the country. Some – some people have tried to murder me—' He caught his breath and licked his lips. 'I wish – I wish the English people to know I am not a drunkard. I am a religious Buddhist. I have given up the crown jewels – Let me stay an hour more, an hour more, an hour only, an hour—'

'No,' Prendergast said, 'no more time. We have drawn up one of your coaches. Will you and your Queens mount so that you may ride in fitting style to the river?'

Maria fought back her tears. If she wept, she would not be able to see and she must see, she must—

Thibaw rose to his feet, a strange, small, plump figure, dignified and absurd.

'I scorn to ride,' he said, 'I scorn it. My Queens and I will walk.'

He stooped and with a sudden and heart-breaking tenderness offered a hand to either Queen. Prendergast stepped back and all the soldiers with him, back until they formed a wide aisle across the green gardens to where the great royal red gate stood flung open, the gate used only by the King, the gate scarcely opened for Thibaw in all the seven years of his reign. Slowly and with irreproachable dignity, the King and his Queens walked across the gardens hand in hand, the sunlight glancing irreverently off their jewels and gold ornaments so that they moved in a halo of dancing lights. Maria longed to follow and would not, would not for these final and fleeting moments take from them their last glory in even the smallest measure. She put her hand to her face and found it slippery with tears.

'Miss Beresford,' Colonel Sladen said and pressed into her hand an immaculately laundered handkerchief.

On the bund, Archie waited behind a double file of men from the Liverpool Regiment. He had waited there through the heat of the afternoon while the royal procession, after the interminable formalities of leaving the palace, made its snail-paced progress through the crowds that thronged the *kalā* town. The SS *Thoreah* lay at the landing stage and round it, on the broad waters of the Irrawaddy dyed apricot by the rapidly setting sun, bobbed the inquisitive boats of the fishermen of Mandalay. The crowd pressed at his back, the dusty-footed, garlic-scented Burmese crowd in its rags and tatters of turbans and pasos, chattering comfortably as if it were about to see a pageant rather than the dethronement of a king. Here and there lanterns began to be lit, glowing yellow in the thickening dusk and then a whisper began, growing to a mutter and a cry, 'The King is coming! The King! The King!'

Two small bullock carts came into view, with eight white umbrellas held over the first.

'Nine,' Archie said to himself, 'there should be nine. As King he is entitled to nine—'

In the second cart Maria sat upright with Mattie Calogreedy beside her, sobbing and dusty, dressed in a peculiarly unbecoming European dress several sizes too small for her. In the dusk, Maria's face was no more than a pale triangle beneath a hat of blue velvet flowers, but Archie felt he could deduce her expression from her attitude and that even, from fifteen feet away, he could sense the distaste she felt for Mattie's lack of self-control and her absurd and inappropriate dress. So strange, he thought, so strange and wonderful – Are the great events of the world always so amazing in their littleness at close quarters? A king is dethroned and a little plump fellow in a pink checked turban is bundled away in a bullock cart in the dusk, without ceremony, without pomp and splendour and hardly any sense at all that an age has passed, that a chapter is closing, that whatever the future brings, it can't bring back kings to Mandalay. I am looking at history, Archie told himself, peering to see clearly, I am looking at the end of an age, at the machinery of the British Empire in visible motion, and what do I see but two little brown Eastern people helping each other to descend from a cart like any fond peasant couple at a market, watched by a few soldiers, a crowd of Burmese and me. The Kingdom of Ava is dying. Even as they step onto the gangplank, with the Queen holding out her hand as if to a child, persuading, urging, cajoling and motherlike, with each step the kingdom breathes slower, more shallowly, and when they are gone we shall be left here with a sense of mission accomplished and an awful emptiness, a hollow aching void because an era is over; every minute carries us farther from it, from any sympathy we felt for it. The spell is breaking, the spell of Mandalay, and those little creatures are taking it with them—

A sudden movement caught his eye. Maria had descended from the second cart and had hurried forward towards the gangplank of the *Thoreah*, followed by the still-weeping Mattie stumbling behind and blotting her eyes on the backs of her grey kid gloves. For a moment Archie thought Maria meant to run up the gangplank behind the Queen and he began to shout, wildly and urgently, pushing his bulk roughly through the crowd that held him from the shore, and then he saw that Maria had halted suddenly and was simply standing there, between two soldiers, gazing up at the side of the steamer where Supayalat was coaxing Thibaw to take his final steps onto the deck. Archie reached her side a moment later, breathless and tumbled.

'Don't go, Maria, I beg you, don't go, reflect a little—'

She shook his restraining hand off impatiently but said nothing, only continued to look almost imploringly upwards at the tiny figure climbing towards the deck.

Mattie said, sobbing, 'I never meant this; I never wanted this to happen, it wasn't the Queen I hated, it wasn't her. Oh, tell her I always loved her, tell her it was Pierre I wanted to hurt, I didn't think, I didn't think—'

Maria said in disgust, without turning, 'Control yourself.'

Archie put an arm about Mattie's shoulders, feeling her warm puttylike flesh squeezing against the fabric of her dress.

'Oh, Mr Tennant, I am so unhappy, I am so confused. And now there is no-one left in Mandalay for me. I am quite alone. What will become of me, what will happen?'

A gleam of grinning teeth among the nearest soldiers indicated to Archie that the darkness did not cover his embrace of Mattie. He took his arm away from her shoulders but found she still leaned against him, sodden and heavy with misery like a damp flour sack.

'You should go to the convent of St Joseph.'

'Oh,' she said, beginning to cry again, 'nuns—'

'They are going,' Maria said suddenly. 'Look, oh, look—'

The *Thoreah* hooted mournfully and the throb of the engines began to pulse in the dark waters of the Irrawaddy. Mattie peeled herself from Archie's side and rushed forwards to the river, screaming for the Queen, her voice quite drowned by the rising note of the engines and the splash of water. Side by side behind her, Archie and Maria stood and watched the *Thoreah* pull away to midstream, bearing with her the doll-like royal couple, upright and motionless upon the deck, their backs turned resolutely upon Mandalay. Archie wanted violently to put not one but both arms about Maria, but her rigidity and concentration deterred him. He stood beside her, peering passionately at her in the fitful light of surrounding lamps, his fists clenched at his sides and at last burst out, 'Shall you go? Shall you go with her?'

Maria said, as if from far away, 'She never turned. She never turned to bid me farewell.' She paused, and then said in a more normal tone, 'Naturally I shall follow her. I have one more thing to do in Mandalay – and if nothing comes of that, then I shall go to India. What else is there for me to do?'

'You know what you might do,' he said urgently. 'You might marry me.'

'Archie, we have already had this conversation—'

'But things are different now. You are different, so am I. You can't follow her, you can't. India won't be like Mandalay, it can't be. Ratnagiri will be some fly-blown bungalow where life will be nothing but staggeringly boring and full of petty intrigue. There will be nothing left of life here, nothing. The Queen will grow ever more whimsical and tyrannical—'

He stopped. Silent tears were sliding down her face and hanging ignominiously on her cheeks and chin. Mattie, stumbling up from the river, looked astonished out of her own wretchedness.

He said, 'I'm so sorry. Forgive me,' and put a crumpled handkerchief of doubtful purity into her hand.

She said furiously, 'I never weep. Never. And this is the second time today.'

'You are tired. And too much has happened.'

'Tired,' she said, 'yes, tired.' She gave herself a resolute shake and straightened her shoulders. 'Would you find me a bullock cart? I think I should like to go to bed.'

'Come to the convent,' Mattie begged. 'Come to the convent with me.'

'No thank you,' Maria said. 'I have had quite enough of pious women but at least I will remain with those who are familiar, however irritating—'

'You are a cold, hard woman!' Mattie screamed, 'You have no thoughts for anyone else, you have no feelings, you are stone!'

'And you,' Maria said savagely, 'are soft and weak and – and *treacherous*.'

Archie caught Mattie as she lunged across him at Maria. They struggled clumsily together for a while but Mattie's instincts would not allow her to interpret a man's touch save in one direction for long. She gave up abruptly and began to wail into Archie's shirt front, clutching at him with her frantic little fat hands. Over her head he looked in despair at Maria.

'Hysterical,' Maria said shortly and then, raising her voice, she almost shouted at Mattie, 'To make a spectacle of yourself is one thing, but to make one of Mr Tennant is quite another! Let go of him this instant!'

Moments later, with Maria upon one arm, touching him so lightly he could hardly feel her, and Mattie dragging upon the other, Archie descended the landward slope of the bund towards Mandalay. Behind them the *Thoreah*, invisible now in the sudden blackness except for the lights strung along her decks like a necklace, swung her bulk slowly around in the river and began the slow journey south to Rangoon and exile.

22

'I want no-one to leave this compound,' Andreino said, 'without my express permission and the escort of either myself, Mr Tennant or Monsieur Bonvilain.'

The lady missionaries, huddled together in a grey-brown serge flock, listened obediently. Some wore the bright smiles that were as habitual with them as breathing, but others, who had found that their spontaneous ability to burst into rousing evangelical song had unaccountably deserted them in the last few days, looked grave and biddable.

'Now that the King and Queen are gone,' Andreino said, 'I am afraid that lawlessness will again take over Mandalay. I have no doubt but that General Prendergast will institute order as soon as he can, but even he cannot prevent the hordes who will pour into the city from the jungle and the villages from being, initially, a great threat. And the Queen has left many spies and supporters behind and you must not forget that for Supayalat, England is first among her enemies and therefore any English civilian will be a prime target for her revenge—'

'I come,' one of the lady missionaries said loudly, 'from Allentown, Pennsylvania!'

Andreino glanced at Archie, smiling. 'My dear signorina, I fear you cannot expect a Burmese dacoit to make the distinction between an American and an English citizen.'

'More's the pity for that, poor heathen soul,' the lady from Allentown declared roundly.

One of the others stood up, a small fresh-faced young woman with more of an air of having spent the last years on a farm than in a steaming Burmese jungle. 'I have a request, Mr Andreino.'

'Certainly, Miss Newman.'

'Three years ago, when I first came to Burma, I spent nine months at the mission school here in Mandalay with Mr Prior. It would ease my mind very much if I might go back to the school and bring out any Christian souls who remain there and are in peril—'

'Miss Newman, if any Europeans had remained at the mission, I should naturally have rescued them myself the moment the British arrived in Rangoon.'

Miss Newman regarded him reprovingly. 'God makes no distinction as to colour, Mr Andreino. I feel you may have overlooked some *Burmese* Christians.'

From his watchful position at the window, Archie said, 'I will go for you, Miss Newman.'

'I should be glad of your company, Mr Tennant, but I should prefer to go myself.'

'I cannot allow it,' Andreino said, 'unless there is excellent reason—'

'I insist upon going,' Miss Newman said levelly. 'There are various mementoes in the school that I should like to take to Mr Prior in Rangoon before they are in danger of being destroyed. You cannot know what to choose.'

'Miss Newman—'

'I am not afraid of danger, Mr Andreino. And I am fully determined to do what I see to be my duty.'

Andreino looked across at Maria, sitting a little removed as she always did, and shrugged. 'You ladies of determination—'

'We become much worse,' Maria said, with a ghost of a smile, 'if thwarted.'

Miss Newman clearly did not relish the thought of being linked with the worldly and aloof Miss Beresford in anyone's mind. 'I am not being perverse, Mr Andreino, merely asking for your help.'

'I'll come with you,' Archie said. 'I said I would. I should be pleased to.'

'It must be daylight, signorina—'

'Naturally.'

Andreino sighed. He showed no outward marks upon his face of the strain of the past week, but his elaborate linen was now grimy to a point that made Maria reluctant to go near him.

'Will you listen to me one more moment? I must outline plans for your leaving Mandalay—'

Marie-Thérèse began to weep again. Her

husband, most solicitous to her in public, despite having been heard, by the shocked missionaries, to speak quite sharply when he did not think himself overheard, tried a smile of male complicity with Archie which evoked no response and put an arm, with elaborate resignation, around his wife's trembling shoulders. Between sobs she was heard to say that she should never live to see Paris again, nor her beloved parents, nor the little spaniel which had been her childhood companion, nor her old nurse, nor the room which had been hers since babyhood, indeed right up to the very night of her marriage, the marriage that had led to so much danger—

'I would beg you, Madame,' Andreino said, 'to weep as softly as it is in your power to do.'

She took her face from her husband's shoulder to glare at him.

'The scheme I have devised,' Andreino said, 'depends upon the patience of you all. The Irrawaddy Flotilla Company, having suspended its steamer service for the past few weeks, now intends to resume it. If an opportunity arises for me to – to borrow, shall we say, a military escort from the British force, I will make sure that you are all upon the first steamer bound for Rangoon. If it is thought that your departure in smaller groups would attract less attention from the bandits, who will, I fear, harass all shipping south as far as the border with Lower Burma, you must be patient and wait your turn. Mr Tennant—' He paused and looked at Archie, 'Mr Tennant is remaining in Upper Burma and will assist me. May I say to you all that I regard you all as my responsibility and I will do everything in my power to ensure your safety.'

A burst of hoarse shouting arose from the lane some twenty yards away and a hail of stones, flung from behind the matting fence which still remained miraculously intact, pattered noisily onto the tin roof above their heads.

'We should hurry—' Archie said.

'As soon as possible!'

'When is the first steamer?'

'Not before I have been to the mission!'

'Will the British give us no protection?'

'If only we were all armed—'

Archie, stooping over Maria, said, 'On my way back to the mission, I will look at your house.'

She glanced up at him. 'If you would. I long to return there—'

'There can be no question of that.'

'I must. I cannot think here. I cannot put my thoughts into any kind of order.'

'But it is the only place where you have any chance of safety.'

'Oh!' she said impatiently, tapping her foot. 'Safety—'

'Maria—'

'Yes.'

'Have you made up your mind? About – about anything?'

'I told you,' she said, 'I have already said so. I

can think of nothing here. All these women, the lack of privacy, the chattering – it is impossible.'

'You are so difficult to persuade to anything,' he said in despair.

She looked up at him again, on the verge of a smile.

'I should have thought, in a situation like this, that it was a relief to have at least one person who knew their own mind.'

Miss Newman was well equipped for her journey to the mission. She appeared before Archie in the serge dress he had begun to think grew upon her like a skin, stout boots and a solar topee, one hand clasping a green cloth umbrella, the other a capacious bag made apparently of carpet. It was but ten minutes' walk to the mission and Archie had chosen the early afternoon as the most suitable moment since a large number of the inhabitants slept then, slumped beneath trees or carts, even at such an excitable time as this. He carried his own double-barrelled revolver in one pocket and Maria's – astonishingly handed to him in silence as he left – in the other. He had offered one of these to Miss Newman, who had said that as a servant of the Lord, she never touched firearms.

'Not even to defend another?'

'The occasion has never arisen, Mr Tennant.'

He held out Maria's revolver. 'It might today.'

'I prefer not to take it, Mr Tennant.'

He shrugged. 'A little illogical, if you will

forgive me for saying so. A dead servant of the Lord is not so much use to Him as a living one.'

Miss Newman gave him a quelling look.

The lane outside the compound was still and empty in the heat. It was lined with compounds and bungalows such as the one in which they had taken refuge, but in a haphazard way, with rough spaces here and there in which Burmese had set up their matting hovels. Goats roamed unsteadily in these dusty clearings, but they were almost the only sign of life beyond a still body or two, humped in the shade, its turban wound about its face.

'I think,' Archie said in a low voice, 'that conversation would be a mistake. The dust is thick enough to muffle much of our tread. Would you be so good as to walk slightly ahead of me?'

Miss Newman struck out purposefully, her umbrella held over her head and casting a round black block of shadow on her serge-clad shoulders, swinging her carpet bag with almost military precision. Archie trod behind her, his eyes moving from side to side, slipping watchfully over matting walls and mango trees, their heavy leaves drooping and motionless in the heat. It was a long ten minutes, following Miss Newman's resolute back and expecting all the time that someone might leap from the foliage – foliage which somehow managed to give an impression of concealing something watchful. Two turnings were safely negotiated and Maria's house came into view. The doors onto the verandah stood open but within Archie could glimpse the gleam of the gilding on those familiar rose-pink chairs. Guiding Miss Newman out of her determined course, he steered her onto the verandah and looked within. The Chinese bowls had been broken, littering the floor with blue and white fragments, but the furniture stood where she had left it around rugs rumpled by hurried feet – but still there. In silence, regarded disapprovingly by Miss Newman, Archie pushed the broken china pieces into a corner with his foot, straightened the rugs and then closed the shutters upon the room. Then, still without speaking, he shepherded Miss Newman back down the lane.

The mission house itself looked almost untouched. Together they climbed the worn steps to the verandah and pushed open the shutters warily to let sunlight into the room where Grace had dispensed tea and the seed cake learned from faraway cookery lessons in her Brighton school. Apart from the dust and a strange greenish-grey mould that had settled like a veil over the cushions and upholstery, the room was just as Archie remembered it; the highly coloured saints still frozen in acts of heroism and martyrdom on the walls, Grace's tea table, the sagging chair in which Tom had crashed to sleep the night of her death, the hooked wool rug the mission school children had made in a thoroughly Burmese mixture of turquoise and apple green and yellow.

'There!' Miss Newman said in triumph. 'Quite untouched! Poor heathens they may be, but not in their souls. They know better than to touch what is the Lord's.'

Archie said, running his finger along the edge of the table and revealing, under the dust, the rings where cups and saucers had stood, 'I fear it's not so much that as fear of ghosts. The Burmese believed ghosts took over when Grace died. Ghosts would keep even the most hardened marauder away.'

'What a sad cynic you are to be sure, Mr Tennant.'

'Perhaps,' he said, 'perhaps.'

'You will remain here,' Miss Newman said firmly, 'while I see if there are any little remembrances in Miss Prior's room that her father might wish to have.'

Archie put a hand on her arm. 'Look by all means. But don't bring anything. It would only hurt him to see—'

'The Lord gives us succour in our grief. He will not suffer us to be long troubled.'

'It has often seemed to me,' Archie said with some energy, 'that Buddhists, for all they are heathen, have an excellent human sympathy.'

'I do not understand you, Mr Tennant.'

'Miss Newman, I dared not hope that you might.'

She returned ten minutes later to the sitting room bearing the picture of St Francis upon which Grace had hung her ribbons and the small china virgin and child which Archie had last seen lost in a forest of physic bottles.

'Of course, there was a lot of girlish foolishness in there,' Miss Newman said, 'which naturally, I left.'

'Naturally.'

'And now, Mr Tennant, the school. The school and the chapel.'

It was evident at once that the ghosts of the house had not been deemed powerful enough to afflict the school and chapel also. Complete devastation reigned, the schoolroom a debris of smashed furniture and broken pictures, the chapel a melancholy scene of heaped destruction surmounted by a crucifix which had been thrust in, like a sword, as a final gesture. Out of the mound of splintered wood in which winked fragments of coloured glass from the broken windows, Christ protruded on His Cross, His face disfigured and His bronze legs obscenely twisted below the knee. Not a thing remained whole, not even the altar, a solid teak structure, which had been hacked at viciously, and stood on its side, as undistinguished as a tea chest, naked of the cloths that forty years of embroidery by lady missionaries had adorned it with – now probably in use as items of apparel somewhere in the Mandalay bazaar. The banners of the Sunday School and the Bible society had gone, the pages of hymn books lay scattered like white leaves over the chaos and above it all, as a sickening last insult, hung the stench of human filth.

Miss Newman gripped her umbrella more tightly. 'Barbarians!'

'Only poor heathens – I thought.'

She moved forward a step. 'I must at least take the crucifix.'

'And show to Tom Prior evidence of the fate that has overtaken the place he loved so much, where he had such high hopes?'

She turned to him. 'Mr Tennant, are you an unbeliever?'

'Not at all.'

A slight sound came from beyond the shattered window frames. Archie looked round at once but the compound between the chapel and the school house was empty of everything but a solitary hen.

'Will you now pray with me in this desecrated place of the Lord?'

'I think we shouldn't linger, Miss Newman. I think we should go now. You see there is no human life here—'

Miss Newman dropped to her knees, laying down her bag and umbrella that she might clasp her hands before her. Then, with closed eyes, she began to pray, calling upon the Lord in strident and demanding tones.

'Please—' Archie said.

Unaccountably, the hair on the back of his neck was prickling, his hearing seemed suddenly intensified, acute. He stooped and seized her arm. 'Miss Newman, *please*—'

'Amen,' she said loudly, glaring at him and getting to her feet. 'My bag, if you please, Mr Tennant, my umbrella—'

Outside in the still afternoon heat, a small

band of men was waiting. There were four of them, with broad mahogany faces and sullen mouths, naked except for loincloths and, in one case, a ragged shirt of checked cotton. Their feet were bare and white with dust and in each of their right hands a *dah* swung, catching the sunlight on the blades.

Archie put his hand to his pocket. 'Please take the pistol—'

'Certainly not,' Miss Newman said.

One of the men came forward and two began to move sideways so that they were treading in a horseshoe shape of which Archie and Miss Newman were the centre.

'Then get behind me—' Archie shouted, plunging a hand into either pocket.

There was a swish in the air like a sudden gust of wind and the centre *dah* blade went up at the sight of the revolvers. There followed a moment of extreme confusion, Archie much impeded by Miss Newman's frantic grasp at his waist and by his having nothing with which to cock the pistols except his teeth. The men were all coming forward, moving faster now, their weapons gleaming in the cloud of dust they were trailing and then Archie fired, right- and left-handed simultaneously, and saw one man fall. Miss Newman was screaming now, dragging him backwards as she hung upon his waist, but he leaned against her weight with his own and fired again, wildly. One of the men began to shout. Sweat was running down Archie's forehead into eyes already filmed with dust. He had to drop Maria's revolver to reload his own and the *dahs* would be upon him before he could do that, any second now—

'They have stopped,' Miss Newman said from under his right arm.

Stock still, ten strides away, the men stood, weapons hanging. Archie raised his empty pistol. They ducked in unison, flinging their arms up across their faces.

'Get out,' Archie said, using the dialect with which he had learned to swear at the *mahouts* in the forest. 'Move. Quickly. Or I will kill you all.'

They stepped backwards a pace or two.

'Move! At once!'

In a moment the compound was empty except for the fallen man in the centre. It had been over in not much more than a minute.

'Is he wounded?'

'Don't touch him!' Archie said. 'Stand there, holding Miss Beresford's pistol as if you would shoot with it – do not argue, Miss Newman – while I load this one—'

Warily, crabwise, they left the compound, retreating backwards up the steps to the mission house and the safety of the ghosts.

'I have to thank you, Mr Tennant,' Miss Newman said with the air of one doing her duty.

'Please do not.'

'It would, of course, have been a martyrdom—'

'It most certainly would not. A tawdry picture

of St Francis is not worth being hacked to pieces for.'

'I was at *prayer*, I would remind you, Mr Tennant.'

They crossed the dusty floorboards to the verandah which fronted the lane. The lane itself was empty still but Mandalay was waking up in the distance and the sounds of gongs and shouting echoed in the hot air.

'Are you ready to attempt our return?'

'Certainly, Mr Tennant.'

She tried to return Maria's pistol, but he shook his head, pushing her before him.

'My umbrella, my bag—'

'A small price to pay for whole skins, Miss Newman.'

She set out, her head high, holding the pistol stiffly in front of her. Only once did she turn her head, when they passed Maria's house once more.

'Mr Tennant.'

'Miss Newman.'

'I am aware that you saved my life this afternoon. I am also aware that there are other lives which you would have preferred to save.'

Over her shoulder, Archie could see that only a hundred yards now separated them from safety. A quick glance behind him showed him that the lane was empty and before them only a group of children was visible, straggling along in the scanty shade dragging a bullock calf on a rope. He prodded Miss Newman to make her go faster.

'Only one,' he said, 'only one.'

23

'So the Lion Throne Room is to be a church,' Maria said, her voice taut with scorn.

Murray Shaw, uncomfortable in a miserable little upright chair and wondering why on earth he had come, nodded.

'And the passage behind it the vestry? And the Lily Throne Room a club? A *club*. I suppose the sacred Red Gate is open always now. And Lord and Lady Dufferin are coming from Calcutta, I gather, to confer a blessing on the noble work of the Burma Field Force—'

He muttered, 'We expected a fight, Miss Beresford. We thought the King would resist. Indeed we did.'

Maria snorted and looked past him out of the doors. They were seated in a room she insisted upon calling her drawing room which contained nothing whatsoever except the two chairs on which they sat and drifts of dust on the polished floor. She had described in tediously intimate detail all the furnishings the room had once possessed, many of which lay smashed and ripped out in the heavy green tangle of the garden, and there had been an awkward moment when she surveyed the gilt legs and wads of torn stuffing that lay littered about and her chin had distinctly trembled. Murray couldn't take women crying. Never had been able to. He sighed and drew his boot toe through the dust at his feet.

'It was unrealistic of you to expect to find me unchanged, Captain Shaw,' Maria said.

He blushed hotly.

'Miss Beresford, I never – I mean, I hardly, indeed you are scarcely—'

'I am quite changed. So I may say are you. The diffidence of the young man I knew in Bombay is quite gone.' She looked down fleetingly at her dress and remembered with what extraordinary care she had dressed for this interview, what trouble she had taken with her hair and the choice of a hat which would shadow the lines that years of taxing climates had drawn on her brow and round her eyes. 'I believe you have carried about a quite false impression of me all these years and I am sorry for it.'

He did not know how to handle her at all. He did not want to look at her because doing so destroyed the image of the delightful girl in blue that had saved him from various entanglements over the years, and he found himself very much afraid of what she might say next. It seemed to him that she was just as much in charge as she had been at twenty-one but with less charm and lightness, more eccentricity. He said nervously, 'No – oh, no—'

'I am sorry for you, but I am much sorrier for

myself, Captain Shaw. I have learned so much about myself just recently that not only am I quite sick of the subject but also very much afraid that I have nothing left of what I thought I was. When you requested an interview I believed I should recapture some of the buoyancy of my time in Bombay, that you would bring back to me that other Maria with all her optimism and confidence. But how could you? I don't even look the same. And my sharp tongue alarms you. I shall try not to let it alarm you further, although it is difficult for me to express approval of what the British have done to Upper Burma. Perhaps in time I shall get to think such interference a good thing. At the moment the desecration of the palace by your army only disgusts me. A club! No doubt the green edges to the moat will provide a splendid track upon which to run the first Mandalay Gymkhana.'

'It has been mentioned—'

'And so I believe has the erection of a brewery and a distillery since, I am told, you cannot keep an army here without beer and gin—'

Murray stood up. 'It was better for the Burmese to be conquered, Miss Beresford,' he said stoutly.

'Conquered! Better! Yes, better in the sense that the natives will be fed and policed and doctored and governed, but that is only half the story. I will not bore you with the other half because you would not understand me.'

'I must go, Miss Beresford.'

'Yes,' she said, 'yes, you must.'

He shifted his feet and looked about him. 'This is really your house?'

'Certainly. It was built for me by the Queen. I have no servants just at present but that is a small matter.'

He held out his hand, forcing himself to look at her and finding, to his resentment, that her face, close to, was quite as captivating as it had been in Bombay six years before, lines and gauntness and all.

'Goodbye, Miss Beresford.'

Her hand in his felt as fragile as a bird. She smiled at him but her eyes were cold and blue. 'Perhaps you would find your own way out, Captain Shaw.'

'Yes,' he said, 'certainly.'

'And I am sorry for your disappointment.'

He flushed with indignation. 'It was not a disappointment, Miss Beresford.'

Seconds later, negotiating fragments of porcelain which littered the verandah, he reflected that although the interview had indeed been a disappointment, that was not what he had minded so badly. What he minded was her continuing upper hand, a supremacy which the young Murray Shaw had found exciting, but which the older one found only intolerable. He had come away, he told himself crossly, shaking like a disgruntled dog, thoroughly worsted; even if he didn't want her any longer, he had not been prepared to be so absolutely unwanted himself.

What the dickens she had sent for him for, he could not imagine.

In the lane a second bullock cart was pulled up behind his own. It contained a handful of Burmese and the fellow from the Bombay-Burmah Corporation who was chatting away to the natives with what seemed a pretty astonishing degree of familiarity. Murray said, 'Afternoon, Tennant.'

Archie demanded, without preamble, 'What are you doing here?'

Murray shrugged. 'Renewing old acquaintance. Talking over old times.'

Archie grunted.

'I was just leaving,' Murray said. 'You'll have to announce yourself. She hasn't any servants.'

'I know. I've brought her some.'

'Funny place, Mandalay. Seems to affect people a bit. Know what I mean?'

'No,' Archie said. 'But then, I am affected too.'

'Going out into the forests again?'

'In due course.'

'Best of luck, then.' Murray moved away and then retraced his steps. 'Do you know something, Tennant? Six years ago, Maria Beresford was the best-looking girl in Bombay. And the most spirited.'

'Yes, I know,' Archie said. 'You told me.'

Maria was standing with her eyes closed in the middle of her empty drawing room. The hem of her skirts had gathered up fragments of fluff and horsehair, but apart from that, she looked dressed for a reception. And she was wearing all her rubies.

'I've brought you Ah Chun for a few days,' Archie said from the doorway. 'And two boys he recommends. And he will find you a maid tomorrow. I wish you wouldn't sleep here.'

'I want to.'

'Just because the British are here doesn't mean Mandalay is safe. There are hordes of bandits loyal to Supayalat and hordes more loyal to no-one. Ah Chun says he will sleep across your door tonight but I can't feel that's enough.'

'I couldn't bear another night with the hymn singers. I simply could not. This is my house, in any case. I belong here.'

'Until you go to India.'

Maria began to walk slowly up and down the gritty floor, little plumes of dust rising with her sweeping skirts.

'Until I go to India.'

'Then – then you really are going? Whatever it was you had to do, nothing came of it then?'

'Nothing.'

Archie crossed to the doorway and stood gazing out, his shoulder propped against the frame.

'Maria. Maria – is it a personal objection to me that makes you refuse me still?'

'No,' she said.

Knowing her by now, he did not turn, but waited, his back to the room and to her.

'I have money now,' he said after a while. 'I had much rather have had the old man still but that's something I can do nothing about. I shall stay in the East for a while because he would have wanted that, but I shall go home in the end. Home to a square brick house with its own frontage on the Thames. Even if you don't want me, wouldn't you rather that than a dusty bungalow in India with Thibaw drinking and Supayalat scolding?'

'You forget,' she said, 'I don't know England.'

'I don't forget. I suggest that I am the very person to introduce you to each other. I don't forget anything. I don't forget Maymyo. We might have a house up there where you could spend the forest seasons. Or you could come into the forests with me.' He spun round and said with a piteousness he did not intend and much regretted, 'Maria, do you care nothing for making me happy?'

She put her hands to her temples.

'Did you think yourself in love with that military oaf out there? Did you dream that you were the same as six years ago in Bombay? I wish – I wish that at the very least you would tell me what you think of me!'

Maria took her hands away from her head. 'Archie, you have the most attractive and admirable character I have ever met. You have a natural candour and sweetness that makes me trust you, confide in you. But I don't know that I want a good man like you. I don't know that I shouldn't prefer a fascinating but reprehensible creature like the Queen. To be truthful, I am horribly confused. Perhaps it is recent events, perhaps it is just too long in Mandalay. Mandalay, oh, Mandalay—'

He shouted, 'You are infernally obstinate!'

She smiled at him. He crossed the dusty space between them with huge strides and clamped his arms about her. She remained still in his embrace, but she did not resist him, even when he lowered his head and kissed her with more vigour than subtlety.

'Please,' he said, 'please marry me. I'll do everything to make you happy, I swear it. Think of life with me, think how much lies ahead—'

She detached herself gently, but she did not move away. A faint colour lay along her cheekbones.

'I can't seem to believe in anything,' she said, 'so much has vanished here, died – Grace, my father, Tom Prior, Denzil Blount, ambition, pride, glory—'

'Then don't insist upon making it worse!' he cried in despair, seizing her again, 'Don't throw yourself away to live with a myth, the ashes of a legend. Her reign is over. Yours might just be beginning. New Burma! New beginnings!'

She said, 'The old one meant so much to me.'

'That man out there—'

'Oh,' she said tiredly, her head drooping so that it almost touched his shoulder, 'a great mistake, Archie. A very foolish thing to do.'

'He boasted—'

'Yes,' she said, 'yes. I am sure he did. He told me how they are turning the palace into a merry military compound complete with club room and chapel. I can hardly bear to think of it.'

'That is how Ratnagiri will seem to you,' he said stooping so that her hair might brush his cheek. 'A sham. A tawdry imitation of things vanished.'

'I promised that I would go.'

'Promised?'

'Myself.'

'And me?'

'Oh!' she said angrily, tearing herself free. 'I don't know, I don't *know*—'

He stood back and regarded her. Her face was pinched with fatigue and she was clasping and unclasping her fingers nervously.

He said, 'If I leave you alone tonight to think everything over, will you give me an answer tomorrow?'

She said nothing, only stared down at her twisting fingers.

'I have to go back into the forests quite soon. I don't suppose it will be much fun, I should think the jungle even more lawless than Mandalay now, but I am contracted to go when I can. I had much rather go, knowing.'

She straightened up suddenly, lifting her chin, folding her hands, giving him the old, imperious blue look.

'Certainly you may have an answer in the morning.'

'Whether it be Supayalat or me?'

'Whether it be Supayalat or you or neither of you.'

'I shan't sleep,' he said. 'I dread tonight.'

'I shan't sleep either.'

'I suppose I should derive some consolation from knowing that periodically I shall be in your thoughts.'

'If you wish,' she said.

He came close to her and stooped to put his mouth gently on hers without touching her with his hands.

'Until tomorrow,' he said.

'Yes,' she said, 'until tomorrow.'

On the verandah steps Hnin Si was crouched combing her hair with a wooden comb. She had had no instructions to come with Ah Chun but these days she ignored instructions anyway. As Archie passed, she stopped the sweeping movement of her arm, put down the comb and shikoed to him. He paused and looked at her for a moment sadly, at her curious high-coloured Shan face, her flexible wrists and hands, her slanting brown eyes as blank as almonds. He could not now remember at all what it was like to desire her.

'*Thakin* wants me?' she said.

Archie sighed. 'No,' he said, 'no, I don't.'

She leaned forward and in an echo of a year before said, 'I don't please you, *thakin*?'

A great melancholy was settling on Archie like a fog. Through it he peered down at Hnin Si.

'Not in that way,' he said, 'not any more,' and then he stooped and laid two silver rupees on the step beside her before he went on down to the lane.

THE END

A SELECTED LIST OF FINE NOVELS
AVAILABLE FROM CORGI AND BLACK SWAN

THE PRICES SHOWN BELOW WERE CORRECT AT THE TIME OF GOING TO
PRESS. HOWEVER TRANSWORLD PUBLISHERS RESERVE THE RIGHT TO
SHOW NET RETAIL PRICES ON COVERS WHICH MAY DIFFER FROM THOSE
PREVIOUSLY ADVERTISED IN THE TEXT OR ELSEWHERE.

99755	2	**WINGS OF THE MORNING**	*Elizabeth Falconer*	£6.99
14537	8	**APPLE BLOSSOM TIME**	*Kathryn Haig*	£5.99
99774	9	**THE CUCKOO'S PARTING CRY**	*Anthea Halliwell*	£5.99
13872	X	**LEGACY OF LOVE**	*Caroline Harvey*	£5.99
13917	3	**A SECOND LEGACY**	*Caroline Harvey*	£5.99
14299	9	**PARSON HARDING'S DAUGHTER**	*Caroline Harvey*	£5.99
14407	X	**THE STEPS OF THE SUN**	*Caroline Harvey*	£5.99
14529	7	**LEAVES FROM THE VALLEY**	*Caroline Harvey*	£5.99
14553	X	**THE BRASS DOLPHIN**	*Caroline Harvey*	£5.99
99778	1	**A PATCH OF GREEN WATER**	*Karen Hayes*	£6.99
99736	6	**KISS AND KIN**	*Angela Lambert*	£6.99
14333	2	**SOME OLD LOVER'S GHOST**	*Judith Lennox*	£5.99
99771	4	**MALLINGFORD**	*Alison Love*	£6.99
99689	0	**WATERWINGS**	*Joan Marysmith*	£6.99
13910	6	**BLUEBIRDS**	*Margaret Mayhew*	£5.99
14499	1	**THESE FOOLISH THINGS**	*Imogen Parker*	£5.99
10375	6	**CSARDAS**	*Diane Pearson*	£5.99
99733	1	**MR BRIGHTLY'S EVENING OFF**	*Kathleen Rowntree*	£6.99
14549	1	**CHOICES**	*Susan Sallis*	£5.99
99494	4	**THE CHOIR**	*Joanna Trollope*	£6.99
99410	3	**A VILLAGE AFFAIR**	*Joanna Trollope*	£6.99
99442	1	**A PASSIONATE MAN**	*Joanna Trollope*	£6.99
99470	7	**THE RECTOR'S WIFE**	*Joanna Trollope*	£6.99
99492	8	**THE MEN AND THE GIRLS**	*Joanna Trollope*	£6.99
99549	5	**A SPANISH LOVER**	*Joanna Trollope*	£6.99
99643	2	**THE BEST OF FRIENDS**	*Joanna Trollope*	£6.99
99700	5	**NEXT OF KIN**	*Joanna Trollope*	£6.99
99788	9	**OTHER PEOPLE'S CHILDREN**	*Joanna Trollope*	£6.99
99591	6	**A MISLAID MAGIC**	*Joyce Windsor*	£6.99
14640	4	**THE ROMANY GIRL**	*Valerie Wood*	£5.99

All Transworld titles are available by post from:
Book Service By Post, PO Box 29, Douglas, Isle of Man IM99 1BQ
Credit cards accepted. Please telephone 01624 675137,
fax 01624 670923, Internet http://www.bookpost.co.uk or
e-mail: bookshop@enterprise.net for details.
Free postage and packing in the UK.
Overseas customers allow £1 per book (paperbacks) and
£3 per book (hardbacks).